Coventina's

Daughters

Alan Rafferty

First edition published in the UK in 2023.
ISBN (Hardback): 978-1-7392155-1-4
ISBN (Paperback): 978-1-7392155-2-1
Imprint: Independently published
Typeset by Matthew J Bird

A CIP catalogue record of this book is available from the British Library.

For further information about this book, please contact the author at: abrafferty@aol.com

*Dedicated to all those who asked for a second instalment,
particularly my wife Wendy and my mother, Sheila.
Also, to Coventry, the city that made me who I am.*

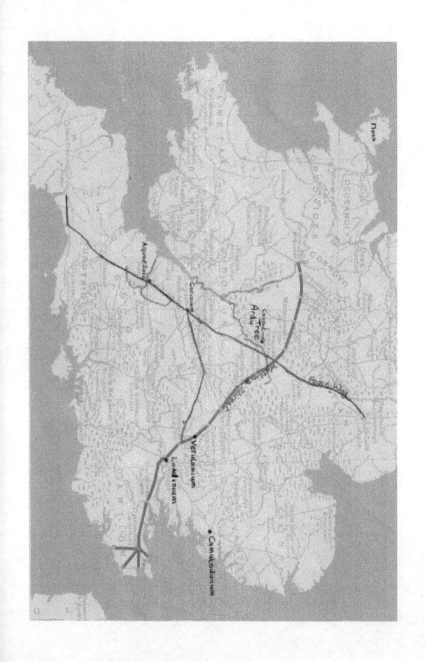

Characters

Britannia

Andronicus – Greek merchant

Brann – regent in Aquae Sulis

Bronwyn – Rivalin's sister

Deedee – Coventina's son

Eirwyn – Man in Rivalin's clan

Ffion – Miriam's maid

Jenna – clan woman

Livia – Quintus's wife

Marcus – son of governor of Aquae Sulis

Nevanthi – Coventina's daughter

Quintus Perpetua – Roman governor of Aquae Sulis

Regus Aurelius – Garrison commander at Ardu

Rhian – Coventina's maid

Rivalin/Felix Britannicus – king of the Dobunni

Sextus – Bronwyn's son

Tara – Miriam's daughter

Carthage

Abigail – Hebrew woman escaped from Jerusalem

Eirwyn – Salome's bodyguard

Junia – Apostle in Rome

Joanna – St Peter's granddaughter

Nerilla – Salome's maid
Pygmalion – Phoenician Trader
Seraphina/Sera – leader of women for the Jerusalem expedition

Galilee

Alexander – Trader, son of Photina
Coventina/Tina/Tira – Salome's daughter
David – Naava's grandson
Demetrius – Photina's husband
Demetrius (II) - Photina's son
Eban – Martha's maid
Esther – Mary of Magdala's housekeeper
Jonah – Mary of Magdala's cousin
Martha – Jonah's mother
Mary – Mary of Magdala's adopted daughter
Mary of Magdala – follower of Jesus of Nazareth
Miriam – Miriam and Jesus's daughter
Naava – Silas's cousin, grandmother to Rachel and David
Naomi/Photina – Samaritan woman at the well from Sychar
Photina/Naomi – Samaritan woman at the well from Sychar
Pygmalion – Phoenician Trader
Rachel – Naava's granddaughter
Sarah – Mary of Magdala's adopted daughter
Silas – Miriam's paternal grandfather
Tabitha – Jonah's wife
Yeshua/Jesus – Tabitha's son

Gaul

Mary of Magdala – follower of Jesus of Nazareth
Quaid – king in Gaul
Quintus Perpetua – Roman governor in Gaul
Sarah – Mary of Magdala's adopted daughter

Jerusalem

Ariza – Deborah's maid
Coventina – Salome's grandmother
D'vorah – Salome's aunt by marriage, Jacob's wife
Deborah, Talia – sisters and co-wives
Demetrius – Photina's husband
Isaiah – Jacob(II) brother
Jacob – Salome's uncle in Jerusalem and her master
Jacob(II) – Salome's second master in Jerusalem
Jonah – Mary of Magdala's cousin
Jonathan – fictitious brother of Salome's Uncle Jacob
Mary of Magdala – follower of Jesus of Nazareth
Matthias – Carter and trader
Matthias (II) – Salome's son
Naomi/Photina – Samaritan woman at the well from Sychar
Photina/Naomi – Samaritan woman at the well from Sychar
Saul – Jacob (II) brother
Seth – Salome's uncle in Rome
Shulamit (Shula) – Talia's maid
Tabitha – Saul's wife
Talia, Deborah - sisters and co-wives
Tira – Maid in Jacob (II) house
Tirzah – Salome's mother
Zilpah – Jacob's wife

Coventina's

Daughters

Alan Rafferty

Prologue

The tribe had been gradually dwindling since they came to this new land. They had gone far enough up the river to get past the coastal marshes but there was very little land between the river and the impenetrable forest. The headman had called a meeting. This could not go on. Some argued for a return from whence they had come, but they could not agree on which direction that was. Others argued that this was just their new land becoming acquainted with them and that it would become more benign. They were a minority. Still others argued that they should explore further up the river for better land. That was felt by most to be the last resort. In the end, the only decision of the meeting was that the shaman would seek the counsel of the ancestral spirits.

He took the holy drugs, derived from the white-spotted, red-capped mushrooms that abounded on the edge of the woodlands. His trance lasted all day, then he slept the night through and could not be woken. The following morning, the meeting was resumed and extended to include the women and children so that all could hear the wizened, still weak, shaman tell them his visions.

'Which of the ancestors came to you?' asked the leader of the tribe.

'I saw no ancestor,' he replied.

Every person, sitting in the large multi-rowed circle, sighed and their shoulders dropped, from the youngest to the oldest. Some wept. They had been abandoned to their fate. Every head was bowed but one. The shaman's assistant shouted indignantly, 'But I heard you. You were talking to the ancestors.'

Every eye turned to the holy man; some faces puzzled; others angry at the lie.

'I saw no ancestor,' he repeated, 'I saw the face of a stranger, a goddess.'

The word was not unknown to the people of the tribe but was strange. Other tribes had gods. They always relied on the wisdom of the ancestors. There was an uneasy shifting in all directions. Could the ancestors save them from this new menace? Some thought one way, some another and heated discussion immediately ensued. The shaman pounded the stones for silence. Out of long-ingrained habit, the silence was immediate, from all but the youngest. Their mothers quickly quieted them.

'This land we have come to belongs to a goddess. She is quite happy for us to stay, but we must visit her and obey her commands. We have no choice. We cannot leave again. We don't know which way to go. If we obey her, she offers prosperity and abundance. If we don't, the land itself will turn against us.'

The old man sat cross-legged, waiting for the words to sink in. He watched everyone's face as they gradually came to acceptance, the pragmatic first, the stubborn last. Finally, only his assistant held out. The shaman knew why. This was the end of their world. The years of training meant nothing now. He held his assistant's eyes, compassion in his own. After a couple of minutes, the man's tension eased, and the shaman saw a reluctant acceptance in his face.

'The goddess lives a long way from here, up the great river. We must all follow it until we find a clear stream. At the source of the stream is her dwelling place. She has promised to guide me to her, herself.'

With that the shaman passed the pounding stones back to the headman, signifying a return to him of control of the council. All eyes turned to their leader. The shaman interpreted the voices of the ancestors or, in this case, the strange new goddess. The headman had the responsibility for the decision. Normally he would take advice from members of the council. In this case, they knew, no advice was needed. Either they heeded the words of the goddess, or they ignored them. There were only two courses, to go or to stay. The chief delayed his words to give them weight, though he knew well enough there was only one decision he could make.

'We will go and find this goddess. Prepare the boats we sailed here in and load them with as much as they will carry, leaving only enough room for everyone to sit in them that needs to. Priority is to be given to food and shelter.'

He pounded the stones twice to mark his decision, excluding any further discussion. Then he pounded them six times to mark the end of the meeting. Everyone dispersed.

The men started by checking the boats and making repairs as needed. The women set to packing the food in leaves for the journey. By the time the boats were ready, so was the food. The men stowed it in the boats, made spaces for all the people and then packed what woven shelters they could around those gaps. It was almost nightfall by the time they were finished.

'We leave first thing in the morning,' was all the headman said. There was nothing else to be said.

The following day they set out after eating their last meal in their village. The shaman sat on the prow of the lead boat, which was paddled and steered by the chief and his household. He sat gargoyle-like, brooding. A lament was sung as stroke by stroke they moved the boats upstream, leaving their dwellings behind. Tears were shed. No one expected to see their home ever again. They turned a bend in the river when a miracle occurred. A large wave came up behind them and swept them rapidly up the river.

'See,' shouted the shaman, 'the goddess sends us her assistance.'

It was a good start. The mood soon dropped though. Each day they went deeper and deeper into the wooded land. At each river, stream, rivulet or brook, the shaman would seek the guidance of the goddess. The command was always to go on. The river gradually narrowed. They had to ditch the shelter materials as the draft became too great for the river to take. Then they had to get out and pull the boats, leaving only the youngest children and the frail old in the boats. Finally, everyone had to walk, carrying as much food as they could on their backs. The headman insisted that they still pulled the boats though.

They lost count of the number of days of this gruelling labour before the goddess gave direction that they take the northern fork where two rivers converged. This was not the main branch of the river, but a muddy stream, flowing blood-red as it carried the clay soil down to the main river. It was not a good omen. They reached another point where two streams converged. To their relief, the smaller ran clear and pure. The shaman prepared himself, took a small amount of his sense-enhancing drug and stayed there for over an hour communing with the deity. He almost felt that he didn't need the potion, her presence was so strong.

'The goddess dwells in a grove at the source of this stream but she wants us to follow the other river. She says that a short distance up the river lies a pool. Swimming in this lake we will find large white birds, swans she called them. They are her gift to us for a celebration feast tonight. Tomorrow, we are to purify ourselves and go and meet her.'

As the woods came down close to the riverbanks, the people all had to wade up through the current. They came to the pool the goddess had spoken of and the lead man cried out as the riverbed fell away beneath him and he fell forward into the suddenly deep water.

Around the edge of the lake, the trees were less dense, allowing them to weave to an area of flat land where they could camp. A shout of joy went up from one of the hunters as he noticed six large white birds tangled in weed near the edge of the water, completely helpless.

The feast that night was joyous and lasted until a few hours before dawn. The following morning, the shaman woke them early. Many were groggy from lack of sleep and grumbled. As they mixed ash from the fires with the fat from animals to make a cleansing lotion, apprehension and fear set in. That day they were going to meet their goddess.

They paddled back down the river until they came to the clear water stream. At that juncture the shaman and headman exchanged glances, and each took a deep breath. With a nod from each other, they led the people up the stream. They found a large glade some way up the stream, by then no more than a trickle. At the opposite end of the glade, where the spring seemed to miraculously rise out of the ground, sat a woman under the shade of a large oak tree.

They stared open-mouthed. She was seated on a giant leaf, her milk-white body completely unclad. Her fiery-red hair streamed out as if caught by a strong wind, though not the slightest zephyr could be detected in the still air. It was her eyes that held the attention though. Green. Green as the leaf she sat on.

'I am Coventina, the queen of all the deities of this land.' The woman's mouth had not moved so they looked this way and that to see who had spoken.

'I am Coventina.' This time there was no doubt that the strange woman in front of them had spoken.

The shaman bowed, followed by the headman and everyone behind them. 'What do you require of us, great queen?' asked the shaman.

'If you are to dwell in my land you must learn to live here without greed and in harmony with the land. I will teach you this. I will teach you how to cut down trees so that you may build houses safely and clear land to grow crops. I will teach you what can be eaten and what may be used as medicine. I will teach you how to harvest the forest, how to find nuts and berries and fruit. I will teach you all you need to know, and I will provide for you abundantly.

In return, I ask for two things. Firstly, that you give an offering to me every year at the autumn harvest. For four years this is to be done wherever you are. In the fifth year, you are to bring your offering here. Secondly, that you nurture my daughters and take them as your queens.

As long as you follow these two commands you will prosper.'

'How many daughters do you have?' asked the headman.

'There will be many. The first I will give birth to myself. The man she marries will be your headman. Her daughter will take over as queen when she dies and the man she marries will be your next chief.'

The headman looked at her dubiously. 'What if there is more than one daughter, or she only has sons?'

'The woman with the leaf-green eyes will be my true daughter. Should the line be broken, mother to daughter, a true daughter of mine will be born to the wife of one of her sons. There will always be a daughter of mine in each generation.'

'When will we meet your daughter?' asked the headman.

'Soon,' replied Coventina.

Each day they went for their instruction and each day the slender goddess became rounder and rounder at the waist. At the end of the month, a child was born. A baby girl with green eyes. The people stayed there for sixteen years. At the end of that time one of the headman's sons, Dobun, married the goddess's daughter.

After the wedding, Coventina spoke.

'It is now time for you to depart. All except my priests, who are to remain in your settlement with their families. Henceforth, no one is to invade this woodland in the high land between the two rivers, on pain of death. A safe passage will be provided along the river to your settlement but no man except a priest is to come along the clear stream to here from now on. When you bring your five-yearly offering it must be taken to the settlement and the priests will bring it to me. My daughters will be my voice.'

They departed the next day, back down the stream to the river and along the river, back to the village they had left at the river mouth. Five years later they took their offering up to the goddess at the place they called *Coventina's Tree*.

Five years after that there was grumbling about the long journey, as the memory faded and pride in their wealth and achievements grew. They were late setting off despite the command of Coventina's daughter. Sickness hit their camp. It started when flies that were always around the nearby marshland began to bite. The sores grew into lumps. Then the victims had a high temperature and sweat, forever thirsty. They gradually weakened, and some died. They hastily sent the goddess's offering.

When the pilgrims returned, they found the village empty and abandoned. They wept. Their journey had been in vain. Tired, they slept in their deserted home, leaving their decision as to what to do next until the morning. They woke to a quiet eerie atmosphere, each imagining that they could hear the call of a loved one or the songs of their people. First one, then gradually all of them sang a lament.

When they had finished, a voice made them turn. 'Who has died? You all seem to be back safe and well.'

They saw their shaman. He was impossibly old now. How old, no one knew.

'The settlement has been moved at Coventina's command. Her daughter has led the way to a new place. A place of hot, bitter-tasting, foul-smelling waters that healed the sores when one bathed. A place by a river in a pleasant valley. Carry on downstream until you come to a river on your left, flowing through a high steep canyon. Follow this river and you will find them. I will not go with you. I am going to a special place, a place where the presence of the goddess is strong. Coventina has given me this as a gift, that I die in her presence.'

The people dwelt in the place by the foul-smelling waters, year after year, generation after generation, in peace and harmony. They revered the place where the shaman had gone to die, and it became known as the *Special place of the Dobunni* and that is what it is still called to this day.

Salome finished her story and looked up to see her green-eyed daughter, Coventina, and her nursling, Miriam, still listening, entranced.

Part 1

Salome

1

On arrival in Jerusalem, Jacob was elated. He was living amongst Judeans, as he felt he should be, and had found a house to buy near the temple. It was not as large as the house in Rome which they had come from. It didn't need to be. In Rome, the house had been for the whole extended family, with quarters for the slaves. The house here was just for himself and his wife, and their children when they came along. Most servants in Judea were hired and had their own homes. The only slave he had brought with him was Salome, his niece. In crowded Jerusalem, most houses, including this one, had two storeys. It was big enough, with separate bedrooms for himself and his wife, and a separate room for business, away from the dining area and his wife's private lounge.

The house's proximity to the temple was good as it enabled him to be seen constantly so that he rapidly became known to the temple authorities. This, in turn, introduced him to the highest strata of Jerusalem society. He found that his time in Rome, where he had been born, both helped and hindered him.

It helped that he could use his contacts in Rome to import and sell high-priced luxuries to both upper-class locals and Romans. It hindered him as he was unused to Jerusalem prices for household goods, particularly grain. He had not realised how heavily the Roman authorities subsidised wheat. The phrase *'bread and circuses'* came to mind. Still, it was not his problem. Slaves did that sort of menial work. It was Salome's task, not his.

He called Salome and, as she entered, he looked at her with distaste. She was tall and light-skinned like the Greeks, but with a pinkish undertone to her skin. Her hair was dark brown with copper-coloured highlights, unlike his own black hair. She kept her head bowed, as was required of slaves, but if you caught a glimpse of her eyes, you would be startled by their leaf-green shade. She was a slave, but also the daughter of his sister who, in turn, had been the daughter of a British slave-cum-concubine. He resented that his father had loved his concubine as much as his wife, Jacob's mother. Even more, he resented that his father had doted on Salome, his beloved granddaughter. Her very presence tainted him.

I could have left her in Rome with my brother, but no, this is better. Sell her here where she has no friends, and her mixed parentage will make her a despised outsider. I can start now and show off the wares.

'I have been invited to dine with a new client. It is customary here to take your wife and to talk business after the meal. D'vorah will be expected to have a maid, so you will have to go with us. Go in and dress D'vorah's hair.'

Salome went to her mistress, who was in a panic. Except for the slaves and the very poor, women didn't go out in Rome. D'vorah hadn't seen anything of Jerusalem except when they entered the city from Rome. Salome set to with D'vorah's hair, making it look as if she were expecting an important visitor, Roman fashion. All the Hebrew women that Salome had seen in the street wore their hair simply, with no more than a hair slide, but they were likely to be poor or slaves, like herself.

They left for their host's house at about noon. It wasn't far but D'vorah had a nervous shake in her right hand all the way.

On arrival, Salome stood in the corner, as was expected of her, whilst their host and two other women lay on the couches by the table. Their host indicated that Jacob and D'vorah should take the other two couches.

Both host ladies wore their hair simply, as Salome had seen in the town, though the house was undoubtedly wealthy. The host indicated to the servants that the feet of his guests should be washed, and he then welcomed Jacob and D'vorah. He introduced the two women as Deborah and Talia, which Salome found interesting. Their host, who was a traditionally conservative Hebrew, had a wife with a Hellenised version of a name and her master, who followed Greek custom, had a wife with the traditional Hebrew version of the same name.

During the first course, Jacob politely complimented his host on his beautiful wife and daughter. There was an awkward silence, in which both women visibly reddened, though their host took it in his stride.

'I know you are well-meaning, Jacob, but we do not follow Greek custom here. In Judea, we only compliment a man's daughter if we intend to follow it with a proposal of marriage. Besides, Deborah and Talia are both my wives. I know having more than one wife is unusual but, unlike in Greek and Roman society, it is not illegal. Deborah was already my wife when their parents died. Talia, her younger sister, was destitute and without dowry, so this was the easiest way to resolve the problem.'

Jacob was startled. He would have to carefully check the old customs, just in case there was anything else he fell over on. He apologised.

'I am very sorry, the temple authorities had me believe that Greco-Roman custom was followed everywhere now except, and these are their words, "by the ignorant".'

'That is what they want people to believe. The Romans have given them Roman citizenship to keep them onside and to make sure they keep any potential troublemakers quiet. Of course, being Roman citizens, they are legally restricted to one wife but, on the other hand, they can break Judean law to their advantage, with impunity. Hence the racket they have going on with the market for sacrificial animals. As with any elite, if they are not allowed something, they don't want anyone else to have it either, which is why they are anti-polygamy.'

After the meal, the men left to talk business and the women were together in the room where dinner had been served. Deborah, the older of the two women, told the servants to clear the table and couches and bring in weaving looms. Then, to Salome's surprise, she told her maid to take Salome to the kitchens so that they could both eat. That would never have been done in Rome.

On entering the kitchen, Salome found that the cook had a meal waiting for her. This was customary in Hebrew society. Salome and Deborah's maid, Ariza, and Talia's maid, Shulamit, ate and talked. Shulamit and Ariza were particularly interested in Salome.

'You have a Hebrew name, but you don't look Hebrew. Not even like the Naphtali in Galilee,' said Shulamit.

'Sorry,' interjected Ariza, 'Shula has a habit of being direct. She doesn't mean any harm by it.'

'It is alright. My grandmother was from Britannia. My great grandfather bought her as a slave and concubine for his son, my grandfather. My mother, their daughter, is still a slave in Rome and my master, my uncle, brought me here.'

'How come your mother is a slave?' Ariza looked puzzled.

Salome was just as puzzled by the question. 'Well, she was the daughter of a slave, of course.'

Ariza still looked puzzled but shrugged. 'Here, if you are the child of a concubine, you are counted as a child of the senior wife. That would make your mother just as much a child of your uncle's father as he is, and she wouldn't be a slave.' Then, after a pause, 'Are you a slave too?'

'Yes.'

'Strange customs Romans have. It is not civilised having someone born a slave like that. Still, it will soon be the Year of Jubilee.'

'Is that custom still followed?'

'It is here. That means that Jacob will have to release you and give you a dowry.'

'Why would he have to do that? It only applies to fellow Hebrews.'

'But you are an Israelite, at least in our tradition. Though why they never taught you Aramaic, I don't know. Your Hebrew is impeccable, though. Oh, I have seen you in the market buying food from Greek traders, haven't I? Is it because you don't speak Aramaic?'

'Yes, with my looks and because I don't speak Aramaic, the Hebrew vendors won't sell to me. Don't tell. My uncle would beat me black and blue.'

After the visit, Salome was sent to the market. On her way, she was lost in thought. Back in Rome, a visiting priest had objected to sharing a Sabbath meal with her Uncle Seth, her mother, and Salome herself. Salome's grandfather had replied, 'Seth is my son, Tirzah my daughter, and Salome my granddaughter. We are all Judeans, whatever our status. Does not the law say that everyone in the household should refrain from work on the Sabbath, even the alien? How, then, can I not invite my own kin, even though slaves, to the table?'

Salome had been perplexed at the time. The Romans regarded the offspring of slaves as slaves and unrelated.

Having sexual relations with a slave was not even regarded as adultery, not that the Romans she had come across seemed too worried about adultery. Her main worry had always been a man waylaying her for sex in the marketplace. Whilst it was frowned upon to take another's slave, no one would have intervened. Her master would have received compensation had she become pregnant. Otherwise, nothing would have happened.

2

On arriving at the market, Salome went to her usual stall. Whilst she waited for the stallholder to serve someone else, she looked around. The sights, sounds and smells took her back to the first day they had arrived in Jerusalem.

Salome had been told to put on her Sabbath clothes and go to the market and buy food. She could still feel the claustrophobia she had felt as she roamed the narrow streets with their high walls on either side. Jerusalem was more compact than Rome and hadn't any open spaces. It was dominated by a central hill on which the temple and the citadel stood. Its seven hills made Rome feel more open and inviting. She had eventually found the main market up near the temple.

The Jewish traders had looked at her with suspicion. Her height, her dark brown hair with its copper highlights and her pinkish pale skin made them suspicious of her, as did her use of imperial coinage minted in Italy. She had heard them speak in Hebrew but, when she spoke to them, they pretended not to understand and switched to Aramaic. There were fleeting words she understood so she realised that they were talking about her, discussing what sort of 'mongrel' she was. Some sort of Samaritan was the eventual consensus, and they pointedly turned their back on her when she tried to speak to them.

'You will do better trading with Samaritans or Gentiles,' said a gentle voice behind her, 'and get better prices too.'

Salome turned. Her eyes met those of a woman whose appearance was that of a local, but her dress was subtly different. Her shawl, showing her married status, was slightly further back, and her dress slightly shorter, like those of Greek women. The man who stood beside her was obviously Greek, tall and strong with black hair and blue eyes.

'If you cannot speak Greek, I can translate for you.'

'Thank you, I speak Greek. We have just arrived from Rome. My master will not like me dealing with Gentiles, but since our fellow Hebrews won't sell to me, it seems I have no choice. He will like going hungry even less. If you could just show me where I go,' Salome replied, in Greek.

Thank you, Grandmother, and the emperor, I suppose. Had he not insisted that my grandmother be thoroughly civilised, to create a Roman ally in Britannia, she would never have been taught oral and written Greek and Latin. And thank you, Grandmother, for insisting on passing the learning on so that your children and grandchildren could earn money to buy their freedom.

As they walked, they talked.

'I heard them say the word Samaritan. What is a Samaritan?'

The woman smiled, 'I am a Samaritan. Naomi of Sychar. We are the descendants of the tribes of Israel, mainly Manasseh and Ephraim, who inter-married with non-Hebrews. We still worship Yahweh but that is not enough for Judeans. This is my husband, Demetrius. He is, as you will probably have guessed, Greek. The Judeans tend to call all non-Judeans, Samaritans; even occasionally the Naphtali.'

Salome was astonished, 'The Naphtali still exist?'

'Yes, they are dwindling and have a lot of Greek blood in them now, but they still exist in Galilee. Benjamin and Simeon and Levi still exist as well but tend to be thought of as Judeans if they live here or Jews elsewhere.'

'But Jew means Judean. Wouldn't it be better to call them Hebrew?'

'Yes, but that would include groups they don't want included.'

'Like me, for instance. My grandfather on my mother's side was Judean. My grandmother and my father were both from Britannia.'

'So, you have a British name?'

'No, my mother and father were both slaves to Hebrews, so I have a Hebrew name. Salome.'

They reached the quarter of the market furthest away from the temple where there were a few stalls run by non-Judean traders. Naomi and Demetrius seemed to know them all. Naomi introduced Salome and then she and Demetrius left.

Naomi's parting shot was, 'Goodbye. We need to start our journey home in the morning so can't stop. These traders will all give you a fair price, I know.' She looked hard at the traders, her eyes saying, *don't you dare cheat her or you'll regret it.*

The trader looked at Salome. 'Any friend of Photina's is a friend of ours. What is it you need?'

'Photina?'

'I see. You are a new friend. Everyone calls Naomi, Photina. Now, what do you need?'

For the first time in her life, Salome found that she didn't have to negotiate a price. They gave her the lowest price at the start.

Salome came back to the present as the woman in front of her moved aside. The transactions were quickly concluded. Flour for the next day's bread, a little salt and various vegetables. Meat was expensive so not eaten often. In the month since they had arrived, Salome had learnt enough

Aramaic to get by when ordering food items. After all, everyone in this part of the empire, from Syria in the north down to the border with Egypt, spoke Aramaic, so the stallholder had taught her as she shopped.

There was a tense atmosphere when Salome returned home. She heard a shout from her mistress as she gave the provisions to the cook. Salome raised an eyebrow.

'Seems the mistress was introduced to weaving whilst out on their visit and wants her own loom. Also wants to accompany you on your next visit to the market.'

The cook picked up the pot with the starter dough kept back from the morning's loaf and started to mix in fresh flour and water for the following day's bread. It would be left overnight to rise, ready for baking when the cook arrived the following morning. This was another difference. Most servants in Jerusalem were paid and lived elsewhere in the city. In Rome, they were mostly slaves and lived with the family.

'I can imagine how the master reacted to that,' said Salome, 'but why does the mistress want to do servant's work?'

The cook was puzzled for a moment, then said, 'You're not local. Spent too much time amongst Greeks and Romans. Here, all women weave and sew. It is usually the mistress of the house that goes to the market too. In some very large households, it might be the steward but, even then, the mistress usually accompanies him.'

'I can't imagine D'vorah carrying even this small amount back herself.'

'They will take a maid or two for that.'

Another shout followed, this time from Jacob.

'Jacob is definitely not happy with D'vorah.'

'That is not all,' said the cook, 'apparently the master raised the subject of selling you to your host today. Your host knew somehow that you were Jacob's niece and made it quite clear that selling you to a Gentile would be regarded as totally unacceptable and that it was highly unlikely any Judean would be prepared to buy you.'

'Why is that?'

'Here, they regard themselves as honour-bound to buy back a family member who is a slave. They would never sell a family member into slavery. And no one would ever sell a Judean to a Gentile.'

The following day, a loom was delivered and Salome was given the task of teaching D'vorah how to use it. On her next visit to the market, D'vorah accompanied her. This time, the Hebrew merchants were only too pleased to help. Deborah and Talia were there as well, accompanied by Ariza and Shulamit. As the three mistresses talked in Aramaic, Ariza whispered a translation to Salome in Hebrew. After that, D'vorah became a frequent visitor to Deborah's house, accompanied by Salome. D'vorah learnt to weave whilst, unbeknown to her, Ariza taught Salome Aramaic.

3

A couple of months later Salome was called in to see Jacob. Another man was standing there, a stranger. He had the standard Judean looks but there was something about him Salome didn't like.

It is the way he is looking at me. It is as if I am a sex object, not a person.

Jacob and the stranger spoke in Aramaic, not realising that Salome understood.

'Here is the document.'

'Says here that the girl was taken as a slave in lieu of a debt owed to you by your brother, Jonathon, her father. How do I know that this document is legal?'

'What do you care? No one is going to be able to check up on it anyway. Rome is a long way away. Besides, you are getting her cheap.'

'And she doesn't speak Aramaic?'

'Again, what do you care? She is an excellent lady's maid for your wife and, as I said, comes cheap.'

'The Year of Jubilee is only two years away.'

'Look, I have gone as low as I am able, either you want her or you don't. Besides Salome has no idea of Hebrew Law, only Roman Law. If you do not release her then it is up to her to go to the courts to enforce the law and if no one tells her…'

'Her or her relatives,' the man said.

'I am her only relative in Jerusalem and it is not in my interests for her to be freed and for me to then have to provide a dowry for her,' Jacob replied.

The man looked at Salome again. This time, the leer and carnal look left no doubt as to his future intentions and made Salome shudder.

The man took off his shoe and handed it to Jacob. Jacob was taken aback for a moment before taking off his shoe and handing it back. The deal was done. After handing their shoes back to each other, Jacob ordered Salome, in Hebrew, to collect her things and go with her new master. When she had collected everything, the strange man took her roughly by the arm and dragged her out of the house and through the streets of Jerusalem back to his own house.

It was obvious that it was not a happy house. All the servants showed signs of abuse, as did the mistress, Zilpah. Her previous maid, whom she had had since turning fourteen before she married the master, another Jacob, had left and no servant would work for them. Salome noticed that Zilpah's dress was shabby. She found a better dress, that Zilpah had worn to a recent wedding, but was promptly informed that it was for special occasions only. Salome was then told to change into her oldest clothes. She was only to put something decent on when she went to the market. To ensure that she complied, Jacob went through her clothes, picked out the oldest and ordered her to change into them, with him watching. Having stripped down to her loin-cloth, she picked up her dress, only to be stopped by Jacob.

'Remove the loin-cloth. I only allow women in the house to wear underclothes during their bleed. Cuts down on wear and tear.'

Salome complied. She hated the way Jacob looked at her, but she was a slave and had no choice.

Jacob then left the house, obviously pleased with himself. Zilpah spoke to Salome in Hebrew and looked relieved to get an answer in Aramaic. They stayed in the main room where they were served lunch.

On his return, Jacob was not in such a good mood. He grabbed his startled, frightened-looking wife and dragged her into the mistress's bedroom.

'You owe me for the present I have given you.'

Salome heard a cry of pain from her new mistress and then an evil-sounding laugh from the master. Half an hour later, the master came out and then looked at Salome. It took all of Salome's control to stop herself from shrinking away.

'Your mistress needs you.'

Salome went into Zilpah's room to find her bleeding from her vaginal region. She got up to go and get the necessary things to minister to her mistress, warm water, honey, olive oil and cloths, but found she didn't need to. A young maid, about twelve, was already standing near, waiting with what was needed. Salome had already been introduced to this maid.

'Thank you, Tira. Could you get better cloths, please, these are a bit rough.'

The maid just shook her head. Salome looked at her quizzically.

'The master won't let us use linen,' Tira whispered.

Salome sighed and proceeded with what she had. No real cleaning was needed anyway, not with this type of damage. When she had finished, she gave the things back to Tira to dispose of and looked around the room. It was a reasonably sized room, about eight feet by six feet. The mistress's dresses were piled in a heap in a corner, not even folded.

That can wait until morning. Dealing with that smelly bed will have to wait 'til tomorrow as well. My mattress, when growing up, was better than that, though directly on the floor. Grandfather would never have let a slave sleep on anything that bad, let alone his wife or family.

The mattress was on a pallet bed. There was a sleeping mat in the corner for Salome. She had slept in worse places occasionally, but this was going to be permanent.

Her duties were light because the master didn't allow any of the women to leave the house and didn't accept visitors. He made an exception for Salome. She was sent out each day to buy food, with instructions to get the cheapest possible. For this six-day-a-week trip, she was allowed to put on a better dress. Her new Samaritan and Gentile contacts came in useful, and Jacob never enquired where she purchased anything.

On her third trip to the market, Salome met Ariza and Shulamit. They were on their own, which was unusual, and appeared relieved to see her.

'Our master has asked us to look out for you. He heard that you had been sold but wanted to be certain that Jacob hadn't just got rid of you,' said Ariza.

'I have been sold, to a man also called Jacob. His wife is called Zilpah.'

The two women looked concerned but only asked, 'Are you alright?'

'I am fine. Jacob hasn't touched me as yet.'

'He has a reputation for treating women, particularly slaves, in the Roman way.'

'What do you mean?'

Ariza remained silent. After a moment's silence, Shulamit blurted out, 'That he regards all the women in the house as his possessions. That he takes them at will whenever, and however, he wants and enjoys inflicting pain. That he cares more for his asses than his slaves or even his wife. That when he goes out, he…'

Ariza's hand on Shulamit's arm and a sharp 'Enough' stopped her mid-sentence.

Ariza carried on, 'Your uncle, Jacob, did not weigh up the consequences before proceeding. There was disgust in the Hebrew community that he would sell his niece to such a man. The fact that he did not provide you with a dowry made matters worse, and he has lost the respect of most of his new friends. It will blow over eventually because of his contacts in Rome, but it has cost him. The only redeeming feature is that your father, Jonathon, owed him money so he did have the legal right to sell you.'

Salome thought about telling them that Jonathon didn't exist, but decided not to. Ariza and Shulamit had evidently forgotten her true parentage or thought she had lied. In the face of the fake document, there was nothing she could legally do anyway.

4

Jacob always went out each day, except Sabbath, though where he went and what he did she didn't know. Salome did not go to the market on Sabbath either. That was as far as the observance of the Sabbath went. There was no refraining from work for anyone in the house, as had been the case with her previous family. So long as there was no outward sign of the breach of tradition, Jacob didn't care. Salome had tried asking where he went each day, but no one would say. The usual answer was along the lines of, 'so long as he is not here, who cares?'

One day, Jacob came home early and in a fury. Salome was sitting with Zilpah. A maid had just entered the room with refreshments. Jacob saw the maid first and barked an order.

'You, my room now!'

The maid froze. Jacob knocked the tray out of her hand, hit her hard across the face, then dragged her out by the hair. Salome could hear the maid's screams, as she cleared up the mess. Then the screams stopped. Jacob emerged from his room, looked around and saw Salome. She feared she was next and almost sighed with relief when, instead, he shouted at her.

'Go and look after her. If she dies, I will hold you accountable for the loss of a valuable slave.'

He then stormed out of the house again.

Salome stayed with the woman for three days, leaving her temporarily in someone else's care when she went to the market for food. At the end of three days, the woman had recovered enough to talk.

'What did you do for him to do that?' Salome asked.

'It will just be that some woman that he is chasing has rejected him. Probably Tabitha, his brother's wife. He has been chasing her ever since their wedding.'

'Why does his wife tolerate his behaviour?'

'It keeps him away from her and the rest of the women servants. He doesn't touch Tira because she hasn't had her first bleed yet and you have escaped so far because he has been so intent on Tabitha, but you won't escape for long.'

He didn't touch Salome. The only explanation she could find was her daily trips to the market. Jacob didn't want her to have visible signs of abuse when she was in such a public place. It couldn't last forever and didn't.

One morning, he came to the mistress's room just as Salome had finished dressing her. Salome went to leave, as this meant he wanted his wife, only to be stopped by Jacob.

'Not today. Zilpah has started her bleed. Today it is your turn to be pleasured by me.'

Zilpah scurried out of the room. Salome, remembering what he had done to the maid, quickly lay down on the bed. He lifted her skirt and, with no preparation, forced himself inside her. Salome swallowed her cry of pain.

'You are useless. I take the trouble to pleasure you and get no response from you. I will keep going until I get a response.'

Jacob entered her again and Salome forced herself to respond despite her pain.

'Better, but still not good enough.'

After a brief rest, Jacob took her again. Salome responded as best she could.

'Still not good enough, but I have wasted too much effort on you already. You must learn to pleasure a man.'

Salome grabbed a loin-cloth to protect her dress from her virgin bleed and followed Jacob out, to wait on Zilpah at breakfast. She was still smoothing her dress down when she entered the main room of the house. Jacob turned to jeer at her performance but stopped, mouth open, as he saw a flash of anger in her leaf-green eyes. Salome felt a power in herself that she had never felt before. Jacob staggered back as if he had been hit, fear on his face.

After that, Jacob would occasionally demand Salome to stay with him in his wife's room, but never took her again. Just to prove he was a man, he might have hit her, but never hard.

5

Some six months later, there was a new addition to the household. Jacob's eldest brother, Saul, had died. There was the funeral on the day after his death, as he had died after nightfall, then the usual seven-day period of mourning. Jacob was assiduous in attending the funeral even though his presence was unwelcomed by the widow. He did not take Zilpah with him, as was customary.

The day after mourning had finished, Jacob arrived home with the reluctant widow in tow. Jacob declared that he was acting as a kinsman redeemer and had married Tabitha. There was dismay from Zilpah who knew the cost that that would incur. Salome looked at the poor young woman, no more than fifteen at the most, with pity.

What happened next was entirely predictable. Jacob dragged the woman to an empty, unused bedroom. Salome agonised as she heard Tabitha's useless pleas and then her cry of pain as Jacob roughly took her. From her cries and his satisfaction, it sounded like Jacob was enjoying causing her pain and was deliberately prolonging it. Thinking of how he had treated her, Salome dreaded what he must be doing to the poor woman.

It was almost a relief when Salome heard Jacob hit Tabitha and shout at her never to resist him again. Jacob then called for Tira, who hurried into the room. No doubt Jacob was intending to use a normal voice, but his blood was up and his speaking volume was only just below a shout. He instructed Tira that she was now Tabitha's maid and then left the house, oblivious to the blood on his robes.

Tabitha was silent and Salome wondered if Jacob had killed her, in his malice. When Tira came out, looking for something to treat Tabitha with, Salome took her and got warm water, olive oil and honey and a clean linen cloth. Zilpah stopped them, insisting that they used a clean but rougher hemp rag. Salome couldn't countermand Zilpah's decision but knew it would cause Tabitha more pain and would not clean the wounds as well as linen, leaving scars. She guessed that Zilpah was hoping Tabitha's wounds would be infected and she would die.

As Tira went back into Tabitha's room, Salome headed for the kitchen where she boiled a cauldron of water. By the time Tira came out again, looking for something with which to wash out Tabitha's dress, Salome had everything ready and waiting. Tira returned to Tabitha's room.

Zilpah was furious. She hit Salome hard, and Salome felt blood trickle down her face from her lip.

'You are my maid. Tira is Tabitha's maid. From now on, you let Tira do her job and you do yours, and Tabitha is to be given the minimum possible to keep her alive, nothing more. That bitch will wish she had never wormed her way into Jacob's affections before I am finished with her.'

That evening, Jacob didn't come home to dinner and Salome was able to see Tabitha for the first time. She was the usual height for a Judean though broader at the shoulder and hip. She also had a darker complexion and a broader, slightly flattened nose. What really stuck out was her wavy, almost curly, black hair. Salome had never seen a Judean like her before. She commented to the cook, wondering whether Tabitha, like herself, was mixed-race.

'She is of Davidic descent,' said the cook, as if that explained everything.

So, she is descended from King David. But why would that make any difference to her looks?

Seeing her puzzled expression, the cook continued, 'David married Bathsheba, which means daughter of Sheba. Sheba is in Ethiopia where they are black. As was customary, when the king married a foreign wife, his close kin would also take wives from the same country to cement the alliance. Hence those of pure Davidic descent tend to have looks like Tabitha.'

From then on, Salome and the other servants never helped Tabitha or Tira openly, but did what they could for them covertly. Most of all, the cook daily risked Zilpah's wrath by making sure that Tabitha had sufficient to eat.

It was easy for the cook to do this to start with as, the following day, Jacob announced that he was going to Damascus on a business trip. Everyone, except Tira and Tabitha, knew what this meant. He was going where he was unknown and would pretend to be a Gentile. For a month after he arrived, he would frequent the drinking houses and temple prostitutes every day. Everyone was relieved, but Zilpah was still angry at Jacob's marriage to Tabitha and insisted that she remained in her room.

The atmosphere in the house changed with Jacob's absence. One of the maids even started singing whilst working. Zilpah was troubled. She needed to do something about Tabitha. The only way to ensure that they kept Saul's estate and the redemption money was for her to have a son and for Tabitha to die childless. But how was she going to achieve that? Jacob was obviously incapable of fathering a child, for a start. Gradually, she formulated a plan. She instructed Salome to seek out Isaiah, Jacob's other brother, when she went to the market. The market's proximity to the temple meant that she was sure to find him in the vicinity sometime.

Tension returned to the house abruptly on Jacob's return. That first night back, he insisted that Tabitha join him and Zilpah for the evening meal. Zilpah resented this as she didn't dare restrict Tabitha to the rations she thought she had been getting whilst Jacob was away.

At the end of the meal, Tabitha was ordered back to her room and Jacob followed her. There was no sound, as there had been before, so everyone, but Zilpah, hoped that meant that Tabitha hadn't resisted and that Jacob hadn't been as rough as previously. Even so, Zilpah couldn't keep a smile from her face as she thought of the plans now in place.

The next day, Jacob left early in search of a new woman to force into sex. Submissive women he had tamed were no longer an attraction to him and none of the women in the house were going to deliberately entice him into bed. They were his fallback should he fail in his conquests elsewhere. Zilpah was chagrined when Tira asked for straw to restuff Tabitha's mattress, but she dared not deny a direct order from Jacob.

Jacob didn't eat with Zilpah and Tabitha again whilst back in Jerusalem. Zilpah dared not confine Tabitha to her room and did not want to. She hoped that if a conquest went wrong that Jacob would go for Tabitha, not her, when he returned in a foul mood. She ensured that Tabitha was served starvation rations at the table, not realising that Tira was getting extra food from the cook to leave in Tabitha's room for when she returned. Zilpah pretended that it was Jacob's parsimoniousness that restricted what Tabitha was given.

If Jacob had a bad day, he came home looking for sex. He would go for any woman in the house who took his fancy at the time. If that woman was Zilpah, she would lash out the following day at the other women in the house, particularly Tabitha.

A couple of months after his return, Jacob came home in a good mood. Everyone guessed that he had made a new conquest. He announced that he was going on a business trip again the following day. In the morning, he left before anyone else in the house was awake.

6

Zilpah's plan, as she outlined to Salome, was simple. Salome was to get Isaiah to agree to sleep with Zilpah whilst Jacob was on his next business trip. Then Zilpah, hopefully pregnant, would sleep with Jacob on his return. The resulting child would lesson Jacob's aggression considerably, as she was sure that part of his problem was the knowledge that he couldn't father a child.

Salome didn't bat an eyelid at this. Adultery was illegal under Roman law but quite safe for the woman. It was counted as primarily the man's fault, violating the husband's property rights. Zilpah might get a small fine, but that was all. In law, Isaiah could be executed, but that hadn't happened in decades. In fact, adultery laws were hardly ever enforced anymore and a brother fathering a child for an impotent man was the normal solution to the problem and done quite openly. It never occurred to Salome that Hebrew law might be different.

When Jacob went on his next trip to Damascus, Zilpah didn't confine Tabitha to her room as Salome had expected. Instead, after a couple of days of buttering her up in the garden, Zilpah broached her plan with Tabitha. Zilpah would get pregnant by Isaiah whilst Jacob was away. Once the child was born, if it was a boy, Tabitha would do the same the next time Jacob was away. Zilpah was convinced that that would reduce Jacob's abuse of the women in the house.

Tabitha was shocked at the idea of adultery and declared that she couldn't do it herself, although she agreed to fall in with Zilpah's plan for herself. This didn't suit Zilpah totally but, for now, it was enough that Tabitha wouldn't betray her adultery. Isaiah had manoeuvred his wife into visiting her family in Bethany and taking their two boys with her. That left the coast clear for at least a month. Zilpah was sure that she was pregnant when Jacob returned.

Jacob was surprised when, on his return from Damascus, Zilpah came to his bed. He had been unusually tired that evening, not realising that she had put a slow-acting sleeping draft in his wine. He fell asleep before he could take Zilpah and was surprised the following morning when she had waxed lyrical about how pleasurable the previous night had been.

It was then up to the other women in the house to keep Jacob away from Zilpah so that he didn't cause any damage to her or cause a miscarriage. Two months later, Zilpah declared that she was pregnant. She needn't have done so, as it was obvious. Jacob was elated and stopped chasing other women in Jerusalem. He left Zilpah alone but still took the other women in the household, though he was less rough than before. When Zilpah's baby was born it was, to everyone's relief, a boy.

Now, for the second part of her plan to succeed, Zilpah needed to persuade Tabitha to do the same as she had done. She started by trying to reason with her, pointing out how much better Jacob had been since the conception of his son. She also pointed out that it was her duty to provide an heir for Saul, her first husband. But to no avail. She decided to enlist Jacob's help.

She pointed out to Jacob that she had conceived, so it must be wilful on Tabitha's side to avoid getting pregnant. She kept this up, day after day, until she had wound Jacob up into a frenzy and he vowed to take Tabitha every day, not even stopping for her bleed, until she was pregnant. He started the very next day, taking pleasure in being rough with her. When Tabitha asked why he was doing this, he told her that Zilpah had conceived so she must be deliberately avoiding conceiving. Tabitha didn't know what to do. She couldn't very well tell Jacob the truth.

Jacob kept this up for a month. Then one day, when he was out, he boasted about his determination to get Tabitha pregnant and was met with jeers and laughter. One particularly mocking comment struck him.

'Why don't you do the same as you did with Zilpah and get someone else to do it for you, you runt?'

Jacob went home immediately and confronted Zilpah. He went straight to her room, where Salome was dressing her for dinner, and hit her hard. He then threatened to kill the boy if it wasn't his.

'You will never get another son if you kill this one, you idiot,' Zilpah screamed, 'You are incapable of making a woman pregnant.'

'Then who is the father?'

'Your brother, Isaiah. It was the only way.'

'Then why wind me up about Tabitha?'

'Think about it. If Tabitha has a son, he will be heir to Saul's estate. If she does not, then she gets the redemption money when you die. Either way, our son does not get his full inheritance.'

'Your son, you mean.'

'Our son. He is your heir, and he is named Jacob for you. People may say you are not his father but only Isaiah can confirm that, and he will say nothing.'

Jacob was silent for a time before his greed got the better of him.

'So, what is your suggestion?'

'Tabitha is at breaking point. We pretend that you have decided to take a trip to Damascus. Tabitha will go to Isaiah, as I did, to lie with him and get pregnant. You will be forewarned of this and, taking witnesses, will burst in on them. You will then take Tabitha to the Sanhedrin with proof of adultery. Your redemption becomes null and void and you will get to keep both the redemption money and Saul's property.'

'It will mean death.'

Salome was disgusted that Jacob would be a party to his brother's death in this way. Also, Zilpah, after what he had risked for her.

'What about Isaiah? He will not go along with this,' continued Jacob.

'He will. His alternative is death by stoning and you seizing his property as compensation. That would leave his own two sons without any inheritance.'

That was the point at which Salome realised that they were plotting Tabitha's death, not Isaiah's. She let out an anguished grunt as if she had been hit hard in the stomach, then started screaming, 'Murder! Murder!'

The two male servants in the house came running. By the time they arrived, Jacob and Zilpah had Salome pinned to the floor and gagged.

Zilpah quickly told the servants that Salome had gone mad and attacked her. Salome certainly looked mad. Jacob said that a demon must have taken hold of her and that it had a powerful voice. It would be dangerous to let her speak until the demon had left her. They were to keep her locked up, away from the other servants, and not give her any food until she had calmed down, in case the demon used her voice to curse them. The two men dragged Salome out.

Tabitha had been in her room with Tira when she heard the commotion. She sent Tira out to find out what had happened. Tira came back to report that Salome had gone mad and attacked her mistress. They thought a demon must have taken hold of her and were confining her until she calmed down.

7

It was two days later that Salome was released, weak from lack of movement. The steward of the house gently gave her nourishment and, when she had revived, helped her stand, and walk off the stiffness. Once she was alright, he told her that she was wanted by the mistress, in her room.

The house was unusually quiet, even for when the master was at home, the only sound being a low whimpering coming from the mistress's room.

Zilpah must be having problems settling baby Jacob.

Salome had always been able to settle him. On arrival, she found the baby fast asleep, the whimpering coming from the master of the house.

He had blood coming from cuts all over his upper body and particularly his head. An inept Zilpah was trying to minister to them. Salome felt like letting him suffer and refusing to nurse him, but she knew that would help no one, particularly not Tabitha, if she was still alive. Salome took over. She started with the deepest cuts, checking for any other damage as she did so. She decided that Jacob must have a head as hard as an ox as, despite the numerous wounds, there was no sign of any serious damage. As she worked, Jacob moaned and complained about how rough she was being. In truth, Salome was being as gentle as she dared. She needed to ensure that no infection took hold.

She had just finished binding the worst of the wounds when Tabitha arrived home. Jacob, who had claimed he was weak with loss of blood, rose quickly, knocking the bowl of water off Salome's lap. He strode to the front door shouting at Tabitha to go away. He was going to divorce her.

'You can die in the streets like the whore you are,' was his final shout as Tabitha turned to leave.

Salome had caught a brief glimpse of Tabitha and was relieved to see that she looked fine physically. She was worried, though. Where would Tabitha go? What would she do?

As she went to return to her room, she heard one of the maids murmur, 'An eye for an eye, a tooth for a tooth.'

Salome knew the scriptural reference. It was the punishment for perjury. The man who bore false witness was given the punishment the defendant would have got, had he been found guilty. Then she remembered the story of Judith. The men who had falsely accused her of adultery had been stoned. So that is what had happened to Jacob.

Her thoughts were interrupted by a shout from Jacob, 'What do you mean, there is no food in the house? So, if Salome can't go to the market for two days, we starve? You are all useless. Salome! Salome!'

Salome turned around and went back to the main room, where Jacob threw his purse at her.

'Go and get some food.'

Salome left in thought. The market square was awash with gossip. She soon learned what had happened to Tabitha and Jacob. Tabitha had been dragged here before a preacher called Jesus. The preacher, although she was confused how, had managed to have the charge of adultery against Tabitha dropped. The crowd had then turned on Jacob. He deserved it of course. He had committed adultery countless times. She was relieved about Tabitha, but still worried.

When Salome arrived at the usual Greek merchant she bought from, she found Photina there. Photina took one look at Salome and knew there was something up. She asked nothing, just put her arm around her. Salome burst into tears, buried her head in Photina's shoulder, and sobbed her heart out. Salome had never done that before. She had grown up accepting everything, because she was a slave. She then poured out her story to Photina, not caring what she thought of her unwitting connivance in what had happened.

'Alexander, quickly give Salome what she needs. There is a friend of mine she must meet, and soon, whilst she can help.'

'Don't wait for me,' replied the trader, 'Just give me your list. I will have it ready for you when you return.'

Salome gave him the wax tablet the steward had given her of the supplies he needed and Photina almost dragged her away in her hurry.

Photina led expertly through the Jerusalem streets, almost at a run. Salome, being tall, was a fast walker, but still had difficulty keeping up. At the Damascus Gate, they found a woman talking to the leader of a caravan of wagons. Photina shouted to her.

'Mary, wait!'

'I am not going anywhere. I am just giving instructions to everyone for the journey back and the keep of the house whilst I am away.'

'Just wait. This is Salome. Hear what she has to say first.'

Salome gave her story a second time and was even more nervous than previously. Mary was obviously Hebrew. She would have less sympathy than Photina. Mary's response took her by surprise.

'I will find Tabitha. I saw her at the square before Jesus, so I know what she looks like. She can go with Judith, here, to the safety of Galilee. But what about you Salome? If you are Tabitha's maid, she has the right to take you with her. You could go too.'

Salome was tempted to lie but couldn't.

'I am the maid and slave of Zilpah, the mistress. I cannot go.'

Photina looked with sympathy at Salome.

'I am sure Alexander will have everything ready, so if you hurry back to the market, your shopping trip will have been a bit long, but not unusually so.'

Salome reddened.

'I don't know the way. I am only allowed out of the house to go to the market, so I don't know Jerusalem at all.'

Mary sent Judith to accompany Salome back to the market, whilst she set out to look for Tabitha. The pile of goods waiting for Salome made her realise that she was shopping for three days. She was a strong woman but there was no way that she would be able to carry the pile in front of her on her own, particularly after her two-day confinement. Judith helped her carry it back before heading off back to the Damascus Gate.

Jacob was too busy whining about his misfortune and whimpering over his pain to notice how long Salome had been. The cook quickly prepared the food and Jacob sullenly ate it. Everyone else ate in tense silence.

8

Jacob was subdued for a few days following Tabitha's departure. Then Isaiah came round. This was a momentous occasion. Isaiah had never visited before. Jacob begrudgingly let him in and, even more begrudgingly, offered refreshment. Isaiah had been afraid that he would be despised for his role in accusing Tabitha but, on his way, he had been greeted by friends in their usual manner. He immediately broached the subject he had come about.

'Tabitha cannot remain in this house as your wife and I feel responsible for what happened. So, if you divorce her, I will marry her and look after her. I am even willing to recompense you the redemption money.'

'And what are you going to say to your wife?'

'My wife knows. I told her the whole story. She understands completely. She knows that, whilst it is technically adulterous to sleep with another's wife, it is common to do so to give an impotent man an heir. I was under the impression from Zilpah that you knew and approved. Like me, my wife feels that we have a responsibility to Tabitha.'

'Humph.'

'Well?'

'I don't know where the bitch is. I haven't seen her since the day she got off with adultery, but I will tell you this. There is no way I am going to divorce her just so she can live in luxury with you. She can die in the gutter as she deserves.'

Nothing Isaiah said could change Jacob's mind. He left, a chastened man. He was so preoccupied that he didn't notice Salome slip out after him and follow him home.

Salome had left the house on the pretext of going to the market. She had intended to tell Isaiah the full story and where Tabitha was, but something stopped her. Still, at least she knew where he lived now. It might be useful. She had learnt from her trader, when she had seen him a couple of days after Tabitha had disappeared, that she was safely on her way to Galilee. Not knowing Jerusalem, Salome initially found it difficult to navigate her way to the market from Isaiah's house. Then she realised the advantage of Temple Mount. Ultimately, wherever you were in Jerusalem, if you headed for Temple Mount you would find somewhere familiar. In that way, she found the market and bought a few things she had intended to buy the following day.

On her return, she found that Jacob had gone out. He came home in a bad mood. He had been jeered everywhere he went. Those who knew him shouted that it was him who should have been stoned. More than one man, whose wife had been forced by Jacob, looked with satisfaction at his wounds from the stones. Some even volunteered to 'finish the job'. Those who didn't know him taunted him about his inability to satisfy his wife. Jacob hadn't bargained on that.

When he got back to the house, Jacob grabbed Zilpah by the hair and dragged her into her room. As he hit her, he screamed that it was all her fault and that he should never have listened to her. He had lost his reputation and would never get it back.

'You haven't lost your reputation; you never had a reputation to lose. Everyone knew about you forcing women to your will. The only reason no one stoned you before was that their wives would have been stoned as well.'

'I should have you stoned.'

'And have to admit that you are impotent and had to get your brother to perform for you, you excuse for a man. It was your reputation that landed us in this. Had the Pharisees not doubted what had happened, Tabitha would never have been taken before Jesus in the first place.'

There was another scream, as Jacob hit Zilpah again.

'I will show you how impotent I am, you bitch.'

There was a thud as Zilpah landed heavily on the bed and hit her head on the wall, but that did not stop Jacob.

He came out of the room an hour later, covered in blood. He shouted back at Zilpah, 'That will teach you to call me impotent.'

Salome rushed into the room. Zilpah was out cold, so mercifully had probably not felt too much of the pain from what Jacob had done to her. She would feel it when she woke. Zilpah needed a physician, but Salome knew that Jacob would not allow one. He never wanted a witness, from outside the house, to the goings on in the house. Salome thought this stupid, as everyone knew anyway. She quickly examined Zilpah.

Zilpah had numerous head wounds and a broken left arm where she had defended herself from being hit with a now-broken chair. She had cuts and bruises all over. Her worst injuries were the tears around her vagina where Jacob had forced himself on her. Salome felt her way inside, checking for any internal injury. Zilpah moaned and flinched, even in her unconscious state.

Salome called Tira to come and help her. Tira had anticipated this and entered carrying warm water, honey, olive oil and loads of linen strips. She had got used to preparing these as soon as Jacob entered Tabitha's room over the last month. Hardened as she was, though, Tira winced at the extent of Zilpah's injuries. After stopping the worst of the bleeding and binding linen strips around tightly to keep pressure on the wound, Salome turned her attention to the broken arm. With Tira holding the upper arm, Salome pulled the fracture back into place and bound it to a splint. She then sent Tira to get a needle and thread to sew up the vaginal tears.

Hopefully, those Roman military physicians know what they are doing when they sew up soldiers' wounds. Good job I am naturally inquisitive as well and asked how they got their scars and what the puncture-like marks along them were.

'And bring some wine laced with myrrh,' Salome shouted after Tira. 'She will need the pain relief when she comes round.'

Meanwhile, Jacob was sitting in the main room of the house, still covered in blood, talking business with his steward as if nothing had happened.

Salome stayed in Zilpah's room for the next three days, with Tira bringing meals and helping in other ways when required. Salome still went to market each day, so Tira then took over the task of tending Zilpah.

The day he had hit Zilpah, Jacob just sat where he was until he fell asleep. The steward and the other male servant took the opportunity to remove his bloodied clothing and dress him in fresh clothes. The following morning when he awoke, he sat up and stared at the wall and didn't move. At mealtimes, they spoon-fed him like a baby. The women servants were noticeable for their absence as the steward and the other male servant waited on Jacob. Seemingly, he didn't notice the lack of women around as he sat, day after day, just staring at the wall ahead of him. They couldn't even get him to toilet himself, so he required a constant change of clothes.

Jacob suddenly came out of his mental stasis on the Thursday of the following week. He got up abruptly and left the house. The steward, who was sitting with him at the time, was taken completely by surprise and cried out for him to stop, but Jacob had disappeared before anyone could stop him.

Salome came running at the steward's call.

'He is gone,' said the steward.

'We need to find him. Where will he go?'

'I have no idea. We will have to wait for him to return. You look concerned.'

'Jerusalem is tense. Everyone is jumpy, especially the Romans. Pilate's men have captured the Zealot, Barabbas, and are planning to execute him tomorrow. In addition, there are rumours that the teacher, Jesus of Nazareth, is going to be arrested. With Jerusalem full of visitors, because of Passover starting soon, no one is sure of anyone. The stranger could be an innocent pilgrim or a Zealot, seeking to free Barabbas.'

'We will just have to wait and hope.'

They waited until the fourth hour after noon, when Jacob burst in through the front door, drunk. Where he had found the money to buy drink they didn't know, but that wasn't their immediate problem. He was wild and angry. The steward tried to stop Jacob but couldn't hold him. Jacob went straight to Tabitha's room.

They heard Jacob shout at Tira, 'Now Tabitha is gone, you will take her place.'

Tira shouted defiantly, 'I am too young. I haven't had my first bleed.'

They heard the thud as Jacob hit Tira and a slap as Tira hit him back. The whole household rushed to Tabitha's room. The two male servants tried to restrain Jacob but, in his madness, he had the strength of Samson and easily threw them off. He grabbed a chair, as he had done with Zilpah, and aimed blows at the steward and the other man. They retreated to safety. Jacob then turned on Tira and hit her with the chair, again and again. He didn't stop until the chair broke, and he was just holding a stick of a leg. He then went back into the stasis, just standing there, staring at the wall.

Salome rushed in to see to Tira. The other women tentatively followed, giving Jacob as wide a berth as possible. It was apparent that Tira was dead. The women gently picked up her body and lay her on Tabitha's bed. Salome, with tears streaming down her face, gently closed Tira's eyes and took a blanket to cover the body.

Seeing Tira covered in death seemed to animate Jacob. He looked from Tira to Salome and saw her eyes flash in anger once more. Salome felt the power surge in her as she had done after Jacob had taken her. Once more, Jacob was out of the room before anyone could react. The steward managed to grab him before he left the house, but Jacob reached for a sword and started swinging it around maniacally, seeing imaginary demons all around him. The steward let go of him and dived for cover behind one of the eating couches. Jacob ran out of the house, followed by the other male servant, but didn't get far. He ran into a Roman patrol. His flailing sword glanced the shoulder pad of one of the soldiers. The centurion drew his sword and, in one swift motion, stabbed Jacob in the stomach and up through the rib cage, piercing his heart. Jacob was dead before he hit the ground. The centurion looked around for more assailants and, finding none, cleaned his sword and sheathed it, then swiftly moved on.

They carried Jacob's body back into the house and sent Salome to fetch Isaiah, as she was the only one who knew where he lived.

9

Isaiah immediately set about arranging the funeral. Since no one wanted to mourn Jacob, there wasn't much to do but buy a shroud and pay the gravediggers. The procession consisted of only Isaiah. Zilpah pleaded that she was unable to go because of her injuries and the servants weren't obliged to, so didn't. Usually, a procession leaving a house would pick up people on the way. In this case, Isaiah was on his own all the way there.

He returned with a second shroud and the gravediggers for Tira's body. This time, all the servants insisted on going and Zilpah made a miraculous recovery to go as well. This was a surprise to Salome, as Zilpah had been abusive to Tira many times, hitting her harder than she needed to. She asked Zilpah about it.

'I was jealous. Tira was the only woman in the house that Jacob wouldn't touch. He hit her, of course, but he didn't touch her if you know what I mean. Then there was her goodness. She never complained, no matter what I did. Then, when Jacob did this to me, she tended me as caringly and assiduously as you did, almost as if I was her mother. Ironic really. No one from my family, my clan, or my tribe cared about me after I married Jacob and then I was looked after by a British slave and a Naphtali girl.'

A tear made a furrow down the make-up which was hiding the bruises on Zilpah's face.

After Tira was buried, there was the weeklong period of mourning. No one visited the house, as there was no mourning for Jacob, and no one knew how to contact the friends and family of Tira. There would have been Galileans, where Tira came from, in Jerusalem for Passover. There may even have been Naphtali, but no one mourned Tira, except Zilpah and the servants.

That Passover was a momentous one. The religious authorities arrested Jesus of Nazareth. There was no case against him, but the religious leaders were worried. People were calling Jesus 'The Messiah'. Jerusalem thronged with Zealot supporters of Barabbas and there was a threat that they might switch allegiance to Jesus and revolt against Roman rule. The Romans were intolerant of failure. The religious leaders were given the privilege of Roman citizenship in return for keeping the peace. It was not just loss of privilege the Pharisees and Sadducees were worried about, their very lives would be forfeited should an uprising occur, whoever won. If the Romans won, they would be executed for their failure. If the Zealots won, they would be executed for collaborating with the Romans.

The Pharisees decided that Barabbas was the lesser threat. They manipulated his release and Jesus's execution. Then came rumours that Jesus had risen from the dead. These even penetrated the walls of Jacob's house, so that the conversation changed from talk of Tira and Jacob.

It was the Year of Jubilee, which made the events even more significant since that was when all debts were cancelled, and the prisoners and slaves were released. The Romans claimed that they had released everyone. If you count execution as release, they were correct. Hence their hurry to execute so many prisoners before the end of Passover, which was the traditional time when they were released.

At the end of Passover, Isaiah came to see them to sort out Jacob's affairs. Most of it was easy, as baby Jacob was his heir and Zilpah had custodianship of the estate until he came into his inheritance when he was fourteen. All the slaves, except Salome, were Judean so they were set free, and the women were given a dowry. They were given the choice of whether to stay on as hired servants or leave. They all decided to leave. That left Tabitha and Salome to deal with.

Tabitha was entitled to the redemption money for Saul's estate and her dowry. Isaiah was shocked that the latter had been withheld from her but managed to extract it from Zilpah. When it came to the redemption money, Isaiah couldn't find it. He eventually ascertained that Jacob had bribed a corrupt judge to certify that the money had been paid when it hadn't. It was then up to Zilpah, who refused to part with either the redemption money or the estate, pointing out that, under the law, the redemption money had already been paid. There was nothing Isaiah could do. He didn't know what he was going to do with Tabitha's dowry either as he didn't know where she was.

Salome's status was easier to sort out than Isaiah had feared. Although in the Year of Jubilee all slaves of Hebrews were supposed to be released, the custom had changed, and it was then usually only applied to Hebrew slaves. Also, she was counted as Zilpah's slave, not Jacob's. With Zilpah's intransigence over Tabitha's entitlement to Saul's estate, Isaiah feared the worst. He started by interviewing Salome.

'Who are you and how did you come to be in Jerusalem?'

'I came here from Rome as a slave to my uncle, Jacob.'

'That is a Hebrew name, not a Roman one.'

'My grandfather was Judean. His father bought my grandmother, who was from Britannia, as a concubine for him. My mother was thus born a slave, and hence so was I. When my grandfather died, I became my Uncle Jacob's slave. After he brought me here, he sold me to your brother Jacob.'

'I understand that your father owed your uncle a lot of money.'

Salome was confused.

'My father was a slave from Britannia. My grandfather hired him from another Hebrew as a breed male.'

Isaiah was shocked. Thus prompted, he remembered the controversy a couple of years before. He hadn't quite understood it at the time, but then it became clear. Salome's uncle and grandfather had acted contrary to Hebrew law and custom.

He left to find Salome's uncle and, on his return, talked to Zilpah privately, and then Salome once more.

'There is a problem with your status. Under Hebrew law, you are not, and never have been, a slave.'

Salome stood looking at him, agog.

'Under Hebrew law, your mother is counted as the daughter of your grandfather's senior wife. As he followed Roman custom and only had one wife, your mother is counted as Jacob's older sister. Under Hebrew law, your mother should have been given a dowry and honourably married. When your uncle brought you here, he realised that he would be expected to find you a husband and provide a dowry, so he invented a story of your father owing him money and sold you to my brother. No one else would buy you because of your parentage. As you know, my brother's servants were all slaves.'

Salome recovered.

'So, what now?'

'That is the difficulty. I have been to see your uncle. He claims that you were a slave under Roman Law, which trumps Hebrew Law. He is right, of course, but at any other time would not get away with it. With the events over Passover, it is not possible to push such a case, as everyone is afraid of the Roman reaction to even a minor challenge to their authority. I have talked to Zilpah, and she has agreed to free you, but will not provide a dowry.'

'But why would she do that if I am a slave under Roman law?'

'Because I pointed out to her that she needs the support of the Hebrew community. Under Hebrew law, she has control of her own money. Any money she earns is hers, her dowry is hers and she controls Jacob's estate. Roman custom is different. Roman women do not control their dowries, even if they have one. If Roman women earn money, it belongs to their husbands. If widowed, it belongs to her family. The Romans have no respect for their women. They treat their wives as breeding mares, fining them if they are unmarried and haven't at least three children. Most are little more than slaves. Actually, they are worse off than their slaves, as slaves can earn money to buy their freedom, but their women can't. If Zilpah is going to survive in Jerusalem, she will need the support of her people.'

Isaiah went to continue but Salome held up her hand to stop him whilst she sorted out what he had said in her own mind. The one thing that kept coming back into her head and made her delirious was that she was free. She wasn't a slave.

'So, what now?' Salome asked.

'You have the choice. You can either stay here as Zilpah's maid, as a hired servant, or you can seek employment elsewhere or is there anything else you would like to do?'

Salome thought about it for a moment.

'I will stay here. I do not have the money to go anywhere else and I have no dowry to get married.'

Jacob nodded, then said out loud to himself, 'Now to find Tabitha.'

'I can help you there,' said Salome.

'What?' said Isaiah, emerging from his thoughts.

'I know where Tabitha is.'

Jacob was alert.

'Where?'

'She went to Galilee and is staying at the house of Mary of Magdala.'

'That will cause some difficulty. Mary was a follower of Jesus of Nazareth and his followers are in hiding. Thank you, though, it gives me somewhere to start.'

Isaiah then left.

10

Over the next couple of weeks, Salome started to run the house. She did everything from caring for Zilpah and baby Jacob, to cooking, cleaning, and going to the market. There wasn't a great deal to do, as Zilpah was recovering well.

The tension in the city meant that most Hebrew women were afraid to go out. Hebrews were being taunted by Romans and Greeks and their women were being harassed. Salome didn't look Hebrew with her copper-infused brown hair. By hitching her dress up a few inches when she went out, as Greek women did, she could easily roam the streets unmolested. She also had the advantage that she dealt with the Gentile traders in the market.

Within two days, the mistresses of neighbouring houses were paying her to get what they needed from the market. By the end of the week, she had borrowed Alexander's cart to bring back everything she needed. It was a month before life returned to normal, although there was still unease. Suddenly, the women nearby, who had been friendly to Salome whilst she was getting their goods from the market, ignored her once more.

Life settled down until Zilpah started complaining about headaches. Salome treated her with valerian but, when the headaches became more frequent, Salome moved on to myrrh. This seemed to work for a time, but Zilpah started getting irritable and having mood swings. Salome thought that she was too young to be having the change. One day, she found Zilpah with the baby above her, as if in a trance, ready to smash its head against a wall. Salome kept the baby in sight constantly after that, taking him with her when she went to the market.

One day, Salome came back from the market to find Zilpah in a rage, smashing things. She realised that she couldn't cope on her own anymore, so after slipping Zilpah a sleeping draught, she took the baby and went to Isaiah. He acted immediately and got a nurse for baby Jacob, who could stay with Zilpah whilst Salome was out. This helped initially, but Zilpah got gradually worse. She started accusing Salome of poisoning her and claimed that she wanted her out of the way so she could care for the baby and get her hands on Jacob's estate. Salome started making sure that the nurse checked her preparation every time she administered myrrh to Zilpah. She even had the nurse check her cooking.

Things came to a head three months later. Zilpah had been sitting staring at the wall all morning, oblivious to everything going on around her. Suddenly she stood up, screamed, and ran out of the house, wailing as she ran. Half an hour later she returned with Isaiah.

When they entered the house, Zilpah pointed to Salome.

'There is the murderer. She has killed Jacob and replaced him with her own brat.'

'I have never had a child,' said Salome.

Isaiah called the nurse, then examined the child. It certainly seemed to be Jacob, as he had the family features. He looked at the nurse.

'Is this Jacob?'

The nurse looked confused.

'Yes sir.'

'Zilpah claims that Salome has switched the children and that this is Salome's child, but she claims that she has never had a child.'

'That is easily settled. If Salome has been pregnant, she will have stretch marks. There is no way of hiding them. I will examine her.'

The nurse gave Jacob to Isaiah to hold. Isaiah felt a jolt go through his body, as he had never held his son before. A few minutes later, the nurse returned with Salome.

'She has no stretch marks, nor is there any indication of damage to the vagina that having a baby would cause.'

'They are in it together. They are poisoning me and planning to share Jacob's estate between them.' Zilpah shouted, deafening them.

Neighbours started gathering to see what was going on. Isaiah made a quick decision, which was unusual for him. He asked two of the women to stay with Zilpah and the baby, then took Salome and the nurse to his house. He went out immediately, leaving the women in his wife's care. It was two hours later when he returned with a tall man, sort of Greek-looking, with blue eyes.

'This is Jonah. Zilpah will not have either of you in her house again, so I am going to have to pay you off. I have found a new maid for Zilpah and a new nurse for Jacob. I doubt they will be as good as you, but it was necessary.'

Isaiah turned to the nurse and handed her a week's pay.

'I hope that this will last until you can find a new position.'

The nurse thanked him and left. Isaiah looked at Salome for a time before handing her a week's pay as well.

'What will you do now, Salome?'

'I don't know. The chance of me finding a position in Jerusalem is slim. Maybe I will go to Sychar and see if Photina can help me. Samaritans seem less worried about someone not being completely Hebrew than Judeans are.'

'Photina is in Damascus with her husband, Demetrius,' Jonah chipped in.

'Then I will go to Damascus.'

'Damascus is at least two weeks' travel,' said Isaiah. 'It is a big city as well. Your chance of finding them is very small. Jonah here is Mary of Magdala's cousin. I met him when I returned Tabitha's dowry via Mary.'

Salome still looked suspicious.

'On the day Tabitha was accused of adultery, you found Photina in the market and told her what had happened. She took you to the Damascus Gate where Mary was preparing to send her household back to Galilee. Mary searched for Tabitha, found her and sent her to Galilee. In the meantime, Judith, Mary's servant, took you back to the market. You knew what had happened to Tabitha because Alexander told you on your next visit to the market.'

'You might have found out about that from other people I have told,' Salome blurted out and then whispered to herself, 'But I haven't told anyone, not a soul.'

She looked at Jonah.

'You look Greek, not Hebrew.'

'You look, I don't know what, not Hebrew,' Jonah retorted. 'I am Naphtali. Like the Samaritans, we have intermarried with non-Hebrews. In our case, Greeks.'

Salome was still reluctant, but something inside her head was whispering to her that all would be well. She tried not to listen and analyse it logically, but the quiet voice was persistent. Finally, she gave in, not knowing whether it was the insistent voice that had won, or that she had decided that she had no other choice.

'I will go with you. There doesn't appear to be any other option.'

The journey to Galilee was uneventful. Salome was on heightened alert all the way. When they arrived in Magdala, she was relieved to find that Jonah was well-known. It was even more comforting that he didn't hide her away but introduced her by name, telling people that she was a Hebrew, in need, from Jerusalem. Her looks weren't so out of place there either, with so many Hebrews looking more like Greeks than the Judeans she had met in Jerusalem.

It seemed that Jonah must have been away for some time, as everyone wanted to stop and talk to him. It took them an hour to get from the edge of Magdala to Mary's house, which was less than half a mile. By the time they arrived, a woman was waiting for them. Salome knew she had seen her before but couldn't place her for a minute. Then it occurred to her. The woman had been seated on one of the carts in the train when she had met Mary at the Damascus Gate.

'Good day, Esther,' said Jonah.

'Hello, Jonah. Welcome, Salome. You probably don't remember me.'

Salome smiled.

'You were on one of the carts when I met Mary about Tabitha.'

'You are sharp-eyed. Mary isn't here, Jonah. She and Tabitha have gone to Damascus.'

'Is everyone in Damascus? I heard that Demetrius and Photina had gone to Damascus too.'

'Demetrius is ill, the baby that is, so Photina has stayed in Sychar. Only Demetrius is in Damascus.'

'Seems I am going to have to take you back to Sychar, Salome.'

Esther looked at Salome for a moment.

'Aren't you a lady's maid?'

'Yes, I was Zilpah's maid.'

'Your mother's maid is incapacitated at the moment, Jonah. Just had her first child. Needs to rest for a few weeks. Leave her there. I am sure your mother will appreciate the help.'

'Sounds good.'

Esther saw the doubt on Salome's face.

'Tell you what, I'll come with you. Need to see how things are going with the baby anyway.'

They all got onto Jonah's cart and headed out of Magdala. It wasn't far, only about five miles, but far enough to have made Salome very anxious if she had been alone with Jonah. She was shocked when they arrived, as it was the largest house she had ever seen. The woman who greeted them, Jonah's mother, wore the most expensive clothes she had seen outside of the highest-ranking Judean and Roman women in Jerusalem.

It was late, so they all stayed the night. Jonah took Esther back to Magdala the following morning before heading back to Jerusalem, leaving Salome in his mother's care.

11

Salome settled in and Jonah's mother soon realised that she was far better trained than her usual maid. She told her maid, Eban, that she should take as much time off as she needed. This worried her until Salome arrived at the end of the month with her usual pay. The maid was surprised, as no one she had ever worked for before had given her money whilst she was sick. They struck up a conversation but found it difficult as the maid's Aramaic was heavily accented and she spoke very little Greek or Hebrew. Salome did understand that the maid had been unable to go to the market and so had run out of flour and oil. She smiled as Jonah's mother had specifically told her to help the maid out if she could.

Salome had noticed a trader on her way into the village and, finding him, took him to the maid's house. Unsurprisingly, they knew each other, and he offered to deliver whatever she needed every week.

After the trader had gone, Salome pointed to each item the maid had bought and said the name, first in Aramaic, then Hebrew and finally Greek. The maid smiled, then started pointing to other objects, saying the name in Aramaic and, when she knew it, in Hebrew. Salome replied with the name in Greek.

After this, Salome spent as much time as possible at the maid's house, learning the local Aramaic and teaching her

Greek and Hebrew. Inevitably, news of this reached Jonah's mother's ears. She smiled. Jonah had judged Salome well, saying he thought that she would be an asset.

Three months after Salome arrived, the maid was well enough to return to her duties, bringing her baby with her, which surprised Salome. In Rome, working women were expected to find someone to look after their children whilst they worked. Salome had another shock. On the first afternoon of the maid's return, they sat down and Jonah's mother handed round fine linen and needles and thread. The other two women started at once, but Salome just sat there, non-plussed.

'Ah, we have found something that you can't do,' said Jonah's mother, in Aramaic.

'I can sew, as any lady's maid can, but I have never embroidered. I have never even seen anyone embroider,' Salome replied, also in Aramaic.

'But you do pick up languages very quickly. I have a proposition for you, Salome. We will teach you to embroider if you can teach my maid to be as good a lady's maid as you. In addition, you can continue Eban's lessons in Greek and start teaching me as well. That way you will earn your keep. Any profit on your embroidery is yours to keep. You look surprised, Salome.'

'In Roman households, you must work outside the home to keep any money you earn. Even then, most Romans would demand that you give them any money you have earned. All of them would demand the money if their wife earnt it. It is why Roman wives never work. They are meant to just have babies, nothing more.'

Salome expected to be ousted at any time, but never was. Then Jonah came for a visit.

'Hello, mother. I have asked Tabitha to marry me, and she has accepted.'

Salome couldn't help herself.

'You mean Tabitha, as in our …?' then didn't know how to continue.

Jonah smiled. 'Yes, I mean Tabitha, as in our mutual acquaintance.'

'Oh!'

'I intend to move back here with her and start up our merchant business again. I still have loads of contacts.'

'How will you deal in Damascus? I understand that Silas has returned to Capernaum.'

'Demetrius, Photina's husband, and I are going into partnership.'

Martha, Jonah's mother, frowned. She didn't mind. Demetrius was a good man, but he was married to a Samaritan. That would not be accepted amongst Hebrews in Galilee.

'We will have to talk about this.'

The rest of the day, Salome and the maid were left to their own devices as Jonah and his mother discussed business.

The following morning, Jonah announced that he was going to Sychar to see Demetrius.

'Before I go, Salome, I have a question to ask you. A favour really. Tabitha is going to be nervous when she comes here, for several reasons, as I think you will understand. My mother doesn't need two maids. Would you take the post of Tabitha's maid? At least, that way, Tabitha will have a friendly face when she arrives.'

The request took Salome by surprise. She hadn't wanted to stay around too long and was about to say no when she was hit by a pang of guilt. It suddenly occurred to her that Tira's death was her fault. Had she not been so anxious to appear perfectly normal when she had returned from seeing Mary of Magdala about Tabitha, she might have remembered that, as Tabitha's maid, Tira was entitled to go with her. It should be Tira here, not Salome. She owed Tira, and she would have wanted her to look after Tabitha.

'You can go if you wish, I can get another maid,' Jonah's voice interrupted her thoughts.

'I will stay, at least until Tabitha is settled in and then until I have trained a replacement.'

Jonah smiled.

'Thank you, Salome. I am sure Tabitha will be delighted to see you.'

12

Salome didn't leave. She had been worried that she would be blamed for what had happened, but Tabitha was delighted to see her. Then Tabitha became pregnant, and Salome wanted to see her through the pregnancy and care for her in the first months after the child, a boy named Yeshua, Jesus in Greek, was born. Then Tabitha couldn't have any more children, so Salome stayed to look after her.

I was in the room when Tabitha suggested that Jonah take a second wife or concubine. I held my breath. The usual candidate for a concubine was the wife's maid. I still don't know whether it was disappointment or relief that the handsome Jonah swore that he would rather have one child with Tabitha than a dozen with any other woman.

Mary of Magdala had fled to Gaul with her adopted daughter, Sarah, because a silly rumour, that Jesus of Nazareth was Sarah's father, had put them both in danger. Mary was Tabitha's closest friend.

Then Jonah, Demetrius, Jonah's distant cousin Joseph and his wife Miriam were killed in a riot in Damascus. Miriam had left their baby daughter, Miriam, in Tabitha's care when they went. Tabitha wasn't a natural mother. Looking after Yeshua was one thing but looking after two infants would be beyond her.

There was another reason, Salome acknowledged. Miriam was Tira's sister. She owed it to Tira to give her niece every possible advantage she could. This was how Salome became a nanny and teacher to the children. Her fluency in Hebrew, Latin and Greek would give the children a first-class education. Her natural maternal instincts meant that the children automatically came to 'Nanna Lomie' when upset or troubled.

Tabitha was busy. She had taken over the merchant business, running it on behalf of Jesus, as Jonah's heir. Photina was running the business out of Sychar. They couldn't travel, of course, because of the children. Photina had two boys, Demetrius and Alexander. They used Matthias, the chief carter, to transport goods for them. Demetrius's main contact in Damascus became their agent there. Miriam's father-in-law, Silas, carried on dealing internationally for them, as he did for all the merchants locally.

Two years after Jonah had died, Tabitha stopped Salome after she had dressed her hair.

'I need to talk to you before breakfast.'

Salome wondered why. Tabitha always included Salome in negotiations if they were dealing with Greek merchants because of her fluency in the language, but there were no pending negotiations. Perhaps Matthias had given notice of something when he had stopped the previous day, dropping goods off from Damascus and picking up goods for Jerusalem. His next stop would be Sychar.

'There is no hurry to decide on this, but Matthias has asked for you in marriage.'

Salome was stunned. It had never occurred to her that any Hebrew would want to marry her, let alone Matthias who was Judean.

'But I don't have a tribe,' was all she could think of to say.

'You do,' replied Tabitha. 'Through my marriage to Jonah, I am now Naphtali. As my maid, you are counted as Naphtali.

Besides, if it doesn't bother Matthias, it really isn't a problem. If you marry him, of course, you will be Judean again.'

'Again? Oh, yes, I'd forgotten. I have never thought of myself as Hebrew, let alone Judean.'

Matthias wasn't due back for another month, so Salome had plenty of time to think. Too much time. She decided almost at once that she didn't want to marry him. She wanted to travel, not be tied down in one place. Then the doubts set in. She couldn't leave Tabitha with two children to look after and a business to run. Even if she wanted to, she realised that she wouldn't be able to just up sticks for years to come. Then, she did want children of her own. A daughter with leaf-green eyes to carry on the royal line. Also, Matthias's trade lent itself to travel when the children were older. Then there was that voice inside her head again, telling her that she should marry Matthias. She swung one way, then the other, not knowing what her answer would be.

When Matthias arrived, bringing goods from Jerusalem and Sychar, it was late in the evening, so he stayed over in the servants' quarters. Salome still hadn't made her mind up and didn't sleep that night, turning everything over in her head. Tabitha called her in when Matthias came into the house after breakfast.

'Have you decided yet on whether to marry Matthias?'

Salome was tired and, prompted by the voice, said the first thing that came into her head, 'I will be honoured to marry Matthias.'

Matthias and Tabitha were obviously surprised, but not as surprised as Salome, who had been determined to say that she needed more time. The marriage contract was signed then and there.

It was decided that the wedding should be when Matthias returned from Damascus in a month's time. He went away in a joyous mood. Salome realised that Tabitha was looking strangely at her, but did not question her decision.

Tabitha talked to Martha, Jonah's mother, and then went out. Usually, Tabitha would take Salome with her, but Salome didn't notice her omission, dazed as she was. When she came back, Tabitha had a smile on her face.

The following day, after breakfast, Martha took the children on a visit to see their cousin, Mary, the adopted daughter of Mary of Magdala and older sister to Sarah, who was now in Gaul. Salome was at a loose end, with nothing to do.

'Salome!' Tabitha called. 'Bring your sewing.'

Salome's heart dropped. Sewing was not her favourite pastime, but there was no excuse not to. Still, it had its benefits, as she could wheedle out of Tabitha what she had been doing the previous day.

She didn't have to ask. Laid in front of Tabitha were wedding clothes for a fitting for Salome, and the local tailoress was with her. Once the fitting was over, and the seamstress had gone, Tabitha took out a fine linen cloth and silk threads of many colours.

'What design would you like on your wedding shawl?' Tabitha asked.

That was a great honour. Tabitha's wedding shawls sold for a fortune and were renowned from Jerusalem to Damascus, and beyond. As with the previous day, Salome answered the first thing that came into her head, prompted by the insistent inner voice, 'Swans in a pool, surrounded by birches and oaks.'

'It will have to be a single design. I will not be able to do a repeat pattern of that,' was all Tabitha said.

Dumbstruck, Salome just nodded. Tabitha changed it a little from her original idea, putting the main design into the part of the shawl that would go down Salome's back, then adding swans, here and there, to balance it on the rest of the shawl. That wasn't the only shock in store for Salome.

Two weeks later, the tailoress brought back the wedding clothes, along with a veil. Tabitha called Martha, Salome, and the children to come in. The tailoress dressed Salome. One or two last-minute alterations were made and then Salome picked up the veil. It was designed to be worn with the standard dowry headdress. Her heart sank.

Tabitha saw the reaction, as Salome's sadness was written all over her face.

'Ezra! We are ready now.'

The local goldsmith entered, carrying a sumptuous headdress. The framework was a strong thread to make it pliable, with the standard ties at the back to fit it to her head. The thread was covered in beads, everywhere except at the sides and the fitting across the front that would cover her face below her eyes. These were covered in heavy gold coins interspersed with occasional semi-precious stones.

Tabitha fitted the headdress attaching the veil and then the frontispiece across, over the top of it. Finally, she put the wedding shawl on, stood back and smiled with satisfaction.

Salome made a muffled protest, 'It's not fair, I don't know what I look like.'

Tabitha sent Eban to fetch a mirror. Salome just stood, staring at herself for a full five minutes, before saying, 'I can't have this; I don't deserve it.'

Tabitha asked the tailoress to take the children into the other room and Ezra to join them.

When they had left, Tabitha looked at Salome appreciatively.

'You do look magnificent, just like the high-status, wealthy lady you are.'

'But I am not high-status, and certainly not wealthy. Why are you doing this?'

'Shall we start with the dowry, Martha?'

Martha spoke, 'When Isaiah contacted Jonah about you, he had tried unsuccessfully to get your uncle, Jacob, to provide a dowry. He had also failed with Zilpah. Isaiah told Jonah your story, so Jonah took matters into his own hands. He first checked with contacts in Rome that you were telling the truth about your grandmother. He then went to see Isaiah and your uncle in Jerusalem. By this time, the furore over Jesus had died down so he was in a better bargaining position. First, he went to Isaiah and pointed out to him that his brother, Jacob, had been duty-bound to provide you with a dowry before he gave you to Zilpah. Isaiah saw the sense, and as he was running his brother's estate, at Zilpah's request, he provided a dowry from it. Jonah then went to see your uncle. He told him that he was not obliged, under Roman law, to provide a dowry and Jonah was not going to challenge that. He also pointed out that custom is greater than law and that, if Jonah put around what Jacob had done, his customers would abandon him again. Only *this* time, Jonah himself would step in to supply the commodities, meaning that your uncle would be ruined. Your uncle provided a very generous dowry. Of course, he crowed about his generosity, but that didn't bother Jonah. Job done.'

'So, this headdress I am wearing is legitimately my dowry and not from you?' Salome wept.

'That is not your dowry, just a token of it,' said Tabitha. 'The headdress is just the dowry that Isaiah provided. Your uncle provided much more.'

Salome's jaw dropped.

Tabitha continued, 'Now, Martha and I would also like to show our appreciation. Not only did you save me by risking your life to go to Photina and Mary, but you have also saved our business. When Jonah and Demetrius were killed in the Damascus riot, we lost a lot of valuable trade goods and a lot of Jonah's capital along with it. Same with Demetrius. Photina decided to go on, using her own money, which prompted us to do the same. Since then, you have done everything; from being a nanny to the children to cleaning the house and negotiating with traders when our Greek and Latin were not up to it. Thanks to you, we have more than made up the losses from that incident. Also, Martha and I now own half the business between us, with Jesus owning the other half, and our personal wealth is greater than when we started. Initially, when we put the money in, we thought that it didn't matter because little Jesus would inherit it anyway, but now we would like to offer you a partnership. As a wedding present, we are giving you ten per cent of the business.'

'You are prepared to give Matthias part of your business?'

'No,' replied Martha, 'we are giving it to you. This is Hebrew law, not Roman law. You control your own money. It is yours, not your husband's.'

'Does Matthias know?'

'Not yet but I am sure he won't mind. His older brother runs the family home, but Matthias is hardly ever there. He prefers travelling, even though he doesn't need the money. We are hoping, with this, to persuade him to move his base here. It won't go down well with his family, but they are not happy with the marriage anyway. Matthias is wealthy in his own right and has Davidic descent, so can do what he likes, but I think that this might go some way to mollifying the family,' Martha replied as she indicated Salome's wedding outfit.

'A long way. After all, who doesn't like money?' Tabitha winked, and they all laughed.

Tabitha and Martha called Eban and left whilst Salome was undressed. On the way out, Tabitha whispered, 'That went well. We have secured Salome's continued presence. There is no way that we could run the business and bring up the children without her. We will have to get new maids, but we can afford it now.'

Martha smiled and nodded, then asked, 'What about the children?'

'There is no way that Jesus and Miriam will let Nanna Lomie go and there is no way that Salome is going to let anyone else look after the children. Besides, it will also mean that now we can look after them whilst Salome negotiates with Greek and Roman traders. As a partner, she doesn't need us there anymore.'

'Do you think that she has realised that yet?'

'There are a lot of things that Salome hasn't realised yet.'

13

After the wedding, things started to dawn on Salome. Firstly, she had a wardrobe of fine dresses. She had never possessed more than three dresses at any one time in her life before. Usually a Sabbath dress, then two work dresses; one to wear whilst washing and drying the other. Then, she was given a new bed, a proper bed, not the pallet she had previously slept on. She was not expected to be Tabitha's maid anymore though she continued to give Tabitha a morning hug; something she had done every day since Tabitha's arrival. She also did her hair on special occasions. She drew the line, though, at having a maid of her own and wouldn't brook the children being taught by anyone else. She was also allowed to negotiate deals on behalf of the business on her own, which was quite a shock. This led to another source of income. As she was known to be wealthy and honest, other merchants came to her to use her services in translation between Aramaic and Greek and Latin and later, after she had learned it, Pahvali. Once she was even asked to translate in a discussion between three groups of merchants for a meeting that lasted five days.

The main immediate change was that Matthias was now part of the family. He not only moved his centre of operations to Tabitha's house, but he also now had his own room in the house. The biggest change came six months after the marriage when Salome realised that she was pregnant. There was great excitement in the house. She was secretly hoping that it was a girl and that her eyes would be royal leaf-green.

She soon realised that she had to slow down. She finally gave in to having a maid and Tabitha took back some of the running of the business that Salome had been doing, but she was adamant that she would continue teaching the children. This was not a chore, she insisted, as they were still under three.

When the child came, it was a boy. They called him Matthias for his father, as was Hebrew custom. Salome fed the baby as she taught the other two children. She had no worries about doing so, or even feeding the child in front of Matthias. Tabitha admired her, as she had never been comfortable feeding Jesus with Jonah in the room. Love gradually grew between Salome and Matthias as well. Salome realised that it would never be passionate, but Matthias was always considerate to her, and she knew from her experience in Jerusalem how valuable that was in a man.

Two years after Matthias was born, a second child came. This time a girl. The pregnancy had been difficult, and the child was stillborn. Encouraged by the physician, who believed that the best way to treat Salome's subsequent melancholy was for her to have another child, Salome was soon pregnant again. The pregnancy was, again, difficult. Matthias stopped travelling and got someone else to take over the cartage for the time being. He wouldn't let Salome do anything except teach the children, doing even the most menial jobs himself.

When the child was born, it was again a girl and, to everyone's joy, healthy. Strangely, as soon as the child was delivered, Salome became her old self again. The physician was convinced he had been right, but Salome was not so sure.

There was something about this child that was special and some reason why the last two pregnancies had been difficult. It was as if the quiet voice in her head was rejoicing. Matthias had wanted to call the child Salome, after her mother, but Salome shook her head.

'I know it will make her stand out, but I would like her to have a British name.'

Matthias was somewhat taken aback but, grateful for the safe delivery of both mother and daughter, he didn't want to object.

'What name would you like?'

'I only know one British name. My grandmother's. Coventina.'

'What does it mean?'

'I have no idea. My grandmother was forbidden to teach any of her children the language of Britannia and she died before I was born.'

'How about Salome Coventina?' said Matthias, hopefully.

Salome thought about it. She didn't want to disappoint Matthias but wanted her daughter to be Coventina. Then she thought of Tira, who would never have a daughter named for her.'

'How about Coventina Tira? We can shorten Coventina to Tina which is a good Latin name. You are a Hellenic Jew so no one will raise an eyebrow if we call her Tina outside the family and Coventina within the family. It will save us choosing a Latin name for her. It is about time we chose a Greek name for Matthias as well.'

'That is no problem. I thought we could keep it simple and call him Mathaios.'

'That is just Greek for Matthias, but it does make it simple. If I agree, can I have my choice for our daughter?'

Matthias smiled to himself. One of the things he loved about Salome was that she always held her own with him. She was never submissive, like most Hebrew women, especially most Hellenic Jewish women. He knew that it was the best offer he was going to get.

'Alright, I agree.'

Matthias then did what he always did after these discussions. He took off his sandal and handed it to her to seal the bargain. The first time he had done that, Salome had thought that it was a form of censure, that she had overstepped the mark. Matthias signalled it by treating her as a man. She had gradually come to realise that he was a rare man and treated her as an equal, as he did Tabitha.

After that, their daughter was always known as Tina both inside and outside the house. Salome insisted on using her full name, which made Matthias smile. He usually slipped into calling her Tira, which made Salome smile. Salome felt vindicated in her stand when, six months later, despite their daughter's dark brown, almost black, hair, her eyes turned leaf-green. Salome was never to have another child, though no one could understand why, not even Salome herself.

14

A few weeks later, Miriam's grandfather, Silas, came to visit. Miriam was then six and Jesus eight. He wanted Miriam to join the annual pilgrimage to Jerusalem for Passover.

'My cousin, Naava, will be going with her two grandchildren, David and Rachel. They are twins, the same age as Jesus.'

'I am not going!' said Tabitha flatly.

They all knew why. Tabitha was worried that she would be recognised.

'You know that Miriam won't go if Jesus doesn't go,' said Martha, 'I could go with them.'

Tabitha smiled and said, 'Jesus would certainly like having his grandma there but there is no way that you are going to be able to cope with those two in a crowded, excited Jerusalem.'

'I could go,' said Salome.

'But you have baby Tina to look after.'

Matthias, who had been listening in the background, said, 'I would like our children to go to Passover when they are older, but they are too young for the time being. Photina always takes her two to Passover just for the experience and for some other reason I can't fathom. As she is a Samaritan, she never goes to the temple but if you stayed at Sychar at her house with ours I am sure that Jesus and Miriam will go with her. After all, they love Auntie Tina. I will take you to Sychar on my way to Jerusalem before going on my usual trading trip to Damascus at Passover.'

Silas thought about it for a moment.

'David and Rachel know Photina as well. Martha would find it easier with her there. Would it be any imposition to ask you to take them all to Sychar, Matthias?'

'Of course not. Salome is as good a cart driver as I am, so she can drive them to Sychar, and no one beats Photina in that way either, though young Demetrius, her son, is just as capable as well.'

That was the start of what became a tradition. David and Rachel and their grandmother, Naava, would come with Matthias to Magdala. Then Salome would drive everyone to Sychar, with Matthias driving the wagon with the trade goods. They would stay with Photina in Sychar for a fortnight whilst Matthias went on to Jerusalem and then came back to pick up whatever Photina wanted to be transported to Galilee or Damascus. Then on to Jerusalem for two weeks. After Jerusalem, they would all come back to Sychar for another couple of weeks. Then Salome would drive them back to Magdala.

When Matthias and Coventina were old enough, they went to Jerusalem as well, though Salome stayed in Sychar. This didn't worry Salome as Demetrius, Photina's eldest, was quite happy to keep an eye on Coventina, who loved Deedee, as she called him. This was necessary, as Coventina was always a live wire and no one else could keep up with her.

Everyone thought that Demetrius would become tired of looking after Coventina, but he never did. Every visit to Jerusalem for Passover, they became closer. By the time Demetrius joined the Legions, they were inseparable.

Matthias, who had been watching with apprehension, was relieved that Demetrius was now out of the picture.

15

Salome carried on as the main teacher for the children. As she was fluent in oral and written Latin, Greek and Hebrew and was well-versed in Roman history and mathematics, she was the obvious person to do it. She remembered the explanation her mother, Tirzah, gave her when she had asked why she had to learn so much as a child.

Another legacy of the emperor wanting to civilise your grandmother. She was determined to give her offspring the means to buy their freedom. When Emperor Augustus asked to have the heir to the throne sent to Rome to be educated in Roman ways, cementing the treaty he had signed with the Dobunni, he was taken aback to be sent a young girl. He had dismissed her education to his advisors. Not knowing what the emperor wanted, and not wanting to ask, they had educated her in Latin, Greek, Roman history and mathematics. To make her into a Roman lady, they taught her how to be a lady's maid and accompany one of the emperor's daughters. After the treaty was reneged on, your grandmother was sold to Hebrews who insisted she learnt Hebrew. The local Rabbi could not be bothered teaching a slave the scriptures so he taught her to read so that she could learn them herself.

Salome taught Coventina the stories of her grandmother's homeland, Albion. Miriam was always in the background, quietly listening. There was no harm in it, so she let it pass. Once again, she thought of the difference between Miriam and her mother. Her mother had always been doing things, always excited to be going on to the next thing. Miriam, even though she was a carbon copy of her mother, was more like her Aunt Tira in character.

When Coventina was five, the time came for her to know about the goddess. Before starting that phase of her education, Salome looked around to check that Miriam was not there.

Salome started the story of the goddess. It was the story of how the people had arrived in Albion and how they had been saved, from starvation and death, by the goddess. It was Salome's favourite story. She was so engrossed in telling it that she didn't notice Miriam creep in and sit down, listening quietly. This was a serious matter. Would Tabitha approve of Salome talking to Miriam about a foreign goddess?

After the session, she sent Miriam and Coventina out to play with the other children before going to see Tabitha. She had been wondering how to broach the subject sensitively and decided there was no way to do so. She went straight into it.

'I have started teaching Coventina about the goddess of my grandmother's people. She needs to know as she is of royal descent. In the, admittedly remote, chance that she becomes queen she will need to know.'

Tabitha nodded, 'And?'

'Miriam was listening, and I didn't know.'

'Ah, I see. How much did she hear?'

'I don't know.'

Tabitha didn't shout or fly off the handle but simply said, 'Well, let's find out, shall we? Miriam!'

Miriam entered immediately. She had been expecting the summons. She was greeted with a smile from Tabitha. Miriam was so quiet it was impossible to know when she was there or not. The other side of the coin was that, if Miriam gave her word, she would keep it. All Tabitha had to do was make

Miriam give her word that she would not listen in on stories about Albion again. Though she decided to see what Miriam had to say first.

'How much of the story Salome told Tina did you hear?'

'All of it.'

'Why did you listen?'

'Because it was about the angel, about Coventina.'

Salome started. Tabitha noticed and held up her hand.

'Miriam, Tina isn't an angel.'

'Not Tina, Coventina. Coventina is the guardian angel of Britannia, like Michael is our guardian angel. I know the British call her a goddess but that is only because they have no word for angel.'

Tabitha looked at Salome, 'Is this correct?'

'She is right that Coventina is the name of the goddess, but she would have heard me say that in my story. I know nothing of Coventina being an angel. We always just refer to her as 'The Goddess' to outsiders.'

'So, you knew the goddess's name from today's story. Is that what happened, Miriam?'

'No, I knew about the angel before today.'

'How?' asked Tabitha.

'I had a dream about my aunt, about Tira. In my dream, Tira was not alone, she was with two other people. I could not tell whether they were men or women. Tira told me they were angels and that angels were just angels, they didn't have children, so they just were, neither men nor women. Anyway, one had fiery golden eyes and the other leaf-green eyes, like Salome and Tina. The one with fiery golden eyes turned into the form of a man, with wings carrying a spear. *This is how men usually see me,* came into my head, *I am the guardian angel of Israel, Michael, though some call me Gabriel.* The other one then turned into the shape of a woman with milk-white skin and sat on a massive leaf, hovering above the ground. *I am Coventina, the guardian angel of Britannia. The Romans do not know my right name and call me Sulis-Minerva. Salome will teach you of me, for you will be my servant and save my people.'*

Tabitha stopped to think. With anyone else, she would have thought that they had concocted the story, but not Miriam. Miriam was always honest, even when it meant that she was going to be punished. Tabitha was unsure what to do. In the end, she reached a compromise within her mind.

'You may listen to Salome's stories but remember that they are just that: stories.'

'Thank you, Mother. Are you going to tell Tina another one tomorrow, Nanna Lomie?'

Miriam was at her most endearing. A smile came on her face and though both Tabitha and Salome knew they were being manipulated, neither could resist.

'Yes, I will tell Coventina another story about the goddess tomorrow.'

16

Miriam listened to Salome's stories over the next year then stopped. Salome asked her why.

'I have heard them all before. I don't need to hear them again.'

'Do you remember the one about the flies in the village?'

'Yes. Of course.'

'Why don't you tell Coventina that one today, then?'

'Alright.'

Miriam then told the story, word perfect. All the emphases were in the right place, everything. Salome was amazed. It had taken half a dozen tellings for her to be able to do that and Miriam had only heard it once. She decided to test Miriam. She got her to tell all the stories, picking them at random. She started with *The Hare and the Moon*. Then, *The Beautiful Place*, *Lapwing Migration* and *The Oak Leaf Message*. Every time Miriam recited it perfectly.

After reciting them all, Miriam asked a question.

'Salome, if these are all stories of the past, why are they so important to learn? And why would The Angel want me to know them?'

Salome stopped to think. Miriam had used her proper name. That meant the thoughtful, enquiring Miriam.

'I don't know why the goddess wants you to know. The story of the flies is so that people remember that disobeying her leaves the community in a bad way until they go back to obeying her. My father told my mother that the tribes of Albion were constantly fighting each other since they had got rid of the true queen. He thought that there would be disaster upon disaster until she was restored.'

'That would be you?' asked Miriam.

'Maybe me, maybe Coventina, maybe someone else. Who knows? What do you think of the stories?'

'*Lapwing Migration* is about change. Things were ready to change but it took something startling the flock to initiate the migration, so it sometimes takes a bad event to initiate the change. *The Hare and the Moon* is about things not always being what they seem to be and the goddess showing she is there, going before us. I guess that *The Beautiful Place* must be like our temple, special because of the presence of the angel. Is it where the shaman died?'

'Yes, it is where the shaman died. So just wisdom in the stories? Is that it, Miriam?'

'I don't know. Like our Hebrew stories from scripture, it is a bit more. Yahweh is always in our stories. The moon or moonlight is always in yours. Seems like the angel is there as the moon, though in *The Hare and the Moon,* it almost seems like she is both. It almost seems like the angel is sending messages to her people. Messages that everyone can see.'

'Do you think that one day the goddess may signal to you in this way? Maybe that is why she wants you to know the stories.'

'Maybe, but why, when I can hear her in my dreams, would I need to know the stories?'

'It is a mystery.'

After that, Salome only ever got Miriam to tell a story occasionally. Just to test that she hadn't forgotten. Not that Salome had much chance to get Miriam to do anything, as she was more and more in Jesus's company. Miriam and Jesus had always been close but now it was almost impossible to find them apart if it was a waking hour and Jesus was at home.

After turning fourteen, Jesus had come into his inheritance. He owned half the family business. Salome's husband, Matthias, started taking him on trading trips. It became usual, when he was home, to find him regaling Miriam with stories from his travels. There was no marvel in Jerusalem or Damascus for Miriam, but Matthias decided that Jesus needed to go to other places. He took him to Arabia, Egypt, Parthia, as well as Cappadocia and far off Armenia and beyond. Matthias proposed a trip to India, but Tabitha contended that the market at the Well of Moses in Nabataea would be sufficient to understand the silk trade.

On his return from that trip, they celebrated Miriam's coming of age at fourteen. Salome noticed that, although Miriam was polite and duly attentive to everyone when she needed to be, she spent as much time with Jesus as possible. He was telling her of the nearby town to the market at the Well of Moses, which the Romans called Petra. Its temples and tombs were hewn out of solid rock. Its theatre. The narrow gorge to get to it. Miriam was lost in wonder.

It was no surprise to Salome when she found Tabitha in a panic the following morning.

'What has happened?'

'Miriam and Jesus came to me this morning. They want to get married.'

'So?'

'Well, they are brother and sister. They can't marry.'

'You have never adopted Miriam. She is no relation to Jesus at all. Not quite true, I suppose. She is no blood relation to Jesus. She is the daughter of Mary of Magdala's adopted daughter. So, as Mary was Jonah's cousin, there is a sort of relationship there. They were always close. Even as children, they never let anyone get between them. Jesus has come into his inheritance and Miriam is of marrying age.'

'I suppose so. I am just so used to them both calling me 'Mother' that I sort of think of them both as mine. But Miriam is too young.'

'Miriam is older than Jesus in character. What is really worrying you?'

Tabitha hesitated, then said, 'Once he is married, Jesus will want to run the business. With Martha's portion, which she will give him when he marries, he will own seven-tenths of the company.'

'You are worried that he will push you out?'

'No. Well, yes, I suppose I am.'

'Did you notice how Miriam hung on Jesus's every word last night when he talked of Petra?'

'What of it?'

'Well, they want to travel. They have a plan to explore the possibility of trading with Rome, via Alexandria. There are always ships plying between Alexandria and Ravenna, or Alexandria and Rome, and ships go between Alexandria and Caesarea. That makes cargo rates cheaper. It will take longer but will cost less than overland via Damascus. Jesus and Miriam have an idea of setting up a family branch in Alexandria. To do that, they would need you to hold the fort here. It is the main reason they want to marry now. They want to have a strong partnership before going to Alexandria.'

'How come you know all this, and I don't?'

'They knew that your reaction would be negative, so they came to Nanna Lomie to talk you round.'

'They don't still call you 'Nanna Lomie', surely.'

'They do when they want to wheedle me, just like when they put it to you, Miriam called you 'Mother'.'

Tabitha laughed, 'I will think about it, but you can't just set up in business in a foreign city with the click of your fingers. Have they thought of that?'

'Yes. They reckon that it will take a year to set up a scouting trip before they go. In the meantime, they will travel together closer to home. Alexander, Photina's son, and their Uncle Jairus, will accompany them.'

'At least with Jairus I know that they will be in safe hands.'

Salome smiled. Tabitha was weakening. She could never resist either Jesus or Miriam for long and certainly not both together.

17

The marriage was set for three months later. To Tabitha's surprise, the first thing that the happy couple did was to move Miriam's things into Jesus's room. Tabitha's parents had shared a room, but it was unusual for a wealthy couple to do so. She asked Miriam about it.

'If we are going to travel, we are going to have to share a room so we might as well get used to it.'

It wasn't long before they started. They went with Alexander and Jairus to Damascus. This made Tabitha nervous, remembering what had happened to Jonah and Demetrius. She asked Alexander when they came back how they had done.

'They are both, individually, very good negotiators. Together, they are unbelievable.'

'How so, Alexander?'

'Well, I remember, when we were children, that they always got their way as to what game we played. None of us could work out how they did it. Watching them negotiate, I was on the outside for a change. They distract you by being seemingly totally engrossed with each other, with the world excluded. Then you feel privileged by being given a chink into their private world, where they draw you in, and you find yourself agreeing with them. By the time it comes to the actual deal, you have already sealed the terms that they wanted all along.'

Tabitha smiled. Now that it was pointed out, she could see all the times, when growing up, that Jesus and Miriam had used those tactics on her. They had worked every time.

After a year of planning and travelling, Jesus and Miriam were ready for their trip to Alexandria. They decided on a short delay when Alexander announced that he was getting married. They were all invited to the wedding, of course.

Three months later, they all gathered in Sychar for the wedding. The bride looked familiar to Tabitha, but she couldn't quite place her. Her suspicions were confirmed by Miriam.

'Rachel, how amazing that you should be marrying Alexander. Come on Mother, you remember Rachel, old Jairus's granddaughter, who used to go to Jerusalem with us for Passover.'

Tabitha asked about Rachel's father. She knew that her mother had died in childbirth. She was simply told that he was not there, so Tabitha assumed that he was also dead. Strange that her brother, David, wasn't there.

On return to Galilee, Tabitha was surprised that Miriam and Jesus did not announce their plans for the scouting trip to Alexandria. After a month in which her tension with the delay grew, Tabitha finally tackled Miriam about it.

They were at the table. Just Miriam, Tabitha, and Salome, when Tabitha decided to come out with it.

'Miriam, when are you and Jesus going to tell me what you are going to do about Alexandria?'

Salome, who was taking a sip of wine, spluttered and almost choked. Miriam just looked confused and then laughed.

'We have decided that we must put Alexandria on hold for the time being, at least until the child is weaned.'

'What child?'

'Our child. The one I am carrying, Grandmother Tabitha.'

'Don't you 'grandmother' me. I am not even your mother, let alone your grandmother. If you think that you are going to get around me that way,' then … 'Baby? You are going to have a baby? I am going to be a grandmother?'

Salome couldn't hold it any longer. She burst out laughing.

'Don't worry, Miriam. Tabitha never was very observant that way. She thought Jesus was a stomach-ache, caused by something she had eaten at your mother's wedding.'

The baby, when born, was a girl. They called her Miriam after her mother. Everything settled into a rhythm for the next two years. Whilst Miriam stayed at home and looked after the baby, Jesus carried on going on trading trips with Jairus and Alexander. Nothing of note happened except one strange incident.

On return from one trip, they caught Jairus, Jesus and Alexander laughing. Miriam immediately wanted to know what had happened. She was met simply by Jesus presenting her with a strange pendant. It was made of silver and pointed like a dagger, but with no handle. The centre was not solid and appeared to have the Greek letters, Iota and Chi, within it. The chain that held it was threaded between the two letters. The three men then laughed again.

Try as they might, Tabitha, Miriam and Salome could not get out of them how they had come by the pendant. They said that it was part of a deal they had done with a Roman commander but would say no more. Despite her misgivings as to the origins of the pendant, Miriam never took it off, insisting on sleeping with it around her neck.

They started making plans again for their trip to Alexandria. It would be complicated by little Miriam but, if they took a nurse, still possible. Everything was set when the little girl became sick. Jesus and Miriam were deflated that they would have to postpone yet again.

'It is only a six-month trip,' said Salome, as they discussed it one night, 'Leave the child with us.'

After some persuasion, it was decided that Jesus and Miriam would go to Alexandria, on a shortened three-month visit, leaving young Miriam in the care of her grandmother and Nanna Lomie.

Four months later, when they hadn't returned, Tabitha started to worry. Alexander went to Caesarea to enquire. The news he had to convey on his return was not good. The ship that Miriam and Jesus had been on had disappeared without a trace. Another ship, that had been in the same area at the time, had reported seeing pirates and only just managed to escape them.

Salome sighed inside. Another child to bring up. Yet more delay until she felt she could leave and travel herself, but there was also sadness. Tears rolled down her face as she thought of Miriam sitting on her lap as a child, throwing her arms around Salome's neck and declaring, 'I love you, Nanna Lomie,' or sitting cross-legged telling the stories of the goddess of far-off Albion. Then she remembered Jesus coming in, after tripping and scraping his knee. He had pointed to the wound, 'It hurt, Nanna Lomie.' Salome's tears became a cascade. Suddenly, an irrational feeling welled up inside her.

I have let Tira down again. I have failed to keep her niece safe.

Try as she might, Salome couldn't dispel the guilt.

18

The next five years flew by for Salome though, at the same time, the days felt as if they dragged. Every day was the same, but the years brought changes. Miriam, now seven, was a handful like her grandmother had been, but didn't get herself into trouble. She was just impetuous and teasing. She particularly liked teasing David, Rachel's twin brother, when he came to visit his grandfather, Jairus, in Capernaum.

Tabitha's language skills had improved to such an extent that she didn't need Salome anymore in dealing with Roman or Greek traders. She had also mastered enough Pahvali and Arabic to deal with Parthians and Arabs, which was a distinct advantage as Alexander had set up links importing silk and wine. This was especially so as the Parthians were now insisting on Pahvali, as opposed to Greek, forcing some of their competitors to use translators. High-quality Muscat and Shiraz were always in demand, especially by the Roman elite.

The biggest change was with Coventina. Matthias had insisted that he and Salome talk to Coventina about marriage as soon as she turned fourteen. It was usual for a father to choose a husband for his daughter after consulting her mother. It reinforced to Salome how good a man Matthias was that he was prepared to take Coventina's preference into account as well. There was no lack of suitors. Matthias's status and wealth, plus Coventina's reputation as an exotic beauty, saw to that. Salome's green eyes in her pale skin, and dark brown hair with copper streaks, had been too alien. Coventina's same green eyes, offsetting her darker Naphtali-style skin and black hair, added an element of intrigue.

Coventina had been adamant. The only man she would marry was Demetrius, Alexander's older brother. If necessary, she would run away to marry him, as Rachel had with Alexander.

'I am not happy with this,' Matthias declared, 'Demetrius is not Hebrew. His father was Greek and worse, his mother is a Samaritan.'

'I am not completely Hebrew either,' said Salome, 'but that has never bothered you. Besides, you do follow Greek custom.'

'You are Hebrew, at least by our tradition. I may follow Greek custom but, in this matter, I am fully Hebrew.'

Salome knew it was a gut reaction and that no amount of argument or persuasion would change his mind. The bad blood between Hebrews and Samaritans, and between Hebrews and Greeks, ran too deep. Both Demetrius senior, when he was alive, and Photina, worshipped Yahweh. It was partly conditioned and partly fear as to how it would affect his standing and his business. Salome knew that she was only accepted because she wasn't any of the local rival races either, particularly not Samaritan. That, and her story of slavery under the Romans and freedom under the Jews, gave them a sense of the superiority of Jewish culture.

On Alexander's next visit they broached the subject with him, hoping that he could dash Coventina's hopes, but he confirmed that Demetrius felt the same way about her. There was a large age gap, of course, but that was no bar and, indeed, was usual in Hebrew culture. Matthias and Salome stalled for time. Demetrius was in a Roman legion; another thing

Matthias instinctively didn't like. It did mean though that he was far away as Roman soldiers were not allowed to serve locally. Coventina would have to wait until he returned on leave.

Now, five years after Jesus and Miriam's disappearance, they were sitting in Photina's house in the post-Passover visit. Unusually, she wanted to talk business.

'We have received word from Demetrius.'

Coventina was all ears.

'The recent revolt in Britannia is over. Camulodunum, Londinium and Verulamium are to be rebuilt and there is a gap in the market.'

Now Salome was all ears as well.

'Most of the merchants from the empire, who traded in those places, were killed in the revolt. Nearly all the rest are too scared to go back. Trade out of Aquae Sulis is dominated by Britons, who didn't revolt, sailing to Carthage within a golden triangle of wheat to Ravenna, luxury goods from Ravenna to Carthage and then cotton and a few luxuries back to Aquae Sulis. Many merchants have tried to break the British monopoly in this but have failed. The trade is controlled by the local king who ensures that the taxes on goods, imported by foreign merchants, offset any attempt to undercut his operation.'

Tabitha nodded. Photina had done her research thoroughly, as usual.

'Demetrius has made contacts in Camulodunum and Londinium. He tells me that there is too much competition from Aquae Sulis now to make it worthwhile opening the Verulamium market. So, what we want to do is establish a base in Carthage to trade with Britannia. Alexander will sail between Carthage, and either Camulodunum or Londinium, and we will trade directly with the British merchants sailing between Carthage and Aquae Sulis.'

'Sounds good. What do you intend to trade?' asked Tabitha.

'British wheat, copper and lead one way. Shiraz wine, olive oil and silks the other. Strictly luxury high-end goods.'

Tabitha raised an eyebrow.

'The Roman commanders will pay handsomely for decent wine. Germanic traders supply white wines from the Rhine, but good red wine is in short supply. Demetrius tells me that his commander, Regus, is very partial to Shiraz wine. I have sent over a couple of shipments to Demetrius as samples and he made a handsome profit on them nonetheless.'

'So, what are you proposing? Fully, that is.'

'Our business, your business and Jairus' business are virtually a single business now, yes?'

Tabitha nodded again.

'I want to relocate to Carthage, with Alexander and Rachel. Then, Salome could take over the operation here and, between you, you could supply me as I trade with Britannia. Dealing directly with Britannia means we can undercut the normal imports of copper and lead for price. Jairus has the contacts to set up the supply chains.'

Salome's heart sank. She was to be marooned here. Still, it was a change from Galilee, and she would be her own mistress.

Tabitha frowned, 'How will Samaritans take to Salome?'

'Samaritans are easy-going. They will trade with anyone. Though Salome will be an advantage. There are increasing numbers of Judeans in Samaria, almost all are Followers of the Way. They tolerate dealing with me because of my association with Jesus of Nazareth but they are uncomfortable because I am a Samaritan who was married to a Greek. They prefer dealing with Rachel because she is Hebrew, even though she is my daughter-in-law. They would be far happier with Salome as, alien-looking though she is, she is Judean and married to a Judean.'

'How will Matthias react, I wonder?' said Salome, mainly to herself.

'I asked him already,' Photina replied, 'He is quite happy about it. He will keep his centre of operations with you in Galilee, if that is alright with you, Tabitha.'

'Fine with me. Miriam will miss her Nanna Lomie though.'

A thought came into Salome's head. *Yes, Matthias will be happy with it. It will remove Demetrius, and any association with him, a long way from Coventina. The increased numbers of Judeans in Samaria will give him an opportunity to find her a suitable match from amongst his people.*

19

It took two years to prepare for the move. Then there was a last-minute hitch. Rachel's daughter, Helen, was ill. There was no way they could take her with them. Rachel was unwilling to leave her in anyone else's care. It was either go now or completely call off the enterprise. After some debate, it was decided that Salome would go in Rachel's place because of her language skills. Photina and Alexander had never mastered Latin, the predominant tongue in the western half of the empire.

Salome was in heaven. She was going to get to travel. Matthias was not so happy. It would take Coventina closer to Demetrius. As a result, Matthias offered to take over the provision of carriage of goods between Jairus and Carthage. Their son, Matthias Junior, would take over the business locally, operating out of Tabitha's house which he thought of as home. Another thing that Matthias told himself was that it was only for two years, and then Rachel and Salome would change places.

Tabitha was worried. She had lost her husband, Jonah, when he had gone to Damascus on a trading trip. She had lost her son, Jesus, and his wife, Miriam, when they had gone on a trading trip to Alexandria. Salome tried to reassure her.

'But those pirates were dealt with long ago.'

'I know, but there is hardly anyone left.'

'Rachel will be in Sychar. You know that you and Miriam will always be welcome there. She has even offered to have Miriam for a month each year to give you a break.'

'But she has a business to run and two children of her own.'

'That won't stop Rachel. She will be fine. She is a better haggler than Photina, and that is saying something. Well, that is finished.'

Salome put the last of the belongings she was taking with her into the sacks ready for transport. She then looked around her room. Nothing but the bare furniture was left. The bed hadn't even got a mattress on it. She had to admit to herself that she had been happy there. The only place she had been happy since being brought to Jerusalem by her uncle. She hadn't achieved her secret dream yet of reclaiming the throne of Albion, but she had gone from being a slave to one of the wealthiest women in Galilee. And now she was going to Carthage, which was over half the distance to Britannia. She knew that she probably wouldn't get any nearer than that, but she may.

It took over a month to get there, but that was mainly due to Matthias insisting on establishing, or renewing, contacts in Caesarea and Alexandria on the way. Vital, as everyone knew, to handling shipments. It also meant that he would not be dependent solely on goods to and from Galilee and Samaria to Carthage and back.

Matthias called Salome and Coventina on deck when they approached Alexandria Harbour. The light was beginning to fail at the end of the day and the lighthouse, the Pharos, had been lit.

'What is that for?' asked Coventina.

'That, Tira, is to guide ships safely to harbour after nightfall.'

'Why don't all ports have them?'

'Close in, you can see the lights of any port, but most wouldn't use them. For a start, it is often too dangerous for a ship to dock at night as hazards cannot be seen. Most captains prefer to anchor offshore and dock in daylight. There is also a significant danger to the town of being attacked by pirates at night, if the way in is lit. Alexandria has few hazards and plenty of docking. It is too well defended to fall prey to pirates.'

The mention of pirates made Coventina shudder, and she shed a tear for her lost friends. Salome took the opportunity to tour Alexandria and dragged Coventina along with her. The city was certainly beautiful with the lighthouse harbour and many fine houses and temples. When they reached the library, though, they forgot about everything else.

There were thousands and thousands of scrolls. Salome and Coventina were stunned into immobility. Neither had seen any Greek or Roman scripts before, except trade documents and contracts. A scholar approached them and asked in which languages they read. When they answered Latin, Greek and Hebrew, they could see the disbelief on his face. He picked two Latin, two Greek and two Hebrew scrolls at random and handed them to the women to read to him. He was astounded when they read them perfectly. He obviously didn't know Hebrew and was faking his understanding. Like all Greek men, he couldn't bear to be outdone by a woman. Salome's instincts kicked in and she asked him to suggest what they should read. Being Greek, he suggested Greek texts and put himself at their service should there be anything they couldn't understand. He put back the scrolls and pointed out where they could find the suggestions he had made and went back to his couch to continue reading.

Coventina fetched the scrolls, and they took couches close to the academic. After one or two well-judged questions of the scholar to 'enhance their understanding' of what they were reading, they settled down and left the man alone. They discarded a couple of things and then found scrolls that riveted their attention. Homer and Socrates were a revelation. The more prosaic Coventina loved Socrates. Romantic Salome loved Homer. It was well after dark when Matthias found them, still reading by candlelight.

The following day, Matthias found that Coventina and Salome had left the ship at dawn, taking breakfast with them. He smiled. When he had finished his business, he wandered the city. He turned a corner to see a familiar face.

'Simon?'

'Matthias, what brings you to Alexandria? Haven't seen you since we met at Jairus's house, years ago.'

Matthias knew that Simon had been one of the followers of Jesus of Nazareth. One of two called Simon. The other was now called Peter for some reason Matthias couldn't fathom.

'I am here on business. Is Thaddeus here?'

Matthias knew that Simon usually travelled with Thaddeus. Thaddeus's Hebrew name was Judas, but because it was a Judas who had betrayed Jesus, he used his Greek name, to save confusion.

'Thaddeus is in Carthage. I agreed to follow him there once I had finished here. I was on my way to the port now to look for a ship to take me.'

'It is your lucky day. We are sailing for Carthage tomorrow.'

'There is no such thing as luck with Yahweh.'

Matthias smiled. Simon hadn't changed, not one bit.

'We could have sailed immediately, but my wife and daughter are happily engrossed, reading in the library.

Tomorrow will do. It is almost sunset and I was about to collect them. Like to join me?' They proceeded to the library and found the two women reading, as he expected.

'Greek again?'

'We did glance at a couple of works by the Roman, Cato, but his history was dodgy and full of how great Rome was. His agricultural treatises were alright but not astounding, so we went back to Greek. Greek epics are really good fun,' said Salome.

'I prefer the Greek philosophers,' Coventina chipped in, 'They treat wisdom so differently to Hebrew scriptures but, unlike the Scriptures, they never really come to a conclusion. Always leave you asking questions, never giving answers. Fascinating, but how do they ever make any decisions, I wonder?'

On the way back to the port, as Coventina talked to Simon, Salome questioned Matthias.

'Why did you leave us in the library so long? We have lost half a day's sailing to Carthage.'

'Well, you and Tira were enjoying yourselves.'

Salome stopped and looked Matthias full in the face, 'Really?'

'Alright, you have rumbled me. I thought that this might entice Coventina back eastwards, further from Demetrius in Britannia.'

There was a quiet voice in her head and, in a thoughtful whisper, Salome said, 'I don't think that Coventina and I will ever see Alexandria again, whatever the lure of the library.'

Coventina and Salome were both sad and excited to leave Alexandria. Sad because they were leaving the library behind. Excited because they were going on to Carthage, with its direct connections to Britannia. A step closer to both their dreams.

Carthage, when they arrived, looked much like Tiberius. It was a very Roman-looking city. They found that Latin was readily spoken, but so were Greek, Phoenician, Hebrew, and many languages that they didn't recognise. They had assumed that Latin would be the main language, but it was not. There didn't appear to be a main language at all. If there was an official language, it was Phoenician. That was the inscribed language on official buildings, but Greek and Latin were heard more often in the streets. Salome realised that she was redundant.

They quickly realised that their choice of Carthage, as a base, was both fortuitous and challenging. Fortuitous, in that it was obvious that Carthage was the predominant trading city of the western part of the empire. Finding partners to trade with and setting up trade with Britannia was going to be simple. On the other hand, the competition was going to be fierce. Also, the area around Carthage, like Egypt, produced significant quantities of grain. It would be difficult to bring grain in from Britannia and sell on at a profit.

Luckily, Demetrius had forged a contact with a merchant based in Carthage; a Phoenician called Pygmalion. Pygmalion had secured a warehouse close to the docks for them. He was interested in their ideas.

'I don't bring grain back here. There is no market for it, and that is Britannia's main export. Trade in grain is dominated by the Britons themselves, mainly from the west of the island. They can undercut us, in delivery to Gaul and the barbarians, and they bypass us with deliveries east of here. They make no profit on the grain, but it pays the bills. They then use extra space on the ships to transport lead and copper from British mines to make their money. It is an interesting business model, though most people here prefer to stick to the old ways and buy what they know they can sell at a profit elsewhere.'

'You look interested, Photina.'

'My husband and his partner used the old ways. After they were killed, his widow and I started using the business model you have just described. They were killed in riots in Damascus and a lot of valuable trade goods were stolen. Most of their fortune was tied up in the goods. When we started, we needed to ensure that we made no losses, so we developed that business model. It has advantages if you have a network of established agents, as we did. As you are selling the grain at cost, so to speak, you can undercut anyone else. That means that, if you are static in one place, people always come to you for their grain. In turn, that means that you can always guarantee to cover your costs. You make less of a profit on the trip, but you never make a loss. Where grain was not appropriate, we used another basic product. For instance, grain from Egypt to Samaria and Galilee, olive oil from Galilee to Damascus, wood imported from Lebanon from Damascus to Egypt.'

'What did you make your money on?'

'Egyptian perfumes to Galilee, silk, Parthian wines, and embroidered wedding shawls to Damascus; and Damascus steel to Egypt.'

Pygmalion was suitably impressed, and asked 'What are you planning here?'

'Demetrius tells us that Camulodunum, Verulamium and Londinium are all being rebuilt after the Boudiccan revolt.'

'If you are thinking of building materials, then forget it. There are plenty at hand.'

'Not building materials, tools. Demetrius says that the local craftsmen cannot keep up with the demand. Then grain via here to Galilee. Olive oil from Galilee to here and Britannia.'

'Why not grain from here to Galilee?'

'If we are using it to just pay the bills, then we can get grain cheaper in Britannia and cover our transport costs.'

'Where is your profit?'

'Luxury wine and silks to Carthage and Britannia. Local wine is not particularly good, I understand, and wine from the Germanic provinces is mainly white.'

'The Britons are doing this already, how do you hope to compete?'

'Their operation is confined to the west of Britannia and Verulamium. We will concentrate on Londinium and Camulodunum.'

'There is one slight problem that will make your task harder. Demetrius has been transferred to Ravenna.'

'What about his contacts? Has his whole legion been transferred?' asked Salome.

'Not to Ravenna. Ravenna is a reward for Demetrius for some heroic act or other, but Regus and the rest of the legion have been returned to Ardu, where they were based, now that Camulodunum is secure. Apparently, Ardu is out of the way and the new governor of Camulodunum feels that Regus is a political threat.'

'Where is Ardu?'

'No idea.'

There was shock and disappointment and a debate ensued. Was the venture viable without Demetrius in Camulodunum? Salome and Matthias were for pressing on. Coventina was for returning to Alexandria. Photina and Alexander were unsure. It had cost a lot of money to get this far, but they could not see how they could carry on.

Salome was desperate. She had got this close to Albion, her ancestral homeland, she didn't want to turn back without seeing it. Coventina was equally desperate to return to

Alexandria, closer to Demetrius. Matthias wanted to keep Coventina as far away from Demetrius as possible and find her a husband within the Judean community in Carthage.

After an hour of fruitless debate, Salome played her final card. It wasn't worth much, but it was all she had.

'What about Mary in Gaul? She must have made contacts by now and Gaul is not far from Britannia.'

'We haven't heard from Mary since we heard that she arrived safely,' said Photina, 'We don't even know if she is still alive.'

Pygmalion looked quizzically. 'Mary?'

'Mary of Magdala,' Salome replied, 'She went to Gaul many years ago with her daughter, Sarah.'

'It has to be the same person. Her daughter married a local kinglet. She controls all the trade in that part of Gaul. A good person to know. She also has many contacts in Britannia.'

That swung it. Not wanting to make a loss or let go of their idea, Photina and Alexander agreed to contact Mary. The olive oil and fine wines they had brought with them would sell equally well in Gaul. Alexander had been the person to go to Britannia, but he didn't really know Mary. Photina wanted to stay in Carthage to establish the base there, so it was decided that Salome should go with Pygmalion to Gaul and, if Mary could provide contacts, on to Britannia. Matthias would return to Galilee via Alexandria to cement his trading ties.

'I would like to get to Britannia, if possible,' said Salome, 'It is where my grandmother came from, and my father.'

Normally Matthias would have frowned on this. He didn't like to be reminded of Salome's non-Judean heritage. This time he saw it as an opportunity.

'Take Coventina with you. It is always good to understand your own people's customs.'

Salome immediately realised what Matthias was doing but, since it gave her freedom to go on from Gaul to Britannia, didn't object. She had to face the problem of Coventina and Demetrius at some time.

Not yet.

It was soon arranged. Pygmalion had a ship waiting, so all that was needed was to transfer the cargo. Matthias would find cargo to take back with him. The basic grain was easy to find, but what else? He settled on Carthage's high-quality manufactured goods and departed five days after Salome. Simon, having ascertained that Thaddeus had returned to Jerusalem, went with him.

20

The ship sailed westwards along the coast of Africa. They hopped over to Hispania at the narrowest point. A huge rock dominated the new shoreline, apes clearly visible on its sheer side, the air filled with their chatter. As they sailed round Hispania, they left civilised parts. The Phoenicians had conquered the southern Mediterranean shore but the wild Atlantic shores were still barbaric.

At least, that was the picture in Salome's mind. These western Roman provinces were semi-autonomous, inhabited by Celts who barely bowed to the Roman yoke. The Phoenicians and Greeks had traded here for centuries for lead, copper and gold but only on a small scale. It was only since the Roman conquest that trade had flourished.

When they finally docked, Salome was disappointed. There were a few Roman buildings. Other than that, just wooden huts, to her eyes. The locals didn't seem warlike at all, despite their fearsome reputation. Their skin had a pink undertone, the same as her own. There was no sign of the fabled woad which their warriors adorned themselves with in battle.

They were approached by a man who introduced himself as Titus. His pale skin, bright red hair and hesitant Latin showed him to be a Romanised Celt. Salome asked where she could find Mary.

Titus pulled himself up to his full height. 'I am the Queen Mother's representative here. You deal with me.'

Pygmalion emerged from the ship behind Salome and Titus's face dropped. He thought he could browbeat a woman as Greek and Roman women were always submissive. Pygmalion was a different matter.

'I don't think so, Titus. Particularly, in this case, I think that Mary will want to see Salome herself.'

Sullenly, he took them through regular Roman streets to a large rectangular wooden house. Salome was surprised. There was none of the stenches one got in Mediterranean towns, where only the wealthy had sluices. Then she noticed a man *fertilizing the fields*. Crude, but it made for a healthier town.

Titus made them wait outside until he had announced who was there to Mary. He came back, Mary with him, along with two armed guards. Mary signalled the three men to stay back and walked up to Salome.

Mary seemed anxious. She looked around and then asked Salome in a whisper, 'Is Coventina with you?'

Salome was taken aback. That was the last greeting she had expected. How did Mary know about Coventina?

'Is Coventina with you?' Mary repeated.

Salome nodded, too dumbstruck to answer.

Mary turned to Pygmalion. 'Please go and fetch Coventina,' she said, then turned and signalled the two guards to accompany him.

'Come in, Salome.'

'But how do you know about Coventina?'

'We will talk inside.' Then when Salome didn't move, 'A mutual friend told me of her.'

The only person Salome knew that had been in this part of the world was Demetrius. He would have gone through Gaul to take up his post in Ravenna. It must be him, Salome decided. Mary had known Photina before Demetrius was born. Demetrius would certainly have remembered his Auntie Mary. She decided not to mention Demetrius. It was probably better, with Coventina around.

Inside, the building was amazing. Costly mosaics on every floor. Rich tapestries adorned the walls, hiding the wood. Stone columns held up the wooden roof beams, adorned by a thatched roof. Apart from the roof, you could be forgiven for thinking you were in a Roman mansion. On a second look, there was one other difference. An open log fire. Not unheard of for Romans, but out of place in such opulence.

'You are wondering why we have a wooden building, perhaps?'

'Yes, I admit I was.'

'The Celts have no strong history of slavery. A stone building takes a lot of work to keep warm in winter and cool in summer. This is much more practicable.'

'But he is a king, I understand.'

'Yes, he is, but that means something different here. The Romans call this his palace, but it is really the clan house of the chief of this tribe. No one here is a servant, though they will serve you. They all have a role in keeping the government going and most of them are eligible to succeed to the throne. Even the king works in the fields at harvest.'

'The king has no children?'

'Sarah has borne him a daughter and a son, but neither is entitled to the throne. His sister's son or daughter will most likely be the next king or queen.'

'His sister's son or daughter?'

'Yes, here inheritance goes through the female line. The Romans are going to have a shock when they find out. They have already given the son a Roman crib and I know that they have everything lined up to ensure that the boy grows up thoroughly Roman.'

Mary took Salome to a private room and stayed there with her, talking. Salome's mind was whirring.

Inheritance went through the female line. So, it was true, she was of royal descent.

The niggly doubt in her mind, that her father's lowly status might disinherit her, vanished. The romance vanished with the doubt. Salome realised that she had always dreamed of being Queen of Albion, without really believing it to be possible. Now it was not just a possibility, but a probability. However, she saw the problems. How would the Britons react to a foreign queen? How would Rome react to a queen of Albion so soon after Boudicca, who was only Queen of the Iceni?

When Pygmalion arrived with Coventina, Mary suddenly switched the subject.

'I assume that you have come on a trading trip since you are in Pygmalion's company. Or have you just bought passage on his ship?'

'I am on a trading trip. Well, really a scouting trip. Demetrius was stationed in Camulodunum, and we were going to set up a trade route there. They have opened up since the Boudiccan revolt.'

Mary nodded encouragingly.

'Demetrius has now been moved to Ravenna, so we no longer have any contacts in Britannia. When Pygmalion said that you were here, we decided to see if you could help us with a contact.'

Mary sighed inwardly with relief. They had been lucky. If Salome had gone straight to Britannia, it would have been disastrous.

'We, being?'

'Oh, I forgot. Photina and her son, Alexander, are in Carthage.'

Mary smiled, 'It would have been wonderful to see my old friend again. How is Photina?'

They spent the rest of the evening talking about Galilee and old times. At some point in the evening, a man brought in a tray of food. At dusk, Salome, Coventina and Pygmalion got up to leave.

'You don't need to go, there are two beds in the annexe there. I am sure that you would be more comfortable here than on Pygmalion's ship.'

Although she loved to sail, Salome never slept well aboard a ship. On the journey to Jerusalem from Rome, the captain noticed her talent and put her in charge of the steering oar.

Pity they don't trust women enough for Pygmalion to put me in charge on this trip. Bad luck, they say. Just superstition if you ask me.

Coventina jumped at it as she had been used to luxury all her life. Pygmalion went back to his vessel.

Before retiring herself, Mary wrote a message in Hebrew and gave it to a messenger to be delivered.

The following morning, Salome, unusually, slept in. There was a smell she couldn't place. A pleasant woody aroma carried about in a mist. Overnight, a contraption had been brought into the room. A small wall of birch twigs. A woman was scooping up water from the trough under the birch and pouring it over the twigs. Salome asked the woman about it.

'We find it has a calming and relaxing effect. Mary thought that you might appreciate it after your long voyage.'

They stayed for a week before a message arrived for Mary.

They were eating breakfast. Mary opened the message and smiled, 'My main contact in Britannia says that they will meet you in Camulodunum. It would be best if you anchored in the river, and they will come out to you. That way they can keep the vultures off.'

Salome thought she understood. If you were taking a risk on a new trader and trade route, you wanted a monopoly to start with. Mary understood more. 'Vultures' was slang for Roman soldiers, referring to their legions' eagle standards.

Salome was surprised that they didn't sail straight across to Britannia from where they were. Instead, they sailed up the coast of Gaul until they could see the white cliffs of Britannia just across the sea. They sailed across, then east around the coast of Britannia, and up the river to Camulodunum.

It looked like a typical Roman town from anywhere in the empire. The brick buildings, temple, wharf and Roman arches. It could be one of a dozen different harbours in the Mediterranean. Except it seemed a bit out of place in the cold damp air of a British autumn. Salome took everything in, seeing the men carrying goods from a ship, a Roman official checking everything for tax purposes, the guards, everything. Everything, that is, except the man who walked quickly away after seeing what he was looking for, the recognisable red Pi on the sail of Pygmalion's ship.

They slept on board the ship, fully clothed. Pygmalion set a watch. Camulodunum was a safe port, but no port was entirely safe. The following morning, in the cold of dawn, Salome woke to hear two people speaking Aramaic. At first, she thought it was two of the sailors but then it penetrated that one of the voices was talking with a Galilean accent. All the sailors were Phoenician.

'Who is that, Ashok?' she called to the sailor.

'The representative of a local merchant who wishes to speak to you,' Ashok called back.

Their conversation disturbed Coventina, who looked accusingly at her mother, then turned over and tried to go back to sleep.

Part 2

Miriam

21

The pirates sailed up a wide channel with mountains in the distance to the north and low-lying salt marshes to the south. They then turned into a tributary with a high-sided gorge and up to a small British settlement with, to Miriam's surprise, a small collection of Roman-style buildings next to it. Britain had only been a Roman Province for about ten years. The pirates had obviously been there before, as their leader, accompanied by two others, went straight to one of the main houses in the Roman sector. One of the pirates dragged Miriam, bound at the wrists, along with them.

The steward evidently knew them and let them in immediately, with the usual proviso of them leaving their weapons at the door. Miriam was startled by the appearance of the steward, with his red hair and pale skin. He led them into a large atrium and then spoke to the pirates in Latin. The pirate leader, and the one holding Miriam, looked at the third pirate. He translated it into Greek for them.

'He asks what we want and who the woman is.'

'Tell him that we have come on our usual trading trip. The woman is a slave that we are seeking to sell.'

The pirate translated back into faltering Latin. The steward told them to wait there, and he would fetch the master. He then turned and left through a parting in a tapestry opposite the main door.

They waited in the atrium. It seemed strange to Miriam. At first, she couldn't work out why. Then it hit her. There was a large conspicuous shrine to a goddess. It was not uncommon in Roman houses to have a shrine, but they were usually inconspicuously hidden away in the family's private quarters. There was a bust of the emperor, as well. She could see marble steps leading away to the right, down into a walled garden, and the sound of a trickling fountain.

When the steward returned, he came from the direction of the garden. He beckoned them and they followed him. A woman of about fourteen was seated on a curved marble bench by a round pond in the middle of which was a fountain. Standing next to her was a tall young man, a little older. Both were dressed in Roman fashion, but both had the same pale skin and copper-coloured hair of the steward.

There was a pungent, acrid smell in the air and steam rose from the pond. A sluice took excess water from the pond and drained it away, out through a culvert under the garden wall. Miriam could not see how the pond was fed, so assumed it must be fed by the fountain. The garden would be pleasant to be in under other circumstances, she thought, with its delicately perfumed plants, neat green hedges, and statues of Greek and Roman gods. Scattered here and there were Roman-style stone benches, made for two.

The man greeted them and then proceeded to business. He dismissed the haggling for the trade goods they had brought with them, telling them to deal with the steward. However, before he decided on the woman, he needed to inspect the goods. Miriam noticed, with amusement, that the pirate who translated struggled to get the meaning. When he did, a grin spread across his face as he translated to the pirate leader.

'Of course,' the pirate leader said, and the translator repeated in Latin.

The man took Miriam by the arm and he and the woman took her into the house. Once in the house, the couple spoke to each other in a strange language.

The woman turned to Miriam and switched to Latin, 'You don't happen to speak Latin by any chance, do you?'

'Yes, my lady,' Miriam replied.

'How came you to be a slave?'

'These pirates took the merchant ship my husband and I were travelling on. They killed all the men.'

'Is that the source of their trade goods?' the man interjected.

'Yes.'

'It has troubled me for some time whether they were pirates or not. We were getting too good a deal on the goods. I cannot, for grandfather's sake, deal with them.'

'Hold on one moment, Rivalin. What is your name, girl?'

'I am Miriam.'

'What will the pirates do if we refuse to buy you?'

'They will not dare to try and sell me anywhere else in the empire. They do not know I speak Latin, so they think they are safe here as you don't speak Greek. They will kill me, probably after using me as sport for the crew.'

'That is what I thought. We have to buy her, Rivalin.'

'She will not be much better off here. You know slaves belong to the whole clan, which means all the men can … well you know what, whenever they like.'

'Then the purchase must be secret, and you must marry her?'

'I'm marrying Sarah, you know that. What will she think?'

'I think that unlikely. Your cousin, the king, wants her. Anyway, she will not think much of you, not rescuing this woman. You can always make this woman a junior wife.'

'A concubine, you mean?' asked Miriam.

'No, a wife, but not the most senior. Of course, in Roman Law, you would remain a slave but not in our laws. The marriage would not be recognised under Roman Law.'

'That would still leave her open to being used by the men in the clan.'

'Yes, but it would then be her choice, not theirs, and, crucially, her children would inherit.'

Miriam turned to Rivalin, 'That means I would have to lie with you though.'

'To formalise the marriage, yes. After that, I am not interested. My heart is elsewhere.'

'I've never met a woman so willing to let her husband marry another woman just to save her. Thank you, my lady.'

'I am not Rivalin's wife, I am his sister. And if you are to marry Rivalin then you must start calling me Bronwyn.'

'Yes, my... er Bronwyn.'

'I will go out and negotiate the purchase price.'

'Wait!' said Bronwyn, sharply, 'Before you go, we are going to have to make you look a bit more dishevelled.'

With that, she tousled his hair, creased his tunic, and loosened the thong on one of his sandals.

The women watched Rivalin go out. The steward had gone with the pirate who had held Miriam as she was taken to the house, leaving the pirate leader and the translator there. The pirate leader left after Rivalin gave him the agreed amount. Rivalin then called for a servant to bring a wax tablet and stylus. He wrote quickly, giving the tablet back with instructions. The servant ran to deliver his message and Rivalin wandered back to the two women.

'What was that?' asked Bronwyn.

'A message to the commander of the marines' garrison, telling him that I have just learnt that the men are pirates and that I have rescued a woman from them. My orders are for him to set sail immediately and wait for the pirates at the other side of the gorge. They are to sink their ship without a trace. There are to be no survivors.'

'Then there is no reason for you to marry Miriam, Rivalin.'

'No, there is every reason. It will explain to the Romans why I want the pirates got rid of. No one could gainsay me that Miriam wasn't a slave then, and the marriage would be valid.'

'What about the steward?' asked Miriam.

'We will tell him that we discovered that they were pirates and forced them to release you by threatening to expose them,' replied Rivalin.

'You are going to a lot of trouble for me. I am grateful, but why?'

'There is a reason. One member of our tribe was kidnapped by pirates and sold into slavery in Rome about forty years ago or so. Before he managed to buy his freedom, he was made to father a child. He claims that the mother of that child was our queen. We do not know whether he was telling the truth but we have, ever since, freed any slaves we came across if we could. Our grandfather was insistent on this, saying that any freed slave could be the descendent of our queen,' said Bronwyn.

'I am not descended from your queen, though my mother was a freed slave.'

'Nonetheless, Bronwyn is right, it was our duty to free you if we could.'

Three days later, the news came that the pirate ship had been sunk. The pirates who survived had been tortured until they revealed the location of the pirate base. They had then been crucified according to Roman law. There was an unexpected bonus. Ten per cent of the value of the goods seized from the ship was given to Rivalin as a reward. It amounted to considerably more than he had paid the pirates to free Miriam. Rivalin and Miriam's wedding was set for two days later.

22

The wedding was like nothing Miriam had ever experienced before. It took place in the round compound of the British village. The first thing she noticed was that all the men wore skirts, tied at the waist. They were bare upwards from there. The women were dressed, as women dressed the world over, in long tunic dresses.

There was food and drink, of course, and a sort of ceremony in which their hands were bound together using ivy vines. Twisted laurel coronets were placed on their heads. After that, everything let rip. There was wild dancing, the like of which Miriam had never seen before, all kept in time by ferocious, relentless drumming. There were four drummers, she noticed. As one tired, another took over, without dropping a single beat.

At about midnight, couples started disappearing into the large rectangular longhouse that dominated the central square. It was unusual, Miriam noticed. All the other huts were round. Rivalin led Miriam to one of these. He seemed strangely shy, not the confident man she had seen up until then.

'I am sorry,' he said, 'I must now do you a disservice and I must stay the whole night. Anything else would look suspicious.'

'I was lucky with my first husband,' Miriam said, 'I was allowed to marry the man I loved. That seldom happens with the women of my people. We are taught as we grow up to respect the rights of our husbands, whether or not there is love in the marriage.'

Rivalin still hesitated. He stood there, next to a low wooden-framed bed with its taut animal-skin base stretched across, and woollen covers. His upper body was bare, as it had been all night. His skin was paler than any Miriam had seen before. The torchlight played red on his torso, the shadow outlining his muscular chest. His body hair was very fine, seeming to be almost non-existent.

Unlike Jesus, who had thick black body hair.

With that thought, Miriam unconsciously touched the pendant Jesus had given her. She stopped herself. If she thought of Jesus, she would not be able to do what she needed to.

Miriam took a deep breath, removed her dress, and then walked over to Rivalin. She undid his skirt and let it drop to the ground. Taking his hand, she led him to the bed, kicked the covers off and lay down. Rivalin stood and looked at her for a few seconds, then joined her on the bed.

Miriam was surprised at how sensual, yet gentle, he was, making sure that she was ready before entering her. Still, try as she might, she thought of Jesus, the only other man she had ever made love to. She tried to hold them back, but the tears flowed in torrents. After he had come, Rivalin shifted his weight off her, saw her crying and put his arms around her, holding her to himself until the tears abated.

'Sorry, I have hurt you.'

'No, it is just the memory of my husband. I could not have asked for a more gentle, sensitive touch.'

'I will leave you; you need to be alone.'

'Stay, Rivalin, if you can. I need comfort, not sex, though.'

Rivalin got up and Miriam thought he was going to leave. Instead, he stooped and picked up the blankets. He arranged them in such a way that they came up to their waists, leaving their tops bare. One section of the blanket was arranged to separate them below the waist. Miriam realised that, to a casual observer, it would look as if they were indeed naked. Rivalin gently kissed her on the head and held her until she slept, safe in his arms.

23

Miriam woke the following morning to find Rivalin still naked beside her. She slipped out of the side of the bed, leaving him asleep. She dressed and left the hut. Outside, she found Bronwyn waiting for her.

'Are you alright, Miriam? I have been worried.'

'Yes. Your brother has been as gentle and sensitive as I could have wished. I need a wash, though.'

Bronwyn smiled, 'Come with me.'

Bronwyn led Miriam back to the house. As they entered, she called a couple of the women servants. She led Miriam through a decorated door in a corner of the room. There was a passageway leading to a room with an acrid smell. A pool of hot water was in the centre. The bath was completely tiled, Roman fashion, with the beige plaster walls covered in frescos. There were several doors each labelled in Latin. Bronwyn undressed and signalled Miriam to do the same. To her surprise, the servants did too.

As she entered the water, she felt the warmth penetrate her muscles, easing them. She also felt the sting of many minute cuts she had forgotten about or hadn't known existed. Her wrists hurt so much where the pirates had bound her that she jerked them out of the water. Bronwyn gently took them under again.

'These are the goddess's healing waters. They will sting at first but will gradually soothe the pain and ease aching muscles. As if by magic, Miriam felt the pain in her wrists subside. Bronwyn took her to a shelf that jutted out underwater and the two of them sat on it. The servants followed and, as Miriam and Bronwyn sat up to their necks in water, they massaged their shoulders.

As they did so, Miriam looked around at the murals. Vines were the main motif. A mixture of grapevines and ivy. There was a woodland scene on one wall. Huts, like the one she had slept in the previous night, in a lightly wooded area next to a large pool. Swans were swimming on the pool. It reminded her of Salome's wedding shawl.

Opposite, there was a large mural of a naked woman with black hair sitting on an impossibly large, bright green leaf. Behind her was a large oak tree, the branches spread over, shading her. A stream of clear water spouted out of the tree. It was the eyes that drew Miriam's attention, though. They were the same green as the leaf, but more than that, they were the same colour as Salome's eyes and those of her daughter, Coventina.

'Bronwyn, who is the woman depicted there?'

'That is the goddess. Her open name is Sulis in Britain, Minerva in Gaul. The Romans call her Sulis-Minerva. She has another secret name in Britain, but we do not divulge it to any but devotees. She is the source of all clear water and of these healing waters. Do your people have a protecting goddess?'

'No, we worship the one true god, Yahweh, and his son Jesus. We do have two guardian angels though. Michael and Gabriel.'

Bronwyn looked at Miriam strangely. Then she got up and said, 'We had better get out of here now.'

Miriam panicked, grabbing for her dress. 'Are the men coming?'

'No,' chuckled Bronwyn, 'Mixed bathing is allowed occasionally but isn't usual. The men won't come whilst we are here. It is just that if you stay in these waters too long, you become drowsy and can easily drown.'

Miriam relaxed again. Bronwyn took her through one of the doors to a plunge pool of fresh water and jumped in, followed by the servants. Miriam took a deep breath and jumped after them. Following the hot pool, the pool felt freezing. Miriam let her breath out with a high-pitched squeak. The women looked at each other and laughed, and then started splashing each other with water. This was a game Miriam knew. She had played it as a child in the cold waters of Galilee. Their heads were soon thoroughly soaked, joining the rest of their bodies.

They got out of the pool, and the two servants went to a recess to fetch towels. Miriam was disappointed that it was over. However, she and Bronwyn were not given the towels, but led through another door into a room filled with steam, where they sat on wooden benches. As they sat, Bronwyn continued the conversation.

'Tell me of this Yahweh and Jesus. I have heard of them before but know nothing of them. And these angels. What are they? I have never heard the word before.'

'That is a big story you are asking for.'

'At least you can give me a start now.'

For the following twenty minutes, Miriam gave a brief explanation. Bronwyn was overwhelmed.

'How on earth do you find the time to tell the whole story?'

'We talk whilst we work. My mother would tell us the stories as we embroidered. I mean my mother-in-law. My mother died when I was a few months old. I was brought up by Jesus's mother.'

'You were brought up by the mother of a god and married to a god?'

'Not that Jesus. It is quite a common name in my country.'

'You embroider? That is a skill I would like to learn.'

With that, Bronwyn got up and led them back to the plunge pool. Miriam was ready this time, but they did not linger after the plunge. They used the towels to dry themselves. Then they went to yet another room. There were six tables there. Bronwyn spread her towel over one and lay down on top, with her face through a hole in one end. Miriam copied her. One of the servants opened rose oil and started to massage Miriam.

Miriam lapped it up, 'I feel like a queen.'

'In a sense, you are,' replied Bronwyn.

'What?'

'Rivalin is our king. His senior wife would be queen. He hasn't taken a senior wife yet. You are his only wife, thus far. So, as the most senior junior wife, you are Queen Pro Tempore.'

Miriam was stunned.

'I thought you were Romans. Who was queen before?'

'As Rivalin's sister, me.'

'Oh.'

After the massage, Miriam was presented with new clothes. They were in the Roman style which Miriam had never worn before. The dress had a hole for the head and a bodice, like all the dresses she had ever worn before. There the similarity ended. There was a slit up the side of the dress from just below the bosom to calf height where the dress ended. The waist was kept together using a band and there was a tie just above knee height. One of the maids showed her how the band went around the waist to keep the dress on. She then proceeded to braid Miriam's hair, again Roman-style. Finally, Bronwyn looked at Miriam.

'Yes, you will pass. Rivalin will join us once he has bathed. He won't take long, he never does. Then our people will be presented their new queen. After that, we will have to greet the local Roman notables. Lucky you speak Latin.'

Bronwyn and Miriam walked out together. As they did so, the side of Miriam's dress billowed open from the waist. 'Oh, how do I stop it?' she shrieked.

'There is a tie just above the knee if you wish to use it.'

'That will help, but it will still open. Surely Roman women don't let men see everything?'

'That depends on the Roman woman. Still, tying up the lower dress is thought modest.'

Bronwyn signalled one of the women, 'Get material for another tie for Miriam's dress.'

'Make that two ties, please.'

The woman left and returned with the material, needle, and thread. 'Where do you want the ties?'

'Here and here,' said Miriam, indicating the top of her thigh and halfway down her upper leg. The woman complied.

'You are certainly the most modest woman from the Roman Empire I have ever come across.'

'My people would still think this immodest. Looks like something one of King Herod's courtiers would wear.'

'As I said. You are now a queen, Miriam.'

Miriam's mouth opened and closed a few times, like a fish, as it sank in. Then she tittered and finally burst into open laughter as the absurdity of her position dawned on her. She moved up close to Bronwyn and whispered, 'Let me get this straight. I am in a marriage of convenience with a man who is not interested in being married to me. Under Roman Law, I am still a slave and the marriage is not recognised. According to British custom, I am not only married but a queen, until Rivalin marries a senior wife. At which point, I become what?'

'That just about sums it up except that Rivalin is never likely to marry a senior wife. If he did, it would be her decision as to what title you had. He may marry another junior wife, of course. Then it would depend on how he ranks you, but you would still be a queen.'

'So as Queen I can command, if I want, though that seems strange. As a slave, I cannot leave on pain of death from the Romans.'

'Even more absurd is that if Rivalin goes away anywhere or dies, you rule in his stead, even though a slave.'

'That is a lot of trust to give a total stranger. Why did you do it? It was you, after all, that made the final decision, and your explanation doesn't feel complete.'

'I mentioned that we have not had a real queen now for many years.'

Miriam nodded.

'Our queen links the people to the goddess and tells us her wishes. A prophetess, I think you would call her. That said, most of our women can sense what the goddess wants, to a greater or lesser degree. Generally, the higher the rank of the woman, the more acute that sense is. There was great disappointment when I didn't have the mark of the queen despite being highly attuned to the goddess. You are important, Miriam. No, vital, for the future wellbeing of our people. I don't know why, and I don't know how, but you are. It doesn't make any sense to me, but there it is. Rivalin knows how strong my connection to the goddess is, so when I made my suggestion, he took it as a command. You were meant to come here, and you were meant to be Queen. That is all I know.'

'That is a lot to take in. I will pray about it.'

Bronwyn took Miriam by the hand, 'Shall we go?'

They went on to the private room behind the atrium, each in silent thought. Then they sat, mute until Rivalin joined them. It was not long, as Bronwyn had predicted, only about twenty minutes. He looked more Roman than ever, so different to the way he had looked at the wedding the previous day and certainly very different to last night. At that thought, Miriam coloured a little. She told herself that she had nothing to be ashamed of, as Rivalin was her husband, but that simply made her colour deepen.

'Are you alright, Miriam?' Bronwyn asked, with concern in her voice, 'You are not ill?'

'I'm alright. I just need a little time to draw breath and collect myself for the performance.'

'Performance?' asked Rivalin.

'Well, that is what we are doing, isn't it?' asked Miriam, 'Putting on a pageant for the benefit of your people and the Romans. For your people, it will be an important occasion to meet their supposed new queen. For the Romans, it is an act to humour, as they will see it, a petty king, in his ignorant pomposity, taking a semi-civilised citizen of the empire as a bride.'

'Semi-civilised?' said Bronwyn.

'I am not a Roman citizen. In Roman eyes, a half-starved Roman citizen, dressed in rags and lying drunk in the gutter, is still more civilised than a king from a subject race.'

Rivalin laughed. A quiet melodic chuckle in his tenor-range voice. It was the first time Miriam had heard him laugh and she liked it. She turned her head as Bronwyn joined in to receive a wink from her sister-in-law.

'Shall we go then, my fellow actors, and play the fool for the benefit of our masters?'

They went out to the front of the house where three chairs were arranged. A central large chair, with two smaller chairs. Miriam supposed they were substitute thrones. Rivalin took the central chair and indicated to Miriam that she should take the one to his left. Bronwyn took the other.

The British citizenry was genuinely joyous on the occasion. So much so, that Miriam had a pang of guilt at the subterfuge. The Romans, when they came for their private audience after the public show, were insincere but careful to lay on the flattery. That would normally have annoyed Rivalin, but he saw it through Miriam's eyes as she made quiet, witty comments that only he could hear and, instead, he had difficulty holding in his amusement at the Roman arrogance.

At the end of the day, Miriam asked about the chairs. Where were they kept? There had been no sight of them before.

'They are kept for visits from the Romans. Our kings do not use such pomp normally, they are closer to their people,' Bronwyn informed her.

Rivalin turned to go, then stopped, and turned back.

'Thank you, Miriam. I usually hate those occasions when I have to suck up to the Romans, but you made it fun. You will make a good queen. You know how to perform and hide your true feelings.' He then left.

Miriam looked to Bronwyn, for reassurance that Rivalin was in earnest, to find her beaming from ear to ear.

'See, already my instinct is proved right.'

That night, Miriam prayed to Yahweh for guidance. As she slept, she had a visit from Coventina, the angel with bright green eyes. As when she was a child, she still could not discern what gender the angel was or even if the term 'gender' applied to this being.

'Yahweh has sent you here, Miriam. He has work for you. You are meant to be Queen, and I will guide you when you need it. Mostly though, you just need to do what feels right.'

When Miriam relayed this dream to Bronwyn the following day, Bronwyn just nodded and smiled.

24

Over the next week, Miriam gradually began to feel safe. It was one thing to know you were safe, she mused, another entirely to actually feel safe. Rivalin kept his promise to leave her alone and Bronwyn was her constant companion. When she wanted to talk, Bronwyn was there; when she wanted silence, Bronwyn was there; when she cried, Bronwyn held her; when she needed space, Bronwyn backed off but was always ready, if needed. Night or day, Bronwyn was there. She asked no questions, gave no platitudes; just listened and, if necessary, talked. She talked about anything inconsequential, as if nothing had happened.

At the end of the week, Miriam broke down. It was early evening, and they were sitting in the garden. Orange-tip butterflies flew from flower to flower in the late spring sunshine. Bronwyn held her, as she had countless times before in the week, as Miriam spoke, her words hardly audible through her sobs, 'Jesus, my poor Jesus, oh Jesus my love.'

Bronwyn, as usual, just held her until Miriam had cried herself out. Then Miriam broke free and began to speak.

'We were on our way to Alexandria by ship from Caesarea.'

Bronwyn knew of Alexandria. Ships had occasionally come to Britain's shores from there. It was more usual for them to come from Carthage. She had never heard of Caesarea but didn't interrupt.

'We followed the coast as that is usually safest. Pirates don't normally operate in sight of land. But we had to go past Sinai. There are no towns in the desert there. That is where they struck, coming out of a hidden inlet. They were on us before we could get the oars out or prepare ourselves.'

Miriam stopped, fresh rivulets of tears meandering down her cheeks. She collected herself once more.

'Jesus drew his sword, along with the other men aboard, sailors all. The fight was swift. None of the crew were swordsmen and nor was my Jesus. He stood in front of me, to protect me, but had three men to face, all seasoned fighters. They chopped him into pieces, just for fun. When he was dead, they kicked him into the sea. Then the men turned to me. I could see their intent.'

Miriam went silent for a second time and shivered. Bronwyn put a comforting arm about her shoulders and waited. Miriam continued, barely audible.

'I pulled my dress tightly around me and backed off, but there was nowhere to go. One backward step took me hard against the mast. My former protection was now my trap. The foremost man grabbed the dress around the neck and pulled me towards him, lifting the hem with his other hand. He was about to force me onto the deck when I heard a shout. The pirate captain called at him to stop.

'Don't spoil the goods or they will be worthless. If you don't stop, I will kill you both and you can feed the fish along with all the others.'

That stopped him and he loosened his grip on me. I pulled free and dashed for the side of the ship, intending to jump in, not caring whether I survived or drowned. I was not quick enough. The pirate captain caught me.

'You are lucky that you are so pretty. You will make a good price as a concubine. Otherwise, I would let the crew have you. I might yet if you cause any more trouble. He took me back to his ship, bound my hands in front and tied the rope to their mast. They transferred all the trade goods from the hold of the trade ship to their own, then they sank it. I could move my hands sufficiently to eat and drink and lift my skirts if I needed to relieve myself, but all in sight of the crew. They just watched and then washed it away with seawater. After a few days, they were bored of the spectacle and I smelt, so they allowed me to wash, with one of their number guarding me; a boy hardly twelve years old I would guess. He was frightened, knowing that if I escaped or anything happened to me, he would be killed. That made me give up any idea of escape. The rest you know.'

Bronwyn was silent as Miriam sobbed once more. When her tears subsided again, Bronwyn asked her first question.

'Rivalin said that he thought you had had a child. Was the child also on the ship?'

'I have a daughter, in her third year. She was ill and, as we were just doing a short reconnaissance trip, we left her with her grandmother. I will never see her again.'

'Why do you say that?' asked Bronwyn but knew the answer even as she said it. She could feel that the goddess didn't want Miriam to go home.

'The angel told me that I must not go back or even try to contact anyone at home. I don't know why.' Miriam's tears flowed once more.

Miriam ate no dinner that night. Rivalin was worried, but Bronwyn signalled him to pretend he had noticed nothing. Miriam retired as soon as dinner was over. She felt dirty, defiled by the pirates, and went to the heated water bath in the spa, to clean herself before returning to her room.

She found Bronwyn there. Neither woman said anything as Bronwyn gently took Miriam to the double bed, lay down with her and held her protectively until, finally, in the early hours of the morning, Miriam slept.

25

At dawn, one of the maids went into Miriam's room. She saw Miriam get up from the bed, lean over a sleeping Bronwyn and kiss her forehead. She then said something in a language the maid didn't understand. All she caught was the name, 'Miriam'. With unseeing eyes wide open, Miriam headed for the door past the maid. The maid followed.

When the maid realised that Miriam was in danger, heading for the spa room, she tried to stop her but could not. She called out as she struggled to hold Miriam away from the water. Rivalin came running. He helped hold Miriam but, even with the two of them, they could barely stop her. Breathlessly, the maid explained what she had seen. In desperation, Rivalin tried a new tack.

He spoke in Latin, hoping it would penetrate whatever barrier was around Miriam.

'Miriam, my love, come back to bed. Our daughter needs you.'

Miriam stopped struggling.

'Come Miriam, come back to our daughter.'

With this, he gently led her back to a still-sleeping Bronwyn. Miriam kissed Bronwyn again, lay down next to her and put an arm across her, holding her tightly. Rivalin turned to leave. Miriam became agitated. Again, she spoke in the unknown language. All Rivalin could discern was the name,

'Jesus'. He lay down behind Miriam, on the opposite side to Bronwyn, and tentatively put a hand on her. Miriam settled.

After a few minutes, Rivalin got up, but Miriam was immediately agitated again. He lay back down. Half an hour later, he tried again. This time Miriam stayed resting. He asked the maid, who was still in the room, what her normal duties were. He then said that he would get them covered by someone else. The maid was to stay in the room until Bronwyn and Miriam woke, then go home.

'From now on, your duties consist of staying in this room every night and making sure Miriam is safe,' Rivalin told her, before leaving the room.

Bronwyn and Miriam emerged from the room about two hours before noon, neither with any memory of what had happened. The night's event was never repeated but the maid was kept there for the next month, just in case. As a bond had then built between her and Miriam, Rivalin had her trained as a lady's maid for Miriam.

26

Over the next month, Miriam and Bronwyn talked. Bronwyn taught Miriam their language and Miriam taught Bronwyn how to embroider. They also explored the local area together. Miriam found it fascinating. Particularly interesting were the wheat fields. There was wheat of different heights altogether, the winter wheat ready for harvest. Not unusual.

'But where are all the harvest men?' asked Miriam.

'Harvest men?'

'Well, women as well. It must take a lot of people to cut and thresh all this wheat.'

'Thresh?' enquired Bronwyn, 'What does that mean?'

Miriam was surprised. Even the children of wealthy families worked to bring in the harvest in Galilee. Miriam picked up a sickle that lay at the edge of the field, bent, and cut some corn.

'This is threshing,' she said, as she laid out a cloth on the ground and then beat the sheaf to remove the grain from the stalks.

'I have never seen that done before,' said Bronwyn. 'We have a different way.'

She took Miriam to another field where two men were pulling, and a third was guiding, a contraption the like of which Miriam had never seen before. They pulled the machine up the field and then back down again. When they reached the edge of the field nearest them, Bronwyn called them to stop. She took Miriam over.

The contraption consisted of a hopper on two wheels, with ropes to pull it and handles behind to guide it. At the front, was a wooden board with a V-shape cut-out, widest at the very front and leading to a series of narrow slots at the back, over the hopper.

'Watch,' said Bronwyn. She signalled the men to carry on.

As they pulled the device, the wheat was pushed into the V by the forward motion of the vehicle. When the stalk of the corn reached the narrow slot, the corn bent, with the slot eventually reaching the head of the plant, stripping off the grain which fell into the hopper. Miriam was delighted, thinking of how this could be sold across the empire.

'But what about the straw?' she asked.

'We cut what we need for bedding, for ourselves and our animals, and let our sheep and cattle eat the rest.'

'What about winter feed?'

'We don't need a lot. Most of our animals are hardy enough to stay out all winter. Anyway, we use the autumn harvest straw and hay for that.'

'There must be far more grain here than you can possibly consume yourselves.'

'We sell most of it to visiting traders from the empire. We were doing this well before the invasion. Since then, we have opened up more land and exported more. Of course, we cannot command Egyptian prices, being so far from Rome. Transport costs, you know.'

This piqued Miriam's merchant instincts, but Bronwyn had no detailed knowledge of actual costs and prices. The main source of the region's wealth now became clear to Miriam.

She had always thought that copper was the main trade with Britain. She asked Bronwyn about this.

'Not here,' she said, 'The land, west of here, produces copper, along with lead. Also, in the hills across the other side of the channel, the pirates sailed down before the gorge.'

'That is part of the empire as well?'

'I don't know, but if it isn't, it soon will be. The lure of the copper would be enough, but they have gold mines there as well. In fact, they say, in some secret places, that you can pick up the gold from the ground as you walk along.'

It was during this time that Miriam learnt Rivalin and Bronwyn's story. Their great-grandfather had usurped the throne from his sister, the rightful queen, who had been forced into slavery in Rome. At first, this had been popular as he had implemented what the people wanted. This gradually turned sour as people realised that what they had wanted was not as good as what they had had. They also lost the guidance of the goddess who spoke to the people through the true queen.

Further, as things went on, it became clear that their great-grandfather was changing things for his benefit and that of his close supporters. At first, it was just the minor people who were dissatisfied, then the chiefs who were not in the inner circle. To maintain authority, the king had to use more and more force. Then his allies wanted greater and greater reward for supporting him. There was constant political in-fighting, even when there was no actual bloodshed. Their great-grandfather had died in one of the skirmishes.

Their grandfather had taken over as king. He tried to heal the rifts but was not in the true line of succession, so lacked authority. He listened to the women who were most connected to the goddess. None could discern the goddess's wishes clearly. He married the woman who had the strongest connection, but still lacked authority, and there were constant challenges to his reign.

That was when the Romans invaded, some ten years before. The invaders did not turn on their grandfather's kingdom until the following year. A common enemy created a temporary alliance but, after initial minor victories, the coalition fell apart. Some powerful men made a pact with the Romans to switch sides if their leader could inherit the throne. Their grandfather and father had been killed in the subsequent battle. The leader of the rebels was also killed. It did not suit the Romans to put one of the other rebels on the throne. Rivalin had been seven at the time, Bronwyn five. They were young enough to be moulded into model Romans and dominated by the invaders.

Their education, since, had been Roman, and Rivalin ruled on behalf of the Romans. Although nominally king, he was totally reliant on them to maintain his authority. He tried to rule well, and in accordance with the goddess's wishes, but that was hard to discern.

'But you have a strong connection to the goddess, don't you?'

'I do, but I do not have the mark of the queen. I can support Rivalin, but my discernment is whether something is right or wrong; I do not perceive what the goddess wants done.'

'So Rivalin is sixteen and you are fourteen. I never thought that I would end up marrying a man who was younger than me. It never happens in our culture. When will you marry, Bronwyn, and how will your husband be chosen?'

'I will never marry. There would be too much competition for my hand, fracturing the people once more. Besides, with my strong connection to the goddess, my husband would threaten Rivalin's authority and, with it, Roman authority. The

Romans would never tolerate that. The people need healing, not more bloodshed.'

'What if the true queen were to return?'

'I would then be free to marry, yes, and Rivalin would have no choice. He would have to cede the throne to her, whatever the Romans wanted. We fear that most.'

'Why do you fear it?'

'Because conflict with Rome would be almost inevitable and disastrous, whether we won or lost. Our people have suffered enough.'

'So, your greatest desire is also your greatest fear.'

Bronwyn's reply was an almost inaudible whisper, 'Yes.'

27

After the first month of her marriage to Rivalin, Miriam started venturing out on her own. She observed the markets, the way people lived, their clothing, everything.

The town was made up of a Roman quarter, built in local limestone, where she lived with Rivalin and Bronwyn, along with several separate enclaves of round huts with a central longhouse. Around each enclave was a low wooden palisade. It looked more for demarcation of the boundary than defence, or maybe to keep animals in.

The closest enclave to the Roman area was the one where she and Rivalin had married, and she had spent her wedding night. The people in this enclave were friendliest to her as well. One day, she noticed Bronwyn there, talking to Miriam's maid. Miriam thought her maid, Ffion, lived in the palace but didn't know. She must ask her, she decided.

It was the people's dress that most interested Miriam. The women wore tunic dresses, much like women wore everywhere Miriam had been. She wore the same, although the material had confused her to start with and she couldn't understand when the women tried to explain. Then one old woman had taken her and shown her. They went into the fields near the settlement. There, the old woman harvested a stinging plant. After stripping off the leaves, which stung, she beat the stalks until a fibre was produced. Miriam was invited to feel it and it was the same soft fibre of her tunic.

Miriam was pleased that she only had to wear the revealing dress on formal occasions. Around the palace, she wore a dress with a tunic base and fine cotton or silk over the top. If she was there as Rivalin's wife she wore cotton, as Queen she wore silk. At least that was the theory. She hadn't had occasion to wear silk yet.

The men's dress was unlike anything Miriam had seen before. They wore skirts as Rivalin had worn on their wedding day. The skirt was wrapped around and held in place by a leather thong or simple piece of rope, with the excess cloth thrown over one shoulder. That was all. She had noticed that workmen often wore a shorter skirt, without any excess for over the shoulder. The men in the fields had had these on when using the reaping contraption.

Bronwyn told her that the longer skirts were used as blankets, when on long journeys. She also told her that when the men went into battle, they would adorn themselves in a blue dye called woad and, at the last minute before the battle, would throw off their skirts.

The market was very small, with little for sale. It seemed more like a meeting place for people to exchange the odd goods or talk, than a proper marketplace. Bronwyn had been asked about this too. She explained that each settlement was self-sufficient so much trade was unnecessary. They didn't have the money to buy imported goods, so the people carried on as they had done for a thousand years. This left Miriam with many questions, but Bronwyn knew little about anything outside Aquae Sulis, which the Romans called the settlement, so Miriam started asking the people in the enclaves.

This was how she became confused again. Outward differences in culture are simply a veneer, like the way people dance and how they dress. Miriam didn't know the actual differences. She went to the houses where her maid came from and started talking, as she had done before, only this time she was confronted by a group of men. They were not aggressive, but they seemed to be having a game of some sort with her. They started by making subtle suggestions and then became more and more obvious in their intent. They were competing to see who could get Miriam to sleep with them. In their eagerness, they surrounded her. Miriam became frightened and froze. One of the men reached out to touch her and Miriam panicked. She hit out at the man, broke through the circle, and ran back to the palace, leaving the man nursing a nosebleed, and the other men laughing and jeering at him.

Bronwyn found Miriam in her room, crying. She had heard what had happened from Ffion. She held her until Miriam had cried herself out, then she spoke.

'I am sorry, Miriam. I taught you our language but nothing of our customs. It is just that it never occurred to me that this would happen.'

'Why did they do it? It was horrible. They had been so kind before.'

'They did not know, Miriam.'

Bronwyn hesitated.

'Are you ready to talk about it? I know that Romans are monogamous, but most of our people don't.'

'I am not Roman, I am Hebrew. Most marriages are monogamous because the men cannot afford to be otherwise, but richer men may have more than one wife. Rulers often do because of making political alliances.'

'Still, when you marry, you have one husband, like the Romans?' asked Bronwyn.

'Yes, of course.'

Miriam was startled by the question.

'In our culture when a woman marries, she marries the clan. Any man in the clan has the right to sleep with her and she has the right to sleep with any of the men she chooses.'

Miriam was appalled. 'You mean I have to lie with any of the men in that enclave who want me?' She shuddered.

'No, Miriam. You have the choice. You can sleep with any of them or refuse to sleep with them at your choosing, even Rivalin. The same thing goes the other way around. The man can choose to sleep with any woman he wishes, so long as she consents and is married within the clan, or he can choose not to sleep with her.'

'Does Rivalin sleep with them then?'

'No, he will not. It would give the woman, and her husband, an elevated status above everyone else in the clan. That would be bad for the clan.'

'How do you know who has fathered a child?'

'We don't always know. By convention, the child belongs to the man the woman is married to, whether he has fathered it or not, but most men and women stick to the person they are married to for sexual relations, with only the occasional fling, unless of course they lean towards members of the same sex.'

Miriam was shocked again. 'So, you don't have any such thing as adultery?'

'Yes, but it is defined differently. Adultery, with us, is sleeping with someone outside your clan.'

'How do you stop someone sleeping with a half-brother or sister, if you don't know who the father is?'

'Women always marry outside of the clan they are born into. That is why I cannot marry. It would not only diminish Rivalin's status, but it would also bring our clan into conflict with the clan I married into. Come, Miriam, we need to talk to Rivalin about this.'

'Must we? Does he have to know? After all, I have made it clear I don't want to sleep with them.'

'The men will just think that you didn't understand. They will be more subtle but will continue until they succeed unless we do something. Anyway, Rivalin probably already knows. We had better head him off before he makes matters worse.'

Miriam was confused but followed Bronwyn, who signalled Ffion to accompany them. They found an angry Rivalin in the atrium, talking to his steward. Miriam's language skills were not yet good enough to know what was being said as, in his haste to get his point across, Rivalin was speaking fast. He dismissed the steward.

'You have heard what happened, then.'

It was a statement from Bronwyn, not a question. She used Latin.

'Second hand, yes. The steward is reporting gossip, not fact. Miriam, could you tell me please?'

Miriam went red, then took a deep breath but, before she could speak, Ffion spoke, 'I was in the village visiting my husband, I can tell you.'

After Ffion had related the story, Miriam blurted out, 'I am sorry, I didn't know your customs, I didn't know what to do.'

The anger left Rivalin's eyes and was replaced by the compassion Miriam had seen on their first meeting.

'You have done nothing wrong, Miriam. Bronwyn and I should have spent more time explaining our people's customs, rather than just teaching you our language. Now, how do we stop this from happening again, and how do we punish Eirwyn? An edict to start with, I suppose.'

'You can't issue an edict and you can't punish Eirwyn,' said Bronwyn, 'An edict would diminish the clan in the eyes of the other clans. That would lead to trouble with maybe one or two men from the other clans trying it on with the clan women because none of the men can satisfy them. They might even make a play for Miriam. And Eirwyn has done nothing wrong. He pushed his luck a bit further than he should have but the nosebleed, that Miriam gave him, has given him enough loss of face.'

Rivalin turned to Miriam.

'You gave Eirwyn a nosebleed?'

'I didn't know, and I panicked and ...'

Rivalin, laughing, put his hand up to stop her. 'It is alright, Miriam, it is no more than he deserved. It is a good reminder to all the men that our women have a choice too.'

'Alright, no edict, but we can't just let it pass. What are we going to do?'

'Leave it to Ffion and me. We will sort it.'

'How will you do that? On second thoughts, don't answer that. I am not sure I will like the answer.'

Once Miriam, Bronwyn and Ffion got back to Miriam's room, she couldn't wait. 'How are you going to sort it?'

'Fairly easy, wouldn't you say, Ffion?' said Bronwyn.

Ffion smiled and nodded.

'The way we always tackle this sort of thing. I am sure we will get total support.'

'But how?' shouted an exasperated Miriam.

'A threat to refuse sex to all the men, if any of them try it on with you again,' Bronwyn smiled.

'What?!' exclaimed Miriam, 'But a husband has a right to sex with his wife and the wife has a duty to give it to him.'

'Not in our culture, Miriam. As I said earlier, here both men and women have the right to choose, not only who they are going to sleep with but whether they have sex at all.'

Miriam sat down on her bed, open-mouthed.

28

The following day, Ffion reported back.

'The women have made it clear that Miriam is off-limits, not that they needed to. There is more than one shame-faced man. All those involved were berated by those men not involved. The added threat of a sex strike will easily keep them in order. Particularly after we reminded those not involved what they would be missing.'

'What about the men involved?' asked Miriam.

'Their enforced abstinence, when the other men were having fun, served as both a punishment and a reminder of the boundaries. They will stay in line from now on.'

Bronwyn got up to leave and join Rivalin, to consider another matter that had arisen, with a satisfied smile on her face. Miriam found herself with just Ffion for company for the rest of the day. It was a lovely sunny day, so she took her embroidery out into the garden. They sat in silence to start with.

'Ffion?'

'Yes, My Lady?'

'Please call me Miriam, not "My Lady".'

'Yes, Miriam?'

'Could we talk? I mean, woman to woman. There is so much I don't know about your customs. Bronwyn is very good, but she is not married.'

'What would you like to know?'

'Well, have you ever slept with one of the other men, not your husband?'

'Yes, when I was first married. It was sort of expected, but not for many years now. Most women come to love their husbands after a time and don't really want to sleep with anyone else. I have a good husband, why go elsewhere?'

'That is something in common at least. The same is true of my culture. I was lucky in that my first husband was the man I loved anyway before I married. Did you have a choice of husband?'

'Yes and no. There were several suitors from different clans. I had the choice of which I could marry, in theory. With my husband being from the king's clan, though, there wasn't any choice. Even without the pressure from my father, I knew that the prestige of the clan, and hence its power and wealth, would be enhanced by the marriage. As I said, though, he is a good man.'

'So is Rivalin.'

'There is envy of Rivalin because he is king. People know also that his great grandfather usurped the throne, but it is not just Roman power that keeps him on his throne. He has not played favourites, the way his great-grandfather and grandfather did. He has also respected our customs and made it quite clear that if the queen returns, he will cede the throne to her.'

'That is not likely to happen, is it? Surely, she would be dead by now.'

'The original queen whose throne was usurped, yes, but her successor will come someday.'

'How will you know that she is the rightful queen?'

'She will have the mark of the queen.'

'Bronwyn said that. She said that there was disappointment when she did not have the mark of the queen. What is the mark of the queen?'

Ffion hesitated, but then said, 'I think it will be alright to tell you. Apart from the fact that I have the feeling the goddess wants you to know, I think that you have already worked it out. The mark of the queen is the eyes. They are leaf-green, like the goddess's eyes.'

Miriam thought about it in silence. She had never quite believed Salome when she said that she was descended from a British princess. She had started believing it might be true when she had heard the story from Bronwyn that was so similar. Now she knew it was true. More than that, she knew that Salome was the rightful queen. With what Bronwyn had said about the Romans, she now understood why the angel told her that she could not communicate with her family back in Galilee. She also realised that it would not be good for the people here to know the whereabouts of their queen. They would want her back immediately and the delicate balance Rivalin had achieved would be shattered.

Miriam came out of her reverie. 'Anyway, that is an aside. I want to know how the balance is achieved in a marriage where you are effectively married to the whole clan. How do you manage an inheritance, for instance?'

'Your children inherit from your husband, no matter whose child they are. Since most things are held in common in the clan, it makes very little difference anyway. Status and most inheritance are through the female line anyway.'

'In general, men, where I come from, marry later than they seem to here. They wait until they have established themselves and have the resources to look after their wife.'

'That is not necessary with us. We are dependent on the resources of the clan, not our husband.'

'What happens if a wife does something of which her husband disapproves? In my society, the husband has the authority to sanction her.'

'The whole clan would have to agree, women included. Anyway, approval from your husband is not required, any more than he needs to seek his wife's approval. Usually, they will agree beforehand anything that might be contentious.'

'What about divorce?'

'I have heard of that from the Romans. I do not understand why it is necessary. You are married to the clan. You are not dependent on your husband for anything.'

'What if your husband is abusive?'

'You move out of his hut.'

'I mean, er, in bed.'

'Oh, you mean rough with sex. It rarely happens. Men are taught, when young, how to pleasure a woman by the older women in the clan. They know that if they get a reputation for being rough then no woman will sleep with them, even their wives.'

Miriam thought of Rivalin on their wedding night. 'I suppose they then have to go to a prostitute if they want sex.'

'What's a prostitute?'

This took Miriam back for a moment.

'A prostitute is a woman a man pays to have sex with.'

'Why would a man pay for sex? And why would a woman have sex for money when she doesn't need the money and can sleep with any man in the clan anyway?'

That stumped Miriam. 'What about a slave? Rivalin said that women slaves were the property of the clan, and all the clan men had the right to sleep with her and she had no right to refuse. Surely a man who wanted rough sex would use a slave.'

'In theory, yes, but we only take women slaves after warfare when their clan men have been killed. We do not purchase slaves. There hasn't been any tribal warfare for ten years now since the Romans came. There are very few women slaves, and they are old now. Even so, the women would stop the abuse of women slaves. It might be them one day.'

So that is one way in which Rivalin has broken with tradition. No wonder he can get away with people not believing I am a slave.

'What about the widows of the conflict with the Romans?'

'Some were enslaved by the Romans. Where there were sufficient men left in the clan, the widows stayed with the clan. The rest remarried. Rivalin's mother committed suicide to prevent anyone from marrying her to claim the kingship.'

That shook Miriam. 'That was hard on Rivalin and Bronwyn.'

'If she hadn't, and a man had married her to claim the throne, Rivalin and Bronwyn would have been killed shortly afterwards.'

Again, Miriam fell into silence. She was not used to such brutal politics.

'Tell me of your society,' said Ffion. 'I know nothing beyond Britannia, and we have few Roman visitors.'

'I am not Roman. I am Hebrew.'

'Hebrew, what is that? Do you come from as far as Rome?'

'Further.'

'As far as Greece or Egypt?'

'Further still.'

'You must come from the ends of the earth then.'

'No, not that far. There is Persia and India beyond us and rumours of lands beyond them.'

'Are your people monogamous, like the Romans?'

'No. We allow a man to have more than one wife, but a woman can only have one husband.'

'I thought everyone was monogamous except us. That is what the Romans made us believe.'

'Only the Romans and Greeks are monogamous, at least in law. There are many other races out there.'

'What do you mean, 'at least in law'?'

'In Roman Law, marriage is monogamous and adultery is a punishable crime. They do make exceptions though. Sex with a slave or a prostitute is not counted as adultery. Nor is sex with a temple priest or priestess.'

'The men have sex with other men then?'

'The priests and priestesses have sex with anyone they want, male or female. It is rare for women to visit a temple for this purpose, though. As a result, the main reason men visit the temples is for sex.'

'Why would a man use a prostitute then?'

'It is more discrete.'

'So, except for slaves, prostitutes, priests and priestesses, Romans are monogamous.'

'Officially, yes. Even those who adhere to the law practise serial monogamy.'

'What is serial monogamy?'

'A man divorcing his wife and then going on to another wife and then another and so on, or a woman doing the same with her husbands.'

'Women can divorce their husbands?'

'Yes, simply by reclaiming their dowry from their husband.'

'I had always thought that the Roman women were owned by their husbands.'

'Yes, which is why adultery is illegal and the man is punished more than the woman. He has infringed another man's property rights, stolen from him. Again, that is the theory. No one bothers anymore.'

'What a messy way of doing things. I think I prefer our way better. Seems they are doing the same as us, just pretending differently.'

'You know the Roman-style dress I wore the morning after my marriage to Rivalin?'

'Yes, what of it?'

'It undoes very easily to just under the breast. One of the Roman women told me that if you go to a banquet at the Imperial Palace, you are expected not to wear anything underneath.'

'I suppose the emperor enjoys the view.'

'And more. It is so that the men can have sex with the women without either having to undress.'

'A man will have sex with his wife in public like that?'

That time it was Ffion who was scandalised.

'Not just his wife.'

Both fell silent for the rest of the day.

29

After that episode of misunderstanding, Ffion took over Miriam's education in British customs. As she rightly said, 'Bronwyn means well, but she has been brought up by Romans, with a largely theoretical knowledge of our ways.'

Ffion took Miriam to the clan enclave to meet the family. The first person she met was Eirwyn. He apologised profusely and said that he would never repeat his behaviour and, that if she needed any help, to contact him. He would be honoured to escort her if she wanted to visit any of the other enclaves or even further afield. Miriam looked at Ffion, who nodded, 'He will keep his word.'

'Maybe, once I have got to know you better, Eirwyn. Just one question for now though. In my culture, names very often reflect something about the person the name is given to. My limited knowledge of your language suggests that your name means 'snow', but you are the darkest Briton I have seen.'

Eirwyn smiled. *A smile that could melt any heart.*

'My mother was a Moor from Africa. They called me 'Snow' because I was born in a snowstorm.'

Later, Eirwyn was as good as his word and took it upon himself to be Miriam's personal bodyguard whenever she was out and about in the town. If they went further afield, Eirwyn went armed. There was never any trouble that he needed to deal with but, Miriam supposed, who would cause trouble with a six-and-a-half foot, heavily armed, dark, curly-headed man with the muscles of a wrestler standing next to you? A frown from Eirwyn was enough to get a profuse apology for even the slightest wayward remark.

Two months later, a Greek merchant ship arrived with no one on board who spoke Latin. Rivalin sent for Miriam and asked if she could translate. She agreed but then asked him a series of questions which took him by surprise.

'What are they selling and how much are they asking?'

Rivalin looked at his steward, who told them he was selling cotton, silks, olive oil, nard, and wine and gave the usual price that was asked. 'They usually buy grain', he proffered and again gave the usual amount offered.

'What do they do with anything we do not buy?'

'They travel up to Verulamium, using the Roman Road, and sell it there.'

'What is the usual toll charged?'

The steward was confused. 'Toll? What is that?'

Miriam looked at Rivalin. He was just as confused. 'It is obvious that the Romans have only taught you what they want you to know about their world. They are cheating you.'

'What do you mean?' asked Rivalin.

'I am the daughter of a merchant, brought up by a merchant and was married to a merchant. The Romans don't like dealing with women, they think men are superior, but will if they must. Greeks are more amenable. My husband, my first husband that is, and I had our own system of signals during negotiations to strike a deal. I could sort something out with you quickly. Plus, the usual toll, fee that is, when you take goods into a Roman province from elsewhere is one percent of the value of the goods, payable to the ruler of the province. That is you, Rivalin.'

'So could you translate for the steward?'

The steward looked forlorn. 'It looks like I don't know what I am doing. I think it would be better if you just let the queen negotiate for us. I had no idea what prices were fair and have never even heard of …' he looked at Miriam, '… tolls.'

Miriam went to the quayside to talk to the merchant but stopped off at the family enclave to enlist Eirwyn as an escort.

'What do I do?' he asked.

'You look imposing, threatening and ready to reach for that sharp sword of yours at the least provocation.'

'You are not planning to raid the ship, are you?'

'No, you are providing two purposes. First, to distract him and, secondly, as insurance against him trying to cheat me because I am a woman.'

To Eirwyn's surprise, they didn't go straight to the docks but stopped off at the marine base on the way.

The merchant captain was all smiles when they arrived. He obviously didn't like the look of her escort and, as Miriam had thought would happen, his eyes kept straying Eirwyn's way.

The captain started by asking for the prices he usually asked for his goods. He was surprised by Miriam's counteroffer and soon realised he had a formidable opponent. When they hadn't agreed on a price, the merchant suggested that they negotiate on the grain as well.

'Perhaps if I can get the grain at a good price, I can move a little on the charge for my goods,' he said.

Again, he offered the usual amount. Miriam countered by asking for four times what he offered.

'That is more than I would pay in Egypt and the transportation costs are a lot higher.'

He offered half of what Miriam asked and said, 'I will be hard put to make a profit on it at that.'

'Nonsense,' replied Miriam, 'That is only two-thirds of what you would pay in Alexandria and the transport costs are not so much greater. Also, you are here now. You will have to pay the transport costs whether you take any cargo back with you or not.'

The merchant's face dropped.

'As a goodwill gesture, though, I will accept your offer,' Miriam continued, 'Your prices on what you are selling are still much too high. They are a luxury here that we do not need.'

'I heard that the king here has a new queen, from the empire. I am sure he would be prepared to pay the going price for them for his new love.'

'I will not and nor will he.'

'Kings don't like subjects presuming their wishes.'

'It is a good job I am not a subject then, isn't it?'

'You think yourself safe from the king's wrath, then?'

'Yes. You see, I AM THE QUEEN.'

'In that case, I will buy your grain but take my goods up to Verulamium.'

The merchant turned to go.

'One moment, merchant. You still owe the tolls for bringing the goods into the province.'

The merchant turned back, angry, but one look from Eirwyn made him suppress his anger. Then he smiled again.

'I have never paid duty on my goods here before and you can't make me now, even with that brute of an escort.'

'No, I can't, but they can,' Miriam indicated behind the merchant.

Whilst they had talked, three Roman biremes, loaded with marines, had manoeuvred into position on the river behind the merchant's vessel.

'You know how tetchy Romans are about people not paying their due taxes. I calculate you owe this amount.'

She wrote the figure on a wax tablet. The merchant looked at it.

'That is double the usual rate,' the merchant raged.

'Either that, or you were trying to sell me your goods at twice their worth.'

The merchant looked at Miriam and then laughed.

'You have me either way. Alright, I will let you have what you want, at the proper price, and will take the rest to Verulamium with the tax, based on the price that I charge you for the goods. I could just take the whole lot to Verulamium and get the higher price there.'

'With the higher rate of tax, of course. But if you sell me the goods I want, at the price I want, I will only charge the lower rate of tax. As a bonus, I won't tell the Romans that you have cheated them out of revenue previously.'

'And the price I charge in Verulamium?'

'Verulamium is not in our territory. What business is that of mine?'

'What do you want?'

Miriam bought all his cotton and half his olive oil and some silk she knew she could sell to the Roman governor's wife. As she went to go, the merchant stopped her and gave her a tiny ampule. Pulling the stopper, Miriam realised it was nard.

'We cannot afford this, merchant.'

'It is a gift. I have not enjoyed myself so much in a long time. A beautiful, intelligent queen deserves such luxury.'

The merchant bowed and returned to his ship. Miriam told Eirwyn what the merchant was unloading and to get it moved to the usual place. She suddenly realised she didn't know where the usual place was, but Eirwyn would know.

30

Rivalin was full of praise for what Miriam had achieved and put her in charge of all dealings with merchants. Miriam was troubled by this.

'What about your steward? He will lose face.'

'He is just relieved that he doesn't have to deal with merchants anymore.'

After they had called the steward, and Miriam had heard directly from him that he was indeed happy with her taking over dealing with the merchants, Miriam sent for Eirwyn. Rivalin was puzzled. Miriam chose to use Latin.

'Eirwyn, have you had any problems with the merchant?'

Eirwyn laughed. 'He tried to give us fewer bales of cotton than we agreed. A frown and a hand on my sword hilt were enough to change his mind.'

Rivalin was concerned. 'I have never known you aggressive, Eirwyn.'

'It is something the queen taught me. Others' expectations are nine-tenths of a bluff. The merchant thought I am a murderous barbarian so even a slight hint in that direction was enough to make him back down.'

'Eirwyn is intelligent and very good at bluff, all he lacks is knowledge of prices and language skills to make an excellent merchant.'

'But we have plenty of Greek merchants coming here. Why do we need to trade ourselves?'

'Because then we control the trade. What if there was a harvest failure in Egypt? Wheat prices would rocket, and merchants would be buying all our wheat at low prices and make a killing, selling it in Ravenna or Rome. If we have a merchant out there, he can tell us, and we can raise our prices. Add to that, even in normal times, the merchants know that we are dependent on them. If we are exporting ourselves, we have extra leverage, as we can simply refuse to sell. If there is one thing that dents a merchant's bottom line it is having to travel home with empty holds.'

'What do you propose, Miriam?'

'That Eirwyn acts as my assistant for the next six months. He can continue to escort me, and I will teach him Greek and how to bargain. The best place to send him on his first trip would be Ravenna. They buy grain for Rome there and top prices are given. Plus, they speak Latin.'

'How will you begin?'

'I think I will accompany our merchant friend to Verulamium. That will be easily arranged. Eirwyn can act as an escort and apprentice. That way I can start teaching him Greek and do some trading, in a small way, in Verulamium to show him how it works.'

'How are you going to persuade the merchant to take you along and what are you going to trade on your behalf?'

'Verulamium is Latin-speaking; the merchant only speaks Greek. I will offer to translate though I will make it clear that there must be no dishonest dealing on his side, with dire consequences if he tries it. Some of the cottons I bought from the merchant will do as trade goods.'

It was easily arranged, as Miriam thought, with the merchant delighted to have a translator. Eirwyn's presence and Miriam's status were a bonus, taking away his fear of brigands. No one would dare attack the queen. There were no brigands in Britannia, as there was insufficient trade to make it worthwhile, but Miriam didn't disillusion him. When he realised that Miriam's trade goods were his cotton, he just laughed.

On leaving Aquae Sulis, they took The Fossa northwards to Corinium Dobunnorum, and then the road eastwards to Verulamium. The merchant was not impressed by The Fossa.

'This road is little better than a ditch,' he said.

'That is precisely what it is,' replied Miriam, 'It is known as *Fossa* in Latin, which means 'ditch'. It is the western boundary of Roman rule.'

The merchant looked uneasily westwards.

'Don't worry. Rivalin, my husband, rules west of Rome's territories as well.'

'So, the king has land on both sides of the boundary. That must be difficult.'

'It has its challenges, but the Romans find it useful.'

'How so?'

'His land west of here acts as a buffer to more hostile tribes. Of course, it also means that he is regarded with suspicion as to where his true loyalties lie. For us, it means that we are safe as I am queen whichever side of the border we are on.'

Corinium was little more than a few huts and a couple of stone buildings, next to a Roman encampment. Not even a proper fort. Again, the merchant was not impressed.

'I don't see what is so special, or beautiful, about here.'

'So, you know some Latin, then.'

'Not really. It is just that a friend of mine has his own *Corinium* in his estate garden outside Rome.'

The road to Verulamium was not much better than The Fossa but, when they reached Verulamium, it came as a surprise. It was a proper Roman town, built at the bottom of a hill by a lake.

'This is much more like it,' said the merchant, 'Why is this place so different?'

'It has been in Roman territory longer and is nearer the main Roman base of Camulodunum. It is also on a major road from Londinium.'

'You mean I could have got here easier via Londinium?'

'Yes, but then you wouldn't have monopoly prices as in Aquae Sulis. Londinium is a saturated market, and the deals you did with us paid for your trip, I would guess. Anything you sell in Verulamium will be icing on the cake.'

'How does a queen know so much about trade?'

'I was not always a queen. My first husband was a merchant. He died before I met Rivalin.'

The merchant did not ask for any further details, but he watched as Miriam worked. He noticed that she didn't immediately set up stalls when they arrived. She frequented the other stalls, sometimes asking for things she couldn't immediately find. She took Eirwyn with her and it looked to the merchant as if it was not just as a bodyguard. She would talk to the merchants in Latin but to Eirwyn in their own language.

'You take your bodyguard into your confidence a lot.'

'Eirwyn is not my bodyguard. Well, not really. He is my apprentice.'

'Then when you dealt with me?'

'He was there to impress and to distract. And to keep you honest, of course.'

'Don't you trust me?'

'I trust no one on first meeting, and don't say that you didn't try it on, I know you did.'

When it came to selling his goods, the merchant found that Miriam did all the bargaining and then just asked for his approval over the agreed price. It was always a better price than he could have got. He had to concede that she was good. Eirwyn was always there, listening intently, whilst seeming not to.

He then watched as she sold the cotton. She got a good price, but not exceptional. She seemed to be playing a different game. Afterwards, he asked her about it.

'I will never deal in the likes of nard again and there is none to be had in Verulamium. I could have asked what I liked. With cotton, I am looking to establish a long-term relationship. I have loads more of it in Aquae Sulis and I would guess that it is not worth your while to bring it up here to trade.'

'How did you know there was no nard in Verulamium?'

'I played the pampered barbarian queen, prepared to pay anything to get hold of some.'

The merchant smiled. 'The vial of nard I gave you has more than repaid me. In fact, I would like to give you the usual agents' fee. I will still be better off than if I had tried to sell my goods here myself.'

'There is no need. It was not part of our bargain.'

'No, it wasn't but I will do so just the same. I have a business proposition for you.'

'Oh, and what might that be?'

'Am I right in saying that the only reason that you didn't buy all my olive oil off me, was that you couldn't afford to?'

Miriam nodded.

'Am I also right in saying that next time you come to Verulamium, that olive oil will come with you?'

Again, Miriam nodded.

'So, you didn't bring it this time so as not to compete with me to sell it?'

'Correct.'

'How about we come to an arrangement then?'

'What sort of arrangement?' asked Miriam.

'Until you have established yourself, I supply the goods and you pay me for anything for your own use. The rest you pay me for, at the same price, when I return on my next trip.'

'That will leave you out of pocket to begin with, by a lot.'

'I can stand it; besides it is too good an opportunity to miss.'

'I have two conditions.'

The merchant was wary but left a silence for Miriam to continue.

'Firstly, I do not deal in substandard goods. I deliver what I say I will deliver at the quality and price I say. If I find anything substandard, I will break our relationship immediately.'

'And your second condition?'

'That the price you pay for our wheat reflects the true price in Alexandria. Again, if it doesn't, I will break our relationship immediately.'

'I agree. Do you want formal documents drawn up?'

Miriam reached into her pack and pulled out two identical parchments with the agreement already set out in both Greek and Latin. It took a full five minutes for the merchant to stop laughing.

'I really am glad that I am working with you, Your Majesty, not as your competitor. No one has managed to manipulate me like this for a decade or more.'

'You wish for changes to the deal?'

'No, Your Majesty, I do not.'

He then signed the parchments and Miriam did the same. They took one copy each.

'Shall we celebrate, Your Majesty?'

'I am tired, so will retire for the night. As we are now partners, please call me Miriam in private.'

The merchant bowed his head slightly.

'I am Andronicus.'

31

Miriam and Andronicus headed back to Aquae Sulis. They had made a good profit on the trip, but it really hadn't needed both to go. Plus, they couldn't find anything worth taking back with them. Miriam had bought some locally-produced wine to use at the palace on their return. It was cheaper than imported wine. Other than that, nothing. As a trader, she was irked by this. She could see it irked Andronicus as well. The problem was that British society was still at the self-sufficiency stage and there weren't enough Romans to create a large market. She spent most of the return journey wondering how she could open Britannia to trade.

Andronicus's ship was already loaded and ready to sail when they returned, so he was anxious to leave immediately. As he set sail down the river, Miriam was still puzzling over what she could bring back with her from Verulamium on their next trip. She had several ideas about what she could sell there. Cloth was mainly imported or woven, by local Roman women, from imported cotton. Embroidered shawls were all imported and very expensive. They needed wheat but then she would be in competition with local farmers. There was another conundrum. She knew she could export as much wheat as they produced, but how could she get farmers to produce more than they needed so there was a surplus to export?

She went back to the palace, deep in thought. Rivalin broke her out of it, obviously angry and upset. He was civil and, when she reported on her trip, was full of praise, but still surly. He then left abruptly, ostensibly to prepare for dinner, which was three hours hence. Miriam noticed he headed for the garden, not his chambers. As she watched him go, Miriam saw Bronwyn out of the corner of her eye. She turned to her and raised an eyebrow.

'We had news two weeks ago. Sarah has married his cousin, in Gaul.'

'That was expected, surely?'

'Yes, it was always a fantasy, but Rivalin never gave up hope. There was no way of telling him, but he never really knew Sarah. He saw a beautiful, exotic lady from afar who, in his mind, was a princess. He never really saw the woman.'

'And you did?'

'Sarah always knew that her fate was to marry the king on whom she and her mother depended. What her personal preference was, she never divulged. Like Rivalin, he is a good man and that was enough for her.'

'Where did she come from?'

'From far to the east of the empire. The Romans wanted to kill her when she was a child, so her mother fled to Gaul with her. The Gauls are part of the empire but maintain their independence. As her mother guessed, they were quite prepared to keep her hidden from the Romans.'

'Why did the Romans want to kill her?'

'There are rumours that she is the daughter of Jesus of Nazareth. That added to her mystery. The daughter of a god. There was no way that the king, her protector, would not marry her.'

'But Jesus never had any children. My mother-in-law met him. I know many who knew him. This is very strange, though

I can see why the child would be in danger if people thought she was his daughter. Both the Jewish and Roman authorities would be concerned.'

'Why is that?'

'Jesus was popular. Both the Jews and the Romans were worried that he would lead a revolt against the Romans. He was from the line of David. After they crucified him, any child of his would be seen as a rallying point for extremists trying to overthrow Roman rule.'

'But you said Jesus didn't have any children. What does *the line of David* mean? I have heard this before as well, but I don't understand.'

'It wouldn't matter whether Sarah was his daughter or not. If enough people believed she was, she would still be a danger. The *line of David* means that Jesus was descended from our ancient great king, David.'

'So, like we are waiting for the return of our true queen, you are waiting for the return of your true king?'

'Sort of. Is the spa free? I could do with getting this travel grime off me. We can continue to talk there.'

They headed off to the spa to find Ffion and Bronwyn's maid waiting for them. 'Anticipated me, Ffion?'

'You always head for the spa on your return from a journey, Miriam.'

Miriam thought about it. 'Yes, I do, don't I?'

Bronwyn and Miriam continued talking whilst in the spa, until they came to the massage room. As their maids rubbed them, they stopped talking and lapped up the luxury of it all. Miriam fell asleep.

The angel with the green eyes came to her. Her presence was comforting as it always was, and Miriam basked in it. The angel was particularly caring this time as if trying to reassure Miriam. Then she spoke.

'Rivalin needs to know his worth as a man. He is still young. Sarah, marrying his rival, has dented his confidence. He needs to be whole for what lies ahead. You know what you must do.'

Miriam woke with a start. Ffion was concerned that she had hurt Miriam in some way, but she assured her that she hadn't. Miriam was quiet for the rest of the day and through dinner. Bronwyn sensed that she had had a visit from the goddess and wondered what it meant.

32

After dinner, Rivalin retired to his room immediately. Miriam had tried to engage him in conversation, but nothing had worked. Even making absurd comments about the Romans had not diverted him. She suspected he hadn't even heard; he was so self-absorbed.

Miriam retired as well, signalling Ffion to follow. She was concerned as she dressed Miriam.

'Are you sure about this?'

'I am, Ffion. The angel has assured me I will be alright.'

'The angel?'

'You would call her the goddess.'

'Oh. But I am still concerned. I know how men can be when in this humour.'

'I will be alright, Ffion. I will need another spa in the morning.'

'I will stay here tonight to make sure I am ready.'

Miriam left her room with a determined walk. No one saw her, except Bronwyn, from behind the door to her own chambers. As Miriam swept past, dressed Roman-style, with all the ties undone and only the band underneath her breasts keeping the dress together, Bronwyn smiled. It was obvious that, under the billowing dress, Miriam was not wearing anything.

Miriam stopped at Rivalin's door, took a deep breath, opened the door and entered. Rivalin, lying naked on his bed, looked up. Miriam closed the door behind her and moved to the bed. She lay next to Rivalin on the bed, and then pulled her dress aside to reveal herself. Rivalin, as she expected, was hungry for her. She was glad she had thought to prepare herself before coming.

Afterwards, Miriam held Rivalin as he cried. He started apologising profusely to her and asked her why she had done it.

'You are my husband, Rivalin. It is my duty, as your wife, to give you comfort when you need it.'

'But ours is a marriage in name only.'

'There is no such thing as a marriage in name only, Rivalin. I did not want to remarry after Jesus died but I do not regret it. I could not have asked for a better man to marry, nor a better husband. Even if you take a senior wife, and I am relegated, I would still consider myself blessed.'

Miriam rose and Rivalin expected her to leave. Instead, she removed her dress and lay back down, next to him. Rivalin held her for a few minutes then gently kissed her, making love to her sensitively, but passionately. He lay back afterwards.

'That was beautiful, Rivalin,' said Miriam.

A gentle snore was his sole response. Miriam lay awake thinking, looking at her husband. As she now realised, the man she loved. There would always be part of her heart that belonged to Jesus, but she loved this man too.

She fell asleep in the early hours, waking to find Rivalin gone.

'I'm glad that you've woken up, sleepy head,' Miriam heard Ffion say and looked around to check she was still in Rivalin's room.

'Rivalin stopped at your room and told me to wake you to be ready for a noon meeting. If we go now, we can just get a spa in and get you dressed in time. Won't have time for a massage though.'

'It doesn't take that long for me to get dressed.'

'It does when I have been ordered to ensure you are dressed in your silks, with the appropriate hairstyle. You know how long it takes to do your hair.'

'What is going on? I have never been asked to wear the silks before.'

'I haven't been told.'

'You must have some idea.'

'If we don't go now, you won't get your spa.'

'Come on, Ffion, give.'

'As I said, I haven't been told. Now come on, let's get you in a shift. Your silks are at the spa, waiting.'

Try as she might, Miriam couldn't get a word more out of Ffion, even though she could tell that she was excited and almost bursting to say something. She relented a little and gave Miriam's shoulders a quick massage in the spa before they both jumped into the plunge pool. After drying themselves, there wasn't time for Ffion to dry herself and then Miriam. Miriam sat down naked whilst Ffion plaited and curled her jet-black hair around her head.

Ffion went to the alcove and brought out the dress Miriam was to wear. It had a fine cotton base, covered in blue silks. Miriam gasped. It suited her best but was her most expensive dress. She had never thought she would ever wear it. There must be visiting royalty. She could think of no other reason.

'Are you sure I should be wearing this dress? That blue dye is easily spoilt and is expensive.'

'Rivalin's orders,' was Ffion's reply.

'What is going on, Ffion?'

'I think Rivalin wants to show you off, that is all.'

'Ffion?'

'Wait and see, Miriam. I am not going to spoil Rivalin's surprise.'

After putting Miriam's dress on her, Ffion tidied her hair and looked at her, satisfied.

'Would you like a quick look at yourself in the mirror before we go, Your Majesty?'

Miriam started at the use of her formal address. 'You have never called me *Your Majesty* before.'

'I have never dressed you as the queen before, only as Rivalin's wife and my mistress. Would you like to see yourself in the mirror, Your Majesty?'

Normally, Miriam would have declined but was intrigued as to how she looked. She grinned and nodded to Ffion, who fetched a mirror. Miriam was stunned, unable to believe how regal she looked. It gave her confidence she didn't feel. Ffion took the mirror back and returned it to its place before leading Miriam out to the palace atrium where the whole of the Royal Council was assembled.

Rivalin addressed her. 'Miriam, I owe you an apology. I have not treated you with the respect that you have earned and your position, as queen, should command. I wish to remedy that immediately and appoint you to your rightful place in the Royal Council. Your duty is to attend council meetings, advise as you see fit, and chair the meetings in my absence.'

Miriam thought before she replied, 'I am greatly honoured, Your Majesty. I thought that was Bronwyn's position. I would not like to usurp her authority.'

Rivalin went to answer but Bronwyn's hand on his arm stayed him.

'You are not usurping my position, Miriam. You are taking up the position that is rightfully yours. The position you should have been given on your marriage to Rivalin.'

Miriam thought for a moment. 'I am not of your people, Your Majesty, and do not know your ways well. I am not fitted to lead your people in the way Bronwyn is but, if you are determined on this, please may I have Bronwyn at my side to guide me on the council?'

A broad grin broke out on the face of every council member.

Rivalin spoke. 'It is a change of custom but how does the council feel about this proposal from the queen? Do you agree?'

The shout of 'yes' from every member deafened Miriam for a moment. She had the feeling that most of them were only just managing to desist from hugging her.

Rivalin led the council out onto the steps in front of the palace, where a crowd was waiting. Every British man, woman, and child in Aquae Sulis was there. As Rivalin took Miriam's hand, and led her to her throne, he whispered, 'Well done. You have just won the heart of every member of my council, along with their undying loyalty. You already have the hearts of most of my subjects.'

After Miriam was seated, Rivalin went to his own throne but did not seat himself. Instead, he stood as he spoke to the crowd.

'The Royal Council has decided this morning to instate the queen, Miriam, into her rightful place on the council. At the request of the queen, the council has also agreed that my sister, Bronwyn, also be allowed to stay on the council in order to assist the queen with her duties. I ask that you support the queen as you have supported me.'

There were murmurs of support from the crowd. Miriam noticed Ffion and Eirwyn, on the edge of the crowd, beaming from ear to ear. Rivalin returned to Miriam, took her hand, and led her to the space between the thrones.

'Please welcome your queen as she comes into her rightful inheritance.'

Rivalin left Miriam standing, as he seated himself on his throne. He then started slapping his thighs. The crowd followed suit, slapping their thighs, stamping their feet, and whooping. It carried on so long that Miriam was becoming embarrassed. Then she heard Bronwyn say, 'When you have had enough, sit down again. They will keep going until you do.'

Miriam moved back to her throne and sat down, rather more quickly than was stately. As she did so, she mouthed a 'thank you' to Bronwyn.

Rivalin let the hubbub die down before he rose again, took Miriam's hand, and led her and the council from the steps back into the atrium. Each council member, in turn, welcomed Miriam and then left. It was only then that Miriam realised that the council was made up of almost equal numbers of men and women. Finally, there was just Miriam, Rivalin and Bronwyn left.

'I am honoured with what you have just done, but I don't understand. Why now?' Miriam asked.

'I have been in a dream world for so long, dreaming of Sarah, not seeing that I had a loyal, dedicated queen by my side. Last night, you reminded me that I am your husband and that you are willing to fulfil the duties of a wife however it may have come about. I have not been a good husband. I will do better for you in future. Today is a token of that promise.'

'I was not aiming for a reward.'

'I know that, Miriam. You did it because it was the right thing to do. That is what makes you fit to be a queen and fit to sit on the council.'

With that, Rivalin bent, kissed Miriam's hand and left.

Bronwyn came to Miriam and hugged her. 'Shall we change out of this finery and get some refreshment? I understand that you didn't get a chance for breakfast this morning.'

Miriam found Ffion in her room, waiting for her. 'You knew,' she accused Ffion.

'I guessed but didn't know,' Ffion responded. 'But why else would he have me dress you in blue, a royal colour, when Bronwyn was dressed in white?'

'Tell me truly, Ffion. What do you feel about this turn of events and how do the people feel?'

'You are not one of our people, so that will automatically make people hesitant. Those who know you are delighted, particularly as Bronwyn is still on the council as well. The rest of the people will accept you because of your kindness to her. In time, as they come to know you more, that acceptance will turn to love as they begin to see the kindness in your heart. You will be a great queen, Miriam, and remembered for ages to come.'

'You flatter me, Ffion.'

'I do not flatter, Miriam. The goddess has told me this.'

33

The next council meeting occurred six months later. Andronicus had visited again and, because of a couple of trading trips to Verulamium, the coffers were healthier than they had ever been. On the first trip, Miriam had gone with Eirwyn to see how he did. She let him do the deals. After each deal they discussed it. The second trip, Miriam let him go alone.

When she was in Aquae Sulis, Rivalin included Miriam in all his decisions as king, large or small. She insisted that Bronwyn was also involved.

'You don't need to include me, Miriam. I won't feel undermined if you don't,' said Bronwyn.

'That would be a good enough reason to include you, Bronwyn, but my motive is more selfish. I have run into enough trouble not knowing your customs. I want to be a good queen, so I need your advice.'

There wasn't any matter that would justify the calling of the council, until Rivalin came back from seeing the Roman governor, Marcus, one day.

'The Romans want to build a public spa.'

'Why is that troubling?'

'They want it for Romans only. Currently, apart from us, everyone uses the huts where the goddess's waters emerge,' said Rivalin.

Miriam looked at Bronwyn for an explanation.

'Our people regard the waters as a gift from the goddess. As it is a gift from her, they share it with the Romans. Everyone in our land has an equal right to the waters. That has held even when we have been in dispute with the Belgae across the river. If the Romans build a spa, which only they have access to, there will be a lot of anger which could result in riots or worse.'

'To make matters worse, they want us to build it for them,' said Rivalin.

'I will have to think about this,' said Miriam.

Now how did those sluices in Ataroth work? I know that they were filling an open-air cistern for water for agriculture but there is no real difference between that and a bath.

She smiled as she remembered how impatient Jesus, Alexander and Jairus had been, waiting for her.

Getting that engineer to explain everything has turned out to have been a day well-used.

Miriam spent the next two days with wax tablets, writing things here and there, and doing calculations. Every so often, she asked Bronwyn a question. Bronwyn had no idea what Miriam was up to, but she got an inkling from the questions Miriam asked.

'Where was the source of the waters? What happened to the waters after they emerged?'

By the time the council was called, Miriam was ready. As Bronwyn had predicted, there was anger in the council. Miriam let them vent their anger. They would not be able to think straight until they had calmed down. The risk was that they would wind themselves up further and explode. This didn't happen, as Rivalin deftly handled them.

'I think I may have a solution,' said Miriam.

Everyone turned towards her.

'If we build the spa complex where there are the two close springs then we can build one for everyone and one for the Romans.'

'That would take years,' said a council member.

'Yes, it would. We will tell the Romans that, during the building works, unfortunately, we will have to share temporary facilities sourced from one of the springs. We build a facility over the other spring. Once this is built, we will charge for use of that spa whilst the other is built. The Romans can then choose whichever they want for their exclusive use. Being built by us, we would expect them to pay for its use, which they are used to. We can agree with the Roman governor what the fees will be upfront.'

'Running the facility will be expensive,' said Rivalin. 'I know how much work goes into maintaining the water in the spa in the palace and how many servants are used to just ferry the water.'

'The palace spa is designed to show off wealth. We could easily divert water to feed it automatically.'

Rivalin was puzzled.

'How? And if the spa is being continually fed, how will we stop it being flooded and how will we empty it to clean?'

'We put in sluices and a dam. Sluices are like gates diverting water through channels so that we can control where we want it to go. The dam would be a wall at one end of the bath that is slightly lower than all the other walls. That way, excess water would flow over the top of it. We build a channel on the other side of the wall to take the water out to the river.'

'I cannot see how it would work,' said Rivalin, 'and I doubt the governor would be convinced either.'

'I agree, your majesty.'

To everyone's surprise, it was Miriam herself who had spoken.

'I am not sure it will work myself, which is why I think we should propose that we try the design on the palace spa first.'

'And if it doesn't work?'

'We put the palace spa back to how it is now. It will cost a bit but would still be far cheaper than getting it wrong on a public spa.'

'I am not sure how I am going to persuade the governor to do this. It would be better coming from you, Miriam, but you know Romans, they won't listen to a woman.'

'They listen to women far more than they let on but, you are right, they will not listen to a barbarian queen.'

There was an angry murmur at this. Roman arrogance was not popular.

'Then how do you suggest we proceed, Miriam?'

'There are ways. Invite the governor here. Tell him that you wish to explain the proposals to him using the Royal Spa as an example. Me being here will be normal.'

After the council meeting, Miriam went into their private quarters.

Bronwyn said, 'I didn't want to say in there, but I don't see how this will work. Even if you are present, the governor is still not going to listen to you.'

'Jesus and I faced this problem with Romans, again and again. We developed a system of signals between ourselves so that we could communicate without them knowing. I will teach Rivalin. First, we must immediately send the governor a message.'

'Why so quickly?' asked Rivalin.

'I will explain in a moment.'

Miriam called for the steward and wrote out a message on a wax tablet for the governor, which she passed to Bronwyn and Rivalin.

'We have discussed your request for a public spa at our council meeting today. We would like to share our proposals with you, using the Royal Spa as an example, as soon as possible. If you could come to the Palace tomorrow, at your convenience, we will be prepared for your entertainment.'

Both Bronwyn and Rivalin raised their eyebrows, but Rivalin set his mark on it and ordered the steward to take it to the governor.

When he had gone, Rivalin asked, 'Will we have time for me to learn your signals by tomorrow?'

'No,' replied Miriam, 'but we won't have to. This governor is the most arrogant type of Roman. Had we not sent the message, he would have summoned you immediately, to demand that you tell him your plans. He will know of the council meeting this morning, of course. By suggesting that he comes tomorrow, making ourselves sound eager, he will delay for at least a week before coming. In his mind, that will be keeping this upstart barbarian king in his place. It gives us time to plan. Arrogance and pride are the two biggest weaknesses in negotiations. They give the whip hand to the opponent.'

Bronwyn and Rivalin laughed.

'No wonder you are such a good trader, Miriam. When do we start on Rivalin's training?'

'No time like the present.'

With that, Miriam took Rivalin's hand and sat him next to her. She told him to look at her lovingly. Rivalin went to remove his hand, but Miriam held on to it.

'You keep hold of my hand.'

'Why?'

'The idea is to make the governor think you are distracted and that he is controlling the negotiation. We can then subtly nudge things our way, without him realising it, using face signals, hand signals and the odd word to guide.'

Miriam started teaching Rivalin. Every time his eyes wandered to the watching Bronwyn, Miriam chided him and told him to start again. An hour of this was more than enough for Rivalin.

'Fascinating,' Bronwyn commented, 'but I think that I will skip future sessions.'

'No, we need you, Bronwyn. This is just the basics. Rivalin needs to be able to keep this up whilst distracted. More than that, he needs to be able to keep it up during the negotiation. Particularly, we need to hold each other's eyes. The eyes give your opponent clues. Shall we have lunch?'

After lunch, Miriam explained her plans for the palace spa in detail. How she would pipe the water in and how they would operate the sluices. Also, the position of the drain holes for emptying the three pools. She seemed to have thought of everything. Then Miriam gave Rivalin another training session. This time he did better.

'Next time, we will do a longer session,' said Miriam. 'We need to be able to keep it up for at least two hours, if necessary. Do you think that you will be able to do that, Rivalin?'

Rivalin grinned.

'You really do have the most beautiful eyes I have ever seen, Miriam. My problem will be taking my gaze away from you when we have finished.'

Miriam coloured and turned her gaze away.

'Come now, Miriam, you need to concentrate. You cannot allow yourself to be distracted.'

'You rotter, Rivalin! That is unfair. You just said that to unsettle me.'

'Not in the least, Miriam. You really do have beautiful eyes. I think I am going to enjoy this game immensely.'

34

As Miriam had predicted, the Roman governor didn't come for a week. He then turned up at the palace unannounced, with his steward in tow. He caught Miriam and Rivalin mid-practice session, with Rivalin looking 'lovingly' into Miriam's eyes. Rivalin 'reluctantly' broke his gaze to see to the governor.

'Hurry up, Rivalin, I am a busy man. Not all of us have time to moon into our wife's eyes all day.'

Rivalin rose, careful to keep hold of Miriam's hand. He moved towards the palace spa, with Miriam ambling alongside him. Once there, he indicated to the governor, with his free hand, where the sluices would be and how they would be controlled. As he was doing this, Rivalin let his eyes constantly drift to Miriam.

Miriam gave him the signal to move on. The governor was beginning to get irritated. Irritation was good, so long as he didn't go off in a huff. They moved back to their private quarters where Bronwyn had arranged for refreshment. They had carefully selected the governor's favourite wine, but not too much of it. They wanted him good-natured but not drunk. He asked a few questions and got answers that indicated that Rivalin wasn't listening. Once, he had to ask the same question of Rivalin three times before getting a coherent answer. Then it dawned on the governor that he could use it to his advantage.

'You will have to build the new baths at your own cost.'

'Uh, oh yes,' replied Rivalin. 'Anything you say, Governor.'

'You did just agree to build at your own cost, Rivalin?'

'Oh, did I? We will have to charge, of course.'

'What did you have in mind?'

'I don't know. What do they normally charge? Perhaps …'

Rivalin whispered a figure in the governor's ear.

'Preposterous!' shouted the governor bombastically. 'I will not pay anything over half that.'

'Oh, as you wish Governor. Half that sum it is. I really can't be bothered to haggle.'

The governor was ecstatic. He got up and left, in triumph, with his hapless steward in his wake. Bronwyn saw him leave and entered the room.

'Did we get what we wanted?'

'And more,' replied Miriam. 'He agreed to let us convert the palace spa first. He agreed to the spa being used by both Britons and Romans whilst the building work is ongoing. He agreed to us doing the building and he agreed to a charge of twice the going rate. These elite Romans leave so much to their servants that they have no idea at all.'

'What happens when he finds out he has been had?' asked Rivalin.

'Who is going to tell him? No one is going to risk the wrath of a pompous ass like that. He is too powerful. Certainly not his steward.'

'One thing still puzzles me though,' said Bronwyn. 'Why do you want us to do the building?'

'I have been puzzling for some time how we could encourage our farmers to clear more trees and open more land to grow wheat. Wheat that, thanks to Andronicus and

Eirwyn's growing trading skills, we will be able to sell very profitably to Rome. Building requires wood. The temporary spa requires a lot of wood. We will give a fair price for it but a royal command, to two close settlements, may still be needed for them to supply it. Once they have chopped the trees down, we can then promise them a fair price for any surplus wheat they have. If we have picked the right settlements, they will jump at the chance to use the cleared land for wheat. That will enrich those settlements and others will see and follow suit.'

'I am glad you are on our side, Miriam,' said Bronwyn. 'I would hate to be the opposition.'

'Funny, that is exactly what Andronicus said.'

Neither Miriam nor Rivalin realised that they were still holding hands and were both comfortable with it.

The governor was elated as he walked back to his house. That idiot Rivalin, allowing himself to get distracted by a woman when negotiating. Still, why should he care? He had got Rivalin to build the spa, which meant that he didn't have to fork out, and he had got the idiot down to half the charge. Everyone knew that, in negotiations, two-thirds of the opening gambit price was the fair one. He had got it down to half.

The governor's steward was less happy. He didn't know why Rivalin and Miriam wanted to build the spa, but he didn't trust them. For all their feigned distraction, they had got the governor to agree to a spa for use by everyone, whilst the building work went on, and they had got the governor to agree to twice the usual entry fee. There was one thing for certain: the governor would not find out from his steward that he had been gulled.

35

Two months later, the double act was called into action again. A week after the spa decision, one of the council members asked for a meeting to be called. The Britons living in Aquae Sulis had learnt of the building of a spa for the Romans and were grumbling. Why was a spa being built when they were still living in mud huts? They were being shamed by the Romans.

'I didn't realise people were unhappy about it,' said Rivalin to Miriam and Bronwyn after the meeting.

'I don't think they are,' said Bronwyn. 'They just feel belittled by the Romans in their stone houses. This really is a big problem.'

'It is easy enough for us to build houses,' said Miriam. 'There is plenty of wood and local stone. It will give us an excuse to get more settlements to clear extra woodland. What is the problem, Bronwyn?'

'They will not be happy in Roman-style houses. We live in clans where everyone has as much, or as little, privacy as they want. We do not live in small family groups like the Romans. And where will they keep their animals? Roman gardens are no place for them,' Bronwyn replied, indicating the palace gardens.

Miriam thought about it and came up with a design a couple of days later. It had all the houses for a clan facing inwards to a central courtyard, most of which was sectioned off for animals. There was no Roman-style garden, but there was a herb garden. The idea would be sold to the Britons as British houses, not Roman houses, and much more practical. After a lot of discussion and a few minor modifications, like the addition of a central meeting hall for each clan, everything was agreed upon.

Two months later, Rivalin and Miriam went to the governor's house to get his permission. They had prepared the ground by always being together during those two months as if they were inseparable. That way, they got to know each other and started laughing and joking together. Rivalin realised that there was more depth to his wife than he had previously discerned.

Miriam told him of her childhood in Galilee and the beliefs of her people. Of how they had once been a mighty nation but, after invasions by various other nations, they were now all but gone, except for the Judeans.

'Are you Judean?' Rivalin asked.

'No. I am Naphtali, but it is a long time since we were even remotely pure Hebrew. We intermarried with, firstly, the Parthian invaders and then the Greeks. Our elite look more Greek than anything now.'

'You look more than a little Greek. Are you from an elite family then?'

'My mother was born to a fisherman but was adopted by an unmarried woman from an elite family. My father was from an elite merchant family. My parents died when I was only a few months old. I was brought up by the woman my mother regarded as her sister, but who was no relation. She was Judean by birth but Naphtali by adoption. I married her son, but he was killed by the pirates.'

Miriam started to weep and Rivalin put a protective arm around her. As he did so, he felt love stirring inside him. Love that, he now realised, had been there for a long time but had been suppressed by his fascination for Sarah. He had been a complete idiot. How could he have let his wild mooning lead to his neglect of this lovely and very beautiful young woman?

'I miss our daughter,' Miriam cried.

Rivalin held her closer.

'Perhaps you could go there, or we could bring her back here.'

'No. The angel has told me that she is safe and that I must not have any contact with my homeland. The angel is Yahweh's representative. I do not understand but I know I must obey.'

There was that strange word again, *Angel*. Rivalin knew that Miriam used it to mean the goddess. It was strange that Miriam should have such a strong connection to the goddess, stronger than any that had been known in Britain in living memory. Rivalin had thought Miriam would be rejected by his people when he married her, but they loved her. A lot of the initial acceptance was because of her connection to the goddess. A connection, so strong, that every woman in the tribe sensed it as soon as they met her. Since then, her kindness and wisdom had won their hearts. People even talked of her being the 'true queen' even though she was a foreigner and didn't have the mark of the queen.

By the end of the first week of their pretence, it was no longer pretence on Rivalin's part. He noticed that Miriam appeared happy to accept his attention, but he was unsure. He knew how good an actress she was. Still, she accepted his attentions in the palace, as well as in public, so perhaps that was a good sign, although Miriam had always maintained that servants were gossipers, so any performance had to be kept up in their presence. Miriam was regretting that this idyllic interlude would probably end after they had got the plans past the Roman governor.

Their strategy for persuading the governor was simple. Flattery. It worked like a charm. The steward was there again and smiled when he saw how they manipulated his master. He was sure that their supposed infatuation with each other was a ruse but, somehow, this time it seemed more genuine. Perhaps the gossip he had heard was true. Genuine or not, Miriam and Rivalin got exactly what they wanted again, the steward noted, with a smile.

It had been so simple. Just tell the governor how the people were so in awe of the Romans that they wanted to emulate them with their houses and were begging for them. How that, of course, it was not right for barbarians to live as the Romans did. They had condescendingly let the royals do so, but the common people were a different matter. To satisfy the people, they would have to build stone houses, that fitted their barbarian status. There were no gardens, for instance, and animals would be kept in the courtyard and, most of all, the opulence of having separate houses for each family would be reserved for civilised peoples, like the Romans and the Greeks.

Miriam and Rivalin had only just managed to keep straight faces during the brief meeting they had with the 'busy' governor, before he went back to his garden, bored with provincial life. On the way back to the empty palace, they laughed and joked, still holding hands. Bronwyn was out.

In the atrium, still holding Miriam's hand, Rivalin asked, 'Miriam, can I come to you tonight?'

'Of course, you are my husband.'

'Not as your husband, Miriam, as your lover.'

Miriam's heart jumped and the whole of her body involuntarily followed suit. Rivalin misinterpreted the reaction and, with a short 'sorry', let go of her hand and turned to leave. Miriam quickly grabbed his hand tightly and pulled him back.

'I love you, Rivalin.'

His retort that she would say that because it was her wifely duty died unsaid in the light of the obvious love in her eyes and the tender kiss she gave him.

'Come as my husband and my lover.'

'Tonight then.'

Rivalin went to go but Miriam still held his hand.

'Bronwyn will not be back for an hour, what is your hurry? I have a very comfortable bed in my room.'

Miriam squealed as Rivalin quickly, and easily, picked her up. Carrying her to her room, in between kissing her, he said, 'We still have an engagement for tonight, remember.'

'Only a rascal would break that sort of undertaking to a lady,' she replied, laughing.

36

When Bronwyn returned, she initially thought the palace was empty, then she heard a squeal from the newly-modified spa. Since it didn't need servants to fill and empty anymore, it was available any time, any day. There had only been one change from the original plans. The healing waters were so hot that Miriam had to add an extra supply of fresh water to cool them. The Romans insisted that the healing waters should not be diluted so Miriam modified the public spa plans to include a cooling pond before the water flowed into the spa pool.

On reaching the spa, Bronwyn saw a naked Rivalin carrying a naked Miriam into the room with the plunge pool.

'Put me down, Rivalin, I want to go back to the healing waters.'

'Bronwyn will be back soon; we need to get dressed.'

There was silence and, although she knew she shouldn't, Bronwyn crept to the door of the plunge pool room and peered in. Rivalin was still holding Miriam whilst they passionately kissed, both oblivious to anything else.

'Dinner isn't for ages. Let's go back to the pool, or my room.'

Rivalin shook his head.

'At least put me down, so I can go back.'

'Alright.'

With that, he let her go so that she landed with a splash in the water. He then jumped in after her.

'You rat!' laughed Miriam. 'As recompense, I want at least five kisses.'

As Rivalin delivered the recompense, Bronwyn crept out into the garden.

Miriam and Rivalin joined her half an hour later, still hand in hand, and sat down opposite her. Bronwyn started telling them about her visit to a nearby settlement and the problems they were having, but it was obvious Miriam and Rivalin weren't listening.

'Would you like me to leave you alone?' Bronwyn asked.

'Would you like me to leave you alone?' she repeated.

Bronwyn got up to go and her movement caught Rivalin's eye.

'I thought you were going to give us your report.'

'I will do that at dinner when you are less distracted.'

'I am not distracted.'

'I asked you twice if you wanted to be left alone but didn't even get a flicker of a response. I rest my case.'

Miriam giggled, 'Sorry, Bronwyn.'

'I will go and get dressed for dinner.'

At dinner, Miriam and Rivalin were less distracted so they could concentrate on Bronwyn's report. The settlement ground was waterlogged and boggy, and the main upright timbers of the roundhouses were leaning over and had to be constantly put back in place. There were mosquitoes in the pools and the people were being bitten and had sores all over. The cattle had blisters in their mouths. So, it went on.

'That settlement hasn't been there long, has it?' asked Rivalin. 'It seemed such a good place. What do the people there think?'

'They have identified a better place further along the river. Not only does it have better land, but a jetty could be built there so that they could load boats. They only ask for permission to move. I gave it, of course.'

'That is a lot of work for them though. We should send help,' said Miriam.

'They could not pay for it,' said Rivalin.

'What did you have in mind, Miriam?' said Bronwyn.

Miriam raised an eyebrow.

'Come on, Miriam, you always have something in mind. Give.'

'If we provide labour to help clear the land and build the houses and jetty, we could take payment in kind. The timber.'

'Where will we get the labour?' asked Bronwyn.

'We will invoke clan aid,' said Rivalin. 'It is time we reminded our people that they are a tribe and that tribes help each other in need. We will pay for the timber. That will help establish the new settlement.'

'How did the meeting with the governor go, or were you too distracted to concentrate?'

Miriam and Rivalin both reddened.

'We got everything we wanted,' said Rivalin. 'It wasn't until afterwards that we got, er, distracted.'

Miriam and Rivalin both retired immediately after dinner. Rivalin changed into something less formal before going to Miriam's room. He was spotted at her door by the eagle-eyed Bronwyn, as he softly knocked before entering. Bronwyn was pleased for Rivalin, even though she knew she would never be able to marry.

He found Miriam on the bed, in her Roman dress, with all four ties done up in bows.

'Modest,' he said.

'These dresses could never be modest. You can take your time getting into it, though, we have all night.'

'We do tonight,' said Rivalin, 'but tomorrow we must plan the clan aid and then I will need a good night's sleep before I go to help with the settlement. No one is excused clan aid, not even the king.'

'We had better make the most of it then.'

Rivalin moved his hands to Miriam's waist, and she put her arms around his neck as they kissed. She then moved his right hand down over the dress, onto her bare lower leg. When she let go and put her left arm back around his neck, Rivalin moved his hand slowly up her leg, undoing each tie as he went.

37

The following morning, Miriam and Rivalin were woken by Ffion.

'You just have time for a spa before the council arrives.'

Ffion then left.

Lucky we are covered by a sheet, thought Miriam.

Rivalin got up and grabbed a shift, which he threw at her. He then saw that Ffion had left a light wrap-around robe for him. They put them on and then headed, hand in hand, to the spa.

At the spa pool, they took off their clothes and entered the water. Ffion and another woman appeared and took the clothes into the massage room. The two women emerged from the plunge pool room a few minutes later, naked, and got into the spa pool. Miriam was shocked.

'Sit on the bench and Ffion will massage you. It is alright, they are both clan women,' said Rivalin.

'But you aren't a woman.'

'Oh, I forget sometimes that you come from different customs. Here, there is no problem with men and women from the same clan being naked together.'

Ffion had a twinkle in her eye, and said, 'Normally Rivalin would have a male masseur but, in deference to your sensibilities, he asked that he only do the main massage in the massage room.'

'We will be going in there separately?' asked Miriam, desperately.

'No time for that,' replied Ffion. 'Don't worry, he will be clan too.'

Ffion felt Miriam tense under her fingers and laughed. The other woman spoke, 'Don't worry, Madam, Ffion is just teasing you. I will be doing Rivalin's main massage as well.'

Miriam looked at the woman. She was young and beautiful. Newly married into the clan. Miriam couldn't remember her name. Then she remembered what Ffion had said about it being expected that you sleep with many of the men in the clan on first marrying. An apprehension arose in Miriam, followed by a pang of jealousy.

She heard Ffion whisper in her ear, 'Rivalin has never slept with the women of the clan, and most have tried. In fact, after his training by the older women of the clan, the only woman he has slept with is you. It would give any woman too much status if he slept with them and would cause arguments. Besides, he loves you. You are the only woman he has ever loved.'

'What of Sarah?'

'He was infatuated with her, yes, but he never really loved her.'

Miriam was thoughtful as they moved from the spa pool to the plunge pool. Ffion and the other servant got out first. As the women dried themselves and dressed, Miriam and Rivalin went into the massage room and lay on adjoining tables. As they waited, Rivalin took Miriam's hand and gave it a reassuring squeeze. The two women then came in and set about their work. To her surprise, Ffion massaged Rivalin.

'Ffion thought that you would be more comfortable with her massaging Rivalin.'

'Thank you. You are new to the clan, aren't you? What is your name?'

'I am Jenna. Yes, I am new to the clan, but not so new as to have not already been warned that Rivalin is off-limits. Just to make sure, Bronwyn gave me a stern warning too, this morning before I came.'

'You are skilled in massage.'

'We learn from a young age in Aquae Sulis. My clan, my birth clan, specialise in tending those who come to the goddess's healing waters for ease of their conditions. Bronwyn's maid has left to marry into another clan, so I have taken her place.'

Jenna was quiet for a time and then asked, 'Which clan are you from? You speak with a strange accent.'

'I am not from your tribe, or even from Britannia. I come from a country a long way east of here.'

Jenna was puzzled.

'I feel the power of the goddess in you, even more than in Bronwyn, and it is strong in her. I have never heard of anyone but a Briton having the goddess's power.'

After the massage, Ffion and Jenna laid out clothes for Miriam and Rivalin and then left. As they dressed, Miriam asked Rivalin about the goddess. She didn't feel like she had any of the goddess's power. He replied that all the women felt the power in her. Bronwyn had, on the first day they met. It is why the people trusted her since all her decisions were guided by the goddess and, hence, would be for the good of the people.

Miriam was still pondering this when they entered the room where the already-assembled council was waiting. She was sad. Their period of intimacy had been less than twenty-four hours, but she knew that duty called and she would not be alone again with Rivalin for another month or more.

The council took under ten minutes to confirm the clan aid. They agreed, with a nod, to Miriam's plan to use the cleared wood for building material in Aquae Sulis. As everyone had expected, Miriam was left in charge in Rivalin's absence, with Bronwyn as her advisor. It was the shortest meeting in the council's history.

After the meeting, Miriam and Rivalin changed into everyday clothes and preparations began. Though they were told that they didn't need to, Miriam and Bronwyn pitched in with preparing travel food. Bronwyn looked at Miriam wide-eyed, and asked, 'Is there anything you can't do?'

'Result of having to,' replied Miriam. 'I wasn't brought up in a palace.'

A mischievous smile came over Bronwyn's face as she said, 'And what will you do with all your spare time with Rivalin away?'

Miriam stuck her tongue out at Bronwyn and they both laughed.

38

As it turned out, Miriam was busy. With the men away, the Romans thought that the women would be a pushover. After all, it was well-known that British women had sex with all the men. They would be desperate, surely. It started with them bothering some of the unmarried women, and complaints started coming in. Miriam went to the Roman governor on three consecutive days to try and get him to act.

'It is only a little horseplay,' was all she got from him.

On the third occasion she remonstrated, 'If you do not take action, I will.'

The governor laughed.

The following day it happened again. That time, Miriam didn't bother going to the governor, and she called the council. All that was left of the council were the women members, apart from one old man too frail to help in clan aid. Miriam outlined her plan. The women giggled and the old man was aghast.

'What will the governor do when he finds out?'

'He will pompously protest, but I will simply tell him that I gave him plenty of opportunities to deal with it himself.'

The next day, Jenna and one of the other younger women went to the stream to do the washing. As expected, they were followed by two young Roman men. Jenna and her companion were under instruction to pretend not to notice.

When they arrived at the secluded place, where the laundry was done, the two women pretended to look around to check they were alone, then undressed and went for a swim.

The two men came out of hiding, walked over to the clothes, and started heckling them.

'Go away,' said Jenna.

The two men looked at each other, picked up the women's clothes, and started to walk away.

'Hey, bring those clothes back,' shouted Jenna.

'Make your mind up, beautiful. Either you want us to go, or you want us to stay. If we stay, we could give you some entertainment you have been missing,' as he mimicked sex.

'There is no way that you can match up with our men, so leave our clothes and go away.'

'How do you know if you haven't tried?'

'You are talking a lot, but I don't see you doing anything.'

The men took this as an invitation and stripped.

'We're ready for you now.'

'So you are.'

The men turned at the new voice to find themselves faced with a dozen women, including the queen.

'You know what to do,' said Miriam.

The women grabbed the men and took them to where they had prepared four pegs driven into the ground. They forced them to the floor, with their backs down, and tied their hands and legs to the stakes. They then drizzled honey on their genitals and onto a mound on one side of the helpless men. They started to leave.

'Is that all you are going to do?' jeered one.

'I don't need to do any more,' said Miriam. 'That mound is an ants' nest. You will soon have all the stimulus you could wish for where you craved it most.'

'Black or red ants?' the other one blurted.

'I really wouldn't worry yourself about the detail,' Miriam smirked. 'I hear that a hungry bear has been seen around here.'

'Don't leave us,' screamed the first.

'We will send help when we get back.'

A suitable interval after they got back, Miriam sent word to the governor where the two men were and that they would need rescuing.

On arrival, the rescuers found them, squirming, with their genitals covered in black ants, and begging to be freed quickly. It didn't happen. The men sent to free them couldn't do anything except laugh for five minutes. They then freed the men, who immediately ran for the relief of the stream.

Their humiliation was not over though. Their clothes were nowhere to be seen. They had been left a woman's dress each. There was nothing they could do but wear them. On arrival back at the town, they had to go through two lines of jeering women. This tipped their rescuers over the edge, and they started making lewd comments to the men as if they were prostitutes. Even some of the marines from the boats joined in.

The governor was at the palace ten minutes later, demanding to see the queen.

'How dare you humiliate my son in that way,' he demanded.

'Oh, one was your son, was he? Surely you warned him that I was going to act if it happened again. If not, it is your responsibility that he ended up humiliated, not mine.'

'But to stake him to the ground like that, and leave only women's clothes for him to wear, that is going too far.'

'Let me make one thing clear, Governor. The next time this happens I will have the culprit's balls cut off. Is that clear?'

The governor was shocked, and said, 'This must never happen again. Do you hear?'

'That, Governor, is entirely in your own hands.'

Two weeks later, a Roman was caught stealing a boar, and dragged by the women before Miriam. Ten minutes later the Roman governor burst in, with a centurion and five soldiers.

'That man is a Roman citizen. Under Roman law, he has the right to be tried by me.'

'But Governor, he is not being tried under Roman law, but British law. He strayed across the boundary, still in our territory, but no longer in Roman jurisdiction. Since you insist on Roman law, though, what is the penalty in Roman law for theft? And remember, I am not a Briton but from the empire.'

The governor shifted from leg to leg uncomfortably.

'Come, Governor, I am sure you must remember. Crucifixion, I believe, if you are not a Roman citizen. If you are, then…?'

The governor mumbled something inaudible.

'Sorry Governor, I didn't catch that. Could you say it louder, please, so we can all hear?'

'Beheading.'

'Thank you, Governor.'

The thief's face went ashen.

'I was just about to ask Bronwyn what the penalty is in our law. I have never known a Briton steal anything since I have been here.'

Miriam turned to her adviser, 'Bronwyn?'

'The penalty is that the person is stripped naked and sent out into the wild. No assistance will be given to them by any member of the tribe or our associate tribes. If they survive six months, they are taken back into the tribe as a slave.'

'But that is only a slow death,' pleaded the thief.

'Which sentence would you prefer, thief? Instant certain death or to take your chances in the wild?' Miriam asked.

'Come, it was only a boar,' said the governor, ingratiatingly.

'The theft of food is especially heinous, Governor. It leads to slow starvation for those stolen from. That is why the penalties are so harsh. You have lived a life of luxury for too long. Well, thief?'

'I will take my chances in the wild.'

Bronwyn whispered in Miriam's ear, 'You do have the power to give dispensation.'

Miriam smiled.

'You are sentenced to be stripped naked and driven into the wild, there to live with no man's aid for six months. On your return, you will become the slave of the clan you stole from.'

Miriam paused.

'However, if the boar is returned and the governor is prepared to provide a second as compensation, I will commute this sentence.'

All eyes went to the governor. He decided to give the man up to British justice and tell everyone he had pleaded for him but that the hard-hearted queen had refused to listen. He looked to go but saw the disgust in the centurion's eyes. He suddenly realised his plan wouldn't work. The truth would get out and it would be him who would look hard-hearted and the queen magnanimous.

'Agreed. Come, thief.'

The governor stormed out, followed by the thief, the centurion and the five soldiers.

The following week, the governor came to see Miriam again. This time he demanded that she keep their agreement that the temporary spa was just for Romans.

'But Governor, you agreed to everyone being able to use the temporary spa until separate ones could be built.'

'As if I would agree to that,' he huffed.

'But you did, Governor. I was there at the time or, should I say, I was here at the time.'

The governor had forgotten.

'You cannot prove that.'

'Oh, but I can, Governor. I was expecting this at some time, so I have kept the agreement at hand. Would you like me to read it to you? As you can see, it has your signature and seal.'

'You read Latin?'

'And Greek, and Hebrew. But perhaps you would like to read it for yourself?'

'Uh, no. That won't be necessary. I will take it up with Rivalin on his return.'

The governor left.

Bronwyn moved to Miriam's side and asked, 'Why didn't he take you up on the offer to read it? Did he already know the contents and not want to lose face?'

'He certainly didn't want to lose face, but it was not the contents that bothered him. Like a lot of Romans in his class, he can't read or write. He depends on a scribe for that.'

Bronwyn's jaw dropped.

39

When the men returned, Rivalin looked a good deal fitter than when they left. He had calloused hands where blisters had been treated. The main change was that he was decidedly happier. This was partly due to his change in relationship with Miriam and partly because he felt useful for a change. The fact that he hadn't had to deal with the Roman governor for three months helped as well.

Rivalin threw himself into the building of the new spa. He couldn't do manual work as he had in the clan aid. This was under Roman gaze and doing so would demean him in Roman eyes. Personally, he wouldn't have minded but he had to deal with the Romans as the representative of his people.

About a week after his return the Roman governor sent a message that he would come and see him that day on the matter of the new spa. Typically, he had not given a time, so Rivalin had to stay at the palace all day. It was now mid-afternoon and Rivalin was kicking his heals in the garden with the women. The women were sewing as was their want.

'Miriam, how about a walk around the garden?'

'If you wish. Just let me finish this section. I will only be a couple of minutes.'

'Oh, alright. I forgot to ask; did you have any trouble whilst I was away.'

'Nothing I couldn't handle.'

Bronwyn laughed.

'Come on. Give.'

'A few Romans were bothering the women,' said Bronwyn, 'so we trapped them down by the stream and staked them out by an ant's nest naked and covered in honey. I wanted red ants, but kind-hearted Miriam would only allow black ants. We left clothes for them when they were rescued. Women's clothes. One was the governor's son, I believe. Then there was the theft of a boar. It was returned and the governor kindly donated a second to compensate. Also, the governor tried to get Miriam to make the temporary spa only available to Romans but backed down on that too. I think, all in all, that he is quite relieved to have you back.'

All the women laughed at that.

'Is that all I should know? No, don't say any more. Ignorance is bliss. Have you finished that section yet Miriam? You have put on weight whilst I have been away and need to get it off again.'

There was a sudden silence from all the women. Their eyes turned to Miriam.

'It is going to get worse before it gets better,' she said, 'but it will come off again very quickly in six months or so when the baby is born.'

'Six months! You shouldn't let it stay on that long.' Rivalin stopped. 'Baby? Did you say baby?'

'That is the usual result of the sort of fun we had before you left.'

'Are you sure? But you let me make love to you when I returned. Is it a boy or a girl? Shouldn't you be resting? What shall we call it?'

'Whoa!' shouted Miriam, 'Yes, I am sure. It is not my first, remember. You won't hurt me making love, certainly not with you being as gentle and sensitive as you are. We will know if it is a boy or girl when the child is born. That will be soon enough to decide on a name. Normal exercise is fine. With that in mind, shall we take that walk?'

Miriam got up and took Rivalin by the arm, leading him around the garden. They hadn't gone far when the governor arrived. Miriam surreptitiously gave Rivalin a scroll before he went into the palace to meet the governor.

'What is this for?'

'It is the agreement on the spa, including that the temporary spa be shared by everyone. I think that our governor, having failed to get round me, will try it on with you.'

Rivalin returned about half an hour later.

'You were right, Miriam. He wanted the temporary spa exclusively for Roman use. He has also caught on to the amount of money we will make from the new one. He wants in on it.'

'What did you say?'

'I held my ground with the temporary spa. Said I would talk to you about letting him have a cut.'

'How did he react to that?'

'Somewhat crestfallen, I would say. What do you think?'

'Well, I don't particularly want him around too long, so I would suggest that we offer to include in the contract that the governor receive five percent of any profits.'

'Won't that just make him stay?'

'How long he stays governor here is not up to him. I said to include in the contract that the governor gets five percent of the profits, not him personally.'

'I don't think that would wash.'

'It will. We just tell him that we are including in the contract that he gets five percent and leave it at that. We then draw up the codicil and get him to sign it, countersigned by a notary to be certain. He can't read or write so there will be no problem.'

'Won't his scribe spot it?'

'He won't say anything. He hates our governor more than we do. The governor will ask if it provides for five percent for him and the scribe will say yes. Our governor fancies he has the love of his people like Alexander and the wisdom of Solomon. He is totally blind to reality.'

'Who is Solomon?'

'I will tell you as we walk along. How about a proper walk? To view the building works for the new spa. You know that you are itching to get out there.'

Rivalin walked out to help supervise the work on the new spa every day from then on. Every day Miriam walked out in the cool of the evening to meet him and bring him home for dinner. Their pace slowed over the months, but Miriam was fine with it until just before her child was delivered. A healthy boy they called Brennon.

A second child, a girl, came along two years later. They called her Aoife.

40

Just after Aoife was born, Miriam woke up from a nightmare. In her dream, the Romans had attacked them in the palace and, in the fighting, Aoife and Brennon had been killed. Miriam ran to the cot, found Aoife alive and well, picked her up and held her close.

The shock of being grabbed woke Aoife and the obvious distress of her mother was transmitted and she started bawling. Ffion came running and found both mother and daughter sobbing. She took the baby, no easy matter, and had her comforted by one of the palace maids who was nursing her own child. She then set about comforting Miriam.

By the time Miriam was able to speak again, her room was full. Ffion had been joined by Rivalin, Bronwyn and Jenna. The maid had taken Aoife out to the garden, along with Brennon.

It still took them a long time to get out of Miriam what had happened. When they finally did, Rivalin was inclined to dismiss it, but not Bronwyn.

'Miriam has a strong connection to the goddess. This is a warning. We must leave Britannia.'

'I agree, we must get Miriam and the children away, but I must stay. We cannot leave the palace empty.'

Bronwyn looked at him.

'No, we must all go. You included. We will need Eirwyn with us, as he is the best mariner. We could leave Brann in charge. It is about time that we gave him some responsibility.'

'But Brann cannot do everything, you know that.'

'He will be fine,' said Bronwyn, in a voice that brooked no opposition. 'So that is decided.'

'Just the matter of getting it through the council.'

'I will do that,' said Bronwyn, and left.

It was an extremely short council meeting. Bronwyn told them that the goddess had ordered them to leave Britannia temporarily and that Brann would be left in charge as Regent. One man asked if there was an alternative and was told, curtly, to argue it out with the goddess, if he wished. Bronwyn took it to a vote, got a 'yes' from everyone and closed the council, all in under five minutes.

A week later, they were packed, loaded aboard the ship, and had set off.

'Where are we going?' asked Miriam, holding Aoife to her breast to feed whilst the baby got used to the motion of the boat.

'To our cousin, Quaid, in Gaul. The one that married Sarah. We owe him a visit,' replied Bronwyn, as she sat holding Brennon's hand.

'How will Rivalin respond to Sarah, do you think?'

'Most likely realise what a fool he was, even contemplating marrying her. I hear our cousin is regretting his choice of queen. Don't know why but I am sure we will find out soon enough.'

As they sailed down the river towards the sea, Miriam was deep in thought. She hadn't been on a boat on the river since her arrival as a slave. She was still a slave, technically, but she was leaving as a queen. The trepidation and the sense of danger were the same, though. Something was drawing ever nearer, she could sense it, and she had no idea what it was or even if she would survive it.

41

When they reached Quaid's court, the difference to Aquae Sulis was obvious. They were not as firmly a part of the Roman Empire, as in Britannia, and the court was traditional. A long house served as the king's hall. Some sophistication was given by rich tapestries. The whole court, and the local Roman governor and his wife, were there to greet them. First, there was the formal greeting by the king and the introduction to the Roman governor, Quintus Perpetua.

Quintus was a small lean man in his thirties, with prematurely thinning hair. He listened intently to all that was said and spoke little in return. A diplomat more than a governor, Miriam decided. She was pulled out of her contemplation by a woman's voice directed at her.

'You look just like your mother, Miriam.'

'You knew my mother?'

'Yes. She was very pretty. You are slightly more Greek-looking. Your father being high-class Naphtali, that is not to be wondered at. How are they both?'

'They died when I was young. I was brought up by Tabitha and her maid Salome.'

'Who is that you are talking to? What are you saying?' asked Bronwyn.

Miriam suddenly realised that they had been talking in Hebrew. Hebrew, not Aramaic.

Miriam replied in Latin, 'I don't know who she is. Her accent is Galilean, and she is telling me that she knew my mother, but she doesn't know that my parents are dead, even though they died when I was just a few months old.'

The woman also switched to Latin, 'I am Mary of Magdala.'

Miriam stared open-mouthed at the woman, the grandmother she had never met.

'Grandmother?'

The woman rose, came over to Miriam and hugged her.

'Didn't they tell you I had come to Gaul?'

'Yes, but I never expected to meet you. What are you doing at the court here?'

Quintus interjected, 'Let me formally introduce you. Miriam, Queen of the Dobunni, this is Mary of Magdala, the queen's mother. There is an intriguing story here, I can see.'

Mary answered, 'I adopted Miriam's mother so that she could marry the man she wanted, even though she was only a few years younger than me. I later adopted Sarah and her older sister, Mary. I came to Gaul with Sarah before the queen was born, so we have never met before.'

'Hold on!' said Rivalin. 'Are you saying that Queen Sarah is Miriam's aunt?'

'Yes, but I doubt she will take kindly to being called Auntie Sarah. I would, however, be honoured if you called me Grandmother, Miriam. You must sit next to me at the feast tonight and tell me all the news.'

'Of course, though I don't know anything about what has happened over the last few years. But you must visit our quarters this afternoon. There are two little ones there who would love to meet their great-grandmother.'

At their quarters, Brennon was delighted to meet Great-Grandma. Aoife giggled with glee at the extra attention. For

Rivalin and Bronwyn, seeing the children with a grandmother was more than they had ever hoped.

'I can't wait to hear your news. Your parents died when you were young?'

'Let's speak Latin. Bronwyn and Rivalin have as much right to know as you do, and I have never really talked of home because of Jesus.'

'Tabitha's son?'

'Yes.'

Miriam was quiet for a time.

'I was left with Tabitha in Galilee when my parents were killed in riots in Damascus. Demetrius, Photina's husband, and Jonah, Tabitha's husband, were escorting them and also died.'

Tears fell down Mary's cheek.

'Jonah was my cousin. He was my guardian after my parents died.'

'Tabitha brought me and Jesus up, as brother and sister. Jesus and I were always close and married as soon as we could. I have a daughter by him, who is with Tabitha now. At least we left her with Tabitha when we took our ill-fated voyage.'

Rivalin sat down next to Miriam and put a protective arm around her. She nestled her head into his shoulder and continued. She told of the pirate attack and her journey to Britannia, of Rivalin's purchase of her, and their marriage and how she had found happiness with him.

'There is one thing that puzzles me. How did Tabitha manage to rear the two of you by herself? She is not the most motherly of women and with a business to run as well.'

'We spent the summers in Sychar with Photina.'

'And the rest of the time?'

'Salome, Tabitha's maid, looked after us.'

'Salome is still there? I would have expected her to marry long ago.'

'She married Matthias, one of the carters who was already trading on his own account. Tabitha made her a partner in the business to keep her there. Afterwards, her own two children were born.'

'Have either of her children inherited her startling leaf-green eyes?'

Miriam snuggled deeper into Rivalin and looked at Bronwyn for a reaction. Not seeing any, she realised that it hadn't penetrated yet.

'Yes, her daughter, Coventina, has them.'

Bronwyn jerked as if hit by lightning. Rivalin jumped up so suddenly that Miriam almost fell off her chair.

'Where did she get the name Coventina?' Rivalin demanded.

'It was her grandmother's name,' said Mary. 'Salome always claimed that her grandmother was a British princess.'

'It is the name of the goddess,' said Bronwyn. 'The secret name we tell no one. That means that Salome is the true queen.'

'Why didn't you tell us before, Miriam?' Rivalin asked.

'The goddess didn't want us to know,' replied Bronwyn. 'She didn't want us chasing after Salome. Something must happen first, before Salome becomes queen. It is tied up with us being here as well. I can feel it.'

Bronwyn looked around and, seeing Ffion and Jenna, called them over.

'Did you hear what was just said?'

The two women nodded their heads slightly.

'Nothing said here must leave this room.'

'When do we start looking for Salome?' asked Rivalin.

'We don't,' said Miriam. 'She will come to us. We just need to be ready when she does. Salome knows you came here, doesn't she, Mary?'

'Yes, she suggested it, why?'

'I think that this will be her first port of call before she goes to Britannia. It would make sense to her to go somewhere where you are known before striking out somewhere new. We must know where she is headed. It could cause no end of division if there is a delay in acknowledging her rights.'

42

That night at the feast, Mary and Miriam took the opportunity to get to know each other. Miriam knew the story of why Mary had fled Galilee. False rumour had circulated that Sarah was her illegitimate daughter by Jesus, the Galilean preacher, executed by Pilate. It had become dangerous for them.

After Miriam had given her a resumé of what had happened since Mary had left, Mary called a halt.

'Do you embroider?'

'Yes.'

'We can continue this, working together for the next couple of days. That way, Sarah can join in too. Not that she remembers much about Galilee. Now, what do you think of people here?'

Looking up, Miriam saw Quaid at the head of the table, with a woman next to him ingratiating herself. At one end of the table was a pregnant Sarah, with her maid fussing over her.

'I was told that it is not a happy marriage between Quaid and Sarah. It would seem the report was right.'

'I warned Quaid against the marriage, but eventually had to give in. Sarah does her marital duty, but no more.'

Bronwyn chipped in, 'They are lucky that Celtic society has clan marriage. It allows Quaid and Sarah to satisfy their needs elsewhere. If she were not the king's wife, Sarah would not even have had to get pregnant.'

Miriam was puzzled.

'You mean that Sarah is not pregnant by the king?'

'I see you haven't quite picked up all the nuances of Celtic society yet,' said Quintus, who had been listening in. 'It clashes so strongly with Hebrew society that I am not surprised.'

'To be fair, things are slightly different in Britannia, Quintus. Sarah's child is Quaid's. She will be hoping it is a boy so that she does not have to have another one. Sarah prefers lying with women to lying with men. See how close she is to her maid. Quaid satisfies his needs by lying with clan women. That one with him now is his current favourite. It will inevitably lead to trouble. The clan men are vying for status, using their wives as bait. Sarah's child will be the next king if it is a boy. If she only delivers girls, then there will be competition between his sons by clan women to take the throne. Inevitably that will lead to bloodshed. Whichever man it is, will have to marry the king's niece to satisfy the traditionalists,' replied Bronwyn.

Miriam was shocked.

'Now you know why I was against the marriage but, in Gaul, Sarah is an exotic beauty. However, I have seen Quaid looking at you all night. I think he might be more than a little jealous of Rivalin. And I think Rivalin might be more than happy at his lucky escape,' said Mary.

'What about in Rome, Quintus? You have monogamy for life. That leaves little scope,' asked Bronwyn.

'There are always the temples, of course,' said Quintus. 'You can get whatever sex you like there, whatever your bent. However, it is not as restrictive as it first appears. It doesn't happen often but it is not unknown, and perfectly legal, to marry someone of your own gender. However, the strong custom that marriage is for producing children means that it is frowned upon, even by those who would prefer otherwise. Of course, in marriage by purchase, the woman has no choice. And if you are married to someone who either won't, or can't, have children, or you just don't get on with them, you can divorce. Some do it just because they fancy someone else for a time.'

'That sounds a bit of a rosy picture to me,' said Bronwyn.

Bronwyn and Quintus stayed deep in conversation for the rest of the evening. Watching them, Miriam was a little sad. They were very suited to each other but, with the possibility that Bronwyn could be the mother of the next true queen in the minds of the Britons, it simply would not be acceptable.

On the other hand, Quintus was already married, through an alliance marriage. It was not a happy one, but not one Quintus could easily get out of. His plain-looking wife, Livia, was one of the emperor's distant cousins. Not close enough to give Quintus a lot of clout but too close for him to be able to risk upsetting her family.

Miriam noticed that Livia had left as soon as the dinner was concluded. She had obviously not wanted to be there and had spoken to no one. The only time she spoke, was to tell her husband that she was leaving. Even when anyone had tried to talk to her, she had pretended not to hear.

43

Over the next two days, Miriam, Bronwyn, Mary and Sarah sewed together. Miriam and Bronwyn were accompanied by Ffion and Jenna, who also sewed. Miriam was surprised that Mary and Sarah were not accompanied by their maids.

'I don't have a maid,' said Mary. 'I couldn't afford one when we arrived. Since Sarah married Quaid, I could have had one, but it seemed too Roman somehow and I wanted to integrate with society here. Sarah's maid is not interested in sewing. If it is not traditional to the tribe, it is not something she should be doing. Unless it is something she wants to do, of course.'

Mary and Miriam started to discuss their relations in Galilee. Bronwyn soon got lost with the inter-relationships but listened, fascinated by a culture she had never known existed.

That was how Quintus, obviously flustered, found them.

'Rivalin is with the king. There is news from Britannia. Rivalin insists that Miriam and Bronwyn must be there when it is discussed. The messenger who fetched me was to come for you afterwards. I told him I would fetch you and sent him back to the king to let him know that we would be there as soon as we could.'

It also gives you a chance to be with Bronwyn alone, or alone-ish, thought Miriam.

She and Bronwyn rose, and Quintus offered each an arm. It was obvious he only really wanted Bronwyn's arm, but it would have looked odd, so Miriam obliged as well.

When they entered Quaid's reception hall, there were two messengers from Aquae Sulis; one from the Roman governor, another from Brann. Each gave his message. Rivalin held the one he had received so that Miriam and Bronwyn could read it at the same time. Quintus read his message privately. Miriam noticed that he read it carefully, twice.

Quaid waited until they had finished but did not ask for any information about the contents.

'Do you wish to proceed alone, or with me present?'

Quintus answered, 'This seems a simple thing to resolve, so long as we are open and honest. So, I have no objection to Quaid staying. In fact, it may be better if he did.'

Rivalin nodded.

'There has been a revolt by some of the eastern tribes in Britannia, led by Boudicca. It seems that some idiot of a governor in Camulodunum went too far in his dealings with her and inflamed the situation there. It was already delicate because the same governor had been taking advantage of them over the treaties. Camulodunum has been destroyed. The governor in Aquae Sulis has requested Brann to aid the Romans in putting down the revolt. Brann has refused. The governor is worried that Brann will raise a revolt in the west, so he has requested troops from Gaul to, as he puts it, 'stabilise the situation'.'

Quintus nodded towards Rivalin.

'Brann says that the governor did request aid against Boudicca and that he explained that he did not have the authority to wage war, on either side. The governor then threatened him with the garrison in Aquae Sulis. Brann explained that, though he did not have the authority to go to war, he could defend his people, and was expected to. He pointed out that he did not want conflict but that the garrison in Aquae Sulis was outnumbered ten to one, even with the warriors immediately available to him.

The governor told his advisors that the Britons hadn't the stomach for a fight. That led the governor's son and two of his friends to claim conquerors' rights and they attempted to rape two women. Brann and two others caught them, disarmed them, in both senses of the phrase, and marched them back to the governor. He wasn't particularly diplomatic in the heat of the moment. He told the governor that, the next time any of his men were caught doing that, he would cut their balls off. If that warning didn't work, he would slit their throats.'

Quintus had started smiling when Rivalin said 'disarmed them, in both senses of the phrase'. By the time Rivalin had finished, there was a broad grin on his face.

'What do you find so funny?' Rivalin asked.

'That governor, with his Roman superiority stance, has needed taking down a peg or two for years. His son is even worse.'

'Ah, but that is not the first time,' said Bronwyn. 'Miriam already took the governor and his son down a couple of pegs.'

'Do tell,' said Quintus.

'Some other time,' said Rivalin. 'What do we do about the problem at hand?'

Quintus looked at Quaid.

'What would happen if I tried to send troops from Gaul to Britannia as requested?'

'They would never get there. You know how volatile Gaul is at the best of times. The fact that they are headed for

Britannia to subdue a peaceful tribe, our cousins, would make matters worse and you would have a revolt on your hands here as well. I am not threatening, you understand.'

'I understand. I am not the governor of Aquae Sulis. Thank you for being so frank. Rivalin, what will Brann do?'

'He will use the minimum of force necessary to keep the peace. If it comes to war, he is a masterful tactician and ruthless warrior. If attacked, he will have the support of every tribe in Britannia, not just his own.'

'That is what I thought. I know the commander of the fort on the edge of the forest, in where you Britons call 'Ardu'. I will explain the situation to him and get him to send a message to the governor to cool him down.'

'He won't send troops, will he?' asked Miriam.

'He won't, even if he had the troops to send. I expect that the legions have already been recalled from Cambrai. He will reinforce them.'

'I hope he is firm with the governor,' said Rivalin.

'Regus doesn't suffer fools gladly. He might even decide that the best way to cool the hotheads is to draft them into his army. That would be a mighty shock for the governor's son who, although he has centurion rank, has never wielded a sword in anger in his life. Do him good, though.'

Quintus called for vellum. He wrote a note to Regus and gave it to the messenger, giving him strict instructions that he was to go straight to Regus and go nowhere near Aquae Sulis. Regus would give him further instructions. Once the messenger had gone, Rivalin gave the other messenger a verbal message in their Celtic language.

'What did he say?' asked Quintus.

'Simply to tell Brann that he is doing well and has Rivalin's full backing for his actions.'

Quintus said, 'Maintain the stalemate. Good idea. Just one more thing. You said that Brann didn't have the authority to declare war. What if you had been there, Rivalin?'

'Then, as war duke, I would have had to call a council of the tribes to vote on war. That would have been tricky, with half the tribes voting one way and half the other. It would have thrown up questions as to my legitimacy, which could end in civil war. If I may, cousin, I will trespass on your hospitality until this situation is resolved.'

Quaid nodded.

Quintus looked at Rivalin, wondering what the questions of legitimacy were but decided not to ask.

'So, being here, you can let things resolve themselves without having to take sides. Lucky you were here. If you ever need to adopt a Roman name, you could do worse than Felix Britannicus, *Lucky Briton*. I will escort Lady Bronwyn back to her quarters.'

Quintus held out his arm and Bronwyn took it.

'Now do tell, how did our clever queen, Miriam, take that stupid man down?'

As Bronwyn started to explain, Quintus started to chuckle.

Miriam looked at Rivalin, thoughtfully, 'You didn't say everything that Brann reported. Why not? If that had happened in Judea, the whole country would have revolted.'

'I don't know that Quintus would have understood, and it would have simply muddied the waters when what we need is to prevent all-out war in the west.'

'What is it you are holding back?' asked Quaid.

'I don't know if what happened was due to Roman arrogance, a misunderstanding, or desperation on behalf of the Roman governor of Camulodunum. Prasutagus was not completely innocent either.'

Quaid was puzzled and asked, 'What has Boudicca's late husband got to do with it?'

'It has troubled me for some time. Prasutagus is of royal descent, but the throne goes down through the female line. The most likely next ruler would have been his sister's son or daughter. Boudicca is of royal descent as well, but well down the pecking order. Prasutagus's solution was to leave his possessions jointly to the emperor and his daughters. That would just be his personal effects of course. It was a bribe to the governor in Camulodunum to support his daughters' claim to the throne. The governor interpreted the will in a Roman way. I know he was desperate for land to give to retired Roman legionaries. He has assumed that, as Prasutagus was king, he owned all the land of the Iceni, which we know is not true. When he tried to take land to give to his retirees, Boudicca protested. Again, the governor's Roman thinking made matters worse. He presumed that Boudicca, being Prasutagus's wife, and his two daughters, were Prasutagus's property and thus, by dint of the legacy, now the property of the emperor. He put Boudicca in her place by exercising the emperor's property rights, as he saw them, and had her flogged and her daughters raped.'

Miriam flinched.

'So why would half the tribes not want to revolt? I know from living amongst you that you take great care to protect your women.'

Quaid answered her by saying, 'If a tribe chose to support Boudicca, then it could lead to in-fighting within the tribe, or between tribes, on who would become the next ruler. By convention, the choice of the next monarch is an internal tribal matter, chosen by the elders. If they support Rome, then they are giving the Romans the right to take whatever they like. Rivalin, I think that Quintus would have understood.'

44

Regus Aurelius was pacing his quarters. That was the last thing he needed. They were going to be hard-pressed to defeat Boudicca, and that idiot of a governor in Aquae Sulis was stirring up the locals there. Regus could do nothing until the legions returned from Cambrai. He didn't believe in gods but the reckless attacks on religious sites had caused more resistance from the Britons than was needed. It had resulted in an enforced attack on the druid site on Mona. All to show the superiority of the Roman gods. Madness. His fort was a large one and well-manned, but he had been ordered to stay put for the time being.

When he had arrived to take command of the fort, he had thought it was an odd place for one. It was on the edge of a forest, miles from any major Roman centre, or even any major Roman road. Behind him, however, in the forest, was the reputed dwelling of a powerful local goddess. Initial forays into the forest had been disastrous. Any men who returned were dead. The previous commander had told him that he too had tried scouting missions, but the same had happened. They had seen the returned men being dragged back, by huge wild beasts, during the night. They had not dared go out of the fort to retrieve them until morning.

Regus called the messenger who had arrived from Quintus the previous night.

'Here is a message for the governor at Aquae Sulis, and a duplicate for the garrison commander, who is to receive his first. Give him the governor's message to deliver. It tells the governor to use all possible diplomatic means to maintain the peace with the local populace, as we cannot send any reinforcements. If that fails, he can either fight to the death along with the local militia or make a cowardly retreat by ship. It also instructs him to send any Romans of fighting age here to reinforce our regulars.'

The messenger smiled. He knew exactly what the commander wanted. The garrison commander in Aquae Sulis was to keep the governor and any other non-Britons in order. The governor was to concentrate on keeping the peace. He, himself, was to spread gossip amongst the troops, to ensure that they watched their step, and to undermine the governor should he try anything covert. It was impossible to keep anything underhand fully from the rank and file. The request for reinforcements was simply to remove the hotheads from the situation. If they wanted conquerors' rights, they were going to have to earn them.

As he rode to The Fossa, and then down to a landing on the river for the boat that would take him to Aquae Sulis, the messenger was still smiling. He would have to go back as one of the reinforcements of course, but it would be worth it. The governor's son was a bullying coward who had never seen real action in his life but would have to go. The alternative was being beheaded for cowardice.

45

Brann had already received his verbal message from Rivalin when the governor came to see him. He could tell from his demeanour that he was not happy. He seemed nervous that the garrison commander was accompanying him.

'I have received word from the garrison commander at Ardu. He tells me that his garrison is at my command should I need it.'

The garrison commander behind him shook his head and smiled.

'I hope that this means that we will have no more trouble,' the governor continued.

Brann thought about his reply. It was obvious, from both the governor's face and the garrison commander's covert signal, that the governor was lying.

'Governor, indeed it will be good to have no more trouble. That is in no one's interest. I have received word from Rivalin to keep the peace but do no more, which is what I will continue to do. Perhaps we could sort something out that would reduce the friction. I would not want this situation to get out of hand. Perhaps I could work out the detail with the garrison commander here.'

'So long as you understand that we will brook no more incidents.'

'I understand perfectly, Governor.'

The governor left. After he had done so, the garrison commander burst into laughter.

'Pompous ass! Alright, Brann, shall we get down to business? It shouldn't take long. For a start, the garrison commander at Ardu has been ordered to take all available men to meet the legions coming back from Cambrai. They will then engage Boudicca. He has also demanded that all men of fighting age be sent from here to reinforce him. That will only leave the veterans to man the garrison here. I would say we could probably hold off an attack from you for about ten minutes tops. It will also mean that the hotheads that have been causing trouble will be taken out of the equation.'

Brann smiled.

'Including the governor's son, I presume.'

'Oh yes. He is begging his father to get him out of it, but there is nothing the governor can do. He is too late in promising not to cause trouble. Anything not to go. Anyway, the governor is to be diplomatic and keep you out of the conflict whilst I am to maintain order amongst the non-Britons so that you aren't provoked. I would suggest that if there are any more incidents, that you come to me.'

'I would much rather deal with you anyway. The governor's idea of diplomacy leaves a lot to be desired.'

'The governor's idea of diplomacy is to hide behind the legions. In a situation like this, he is lucky to be dealing with someone reasonable. In most of my postings, when a regular, his diplomacy this morning would have got his throat slit. Shall we go down to the riverbank with some of our men? We can have a few goblets of wine together whilst we watch them load our troubles into the boats and see them sail away.'

An hour later, whilst half a dozen Romans sat with half a dozen Britons sharing a skin of wine, the governor's son and twenty other men were being loaded onto barges. The governor's son was struggling to hold his shield up, obviously unused to the weight.

Brann was confused.

'Why is the idiot holding his shield ready for battle? Does he think we are going to attack?'

'All high-class Romans are supposed to do drill in case they are called upon to fight. Our governor's son has never done so. Too far beneath him. He has only ever watched the battle drills whilst in Rome. He thinks that that is the way you carry shields all the time.'

'But everyone else has theirs on their backs. Why don't they tell him?'

'For the same reason that I am not going to tell him. He was the main instigator of the trouble that led to them being ordered to join Regus Aurelius, the garrison commander in Ardu, and he will sneer at them for not carrying the shield properly. He will soon learn.'

'The governor is not here?'

'No, he is too angry to witness his humiliation. His wife is over there, with the other women, weeping. Why she didn't divorce the idiot years ago beats me. She could have done a lot better than him. Now this will be interesting. The young pup is trying to board the boat.'

Brann almost spat his wine out as he turned to look. The governor's son was not only fully dressed for immediate battle, but he was also carrying his pack. A bargeman was waiting to take it from him, but he was refusing. Brann saw one of the loaders surreptitiously put a rope around the governor's son's waist. As he tried to board the barge, it rocked, and he fell into the water. The rope was pulled to bring him to the surface and stop him from drowning, but he dropped his pack and shield. His helmet came off as well. His shield was heavy enough to stay on the bottom of the river and was retrieved by a boatman. The helmet and pack sailed off down the river.

The garrison commander laughed.

'Now he will have to strip naked until his clothes dry. Good job it is a warm day. I hope he had his money on him. He will have to pay for a replacement helmet and new spare clothes and a blanket. All in all, this has been a pleasanter day than I anticipated. Another skin of wine?'

The garrison commander didn't wait for an answer. He signalled a man to bring it. Whilst they sat talking, they didn't see the governor watching them resentfully. The governor knew that he had been effectively put under the command of the garrison commander. Further, he knew that they were all being governed by Brann. He would get his revenge once things were back to normal. Unfortunately, he couldn't touch Regus as he was too close to Vespasian, the darling of Rome after the successful invasion of Britannia.

46

Ten days later, the men from Aquae Sulis arrived at the Ardu garrison. Regus took one look at them and realised that they were in no shape to go into battle. He called for his best centurion. It was not going to be popular, but the new recruits were from good families, and he couldn't let it be levelled at him that he had fed them to the wolves.

'See what you can do with this sorry lot. They are assigned to you, as of now.'

One of the men objected.

'I am not going under him. He is low born!'

'And you are?'

'I am the son of the governor of Aquae Sulis. My name is Marcus.'

'Well, Marcus, let me see. This man has ten years of experience in the legions. You have none. This man is the best commander I have. You and your father are lucky that you haven't had your throats cut for your incompetence. If you prefer, I can put you in a lesser unit and you can be cut to pieces.'

'But I am noble born and …'

At that point, Marcus was kicked by one of the other recruits. He turned and protested, threatening the other with dire consequences. He was quietened by a punch. He turned back to Regus.

'Are you going to let him get away with that? I demand justice.'

'Centurion, how do we settle disputes between rank and file?'

The centurion smiled and said, 'Well, usually we either make them box or wrestle. Since the other man is smaller, but obviously the better boxer, how about a wrestling match?'

'Good idea. Summon your unit.'

The men were marched to the horse-training circle. With its fencing, all the way round the perimeter, Marcus realised that there was no way of escape. Besides, the whole unit was watching as well as many from other units who had come, out of curiosity, about 200 in all. Marcus had no choice. For the first time in his life, his rank counted for nothing. Still, he was a good wrestler. He had won every contest he ever entered. He had beaten this opponent many times. It was going to be fun.

The two men stripped to loin cloths and started to weigh each other up, dancing around each other. Marcus knew the other man's main weakness. He tended to put too much weight on his trailing leg. A sweep of the ankle and he would be over. There, he was still doing it. He never learned. Next time!

Marcus's opponent went onto his back leg again. He went for it, a move he had made against that man a hundred times. He swept his right leg across, to take the left leg from under him, but he shifted his weight forward onto his right leg and Marcus's leg met thin air. His opponent used the momentum to twist him onto his back and Marcus met the ground with a thud, his opponent on top of him. Not ever having been thrown before, Marcus didn't know how to fall. The other man got up for the next pass, only to find Marcus was unconscious.

'Well,' said the centurion, 'that is the shortest wrestling match I have ever seen. Lucky he didn't break his back, falling like that. Throw some water on him, then get these new recruits bivouacked.'

Over the following days, the centurion put them through their paces in battle drill. The other recruits had the rudiments of swordsmanship and formation, but Marcus knew nothing.

'Right, form a battle line,' shouted the centurion. 'Marcus, interlock that shield. No, not that way, behind the shield of the man on your left, in front of the shield of the man on your right. Right forward, stab! What in the name of Mars are you doing, Marcus? You open your shield to the left slightly and stab underarm forwards, up through the stomach and rib cage into the heart. Let's try that again. That is better. Marcus, you idiot, don't leave your sword there. It is a quick stab and out again, sword pointed downwards on the out. Do you want to disarm yourself after one kill?'

After fifteen minutes, Marcus was complaining about needing a rest. The centurion stood before him.

'The enemy will not give you a rest every time you get tired. I'd call you a moany old woman, but that would insult moany old women.'

An hour later, the centurion called a halt to the drill.

'Hold on, Marcus. Andronicus!'

Andronicus came out of the watching crowd.

'Take Marcus and see if you can make a soldier of him. Work him till he drops, then work him tomorrow till he drops. At the moment, he isn't even fit to be left in charge of the cooking pots.'

Two weeks later, word came for them to march to just north of Verulamium and meet up with the legions returning from Cambrai. The centurion bringing the message was a Greek; Demetrius of Sychar.

Regus asked Demetrius if he had come across any rebel Britons on his way.

'None we couldn't handle,' he replied.

'I understand that you were very instrumental in the campaign on Mona.'

'Nothing really. Just dealt with some Berserkers.'

Regus's respect immediately increased for the man in front of him, as Berserkers were the Briton's shock troops. He wondered how he had done it.

Two days later, Regus found out. The column had come to a halt, at a point where there was woodland on both sides of the road. In the woodland were Britons in ambush. Well, more open defiance than ambush. They obviously wanted the Romans to come in, where their shields and battle formations would be useless. Amongst the trees were the unmistakeable frenzied cries of Berserkers.

Regus called for Demetrius.

'You have the experience; how do we manage this one?'

'We wait.'

'If we do that, the Britons will just attack under cover of darkness.'

'We won't have to wait that long. The Berserkers are on a drug-fuelled high. They can't afford to wait for more than an hour, two hours tops, before they will have to attack. Until then, I suggest we use javelins to keep them on their toes.'

Regus thought about it. It was only two hours after dawn. Another two hours wouldn't do any harm, so he gave the orders.

'A volley of half a dozen javelins, each side, every fifteen minutes. Other than that, just hold steady in a square formation. If arrows fly, then go turtle. Don't wait for orders.'

The standoff lasted about an hour and a half, before the Britons charged out of the woods, Berserkers at the fore. One or two of the Berserkers didn't even make it to the Roman lines, collapsing in exhaustion before they got there. Those that did get there were easily dealt with as their drug-induced frenzy was wearing off. The Berserkers did achieve one thing though, they allowed the men behind to get close to the Romans. The main contingent went for Regus and his guard. It soon became apparent that they wouldn't be able to hold out much longer. Just as the shield wall was about to break, the Britons turned in dismay. Demetrius and his unit came on their rear. They looked to bolt along the line, a last resort as they would have to run the gauntlet of Roman swords all the way, but Regus had anticipated the move. He ordered his flanks forward, trapping the Britons. The battle was soon over.

Regus took stock of the aftermath. Five Romans were dead and a couple of dozen wounded. Without Demetrius's action it would have been at least fifty Romans dead, himself amongst them. Without Demetrius's knowledge of how to deal with the Berserkers, maybe a thousand Romans would have died.

When they met with the forces out of Cambrai, Regus was summoned to see the commander.

'This is the situation. We are at the bottom of the hill; Boudicca is at the top. She will send scouts under cover of darkness to probe our defences and keep us awake. Tomorrow, she will attack. She is no fool. She knows that we have dug a ditch and set up a rampart, so she will draw us out with a mock attack and then send in her Berserkers. It is going to be a close-run thing even if we prevail. The only thing I can think of doing is to put your contingent out of sight somewhere, Regus, and hope you can outflank them or something. Does anyone have any other ideas?'

Regus smiled and said, 'Yes. Wait!'

The commander raised his eyebrows.

'There is no cover anywhere nearby except the woodland. The Britons would pick us off in there, no problem. Boudicca won't be able to hold her Berserkers in check for more than a couple of hours. We let the Berserkers attack and break upon our ramparts, then march out to mop up the rest.'

Even with those tactics, the Romans only just prevailed. The initial Berserker attack was more ferocious than Regus had anticipated. Once weathered, though, the rest was child's play. Regus looked at his men. He had lost about a third. Other units had lost half, so he had come off lightly. One of his dead was Marcus.

'What happened?' he asked the centurion.

'Despite me having him drilled and drilled, he broke the shield wall and ran. Hit on the back of the head by a Berserker club. Luckily, the man behind him stepped into the breach quickly enough to prevent the Britons breaking through. Just before the Berserkers started dropping from exhaustion too.'

News of the victory arrived in Aquae Sulis with the returning men. There was great rejoicing except in the governor's house. The governor was a broken man. Regus had kindly praised his son's heroism and the returning young men said nothing. They pretended that they had lost sight of Marcus during the battle. Only one other man of their contingent had died, though another would never walk again.

Although Marcus's body had been burned after the battle, according to Roman custom, Brann arranged for a funeral pyre to be built at Aquae Sulis for him and the other man. Everyone in the town attended, Briton and Roman.

Brann expected trouble on the return of the young men but didn't get any. He asked one about it. The man, a Greek, gave him an answer he hadn't expected.

'The trouble was always fomented by Marcus. Without him around, there will be no more problems. Most of the rest of us are Roman citizens of Greek origin. It is not that long ago that we lost to the Romans ourselves. We know the retribution the Romans take, but we also know the lingering resentment it leaves. Carthage still resents Rome, over 200 years after their defeat. Concluding with Rome peacefully is far better than war. Besides, it was a close-run thing. The battle has given even the young Romans here a new respect for the Britons. Before this, they thought the legions were invincible. They still have pride in the legions, but it is now more sober.'

The governor was transferred out a month later, as a reward for keeping the peace. The day after he left, Felix Britannicus arrived as temporary governor. Brann called upon him immediately. He was astounded to find that Felix was Rivalin.

47

It took six months for a new governor to be sent. The new governor was Quintus. Officially, he had been sent as he had been instrumental in keeping the peace during Boudicca's rebellion. In reality, it was because the previous governor had used his influence in Rome to get Quintus sent there because he knew how much Quintus's wife wanted to return to Rome.

Things immediately changed in Aquae Sulis. Quintus realised that the Britons in the town were already far more Romanised than their Gallic counterparts. After he had settled in and consulted his steward, which was the same one the previous governor had, he went to see Rivalin, who immediately invited him to dine.

'I am here on official business,' said Quintus.

'All the better that you should dine with us. Any official business would need Bronwyn and Miriam present and they are putting the children to bed at the moment. I will send word for Brann to join us as well.'

When Miriam and Bronwyn returned, Miriam greeted Quintus cordially. Bronwyn was delighted to see him.

'Why haven't you come before, Quintus, and why only on business? I enjoyed our conversations in Gaul.'

'Sorry, Bronwyn. The previous governor left everything in a mess. His handover report was scandalously poor. It took me some time to get the truth out of his steward. Seems the steward didn't tell him much, thinking it best that he carried on in blissful ignorance. Also seems that Rivalin has effectively been governor anyway.'

'Shall we leave business until after dinner?' asked Miriam. 'People are always more reasonable on a full stomach.'

They went into the dining room where couches were set out around a low table. Further evidence of the adoption of Roman customs.

'This feels strange after Gaul,' said Quintus.

'It is not how our people generally eat, but Rivalin and I were brought up with Roman customs. We will introduce you to British fare some other time. Tonight, we will dine in Roman fashion. Dormice to start, along with dates stuffed with ground almonds mixed with honey, followed by beef and then fruit,' said Bronwyn.

Quintus smiled and said, 'I think if my wife knew, she would be envious. She is partial to dates served this way.'

'So is Miriam,' Bronwyn winked.

'My mother lived with a Damascus merchant during her childhood as companion to his daughter. The merchant was indulgent. After she came back to Galilee, she insisted on them as a Sabbath treat and the custom stuck.'

'I haven't seen your wife around, Quintus. Is she coming on later?' asked Rivalin.

'My wife asked me for her dowry and has gone back to Rome. She understood from the previous governor here, that you were bloodthirsty barbarians, even worse than the Gauls.'

The conversation was cordial all evening. When it came to business, Quintus wanted to sort out some of the anomalies the previous governor had left behind. They agreed that the spa which had been built would be the only spa. Quintus wanted to forego the money due to him as governor out of the profits from the spa. Bronwyn and Miriam vetoed that, as they felt it was a useful way of keeping any future, less amenable, Roman governors sweet. Quintus did ask for a votive room to be added though, useless though it was.

'No one will use it, of course, but it will show conformity to Roman customs and make the emperor happy. There is another more delicate matter, though.'

Quintus paused.

'I am sorry to have to ask this of you, Rivalin. I used the Roman name I had given you when I had you appointed temporary governor by Regus, because a Briton would not be acceptable. Now, to show your loyalty to Rome, you must remain officially Felix Britannicus.'

'Will it keep the peace?' asked Miriam.

Quintus nodded.

'In that case, Felix Britannicus it is. It matters little what anyone calls him unofficially.'

Quintus smiled and said, 'I was hoping you would say that. It is only an official name that the Romans will call him. It is just to make the emperor think that we have always had a Roman in control. After all, Emperor Caligula was formally Gaius, though most people never knew his formal name.'

After Quintus had left, Brann, who had been suspicious at the start of the evening, smiled.

'This is a fortunate turn of events. A significant improvement on our previous governor.'

'Yes,' said Rivalin, 'Quintus realises that, on the fringes of the empire, diplomacy is more useful than force. They rely on the local people to enforce order. It is a pity that the governor in Camulodunum didn't realise that.'

'What did he mean by his wife asking for her dowry?' asked Bronwyn.

'In Roman alliance marriages, technically the husband holds the wife's dowry,' said Miriam. 'Asking for your dowry is a request for a divorce.'

'Technically?'

'Yes, in reality, the dowry is held by her family. It is a way of making sure the husband keeps to the alliance. As the wife reports back to her family, it means the husband cannot afford to offend or ill-treat her. As in a Bride Purchase marriage, he supposedly owns her but as she has leverage through her family, and is economically independent of him, the marriage is far more equal. Asking for her dowry is just a formality. She would not have done so without consulting her family first and they hold the money. They obviously feel that there is no longer any advantage in her being married to Quintus.'

'Poor Quintus,' said Bronwyn.

'Oh, I don't think so,' replied Rivalin. 'I don't think there was ever very much love between them.'

'Anyway,' said Brann, 'It is to our advantage. It will make Bronwyn's influence on him so much greater.'

Bronwyn reddened.

Miriam chuckled and said, 'Don't get any ideas, Brann. Without a true queen, no Briton will accept Bronwyn marrying Quintus. Besides, any such marriage would not be recognised by Rome, as Bronwyn is not a Roman citizen.'

'Still, could be useful,' mused Brann.

48

For the next two years, things settled down. With Quintus as governor, the old frictions between Britons and incomers eased, though there was no intermarriage. British marriage customs were not acceptable to anyone. Aquae Sulis became a bigger trading port and more Romans and Greeks settled there. But not only these, as people from all the trading nations, Germanic, Nordic, and North African, came through. Aquae Sulis was not as large a port as Londinium, but Londinium was being rebuilt after Boudicca's destruction, and taxes were high to help pay for the work there. The Fossa had become more of a road, and less of a ditch, making it easier to transport goods. Besides, Aquae Sulis had the goddess's healing waters.

Bronwyn and Quintus saw each other at least three times a week and often walked and talked together in the palace gardens. It was not unusual for messengers to turn up at the palace looking for Quintus, even when he wasn't there. Bronwyn and Quintus had started a discussion on the role of women, when a messenger came with an urgent message from the governor of Gaul. Quintus took the message and, when he opened it, found another message inside.

'This is from my replacement in Gaul. Mary asked that he forward the message inside to Miriam.'

'Ffion, could you fetch the queen please. Oh, probably a good idea if you got Rivalin as well,' Bronwyn called.

'Why Rivalin?'

'If it were not an urgent message, Mary would not have used a Roman courier. Add to that, the message inside is addressed in Hebrew. Mary normally writes in Latin, so she does not want the contents known. Hebrew speakers are rare in this part of the empire.'

Miriam and Rivalin arrived together, from spending time with the children. Bronwyn handed the letter to Miriam, who turned white.

'What has happened?' asked Quintus.

'Salome and her daughter are in Gaul. Mary has persuaded them to stay a couple of weeks, but their intention is then to go on to Camulodunum. Photina has set up in Carthage and Salome is going to open the market in Camulodunum and Londinium with contacts Demetrius had there.'

Quintus was puzzled.

Rivalin looked at Miriam, who nodded, and then Bronwyn, who did likewise.

'My great grandfather usurped the throne. Salome is the true queen, not just of here, but all of Albion. Even where she is not queen, she is seen as the goddess's representative and will be followed.'

'So, you need Roman help to keep your throne?'

'No, Miriam and I decided long ago that, if this happened, we would cede the throne and retire to an estate somewhere. I would only marry the queen if I had to, to keep the peace. Salome, however, is already married. Her husband is Hebrew. A lot of Britons will not accept a Hebrew as king. Then there is the question of her legitimacy. Unless we prepare the people, and they are assured of her bona fides, there will be many rulers who will not want to give up their power.

Britannia would be plunged back into the conflicts they had prior to the Roman invasion.'

'Another Boudicca,' said Quintus.

'No, Boudicca was never a legitimate queen in her own right. Someone far more powerful. Boudicca could only rely on the support of the Iceni and their client tribes. Salome would gain support from almost every tribe in Britannia. Both those under Roman jurisdiction and those not. Luckily, Miriam assures me that Salome will not want war.'

'You know Salome?'

'She was my nursemaid. Although I was nominally brought up by Tabitha, it was really Salome who mothered me. Her daughter is a bit younger than me and will be queen after her.'

'She has no sons?' questioned Quintus.

'You are blinded by Rome, Quintus, as I was saying earlier. Here the throne is passed from queen to queen. Usually, but not always, mother to daughter, depending on who has the mark of the true queen,' said Bronwyn.

'Can't it be hidden?'

'No. The mark of the true queen is the colour of their eyes, which are leaf-green. Besides, Salome has already unwittingly proclaimed her right. She has called her daughter Coventina, the secret British name of the goddess you call Sulis-Minerva. Our true queens are known as Coventina's Daughters.'

'Is there no way that you can maintain power, Rivalin?'

'Not that I can see currently but, whatever happens, we need to control it. We must go to Camulodunum and get to Salome before she is discovered to be the true queen.'

49

Miriam walked through the streets of newly-rebuilt Camulodunum, down towards the river and the wharfs. Her guide was the servant of their local host, Vitus, a friend of Quintus. She was dressed as a slave as, here, she was counted as Rivalin's slave. No one questioned her status or that she had two children by Rivalin. There was nothing unusual in that. Nor did they question her authority to deal with this new merchant on Rivalin's behalf. Slaves were often in trusted positions.

The streets were quiet in the early dawn. As a slave, she had a simple light shift on down to the knee and shivered a little in the cold spring breeze. The servant stopped when they came to the moorings and asked a lighterman which ship they needed. The man pointed and the servant negotiated the fee for a passage out. Miriam gave no indication that she understood their conversation. The river was calm, with mudflats at each bank, as the tide was out. They would get muddy feet reaching the lighter. The lighterman didn't question why they wanted to go out before the tide was in. He assumed that, with this being a new unknown merchant, they wanted to get a jump on the competition.

There was trepidation for Miriam as she walked, trying not to slip, which made it harder for her to keep her balance. She had no idea what she was going to say to Salome. How do you greet someone who probably thinks you are dead? The lighterman hailed the vessel and a sailor came to help Miriam aboard. As she was so deep in thought, she missed her step and the sailor had to catch her. She told the servant that he could go back and she would arrange an escort, if needed. As the lighter left, she turned to the sailor. She first tried Latin but to no avail, then Greek. She was more successful with this, though his Greek was faltering. On a whim, Miriam tried Aramaic. The man answered immediately and fluently, though heavily accented. Miriam smiled, she had guessed correctly, a Phoenician probably from Canaan.

A familiar voice called in Aramaic from under the shelter on deck.

'Who is that, Ashok?'

'The representative of a local merchant who wishes to speak to you. She appears to be a Hebrew slave. She says she will wait until you are ready.'

'Hebrew, you say?'

Miriam nodded.

'Yes, she is Hebrew.'

'She will be cold if she is dressed as Romans normally dress their slaves. Give her a blanket and heated wine. I will be out shortly.'

Ten minutes later, Salome emerged from the deck shelter, a wooden frame covered in cloth, to find Miriam and Ashok sat talking to each other, each with a blanket around their shoulders. Miriam looked around, at the sound of Salome's sharp intake of breath.

'Hello, Nanna Lomie,' as she switched to Hebrew.

Salome stood stock-still for so long that Miriam thought she would never move. Miriam arose and tentatively moved towards her. She stopped a couple of feet in front of her and held out her hand, shivering with anticipation.

'Hello, Nanna.'

Salome moved her hand out to take Miriam's hand, slowly, as if pushing against a sea of thick honey. Once she had touched Miriam's hand she held it lightly for a moment as if she had an apparition before her. Then her reserve broke and, grabbing her by the shoulders, she pulled Miriam to herself. The hug became almost desperate in its intensity and then lightened, and Miriam felt Salome's body shake as she sobbed. Miriam realised she was crying too. Eventually Salome let go.

'Coventina,' she called, 'it's Miriam!'

Coventina emerged, somewhat sleepy.

'Miriam?'

On seeing the young woman with her mother, though, the sleep was driven from her.

'Auntie Miriam,' she screamed, and ran to Miriam, almost knocking her over as she jumped up and wrapped her arms around her neck, thighs on Miriam's hips. She then dropped back down, embarrassed.

'Sorry, I was thinking I was a little girl again. We thought you were dead.'

'What happened, Miriam?' asked Salome.

'There will be plenty of time for that, but first we need to take you to safety.'

'Take me to safety, why?'

'You remember that when I was a child you told me that you always wanted to come to Albion? That there seemed to be a voice in your head urging you to come here. The voice of your grandmother, Coventina.'

'Yes, so?'

'You told me that your grandmother, Coventina, was a British princess?'

'Yes, but why should I be in danger from that? Surely it will make trade easier if I can claim local connection.'

'It puts you in danger because you are the rightful queen here. It is proclaimed by your eyes and, more so, by the fact that you called your daughter Coventina. There are many, particularly in this part of Albion, who would resent your claim to the throne. The Romans will be fearful because of Boudicca.'

'But the Romans crushed Boudicca.'

'That is what the Romans tell everyone, but it was a close-run thing. Also, Boudicca could only command the Iceni, you can command the whole of Albion. They would have you assassinated rather than risk you claiming the throne.'

'I have only come to trade, not to reclaim my royal rights.'

'You have no choice, now you are here. Some may already have realised who you are. We received word from Gaul that you were coming. There are enough Britons in Gaul for your coming to be heralded to others.'

'What do we have to do?'

'Sail down to the estuary on the next tide. We will be met there tomorrow. Oh, and we must use Coventina's Latin name, Tina. It might confuse people enough to make them hesitate.'

Salome had Pygmalion woken. He was surprised but gave the orders, as high tide was in half an hour. The ebbing tide would speed their passage downriver. The sailors were woken, and they started to prepare the ship.

Pygmalion turned to Miriam and asked, 'Are you coming with us, Your Majesty, or do I need to signal a boat to pick you up?'

'I am coming with you, Pygmalion.'

'Your Majesty?' gasped Tina.

'Meet Queen Miriam of the Dobunni. The most astute trader in Britannia,' said Pygmalion, laughing.

'Queen Miriam! But you are dressed as a slave. Why didn't you tell us? Auntie Miriam, what is going on? Where …'

Miriam put a hand up to stop Tina.

'Yes, I am Queen of the Dobunni. It is easier to go unnoticed dressed as a slave. No one notices slaves. They are just part of the furniture.'

Salome nodded, remembering her early years in Rome.

'Auntie Miriam?'

Pygmalion was puzzled.

'I am not really her aunt. I was orphaned as an infant and Salome brought me up. I then became Tina's honorary aunt to save confusion after she had come home crying when someone had told her she wasn't my sister.'

The following day, a strange ship came alongside. On board was Rivalin with the children and the faithful Eirwyn at the steering oar. The sea was calm, so the sailors tied the ships together. Miriam jumped across, went to the shelter on the ship, and came out ten minutes later dressed in silks, as Rivalin's queen.

She and Rivalin then stepped back across to Salome's ship, followed by their children. They bowed to Salome.

'I am Rivalin, King of the Dobunni. Welcome to Albion, Your Majesty.'

'What do we do now, Miriam?' asked Salome, in Hebrew.

'Shall we stay with Latin? Everyone here understands Latin. We will sail around the coast, bypassing Londinium, and go to Aquae Sulis where we will call a meeting of all the British chiefs to proclaim you as Queen. Within a month, you will be Queen of all Albion.'

'I shall come aboard your vessel then, for you to take me to Aquae Sulis.'

'That will not be possible,' said Rivalin. 'You must be seen to arrive on your own vessel. There must be no hint of coercion, or Dobunni control.'

'Will the tribes accept me?'

'We have thought of that one. The goddess will have laid the foundation so that every tribe will be expecting you. If you then confirm the current chief of each tribe as their king, it will be in their interests to confirm your right. As for me, I will relinquish my throne to you. Miriam and I wish to retire and live a quiet life.'

'How will the Romans react?'

'We are in contact with Rome via our ambassador and have taken the liberty of announcing that you want peace and no change of status for Britannia.'

Salome nodded.

50

As the ship approached the wharfs at Aquae Sulis, they were astonished to be greeted by a massive crowd. There were large retinues from every tribe in Albion, led by suspicious chiefs. They were outnumbered by more than 30,000 Dobunni warriors. It seemed that the goddess had, indeed, informed every tribe. One noticeable absence was that there were no non-Britons in the crowd.

Salome had the ship stand off the wharf in midstream. She looked to see Miriam and Rivalin, but could not, as they had already merged into the crowd. She spoke in Latin and, somehow, her voice came out booming across the water, so everyone heard her.

'I have not come to take anything, I come to give. In place of strife, I give peace. In place of hardship, I give prosperity. In place of division, I bring unity. The rule of the true queen is restored and with it the blessing of the goddess. But I do not take. I do, at this point, confirm all the chiefs of the tribes as the kings or queens of those tribes, subject only to me. There is only one power I remove. The power of the kings to make war, one on another. Henceforth, I will decide your disputes without recourse to arms. We shall have wealth and harmony, as in the time before the throne was usurped. What say you?'

Rivalin suddenly appeared out of the crowd and shouted, first in British and then in Latin, 'Hail Salome, True Queen of Albion.'

'Hail Salome, True Queen of Albion,' echoed the crowd in British, again and again.

It took a full five minutes for the crowd to stop chanting the proclamation, but the hubbub continued as Salome's ship docked. The crowd cheered, as Rivalin and the other chiefs, now kings, escorted Salome and Coventina past them to the palace. On seeing Coventina, there was much speculation in the crowd. Was the princess married? If not, who would she marry? Would Rivalin claim her?

On arrival at the palace, they found a grave-faced Quintus. He addressed Rivalin.

'Sorry to spoil the party, but such a large gathering has raised alarm. Regus has been ordered from Ardu to Corinium with his legions and he is to be joined by the legions from Camulodunum.'

'You are addressing the wrong person, Quintus,' Rivalin replied. 'Let me introduce you to the True Queen of Albion and Representative of the Goddess to the People, Salome.'

'Representative of the Goddess?'

'Yes, like the emperor, she is both ruler and Pontifex Maximus. Well, not quite like the emperor. More Pontifex Maximus, than ruler. Oh, but she does have the power to make war in the interests of all the tribes.'

Rivalin led Quintus forward to meet Salome, who was then seated on the throne.

'Your Majesty,' Quintus bowed his head.

'Quintus Perpetua, our governor, Your Majesty.'

'Welcome, Quintus. I hope we can have peace with Rome. It is in no one's interest to have war.'

'I am relieved to hear that. Unfortunately, such a large gathering of tribes, so soon after Boudicca's revolt, has raised concern. Regus has been ordered to bring his legions to Corinium from Ardu, along with those from Camulodunum.'

Salome looked at Rivalin.

'Regus? Corinium? Ardu?'

'Regus is the commander of the garrison at Ardu, strengthened with two legions of regulars since the revolt. Ardu is a garrison in the highlands, east of here. Corinium is north of here, up The Fossa.'

'The ditch?'

'Yes, Your Majesty. It is a boundary ditch marking the extent of Roman territory, but also now used as a road. Most of the Dobunni are outside Roman jurisdiction but we maintain a peace with Rome.'

'I see, and what does Rome want, Governor?'

Quintus hesitated, 'There is no easy way to say this. They demand immediate dispersal of the tribes and submission of the whole of the Dobunni to Roman rule.'

There was an angry murmur from all the kings.

'Rivalin?' asked Salome.

'Bronwyn, Miriam, what does the goddess say?'

'I will have to seek her guidance tonight,' said Miriam, 'as she speaks to me in dreams.'

'I can discern nothing clearly, Rivalin,' said Bronwyn.

'We will set the enthronement for tomorrow. You will have your answer after the ceremony, Quintus.'

Quintus bowed his head and left.

When he had gone, the chamber erupted with angry demands for war, to rid Britannia of the Romans once and for all. Salome raised her hand for silence.

'I will not make war without guidance from the goddess. We will wait until tomorrow for that decision. It would be imprudent not to prepare though. I understand that you are Dux Bellorum, Rivalin. What would you suggest?'

'It would be provocative for me to leave now, as Quintus knows my position. I will send Brann to gather the clans and surround Corinium. That will neutralise Regus's immediate threat. If the other tribes can do the same with Camulodunum, Londinium, Verulamium and any other major centre, then we will be ready. It would be wise to send messages to the tribes in Cambrai, to prepare them, in case we need their aid to prevent the return of the legions there.'

Salome nodded.

'Can you keep them out of sight? We don't want to accidentally provoke a war.'

Rivalin smiled and replied, 'Luckily, Albion is heavily wooded.'

'What about Ardu?'

'There will be no need for any force there, Your Majesty. The goddess will take care of Ardu.'

Salome dismissed the kings but signalled to Rivalin, Bronwyn, Miriam and Coventina to remain.

'Can we trust Quintus?'

'He is no fool. He knows that, if it comes to war, the Romans would be wiped out within a month. He also knows that, in that event, Rome would abandon Britannia. It would probably provoke a revolt in Gaul as well. Regus will do as ordered. He will try to avoid war but will not hesitate to fight if commanded to do so. He is a good man, as Romans go, but will do his duty.'

'Thank you, Rivalin. Bronwyn, what do you say? I have not been a successful merchant all these years without learning to read when someone is hiding something.'

'I think the goddess has told me what we must do, but I am not certain. I would rather not say until I am certain.'

'Miriam?'

'I have nothing. As I said, the angel talks to me in dreams. I will know nothing until morning.'

'Coventina? You went white as a sheet. I know I never believed your connection to the goddess before, but it seems I was wrong.'

'Again, I would like to be sure.'

'Alright, we will leave it at that until morning, but I need answers first thing. Rivalin, find Brann and send him on his way.'

Rivalin and Salome left. Miriam noticed that both Coventina and Bronwyn were crying. She took hold of them both and hugged them.

'What did the goddess tell you?'

Coventina answered first.

'The goddess wants peace, but the only way for that to happen is for Mother to abdicate and me to marry Rivalin. I am so sorry, Miriam.'

Miriam sighed and said, 'If that is what must be, but it will hurt you more than me, Coventina. You will not be able to marry Demetrius. Poor Salome. She has looked forward to this day all her life and she must lose it. Do you think she will comply?'

'She will want confirmation. As any merchant would do, she will want to know the demands of Rome first. Even then, I am not sure.'

Miriam looked at Bronwyn.

'I cannot say. I won't say. There must be some other way than has been revealed to me. I will beg the goddess for any other way, even if it means my death.'

No more could be got out of Bronwyn.

51

The following morning, Rivalin, Miriam, Bronwyn and Coventina were summoned to a council. Salome presided. 'Will you now tell me what the goddess has said? Coventina? Bronwyn?'

Miriam responded, 'The angel came to me in a dream last night. The instruction I have is two-fold. Firstly, that I crown you queen, as the goddess's representative. Then, we are to send a message to the emperor in Rome requesting Roman terms for peace in detail.'

Coventina went to speak but saw Miriam shake her head and stopped.

'How are we to send this message?'

'We are to make four copies, in Latin. We retain one. One is to be given to Quintus. The other two are to be sent by Quintus to Regus. One is for Regus himself; the other is to be sent to Rome by fast courier.'

'And the contents of the letter?'

'That you wish for peace and are prepared to bring the Dobunni under your rule, as a vassal of Rome. That you do not wish for warfare but will fight, even the might of Rome, should you have to. That a peaceful and prosperous Britannia is in everyone's interests, especially since Britannia is now supplying a significant proportion of Rome's grain, as well as copper and lead.'

'You built that trade up?'

'Yes, but only to improve the lives of our people. If it must be lost for the good of those people, I will destroy it myself. Even if it is just your command, I will destroy it.'

'How would you do that?'

'The same way I built it up. I control eighty per cent of the trade between the empire and Britannia. As queen, you control it now, I suppose. We can bankrupt any merchant who tries to go against us. Then we simply shut down all trade. We have not become dependent on Roman trade the way they have on British trade. We can live without anything the empire can supply. Rome, on the other hand, is now used to low grain prices, thanks to British competition to Egypt and Carthage. They had a big economic jolt with Boudicca's rebellion which would have unseated the emperor, had grain shipments not resumed from Britannia quickly after the crisis was over.'

'What is our main problem here?'

'Standing firm against Rome and letting them know that we mean business, without sounding belligerent,' Rivalin chipped in.

They spent the next three hours deciding on the wording of the dispatch to Rome. Even then, not everyone was satisfied. Some thought it too strong, some too weak, everyone had a bit they would like to change. In the end, Salome had to finish the meeting and go with what they had, which she ordered Rivalin to draw up personally in quadruplet.

When this had been done and checked, Salome sealed it. She was amused that they had a seal waiting, for the queen's use, for almost twenty years, despite there being no queen to use it. It showed a picture of the goddess, with water pouring out of a drinking vessel next to her.

Rivalin addressed the documents and kept them.

The whole council then waited until the appointed time for the enthronement of Salome. Whilst they waited, Rivalin, Bronwyn and Miriam made the preparations. As the current queen, Miriam had to proclaim Salome as the goddess's representative.

At the appointed time, Rivalin escorted Salome out to her waiting throne. The crowd was nowhere near as large as the previous day. There were only about 500 Dobunni warriors and all the chiefs had reduced retinues. Salome raised an eyebrow and asked Rivalin for the reason.

'We thought it judicious to reduce tension by reducing numbers, apparently complying with Roman demands. The Dobunni warriors are helping to surround Regus in Corinium. Each chief has also sent messengers back to ready their tribes and surround Roman centres in their area.'

'Won't it be noticed?'

'No. The Romans don't venture outside their cities for the most part. When they do, they travel along their roads or major rivers. We have ordered that those should appear normal, whilst movement is monitored. We will know about any Roman troop movements before Regus, even in Cambrai, Gaul or Alba.'

'Alba?'

'Farfetched, I know. But you never rule anything out in war.'

'Let's get on with it.'

Rivalin withdrew and signalled Miriam. Miriam came forward and addressed the crowd.

'The goddess has graciously made known to us the true queen of Albion. She is descended from Coventina, whose throne was usurped, through Tirzah, who was attested as queen by Doran. She has returned to take up her own and to re-establish the peace of the goddess. Let Albion once more be united under the true queen. Hail Salome, True Queen of Albion.'

Miriam crowned Salome with a wreath of ivy and knelt, holding out her hand.

'I submit to your will, my queen, as I submit to the will of the goddess.'

Salome rose and took Miriam's hand. She was very careful to repeat the words she had been taught in British, exactly.

'I submit to the will of the goddess and only her commands will I enforce to the service of her people.'

Rivalin and Bronwyn followed, bowing their heads with the same oath and same response, followed by all the kings of the tribes.

As the last king gave the oath, Salome saw Quintus in the crowd. She wondered how long he had been there.

52

Once the enthronement was over, they retired to the palace antechamber and invited Quintus to join them. He mingled easily. If he was worried at all, he did not show it. He gave all the kings the respect they were due, managing to put even the most anti-Roman of them in a cordial mood. After the kings started to leave, Salome indicated to Quintus to remain.

'Very diplomatically done, Quintus. I even had the king of the Iceni saying that, had you been Governor of Camulodunum a few years ago, there would have been no revolt.'

'Questionable.'

Salome tilted her head in query.

'A governor can only do what he is instructed unless it is standard procedure. The governor of Camulodunum followed standard procedure. I do not wish to, as I think that is not what will serve Rome best, but I will have to consult Rome to deviate.'

'I see.'

'Rivalin, Bronwyn, Miriam and Coventina, please join us. We anticipated your problem. Here is a dispatch for Rome which is in quadruplicate. We will keep a copy. There is a copy for yourself and another for Regus.'

'You don't trust us?'

'We don't want the situation to get out of hand because some parties get confused if they are out of the loop.'

Quintus nodded. He took the dispatch addressed to himself and put his finger under the flap by the seal, 'May I?'

Salome nodded.

Quintus, as was his wont, read the dispatch through carefully three times and then stood in silence.

'What do you think? What will be Rome's response?' asked Rivalin.

'It is dangerous to try and predict Rome's response to anything. These days, it depends more on which faction is in ascendancy with the emperor. I don't have any strong contacts in Rome anymore. Nor do I have an alliance marriage to draw on. Regus is better-positioned. His father is in the Senate. One of the more moderate, sensible senators.'

Quintus took the three scrolls and left.

Back at his house, Quintus sat thinking at his desk for a time. He then took a pen and wrote a note to Regus, explaining the situation in Aquae Sulis and sent it by military courier, along with two copies.

On receiving the dispatch, Regus frowned. He didn't know how disposed Rome was to compromise. Rome was not used to dealing with female rulers and had badly underestimated Boudicca. Still, he would try. There was one glimmer of hope, but it was only a glimmer.

He hastily copied the dispatch and Quintus's personal message to him, adding an addendum himself. He sent them to his father in Rome, under seal. Now, all they could do was wait.

Regus's father looked through the documents sent to him, in dismay. He knew the real situation in Rome. The former governor of Aquae Sulis had persuaded the emperor that the only way to deal with Salome was to crush her before she became too powerful. He would try. The fact that the king of the Dobunni had stayed out of the Boudiccan revolt and had loyally served Rome as temporary governor in Aquae Sulis, after the revolt was crushed, was a help. As was the fact that he was now Salome's chief advisor, seemingly. He took the dispatch to the emperor's chief minister, who read it and looked as if he had been handed a cobra. The minister paced up and down for a few minutes, then handed the dispatch back.

'I don't think that the emperor needs to be disturbed with this minor matter from a far-off province. The Senate can deal with it.'

Regus's father knew what that meant. If the affair blew up, and Rome lost its cheap British grain, the chief minister would want the emperor and, more particularly, himself as far removed as possible. Better to let the Senate take the blame.

The Senate was in session, drinking and arguing over some petty project to repair an aqueduct. It would cost more, feeding the senators as they argued, than would be saved on the project, as the result of their 'discussions'.

When Regus's father entered the chamber, there was immediate silence. He never came to the Senate for those debates, only if there was important business. He went to the Senate speaker, whispered in his ear and passed across a parchment. The speaker read it a couple of times and then stood.

'The emperor has passed an urgent matter to us for consideration.'

He then proceeded to read out the dispatch from Salome, before turning to Regus's father.

'Do you have any more information on this, Senator? I believe your son is the military commander on the ground.'

Regus's father related that the tribes had dispersed, as requested, and that Felix Britannicus was the chief advisor to the new queen and had shown himself as a loyal servant of Rome.

'What surety do we have that the bargain will be kept in Britannia? Who is this Felix Britannicus?' asked a voice.

Regus's father turned to see that the voice belonged to the former governor of Aquae Sulis, and his heart sank. It was the person who had insisted on the original belligerent demand that the tribes disperse, or Regus disperse them by force.

'Felix Britannicus is well known to you, Senator, under the name of Rivalin. I believe that he refused to sanction war against Rome, at the time of Boudicca, resulting in our legions only having to face two or three eastern tribes.'

'True. He was loyal to Rome, but these barbarians only understand force. However, the fact that they are suing for peace shows that they fear Rome and I am not unreasonable. This Salome is an unknown, she is too risky. Women should be under the regulation of men. So, I would suggest the following. It is in the true traditions of Rome, so can have no objection. That this Salome resign her throne in favour of her daughter, Coventina. That Coventina marry Felix Britannicus so that Rome is dealing with a reasonable man rather than an unstable woman. Further, that Bronwyn, who is also in the royal succession, be married to Quintus, the current governor of Aquae Sulis, by imperial order so that she, too, is brought under control. Finally, to show his true submission to Rome, Rivalin's slave-wife, Miriam, be submitted as a slave in Regus's camp for a night. Regus, being a student of tradition, will know what is required of him.'

Before Regus's father could speak, the Senate had shouted for the motion to be carried. They just wanted to get back to their drinking at the populace's expense. Regus's father stormed out. As he did so, he was intercepted by the former governor.

'You just want war. You want the death of Regus because he refused to divert troops to Aquae Sulis during the Boudiccan rebellion.'

'You underestimate me, Senator. I cannot lose this time, whether there is war or not. If there is war, Rome will win eventually but not before Regus and Quintus are wiped out, and then Rivalin and Miriam will be destroyed by Rome. If they accede to my demands, our demands I should say, then I will have my revenge on Rivalin and Miriam, and Quintus will be forced to marry Bronwyn, destroying any future career. I have no doubt that some Briton, probably Eirwyn, Miriam's bodyguard, will then dispose of your son for me. Most of all, the speaker has left it to you to relay the Senate's decision to Regus.'

Regus's father turned away in disgust. That was the man who had committed adultery with his brother's wife, on return to Rome. Her pregnancy led to him divorcing his wife and marrying his mistress. His wife had been sent back to her family, who had no use for an unmarried woman who could not have children. She was just a drain on the family's finances so they had sent her to the temple to be a prostitute.

Regus was worried when he received the Senate's orders. He was not at all sure that Rome could win this war, if war it was to be. Even if they did, the rise in grain prices would cause riots in Rome and could lead to civil war. His own life mattered little, he had always lived for Rome.

The orders had to come from him, he knew. With a heavy heart, he relayed the conditions for peace to Salome and Quintus, in Aquae Sulis.

On receipt of Regus's demands, Salome went into a rage.

'How dare he?'

'It is not Regus. He is just the messenger. I did try to warn you,' said Quintus.

'This will mean war.'

'No!' shouted Miriam. 'We cannot make war without the goddess's permission.'

'You know what this means for you, Miriam?'

'Yes, I know!'

'I won't allow it,' shouted Bronwyn and Rivalin, simultaneously.

'See, it is not just you Miriam, Bronwyn has to marry Quintus.'

'I will gladly marry Quintus. It is Miriam I am worried about.'

'If the goddess says we must accept these terms, then that is what we must do. You have always taught me that a queen's duty is first and foremost to her people, Mother. Miriam has shown us all the way, the way a true queen behaves.'

Coventina was crying.

'I am sorry, Coventina. I forgot that you would lose everything you wanted too. No matter what happens now, you will never be able to marry Demetrius.'

There was nothing more to be said so it was decided that the women would seek the will of the goddess that night. The following morning, Salome, Bronwyn and Rivalin could not be woken. The decision was left to Miriam and Coventina.

53

Whilst continued efforts were made to wake the sleepers, Miriam went for a walk in the early morning mist. Her heart was low. As she walked in the cold autumn morning she shivered, but not with cold. The dream the angel had given her could only be interpreted one way. As she stood by the Spring of the Goddess, she smelt the hot spa water as it emerged from the ground. Strangely, the sulphurous smell calmed her. If she stayed too long, though, she would fall asleep and die from the scalding water. Miriam so wanted to just stay there, where she felt safe. The streets of Aquae Sulis had changed over the years, though not by much. Rivalin's clan compound was just the same as it always had been, though some other clans had stone-built houses around enclosed quads now. Rivalin had insisted that his clan was done last as he didn't want to be accused of favouritism. Miriam secretly thought that Rivalin, having been brought up thoroughly Roman, just wanted to hang on to that vestige of his British heritage. The thought made her smile briefly in her troubles.

Things are changing, my love. They will never be the same again, no matter what happens now.

A screaming bird pulled her out of her reverie and she looked up northwards towards the sound. A flock of lapwings rose into the air as the screeching continued of a bird caught by a lynx or fox. The birds circled in the air then flew towards the full moon in the southwest and the safety of the goddess, migrating to a warmer clime. The message was obvious. The goddess was acting for the good of her people, forcing change. Though the fate of the lapwing, which had been caught, felt like an ill omen.

So, you are hearing my thoughts, Coventina. Confirming your desire for change but warning of the cost to me. One bird sacrificed for the good of the flock.

Miriam looked towards the moon and was surprised to see a hare silhouetted against its pale light. Hares were scarce, mostly ones that were descended from Roman imports. As Miriam watched, the hare disappeared but another appeared in the east, against the grey dawn, as if by magic. The new hare turned north and headed off. Perhaps the angel was going before her. A better omen.

Well, Coventina, are you going before me? It would be a comfort to have your strength. Are you going to Corinium, the special place? I desperately don't want to go but, if you are going to be there, it would be a comfort.

Miriam was met with a silence, as if the world held its breath, waiting for the goddess to answer. No answer came and the world resumed its hubbub, starting with the bubble of the spring. For the first time in her life, Miriam felt alone, cut off from the angel.

Whether Coventina is with me or not, I must go.

That decision elicited the merest echo of the feeling of a smile in Miriam's head.

So, you are still there.

'But I must now leave you for a time,' the goddess whispered in her head, *'What you now do I cannot influence. It must be your choice and yours alone.'*

Miriam wandered past the spa, back through the still-sleepy town to the palace. As she expected, they had failed to wake Salome, Bronwyn and Rivalin.

54

The goddess had spoken clearly to Miriam and Coventina. They were to meet the terms for peace. Regus' first request was for them to show good faith by Miriam spending the night in his camp as his slave.

Miriam and Coventina discussed the 'request' from Regus. They both knew that there was no alternative, the demand must be met.

Coventina called Brann to her, 'I have a special task for you.'

'Your majesty?'

'You are to escort the queen to the Roman camp at Corinium. There you are to leave her to enter the camp alone and then take command of the British force surrounding the camp. The force is to remain hidden. Miriam will be released by noon tomorrow. You are to escort her back here in honour whether she is returned living or dead. The Roman camp is not to be attacked under any circumstances unless they fail to return Miriam by the agreed time.'

'And if that happens?'

'You wipe out the camp to the last man, except for Regus. I have a special fate in mind for him if he is false.'

'May I ask a question, your majesty?'

Coventina inclined her head.

'Why are you sending me? Why not Eirwyn?'

'Eirwyn loves the queen too dearly. The queen needs to do this, even if it costs her life. Eirwyn would try to prevent her.'

Bran looked at Miriam in her queenly silks with a renewed respect.

A woollen cloak was provided for Miriam, and she sat on the platform of the royal chariot as Bran drove her up The Fossa. The two wheeled, wicker chariot was light and bounced on the uneven road. The ponies pulling the vehicle were milk white, their harness adorned in thin light golden tokens in the shape of swans. Not greys, Miriam mused, as she tried to keep her mind off what lay ahead. Two warriors on horseback accompanied them, their long red hair in ponytails streaming out behind them. They were only armed with swords, their spears strapped to the chariot along with their shields.

Soon Miriam ran out of distractions as mile merged into mile. She knew nothing of most of the journey as she tried to stop herself from quacking at the thought of what might happen to her. This journey held no novelty for her as it was the first part of her trading trips to Verulamium. Those had been in carts not on a chariot. She wished that she was in the slow cart now, not this swift chariot.

She was to be as a slave in the Roman camp until the following day at noon. That meant rape by Regus at the least, maybe by his officers as well. It was even known for Roman commanders to declare open season with a captured queen for any man in the camp. Whether she survived this night depended totally on Regus' will. She had thought of committing suicide but knew that Regus would simply demand that Bronwyn replace her.

Just before they reached Corinium, Brann stopped to allow Miriam to stand and smooth her ruffled dress. They then proceeded at a stately pace, leaving their escort behind with the other warriors surrounding Corinium. Brann glanced to his side as they entered the clearing surrounding the Roman camp. Miriam looked queenly indeed, upright, and defiant, without any sign of the fear Brann was sure she felt. His pride in his queen made him even more defiant.

At the entrance to the Roman camp, they were met by a centurion. It was little more than a wooden palisade on a bank surrounded by a ditch. Miriam alighted from the chariot. She took off the cloak, handing it to Brann, then followed the centurion. Inside the wooden picket there were large tents scattered around. A single wooden barracks building stood in the centre. It had the appearance of a new, makeshift fort. Miriam knew that it had been here for years, but it was usually only used as a waystation.

Miriam could smell the cooking pots and see the washed-out clothes hanging from tent ropes to dry. The men sat around laughing and joking. Miriam could hear accents from all over the empire. The women at the cooking pots were obviously slaves, mainly Iceni by the look of them. As first one, then more, became aware of her they stopped what they were doing. Their eyes followed her as she was led to Regus' tent.

Regus had thought about what he would do and given his orders accordingly. He had only had this duty once before and it had not gone well. He found it distasteful, but more than that, the woman had fought him, and he had had to use force, resulting in injury to the woman. He knew the necessity, to show to the errant ruler that everything he had ultimately belonged to the emperor to dispose of as he wished, even his wife and family. That didn't mean he had to like it. He would have refused to do it, but that would simply mean that he would lose honour and some other commander would be ordered to do it instead. He had considered getting one of his officers to do it, as he had known others to do, but then he could not control what happened and it had been known for too rough a treatment to result in a second revolt.

Regus became aware of the camp going silent, got up and opened the tent flap. The centurion was leading the woman to his tent. He was surprised, she was following the centurion unfettered and with seeming calm. He had ordered that she only be bound should she resist. Then he noticed a slight twitch on her face. So, she was afraid but was controlling her fear, like a seasoned warrior going into battle. His estimation of this queen rose with every step she took towards him.

The centurion left her at the tent and then departed. Regus looked at Miriam. She was certainly a beauty, this queen. She was reputedly intelligent and quick witted as well and spoke both Latin and Greek. This might be pleasanter than he had anticipated.

Miriam took in the tent on entering. There was a bed in one corner, a proper one she noticed. So, he had some consideration for her comfort. Near the entrance was a chair and a collapsible desk. On the desk lay the Roman's sword. Miriam was surprised. She noticed, however, that Regus stayed between her and the sword. She realised it was a test. He was trying to judge how much force he might need to use. In the centre of the tent there was a low table with couches at two ends.

Regus saw her survey the room. There was a slight extra twitch as she saw the bed. Her eyes lingered for a moment on his sword, but she made no move for it. Her expression changed but he noticed she registered surprise, not intent to try for it. Finally, her attention moved to the table and couches and then back to him. Regus indicated that she should take one of the couches, he took the other.

Regus clapped his hands and servants appeared with food and wine. The food was good and set in the centre of the table for them to help themselves. Regus took food first to show it was not poisoned and then took a drink of his wine. Miriam had seen both cups filled from the same flagon and given the choice as to which she chose. It would have made no difference to her whether they had poisoned it, but she appreciated the courtesy.

They ate in silence initially, then Regus asked, 'You are not from Britannia, I believe?'

'No, I am from Galilee.'

'Are you Greek, then? You have that look about you.'

'I am Hebrew.'

'Oh, Judean.'

'No, I am Naphtali.'

Regus thought for a moment. Naphtali? He had heard the name before, once many years ago, but couldn't recall when and under what circumstances. Of course, most Romans called all Hebrews, Judeans and most didn't know that there had been twelve tribes originally. He had come across the knowledge accidentally, but just couldn't remember when or how.

'You are a long way from home.'

'Yes and no. I am a long way from the land of my birth, but Britannia is my home now and these are my people. I am their queen; it is my duty to do what I can to protect them.'

'That is a trait that few rulers possess. Most are more interested in their own interests and their own skins. They expect their people to sacrifice themselves for them, not the other way round.'

'It is expected of a true queen of Albion.'

'Boudicca was not that way.'

'Boudicca was not a true queen. Salome and Coventina are true queens of Albion.'

'Yet like you they are not from here. They have not even lived here as you have.'

'They are descendants of the true queens and have the mark of the true queens. That they are not born here is irrelevant.'

'And you?'

'I was given sanctuary in time of need. I have been treated with kindness, respect, and love. I love these people. Especially, I love Bronwyn. She is like a sister to me. If I had not come, you would have demanded Bronwyn. I will not let that happen if I can prevent it.'

Again, Regus was thoughtful. He had never come across anyone like this queen before. Boudicca had committed suicide to prevent this happening to her. The commander who defeated her had ordered all the women of every major family in the revolt to be raped in revenge. It was an object lesson. Evading Roman humiliation led to more suffering.

Miriam realised that in her hunger following the journey she had not touched her wine. She took a sip and raised an eyebrow, 'Syrah?'

'Yes, my favourite.'

'Expensive to be given to a slave. Particularly a wine of this quality.'

'But not to a queen. You must be from a wealthy family to recognise it.'

'I only really drank it at my wedding.'

'Felix imported Syrah wine for your wedding!' Regus was incredulous.

'Not Felix, I doubt he knows what Syrah wine is. My first husband, in Galilee.'

'Your family must still have been wealthy, and if you have only drunk it once how do you know this is a good one?'

'My family were merchants, and were wealthy, yes. We traded in Syrah wine occasionally and so got to know the quality of the wines from a slight taste.'

'Ah, yes. The Trader Queen, who has made this part of Britannia so wealthy.'

They fell into silence again.

After the meats and fruit of the first course, they were served sweetmeats. Miriam was familiar with them and reached for her favourites; dried dates filled with a paste of ground almonds mixed with honey. As she did so she did not notice one of the servants switch her wine cup for a fresh one.

After a few sweetmeats, Regus drained his cup, signalling the end of the meal. He looked at Miriam, 'It would be a shame to waste such an excellent wine.'

Miriam smiled and drained her cup too.

Regus clapped his hands and a maid appeared, 'You know what to do.'

The maid bowed to Miriam and then led her from the tent.

55

The maid took Miriam to the opposite end of the camp and into a small tent, with only a chair. On the chair was the familiar Roman court dress, like the one she had worn the morning after her marriage to Rivalin. The maid removed Miriam's silk dress, putting it carefully on the chair as she substituted it for the Roman one. She put it over Miriam's head and did up the band under her breasts. As expected, there were no underclothes in sight. There were no ties on the dress either, so it opened from the band down her left side as soon as she moved.

The maid stood aside and opened the tent flap. Miriam took a deep breath and exited the tent, heading back towards Regus's tent. She was met with jeers, but they died down as they saw her dignified stride and how she made no attempt to hold onto the billowing dress. Miriam felt a support inside her and realised that she was being sustained by the angel.

If they want a show, let them have one.

Regus had opened the flap of his tent slightly when Miriam left with the maid, then sat at his desk and started some paperwork. From where he sat, he could see across to the tent where Miriam had been taken, which is why he had chosen to have her taken to that tent, to be prepared for him. He heard the jeers as Miriam emerged from the tent and looked up. He saw Miriam's queenly procession and heard the jeering stop.

Regus smiled. He was getting to like this queen. It was a pity that he was honour-bound to rape her.

Regus turned back to his wax tablets and feigned indifference when she entered. It would have taken a sharp eye to see that he was holding his sword in one hand. Without looking up, he said, 'You know what to do.'

Miriam moved to the bed, noticing the straps as she lay down, opened her skirts wide and then her legs. She realised that, despite his courtesy, Regus was prepared to tie her down and force her if she didn't comply.

A suitable gap later, to emphasise his nonchalance, Regus put down his tablet and looked in Miriam's direction. She seemed compliant but he knew of cases where this had resulted in the Roman being stabbed with a hidden knife when he got close enough. Regus was a careful man. It had served him well. Not many men survived over twenty years in the legions.

'Stand up.'

Miriam stood.

'Take the dress off.'

Regus watched as Miriam undid the band under her breasts, putting it over the couch by the table. She then pulled the dress bodice over her head and put the dress on the couch with the band. As she did so, Regus's eye caught the glint of metal. A pointed pendant was hanging around her neck on a chain. He was on his feet, sword in hand, moving towards Miriam before she had the dress on the couch. Not so compliant then. He would have the maid thrown to the men for this.

As he approached Miriam, she didn't flinch nor did she reach for the blade. Getting closer, he realised that it wasn't a knife but a broken pendant and one he recognised. He took the ornament in his free hand, wonderingly. He then dropped it, so it fell back onto Miriam's skin. Moving back to his desk, he picked up a blanket and threw it to Miriam.

'Cover yourself. Now sit on the bed.'

Regus hesitated, then asked, 'Where did you get that?'

'My husband gave it to me.'

'Felix?'

'No, my first husband, Jesus.'

Miriam noticed Regus physically jump.

'There was a preacher called Jesus from Galilee, a few years ago.'

'Before my time,' said Miriam. 'He was executed by Pilate, I believe.'

'He still has a lot of followers. Maybe someone would be named in his honour.'

Miriam tensed.

'Jesus, Yeshua in our language, is a common name. There was a hero of our people, long ago, called Yeshua. He took Jericho when our ancestors first came into the land. He is, to us, like Alexander is to the Greeks.'

Regus was silent for a while, lost in thought. He was brought back to reality by noticing Miriam swaying a little and having difficulty staying upright. The sleeping draft in her last cup of wine was taking effect.

'Lie down on your back and cover yourself with the blanket.'

Miriam complied. It was no surprise to Regus that she was instantly asleep. He did not move for a while. His plan had worked but he was reluctant to see it through. He stood up slowly and walked to the bed, dragged there unwillingly. He pulled the blanket down over Miriam's breasts and stared down, his eyes fixed on the pendant.

Regus was statue-still for some time but his mind was in turmoil. He had a conflict of honour. Something he had never conceived as possible, even an hour earlier. His rigid Roman upbringing had never prepared him for this. The honour code was set, you simply followed it. His family were old-fashioned in this. They saw it as the way to preserve Roman culture and hence Roman power. Tacit acceptance of adultery and divorce, for instance, were not for them. They saw it as weakening their society. Regus finally decided that he needed to work out which of his honour obligations was the greater. He pulled the blanket back up to Miriam's neck and returned to his desk. As he did so, Miriam stirred and turned on to her side, pulling the blanket tightly around her. Regus briefly smiled as he was reminded of his sister, but the smile died as the reminiscence added to his disquiet.

Regus forced the emotion down, determined to examine the problem dispassionately. The pendant. It was really a third of a pendant. He had picked up the pendant, after the Damascus riots, some twenty or so years before, when he had been a lowly centurion. It was in the shape of a fish with five Greek letters making up the body. Although he spoke Greek, he couldn't read it. He was later told it spelt *Ichthus,* fish in Greek. Made of silver, he assumed it must be for a child. He had kept the pendant for a long time, but had given it away some years ago.

That was when he had been charged with going from Damascus to Jerusalem, to collect taxes owed by the Jewish Temple there. Most commanders took a sizeable contingent with them for that task, usually a centurion along with their whole unit. Knowing how touchy the Jews were, Regus had decided to go in civilian clothes, with a minimal guard of just two seasoned centurions. With hindsight, it was reckless. His only aberration during his time in uniform. The minimum escort he should have taken was ten, whether in civilian clothes or not. At least that way, they could have made up their own merchant caravan.

Nothing happened on the way. On the return journey, they joined a caravan of merchants, with a wagon of supplies, as cover. Looking back, Regus realised that they must have stuck out like a sore thumb. No Roman merchants bought goods in Jerusalem, as it was too small and out of the way for them to bother with. The caravan was attacked by a group of a dozen brigands, Zealots it later emerged, who knew exactly what they were after. The caravan scattered, leaving Regus and his escort with their backs to the wagon, facing four opponents each. The Zealots were obviously untrained though as they all tried to attack at once, getting in each other's way. Still, the situation was desperate. Though trained soldiers and used to the rigours of battle, they would tire before the Zealots who were sensible to stay out of stabbing range until that happened. A commotion behind the attackers distracted them, just enough, to allow Regus and his escorts to each take out one of their attackers.

Three of the merchants had returned and were charging the attackers from the rear, although they were obviously not used to using swords. The Greek was alright, but Regus chuckled as he remembered the two Hebrews. The way they waved their weapons, they were more of a danger to themselves than anyone else. The Zealots were still in the majority and could easily have dealt with the merchants, but they weren't counting and panicked at the sudden onslaught, so they fled. Regus had thanked the merchants and given them the pendant as a token of his gratitude. The merchants courteously thanked him and then, laughingly, had broken the pendant in three to divide between them. Their names, he had ascertained, were Alexander, a Greek, and Jesus and Jairus, both Naphtali.

Regus thought about this. He had paid his debt of honour for the rescue. At the time it had seemed sufficient but now it felt like he had bought his honour cheaply, especially since he had found the pendant and not bought it. Then he thought of his duty to the empire, to rape Miriam. It was distasteful, but duty and honour were paramount to him. Normally, he would have regarded it as a necessary evil, but the pendant had rocked his previous certainties. He knew that, if another had presented the same situation to him, he would have advised them to do their duty. Try as he might though, he couldn't suppress the feeling that he owed Miriam's husband the duty to protect her.

Regus looked up as he heard Miriam cry out. She restlessly turned onto her side and the blanket fell to the floor as she did so. Suddenly her pale, Greek skin, turned white. Her dark black hair turned a fiery red and her eyes turned a light green.

Ska? Princess? You cannot be here. You are back in Scythia, my forbidden love.

Regus wept. Miriam turned onto her back once more and the spell was broken. She was Miriam again. She shivered in the cool of the night. Regus walked over to the bed, picked up the blanket, and covered her once more. She caught the blanket and wrapped it tightly around herself as she turned onto her side.

Regus returned to his chair to continue his thoughts, eventually falling asleep, still undecided.

56

Regus woke the following morning, stiff from having slept in his chair all night. Miriam was already awake, sitting up, still wrapped in the blanket and looking at him. Regus's eyes darted to his desk. His sword was still there. He stretched to get the stiffness out of his joints, then looked back at Miriam.

'You drugged me,' she said.

'Yes.'

'But you didn't take me?'

'No.'

'Why not?'

Regus didn't answer. Instead, he said, 'I still could.'

'It is your right.'

That simple statement shook him far more than defiance would have done. Regus knew it was dangerous to his purpose to make her a person to him but couldn't help himself asking, 'Tell me about yourself.'

'What do you want to know?'

'Tell me of your first husband, Jesus. He was a merchant, you say. Where did he trade? Did he have associates?'

'We traded in Judea, Samaria and Galilee mainly but would go to Damascus, on occasion. When I was expecting our daughter, and until she was weaned, I stayed home whilst he travelled. If we were trading locally in Galilee we went alone, if going to Damascus or Judea we went with two associates to cut down on the cartage costs.'

'Two other Hebrews?' he asked, hopefully.

'Another Hebrew, Jairus, and a Greek, Alexander.'

That stabbed Regus in the heart. There was no get-out. It was definitely the man who had saved his life.

'What happened to Jesus?'

Perhaps they were divorced, which in Regus's mind would give him a get-out. The tears in Miriam's eyes dispelled that hope before she even answered.

'After our daughter was weaned, we left her with my mother-in-law and went on a scouting trip to Alexandria. We took passage on a merchant's vessel from Caesarea. Our ship was captured by pirates out of Sinai. They killed Jesus and took me and sold me as a slave to Rivalin. Instead of making me his slave, he married me and has always treated me as his wife.'

Purchasing a wife was the most common form of marriage in Rome, so Regus thought nothing of it. It was not as if Miriam was a real slave. There would not be proper certification of this if she was sold by pirates. Under Roman law, it would be counted as paying a ransom, not a slave purchase.

The pirates, though, brought Regus's father to mind. He had been a member of the Senate for years. Regis remembered his rage, as he had been trying to get the Sinai pirates dealt with for years. It was their duty to protect, as they had promised in the Pax Romanus. He got the same response every time he raised the issue, 'Too expensive.' It wasn't until the pirates became bold and started preying on the trade between Alexandria and Ravenna, threatening food supplies to Rome itself, that the Senate would act. Again, the thought came into Regus's head unbidden. Roman honour is cheap.

'Where is your daughter now?'

'I have not been able to see her or contact her, since coming here. I heard the news that she was well, though, and living with my mother-in-law still, from Salome.'

'You keep referring to *your* mother-in-law. Is it usual for the husband's family to take care of children in the absence of the parents?'

'There is no one else. My father-in-law and my parents were killed in the Damascus riots when I was still a babe in arms. I was brought up by Tabitha, the woman who later became my mother-in-law. Salome was my nurse.'

Miriam saw his eyes drop and his face redden, the first sign of emotion that she had seen in him.

His mind was now decided. The Damascus commander had deliberately delayed deploying his men until the riot had blown itself out. Then, when he did send them out, his instructions were to tell the rioters to go home and only to act if attacked themselves. 'Not worth the Roman blood.' Regus had felt the shame at the time and still did, with the memory.

He clapped his hands and the maid from the previous evening appeared.

'Fetch the queen's dress.'

The maid looked surprised but left, to comply, without question. When the maid had left, Miriam raised her eyebrows at Regus.

'You asked me why I hadn't taken you last night. The reason was the pendant you wear. I wanted to check this morning, but I already knew.'

He pointed to her pendant.

'That is only one-third of the original. I gave it to three merchants who saved my life. They jokingly split it between them.'

'Jesus saved your life! How?'

'I was travelling with two men in Judea and was attacked by bandits. Your husband, along with Jairus and Alexander, charged them from the rear frantically waving their swords. I am surprised he didn't tell you.'

'He wouldn't have done. He was hopeless with a sword. I would have bent his ear for a month.'

'Yes, he was useless with a sword, but the surprise threw the bandits off balance, and they panicked and fled.'

'So, what now?'

'We dress you as a queen once more, share breakfast, and then you leave as I agreed you could, this morning. I have issued orders that you are to be unmolested as you go.'

'Thank you. It is a pity that we had to meet in such circumstances. I feel we might have been good friends otherwise.'

'We might yet be friends. For now, please accept my sincere apologies for the indignities I have put you through.'

The maid entered the tent just then, carrying Miriam's silk dress. Regus made sure that the tent flap was closed all the way and then told the maid to dress Miriam. He politely turned his back as she did so. A cough from Miriam gave him the signal that she was decent. Regus turned.

'I understand from my adjutant's wife that you are the best hair stylist in the camp. Please dress the queen's hair in a style suited to her rank.'

He indicated Miriam to sit in his chair by the desk, and the maid set to work. It was an intricate pattern she chose. Regus was fascinated. He had been in the room as a child when his mother's hair had been done but had never watched.

When the maid was finished, Regus noticed that Miriam quietly thanked her. This took him by surprise. One didn't thank servants. They were there to do your will, without fuss and without being seen, if possible. A smile crept across the maid's face, and she nodded her head in acknowledgement. Regus had heard that this queen was greatly loved by her people, and he understood why. Her willingness to sacrifice everything for them, along with her easy manner with them, made them devoted for life. Who would not die for such a queen?

'Have food brought for us. We cannot let the queen return to her people unfed.'

'Water this time, if you please. I have a journey back to Aquae Sulis to make.'

'Water for both of us,' said Regus.

The maid left.

57

Regus removed the Roman gown from the couch, where Miriam had put it the previous night, and tossed it to one side. He indicated the couch, 'Your Majesty.'

Miriam smiled, 'Thank you. Please call me Miriam. 'Your Majesty' is just for formal occasions.'

She elegantly laid herself on the couch.

Regus's heart skipped a beat and he realised that he had also fallen under the spell of this enchantress. He too would be prepared to sacrifice his life for her. He realised that he may have already sacrificed his career. Strangely, he felt a heavy weight lift from his shoulders as a result. He lay opposite her as servants came with food.

The conversation during the meal was easy and congenial. They talked of their families, finding that they had more in common than they had thought. It made Miriam see the man, not just the Roman commander. An honourable man who loved his family and would be devoted to his wife when he had one. In his way, he was also as dedicated to his people as she was. Regus saw the woman, but also the queen. Inwardly, he sighed with relief that she wasn't a man. Such a king would sweep all before him, a modern-day Alexander.

Regus reluctantly called for the centurion who escorted Miriam to his tent the previous day, and courteously held the tent flap aside as she left. He did not wait to watch as the centurion escorted her to the gate. Instead, he exited by a side gate and sprinted around the outside of the picket fence to join a unit he had ordered to be ready for him. He did not want a surprise attack from the Britons once their queen was released. He was handed a sword and shield and a javelin.

The gates opened and Miriam emerged. The warrior who had escorted her the previous day appeared, as if from nowhere, and came forward. He bowed his head, 'Your Majesty.'

'Time to go home, Brann.'

The man turned and led Miriam away. They had not gone twenty paces when Regus heard a shout.

'She is out of the camp now; she is fair game. Old Regus only ordered that she be allowed to leave the camp unmolested.'

A dozen legionaries started to run towards the two figures. A dozen British warriors seemed to spring up out of the ground and formed a shield in front of their queen. Regus shouted, 'Javelins, bring those men down,' and loosed his own.

The twelve renegade Romans fell, hit by British spears from one direction and Roman javelins from the other. Suddenly Romans filled the gate and sprang up around the camp fence ready for an attack. Then their mouths dropped open as British warriors appeared from all directions, 25000 of them at least. Regus realised that if they chose to attack, his command would not last the hour out. His life was totally in Miriam's hands.

Miriam shouted a command to the British.

'Hold firm, children of Dobun. We came in peace; we will leave in peace. Hold firm and ready. This is the goddess's place. She will avenge if vengeance is needed.'

It seemed to reverberate around like thunder. The British warriors stood alert but rested their spears and sheathed their swords. The sight was still one of menace.

Miriam turned to the Roman camp, switching to Latin, 'I came in peace and fulfilled your requirements of me for peace. You will keep the peace.'

Suddenly Miriam's brown eyes flashed bright green. She seemed to grow ten feet tall, dwarfing the huge warriors around her.

'You will keep the peace or face my wrath.'

She then diminished and walked into the ranks of Britons with her escort.

Regus chuckled, as Ska came to mind. The centurion next to him looked at Regus, wondering what he found funny.

'I thought earlier this morning that had she been a man then she would be a danger, a new Alexander. I was wrong. Forget Alexander. This queen is far more dangerous, as a woman, than Alexander ever was as a man.'

'I had never believed the tales of Amazons before,' replied the centurion, 'but they are always overcome by male heroes, anyway, aren't they?'

'You are Greek?' asked Regus.

The centurion nodded.

'One of the replacements following the Boudiccan revolt?'

'Yes sir.'

'Boudicca would have made you believe in Amazons, but she was not a patch on the real Amazons in Scythia. We Greeks and Romans simply don't want to believe that women could outdo us. It is a weakness. We were very nearly defeated by Boudicca. This queen is far more than an Amazon and infinitely more than Boudicca. She is not just a warrior queen; she has the love and devotion of her people. They know she would give her life for them. They would fight to the last drop of blood in their veins for her. All of them: men, women, and children. If I had not let her go this morning, or if I had let those men molest her, Roman rule in Britannia would have been over in under a month.'

Regus was silent, thoughtful for a moment, wondering how long Roman rule would have lasted if he had done his duty and taken Miriam. He forced his mind back to the present danger.

'Back into the fort and close the gates,' he shouted.

The two sides waited, facing each other in silence, for half an hour. The ranks of the British opened and a chariot emerged, with Brann driving and Miriam standing on the platform. She was dressed in British fashion, with a white dress down to just below her knees and a sword hanging from her belt, with a jewel-encrusted gold hilt. Over her shoulders, she wore a cloak of bear fur, trimmed with ermine. The cloak was held in place by a gold pin in the shape of intertwined snakes. Around her neck and wrists were heavy gold torques and her head was adorned with a royal circlet, her hair hanging free down to her shoulders. As she drew her sword and held it aloft, the morning sun broke through the clouds. The sudden light blinded Regus and, when his eyes adjusted, he saw what appeared to be an avenging goddess, with eyes flashing bright green.

'You will keep the peace.'

The figure waved her sword and then pointed away from the Roman camp towards The Fossa and the road to Aquae Sulis. The Britons behind her picked up their spears and advanced towards the road. Brann turned the chariot and followed. A sudden breeze caught Miriam's black hair and it streamed out behind her. Brann immediately saw the likeness to the mosaic of the goddess in the royal spa. The rest of the

British fell in behind, flowing around the Roman camp like a stream around a boulder.

As the Romans watched them go, the centurion next to Regus said wonderingly, 'If I had known she had such power, I would have treated her with more respect. No emperor has ever had such escort or honour.'

The centurion suddenly realised he had spoken treason. Regus smiled at him, 'Unofficially, I agree with you. Officially, I condemn your heinous words, but if you don't tell anyone, neither will I.'

Out of sight of the Romans, Miriam suddenly felt the weight of the sword in her hand and returned it to its scabbard.

'Brann, what happened?'

'You became the goddess. A rare thing. A unique occurrence. The only woman to have done so without having the mark of a true queen but, mark or no mark, you will be forever ranked as one of the great true queens.'

58

There was great rejoicing when Miriam returned to Aquae Sulis safely. The whole town turned out to greet her. The queen who had sacrificed herself for peace. Most of the British warriors had disappeared just before reaching the outskirts of the town, dispersed to hidden pre-organised camps to protect the city should the Romans unexpectedly attack.

On approach, Miriam once again felt the power of the angel inside her and drew her sword in triumph. Her honour guard walked proudly before her, to the side of the chariot, and followed behind. Eirwyn had met them about a mile outside the town. He and Brann stood at the front of the chariot, with Brann driving and Eirwyn, in his rightful place, as the queen's bodyguard. Their bronze armour glittered in the sun.

The crowd parted before them and, as they did so, Miriam felt the angel reassure her that she had done well. The crowd saw their queen seemingly grow, her eyes turn green, and her hair stream out in a non-existent breeze. Everyone, Roman and Briton alike, knelt before her. On reaching the palace, Miriam felt the power surge within her again before the angel departed. She diminished to Miriam and saw Salome, Coventina, Quintus, the whole court and her honour guard paying her homage.

Her sobs of relief at being safe, and seeing her friends safe, made them lift their eyes from the ground. Rivalin ran towards her and took her sword, which she was about to drop. He handed it to Eirwyn and swept her into his arms.

'I don't care what has happened, you will always be my beloved wife and queen.'

Miriam was suddenly weak and faint. Rivalin carried her to a couch in the palace and Quintus fetched a cup of wine for her.

'You do not need to speak about what has happened if you don't wish to,' said Coventina.

'But nothing did happen, well not in the way you mean.'

Miriam then told them of her stay in the Roman camp. She concluded with, 'I always thought this pendant strange. It never occurred to me that it was only a third of the original.'

Coventina said, 'I have seen the other two pieces. Alexander gave his piece to Rachel and Jairus, his, to Esther. You have the *iota* and *chi*, Esther the *theta* and Rachel the *upsilon* and *sigma*. Who would have thought it? Regus a closet Christian. Are you recovered enough, Miriam? You know what I must do now. We can delay it to give you time.'

Tears came into Miriam's eyes.

'All Rivalin and I ever dreamed of was settling down quietly as a family. Your marriage to him invalidates mine, not that mine was ever valid in the first place because I am a slave.'

Coventina's cheeks became moist in sympathy.

'I am sorry, Miriam, but there is no other way. You know that I would wish it otherwise. My heart has always belonged to Demetrius. The Romans think in terms of kings, not queens. The fact that Rivalin loses his authority to me when we marry, not the other way around, simply has not occurred to them.'

'It is not fair. It is not as if I have any authority anyway following Salome's return. The only reason I can marry Coventina is because Salome has sanctioned it,' said Rivalin.

Salome had turned on the waterworks as well.

'I only sanctioned it because it must be. It is part of the price we pay for the peace and well-being of our people. Like Miriam's sacrifice last night. If we want peace, we must satisfy Regus, and thus Rome, with our subservience.'

The three women hugged and then Bronwyn joined in. Quintus looked on. Each had made a huge sacrifice for their people. He felt especially sorry for Miriam. She had lost everything she held dear, yet was still willing to give. There was nothing he could do for them, much as he wanted to. Except for Bronwyn. There and then, he determined to be the most loving, caring husband he could be.

'Well, we had better get on with it,' said Miriam, taking a deep breath and breaking the huddle. 'No one wants it, except Rome, but Rome must have her way.'

Rivalin and Coventina dressed for the wedding. Miriam had been given dispensation not to attend, but it became apparent that she must. Ffion went to her.

'I need to get out of this get-up, Ffion, but I will not be going.'

'I understand your feelings, Miriam. It is hard for you, but unless you go the people will think you have withheld your blessing. That will cause conflict.'

'Why is my blessing important? You know that I am not, according to British custom, properly married to Rivalin.'

'The people don't know that. You have been a great queen and are greatly loved. Also, this morning showed that you have the blessing of the goddess. Coventina has the mark of the true queen but is unknown and they know what sacrifice you have made. Some will say that, mark or no mark, you are the true queen.'

'This will be a sacrifice for Coventina too.'

'I know, but we have to make sure the Romans don't find out about our subterfuge so that it is only known within the palace. All the people see is this stranger coming to claim the throne and displace the most loved queen in our history.'

Miriam was a little embarrassed but carried on, 'I think the Romans now have more than an inkling that they are not in charge of what is happening anymore.'

'What will they do?'

'That would worry me with most Roman commanders, but not Regus. He understands the subtleties of a show and the uselessness of excessive force. So long as he can point out to the emperor that we have satisfied all of Rome's demands, he will accept the fact that we are still in control behind the scenes. Only stupid Romans, like the former governor here, believe in absolute Roman power.'

Ffion brought out the clothes that Miriam was to wear. Miriam gasped. They were the same as she was wearing except, in place of the plain white tunic, there was a white tunic emblazoned with an embroidered dragon design. The fur cloak was replaced with a red woollen cloak edged with royal ermine and a dragonhead brooch to hold it together. Instead of the heavy torques, she was given lighter ones of intertwined dragons. For a crown, she had a gold circlet of intertwined ivy leaves.

'This is an outfit for a queen, not me.'

'They belonged to Rivalin's mother, except the tunic. Bronwyn will wear her mother's tunic, plus the matching cloak and regalia. Her mother's tunic has a swan embroidered on it in recognition of her descent from the 'True Queens' and hence the goddess. The dragon is the symbol of the Dobunni.'

'But I am not of your tribe.'

'We have done as Rivalin ordered. He wants you to know that you will always be part of our tribe and that you will always be a queen.'

'And how does the clan feel about this?'

'There would have been a revolt if he had not done so. We had already made the tunic and started on the embroidery before he gave the order.'

Ffion removed Miriam's travel-stained clothes and put them reverently to one side. She then brought a bowl of hot water and oils to wash Miriam with, drying her with a soft nettle cloth. She clothed her in the new tunic and finally the torques and crown.

'When do we go?' asked Miriam.

'They are only waiting for you to be ready.'

Ffion led the way to the door and onto the palace atrium. Rivalin was waiting, wearing the wedding kilt, with Bronwyn at his side. Her outfit was identical to Miriam's except, instead of the dragons in the jewellery, Bronwyn's had swans. She was standing to Rivalin's left, leaving the place of honour on Rivalin's right for Miriam. Miriam burst into tears. No one made any remark. They waited for her to compose herself and then Rivalin held out his hands to his two queens to proceed to the royal enclosure for the wedding.

A hushed crowd awaited them and respectfully parted to allow them passage. It was obviously going to be a more solemn and formal affair than Miriam's wedding to Rivalin. As the goddess's representative, Salome was to marry them. She had been frantically learning the words she needed. Not easy in a language she didn't speak. When they reached the front, Rivalin dropped his hands, allowing the two women to take thrones off to one side. He then moved to stand next to Coventina, on her left, and they joined hands. Salome stood and recited the words of marriage, word-perfect.

After the ceremony, there was a cheer from everyone gathered, as was obligatory, followed by silence. Miriam and Bronwyn went forward and knelt before Salome. Everyone who was gathered knelt too. In token of the change in power, they took their crowns off and gave them to Salome who put them on a cushion next to her. She then signalled for them to rise, which they did and returned to their seats. The crowd rose and waited expectantly for Salome's speech.

Salome had thought long and hard about her speech. She had decided to use Latin, not wanting to get the meaning wrong in translation. She started to speak.

People of Albion, I came to you as a stranger, but also as your queen. I came, not only to restore the throne to the rightful line but, to reconcile the people of Albion to their goddess. I came to bring peace, not war, and prosperity, not death and destruction. To maintain that peace, the goddess has decreed that I must leave this place and go into exile. I will leave the three queens, Coventina, my daughter, Miriam and Bronwyn as regents in my place.

There were murmurs in the crowd.

This is the price that the goddess has decreed for our peace, and I humbly pay that price. But mine is a small price. Bronwyn and Coventina have paid a greater price and Miriam the greatest price of all. Next to them, the cost to me is negligible.

There were nods of assent in the crowd.

But don't be dismayed, people of Albion. Had we wished, we could have swept the Romans from this land in under a month and they would have never dared return. We are not doing the will of Rome but the will of the goddess. Nero does not rule here, the queens of Albion rule here. No Roman force can take this land and no emperor can withstand the goddess. Against her, he is powerless. Should she choose, she could crush him underfoot as easily as an elephant crushes an ant. The queens of Albion will, once more, rule this land and we shall have peace. Stand proud, tribes of Albion, stand proud. We have the victory, bought not by arms and war, but by subtlety and sacrifice. We have the victory! We have the victory!

The crowd erupted.

We have the victory! We have the victory! We have the victory! Victory! Victory! Victory!

Salome looked down to see a confused Coventina and Rivalin, Miriam and Bronwyn stood with their jaws dropped to the floor.

'Coventina, why are they cheering like that? It was only a few pleasantries.'

'I have no idea, Mother. You were speaking their language.'

Salome panicked, 'Rivalin, what did I say?'

Rivalin shouted his reply over the continued roar of the crowd.

'You told them that, much as you didn't want to leave, the goddess had decreed that you must, for the sake of the peace and welfare of the land. In your stead, you have appointed the three queens, Coventina, Miriam and Bronwyn, to act as joint rulers. It was a lot more stirring than that but that is the gist.'

'Oh, what do I do now?'

'I have no idea. This has never happened before. I would suggest, though, that you give Miriam and Bronwyn their crowns back, to start with.'

Salome held her arms aloft for silence and the roar died to an excited whisper. She gestured to Miriam and Bronwyn to come forward and kneel before her again. She crowned each of them. The fact that she got the crowns the wrong way round so that Miriam's was slightly loose and Bronwyn's too tight, mattered not one iota to anyone. Making it up as she went along, Salome then signalled Coventina to join them and for all three to turn and face their people. Had they not been outside, the roof would have come off. The shout of '*Victory!*' once more echoed through Aquae Sulis.

The noise brought the Roman populace out to see what was happening and Quintus's guard as well. They arrived just as Salome was signalling for silence. Salome came forward, around the three queens, and stopped. Everyone expected more words. Instead, Salome turned, faced the queens, and knelt before them. Rivalin joined her and then the whole crowd, Briton and Roman alike.

'What now?' asked an uncomfortable Miriam.

'We process back to the palace,' said Bronwyn.

With that, she made an upward motion with her arms for everyone to rise and the three queens walked forward, Coventina in the centre, Miriam on her right and Bronwyn on her left. Rivalin was left to follow on behind and escort Salome. As the queens passed, everyone bowed including Quintus. The governor's guard hastily formed up and drew their swords, holding them aloft in salute.

Salome and Rivalin's progress was somewhat slower. Anyone who could get anywhere near, hugged and kissed them. That was until Rivalin managed to attract the attention of Eirwyn. It took the contingent of men ten minutes to reach Rivalin and Salome, and an hour to push their way through the crowd of well-wishers back to the palace.

'That seemed to go down well,' said Quintus, who had joined them. 'Now Rivalin is back in control, I am sure Rome will be satisfied. At least, once I am married to Bronwyn, and Salome has gone into exile.'

He was unexpectedly met with laughter. Rivalin carried on laughing longer than the rest.

'Quintus, I have just about enough authority to blow my nose if it is dripping,' said Rivalin. 'You have got rid of one queen, only for her to be replaced by three more. Bronwyn, Coventina and Miriam all outrank me now.'

'But you are the king.'

'Yes, but here, a true queen outranks a king and by making them her regents, Salome has given Coventina, Bronwyn and Miriam the powers of a true queen.'

There was a twinkle in Bronwyn's eye.

'Don't forget Quintus, that part of the deal is that you have to marry me. I am thus to be a hostage to Rome. However, with my new powers, I can have you executed on the slightest pretext.'

They all laughed.

59

Regus arrived with an escort of just one centurion the following day. This raised eyebrows. He explained to Coventina, during his private audience with her, that following Miriam's show the previous day, he realised they could wipe his command out anytime they chose. Better to waste one man than a whole army.

'Are Bronwyn and Quintus still planning to go through with the wedding?' he asked Coventina. 'I heard yesterday went off splendidly.'

'We gave our word,' she replied. 'It will happen. Besides, Bronwyn has been in love with Quintus since they met in Gaul. Being forced to marry him is the only way our people would have accepted the marriage. It has turned out rather well for them, really.'

'But not for you or Felix or Miriam.'

'Miriam always knew that if Salome and I returned that she would lose Rivalin. They hoped that I would choose someone else as my consort and they would be able to retire into private life. It is a pity my marriage to Rivalin invalidates hers.'

'That has been puzzling me. Why is that? Is it some strange British custom?'

'As you know, Miriam was brought here by pirates and sold to Rivalin as a slave. Under British law, you cannot marry a slave and Rivalin couldn't free her as he needed a pretext for marrying her to protect her. He had to be able to stay free to marry me, if required, as well. That was for political reasons to prevent a fracture within the people. Under Roman law, he is only allowed one wife, as the previous governor told him, so he had to keep Miriam as a slave under Roman law. Falling in love was not part of the plan.'

'So, he married her under British custom, whilst keeping her as a slave under Roman law?'

'Yes.'

'Is it permitted to have more than one wife in British custom?'

'Yes, but it is not usual for anyone but the king. The true queen is only allowed sexual relations with the king. This is because she is married to the people and is not a member of any clan. The king has a duty to his clan so takes a clan wife. Other men can take more than one wife, but that usually only occurs to protect clan women who have become widows.'

'You say that Felix is only allowed one wife under Roman law. Is he a Roman citizen?'

'No, why?'

'Is Miriam? Are you?'

'No, none of us are. Hopefully, you have brought Bronwyn's deed of citizenship so she can marry Quintus.'

'I have brought the deed. I had thought to make you all citizens but will give you the privilege of not being. A wedding gift if you like.'

Coventina was puzzled.

'Just one more question. Is there a deed of sale for Miriam?'

Coventina shook her head.

'Was there a declaration of slavery before the governor, or before a magistrate, or a deed of slavery witnessed by a notary?'

Coventina continued shaking her head.

'Alright, let's forget Roman law for the moment. Under British custom, if Miriam were not a slave, she would be Felix's clan wife, and he would be your consort.'

'Yes.'

'Then that is what is recognised by Rome. Miriam was never a slave. Her purchase from the pirates would be thought of as paying a ransom under Roman law, not the purchase of a slave. As none of you are Roman citizens, you are not constrained by Roman marriage law. As she was never a slave, she is Felix's clan wife legally.'

'But the previous governor ...'

'From what I know of the previous governor, he was a pompous ass who liked rubbing-in Roman superiority. I do have a further wedding present for you as well. Well, more for Felix than you. I will not be offended should you choose to reject it.'

Regus handed Coventina another scroll.

'This grants Roman citizenship to all of Felix's children.'

Coventina gasped.

'Why?'

'Officially, you have acceded to all Rome's demands and put yourself at the emperor's disposal, recognising the overwhelming power of Rome. We both know that is not the case. You have done what you needed to do anyway and made it look like you were grovelling to Rome. You could have crushed the legions in Britannia underfoot easily, but you chose peace. Miriam, in particular, was willing to sacrifice everything. I wish that there was a way I could compensate her more.'

'Well, there may be, at least in part.'

'Yes?'

Coventina explained and a smile came over Regus's face. He always enjoyed subtlety over force.

At that point, Miriam, Bronwyn, Salome, Rivalin and Quintus were admitted. They were followed by the Queen's (formerly King's) Council and the Roman officials from the town. Miriam was unexpectedly invited onto the dais to sit at Coventina's left, with Rivalin to her right. Miriam went to question this.

'Not now, Miriam. I will explain later. Actually, I will get Regus to explain. He has it straighter in his head than I do.'

Coventina rose and said, 'It is the will of the goddess that Bronwyn marries Quintus. Regus will officiate.'

Following the ceremony, whilst they were talking, Rivalin asked Regus, 'What is this I hear about Miriam not being a slave? Does that mean that my marriage to Coventina is invalid?'

Regus explained.

'So, I needn't have married Rivalin in the first place. I could just have left and gone back to Galilee,' said Miriam.

'Yes,' said Bronwyn, who had been listening from behind Miriam.

All eyes turned to her.

'I have a far greater connection to the goddess than I have ever let on. I have always hidden it because it would be a danger to Rivalin. When you were brought here, Miriam, I was told by the goddess that you were vital to the peace and well-being of our people. That, without you, we would be torn apart by internal strife. That is why I arranged for your purchase and your marriage to Rivalin. It was the only way I could think of to keep you here.

It has been a joy having you here. I was worried at first but saw your love grow for Rivalin and his for you. I knew that as soon as he got past his obsession with Sarah, he would realise what a pearl of a queen he already had. It was a joy to see your children born and how you ruled with such wisdom when Rivalin was away. I realised from the start that you had a strong connection to the goddess.'

Bronwyn stopped and burst into tears. Miriam went over to her and held her tight. Bronwyn wept on her shoulder for a time, then determinedly pulled away.

'I came to love you as a sister. When Salome and Coventina came, I saw the pivotal role you were playing and was proud. Without you, there would have been contention within our people. The love and respect our people held you in meant that when you sided with Salome and proclaimed her legitimacy, the people acted as one and supported her. It was you, being prepared to give up sole rights to Rivalin and let him marry Coventina, becoming her subordinate, that allowed us to placate Rome and avoid war. It was you, being prepared to go to Regus's camp and face humiliation, rape and possible death, that persuaded Rome of our sincerity.'

Bronwyn burst into tears again, but this time would not let anyone comfort her.

'I begged the goddess to let me go to the Roman camp in your stead, but she was insistent. It had to be you. I was going to disobey. The first and only time in my life I have been tempted to, but the goddess made me sleep until you were gone. Miriam, I am so sorry.'

Bronwyn sobbed and sobbed but, this time, she did allow Miriam to hold her. When her crying ceased, she drew away from Miriam and turned to Salome.

'I am not worthy to be your regent.'

'Yes, you are. I was totally intent on gaining my birthright as queen. You have sacrificed everything you ever wanted, and everything you ever loved, in obedience to the goddess and for the good of your people. You gave up your power as queen to Miriam, you guided her as you stayed in the background, you refused to marry so as not to undermine Rivalin and you also backed Miriam when she declared me the rightful queen. Yours has been the path of faithfulness and duty behind the scenes. Less spectacular, but no less vital, than Miriam's role. The goddess has chosen to reward you with the regency and with your marriage to the man you love. You deserve that honour and reward.'

Salome knelt to Bronwyn and everyone else, Briton and Roman alike, knelt too. There was silence when they rose, finally broken by Regus.

'I for one, thank the gods that you did not come in place of Miriam. It was only the sight of her pendant that reminded me where my true duty lay. That and a strange reluctance I had from the moment I stepped inside Corinium. My duty lay in serving Rome to the best of my ability, not in slavishly following the rules. I am sorry, Salome. I would wish otherwise, but you must go into exile. Coventina and I have also come to a compromise over Rome's insistence that we impose our gods over yours. The goddess's shrine in Ardu will remain hidden and inviolate from Romans. Here, at her healing waters, there will be a temple to her under her Roman name, 'Minerva-Sulis'.'

60

Eirwyn sailed the following day for Carthage, carrying Salome into exile. Officially, he was to remain there as a trading representative for the court in Aquae Sulis. His other main duties were as Salome's retainer and bodyguard. There were tears, no one knowing whether they would ever meet again. Regus and Quintus looked on in sympathy.

A few days later, an annexe in the spa baths was ready and converted into a temple for Minerva-Sulis. Miriam was shocked when she found out that she was required to dedicate the temple.

'I can't,' she said. 'I just can't. I worship Yahweh, you all know that.'

'Pray about it,' was Coventina's response.

'It will be fine, you will see,' was the response she got from Bronwyn.

She turned to Regus and said, 'Surely you understand that I can't do it, Regus. As a Christian, you must understand.'

'Me, a Christian? Whatever gave you that idea?'

'The pendant, the one you gave Alexander, Jairus and Jesus, is a Christian symbol. It is an acrostic in Greek and stands for Jesus Christ, God's son, Saviour.'

Regus went pale.

'I had absolutely no idea. I found it after the Damascus riots against the Christians years ago when your parents were killed. I wore it openly because I liked it, up until I gave it away to them. I even wore it to the emperor's palace.'

Everyone laughed.

That night Miriam prayed for guidance. The angel came to her, reassuring her that all would be well. The following morning, she still had her doubts but, buoyed by Coventina and Bronwyn, she went to the temple. Everything was prepared. A statue representation of the goddess was in place and incense was burning on the altar. Miriam was nervous as she stood behind the altar, Bronwyn to her left and Coventina to her right. The Roman citizens of Aquae Sulis entered the temple, laying their gifts for the goddess before Miriam. Finally, there came a sizeable gift from the emperor himself, in thanks for the conquest of Albion.

As the last gift was laid, Miriam surveyed the treasure before her. There were fine silks, jewels, gold, silver and costly perfumes. The Romans had certainly not stinted in their gifts. The last devotee returned to their place and an expectant hush fell on the congregation. Miriam was about to raise her arms when a sound like thunder deafened her. She saw fear on the faces of everyone in front of her and then they all fell to their knees and lay on their fronts, heads down, like whipped dogs.

Miriam turned, reluctantly, to see what had happened behind her. Out of the corner of her eye, she saw Coventina and Bronwyn do the same. There, standing amid the rubble of her statue, was the goddess angel, terrible in her splendour with her green eyes flashing like fire. The three women started to kneel, but a deafening voice roared from the goddess.

'Stand, my daughters. Stand, Coventina, my heir through many generations. Stand, Bronwyn, faithful servant of her people. Stand, Miriam, beloved adopted daughter as dear as flesh and blood could ever be. Stand, my daughters and face your new subjects.'

The women turned back to the congregation.

The goddess continued.

'Yahweh has heard your prayers and read your hearts, my daughters. He has granted my pleas. Bronwyn, you shall dwell in peace with your husband, and your family will defend this land. Great shall be their names through the ages, Arthur, Alfred and Aethelflaed and many more. Coventina, my namesake, your family will range as far and wide as you desire, seeking peace. They will come back from the Germanic lands between the seas and dwell in my holy place, forever seeking justice. Miriam, my dearest of daughters, I cannot give you all I would wish, but yours will be a great honour to come. In token of your coming glory, I give you all that has been laid here in tribute to me. This will be a dowry for you and an inheritance for your children, now that all the wealth you created belongs to the crown.'

Miriam gasped. The gathered people, who had gradually lifted their heads, cheered themselves hoarse. Miriam stood with tears in her eyes. The goddess raised her arms for silence.

Arms still raised, the goddess continued, 'I dedicate this temple to my master, Yahweh, in whose name I have ruled these people and who has allowed me, a lowly angel, to be as a goddess to them.'

A blinding light filled the temple. When they could see again, the angel had gone, leaving only the shattered remains of her statue to show she had ever been there. Regus and Quintus appeared from the back of the temple; Regus was in front of Quintus, who was carrying a golden crown on a silk cushion. When they reached the front of the temple, they bowed to Bronwyn, then Coventina and, finally, Miriam. Regus picked up the crown from the cushion and placed it on Miriam's head, before moving to one side and kneeling before her, with his head bowed. Quintus moved to the other side and did the same. Miriam saw everyone before her kneel as well.

'Bronwyn, Coventina, what do we do now?'

'We process out, of course,' they said in unison. 'We will hold your train.'

Knees knocking, Miriam walked from the temple, in as stately a manner as she could.

Later, in the palace grounds, Regus was beaming from ear to ear.

'Did that turn out as you hoped, Regus?' asked Coventina.

'Better. I thought we would have trouble persuading Miriam to take anything. The goddess's, sorry angel's, intervention meant she could not refuse. It is going to take me some time to get used to that term: *angel*. It is also going to take me time to come to terms with a real god, Yahweh. Before today, I had just regarded the gods as a means of maintaining Roman cohesion, though Miriam's performance at Corinium had already shaken that.'

'How will the emperor react to today's events?'

'The emperor will never know. Like everything else that has happened, he will be told what he wants to hear, that the temple has been dedicated. No one will dare tell him anything else. If anyone says anything else, it will be ascribed to the ravings of a madman. This is the first time in Roman history, that I know of, where Rome has paid tribute to a conquered people.'

Regus laughed.

'I am glad that is all over. Now we can get back to normality,' he said, after a pause, with a satisfied look on his face.

Bronwyn and Miriam overheard the remark and all three queens said in unison, 'Not quite. The angel has summonsed you to her at her holy place. Seems she hasn't quite finished with you yet.'

The blood left Regus's face so quickly that Miriam thought he would faint. She held out a hand to support him and felt him sway a little before he recovered.

'I have faced many armies and there is always fear before the battle. I have never wanted another battle, but never flinched from one either, but I would rather face my deadliest foe than that angel again.'

61

They did not leave for the angel's holy place immediately. It was three months before Coventina was ready to go. Miriam did not see much of Rivalin, Coventina or Bronwyn in the meantime. She was left to rule on her own. She understood. Bronwyn was in the first flush of a love marriage, like Miriam's to Jesus. Rivalin and Coventina may have had a political marriage but there was still the necessity of producing an heir to the throne. The next true queen.

Miriam was both jealous of, and pitying, Coventina. Coventina had Rivalin every night, out of necessity, and Miriam knew that he was a good lover whatever the reason. She pitied Coventina her lost love, Demetrius. It was not like Rivalin had been with Sarah, admiring from afar. Coventina and Demetrius had grown up together, like her and Jesus and Rachel and Alexander. She wondered what made her suddenly think of Alexander. It probably was just that he was Demetrius's younger brother, but she couldn't push away the foreboding.

She felt a sudden pang for her lost daughter. There had been discussion as to whether or not to contact Tabitha and let her know. They had decided not to. Miriam, her daughter, was happy where she was. Tabitha would not fit into British society and was too inflexible to change. Her granddaughter was the only relative she had left. They could not take that away from her, not after all she had done for them.

Coventina announced one morning that she was ready to go to the angel's holy place. She was pregnant and past the stage at which she was most likely to lose the child. Bronwyn was also pregnant and ready to go. Rivalin and Quintus were worried.

'We are not clay dolls,' said Coventina. 'We are not going to break just because we are pregnant and if we wait any longer then journeying will become uncomfortable.'

'But women in their second semester tend to get nauseous,' protested Rivalin.

'Good job that we will be travelling the traditional way, by boat,' replied Bronwyn. 'We can be sick over the side without the inconvenience of having to clear it up.'

'I insist on coming with you,' said Quintus.

'Me too,' echoed Rivalin.

'You can't, either of you. You know that,' said Miriam. 'Rivalin, you need to be in charge whilst Coventina, Bronwyn and I are away and Quintus, as Regus has been summoned, you need to stay behind as well.'

'How is Regus taking the visit now, Quintus?'

Quintus chuckled, 'I have never seen him so troubled, even when he has been in a tight spot in battle. He has always been so sure of himself, but you destroyed that certainty, Miriam. He finally found a situation where his Roman honour code couldn't give him the answer. Once that crack appeared he started questioning it more and more until the whole edifice came tumbling down. Then to be faced with a real goddess and to find out that there is one true god, Yahweh. That shook him. Worst of all, he has been summoned to her, and he is brooding over all the times he has laughed at or insulted, the gods. It is a good job, for his sake, that you are not delaying any longer.'

'Well,' said Coventina, 'the boat is ready and has been for a week. Let's get going now. Go and fetch Regus, Quintus.'

'It might take some time. He will use every excuse he can find to delay.'

'I will go,' said Miriam. 'He won't dare delay with a summons from me.'

Miriam left.

Coventina raised an eyebrow.

'Ever since Miriam became the goddess in front of the Roman camp at Corinium and, more especially, after the goddess appeared at the temple and made known that Miriam was her dear daughter, Regus has been scared stiff of her. If you don't move, they will be at the quayside before you.'

'But Miriam wouldn't hurt a fly. Even as a child, she only killed fish to eat, out of necessity. And she understands that Regus was only doing his duty.'

'Ah, yes,' said Rivalin, 'but she reckons the fear is useful for the time being. Makes conflict with the Romans less likely if they are not sure of their superiority.'

Coventina and Bronwyn signalled their maids, Rhian and Jenna, and left. Ffion followed behind. Miriam was indeed waiting, with a very unhappy Regus in tow. The women got into the boat. Regus opened his mouth to say something, but one look from Miriam stopped him and he hastily followed them onto the boat.

As they were going into the highlands, Regus was surprised that the boat was headed towards the sea. He didn't say anything but wondered why. When they had gone through the gorge, into the sea channel beyond, the boat turned away from the open sea to a new river mouth and they started upstream. Then something miraculous happened. The river started flowing upstream, away from the sea. Looking behind, Regus saw large waves approaching. They caught the boat and pushed it rapidly upstream. Had he been less apprehensive, he would have found the ride exhilarating. Unlike most Romans, he normally liked being in boats.

As they passed each settlement, he noticed the joyous reverence that the British gave their queens. More surprisingly, the Roman settlements did the same but there was fear in their eyes, especially when they caught sight of Miriam. That night, they stopped at a mixed settlement where they were treated royally. Regus asked the Romans why they were afraid of Miriam.

'Three months or so ago, there was a strange night. Quiet and close, as if the whole world was waiting for a storm to break. The wolves were howling and all sorts of beasts came close to the settlement. The dogs, instead of baying at the wolves, sat and watched us, as if ready to attack. The following morning, everything seemed to relax and the air cleared. Suddenly, a storm came out of nowhere, as if the heavens were rent in anger. That queen appeared as an apparition.'

The man pointed at Miriam and went silent.

Just when Regus thought he would get no more out of the man, he continued in a whisper so quiet that Regus had to strain to hear him.

'Her eyes flashed green in anger, and she grew to ten feet tall. A terrible avenging goddess, she seemed. Then she conjured over a thousand British warriors out of the ground, not in seeming, but in reality. They had the garrison, with only a centurion of the militia and his men, veterans all, surrounded. They didn't attack, they just stood there out of javelin range. The queen disappeared, but then reappeared as a warrior queen half an hour later. She looked just like Boudicca, but even more dreadful, and everyone quaked. She drew and raised her sword, and we braced for the attack, but she pointed her sword away. A flash of sunlight blinded us and, when we could see again, the warriors were no longer in sight. We could feel they were still out there but there was no open threat again. A week later, there was a joyous atmosphere and the warriors were gone.'

'The consecration of the temple. The goddess was making sure we stuck to our side of the agreement,' thought Regus.

The following day in the boat, Regus asked Bronwyn about it.

'Why don't you ask Miriam or Coventina? They laid the plans for it, not me,' Bronwyn teased him.

She saw his face drop and heard him mumble something about not bothering.

Bronwyn chuckled, 'Alright, I'll explain.'

Regus mumbled his thanks, suddenly feeling vulnerable again; something he was not used to.

'One of your Roman senators said that if you want peace you should prepare for war. So that is what they did. Boudicca's rebellion is still fresh in the minds of people here, and veterans who had fought with her were summoned. Add to that, we knew, from a Roman perspective, how close a call it had been and how you had defeated her.'

'Quintus?'

'No, not him. Anyway, we looked at Roman weaknesses and British weaknesses and concluded that, should we have to, we could push the legions out of Britain. We were not interested in getting rid of all Romans, just the legions. Our people would prosper, more connected to the empire, even if not a part of it.

So, we realised that the Roman weakness was the thin spread of the legions and their reliance on veterans for local defence. We knew a force would confront us at Aquae Sulis, we guessed probably encamped at Corinium. Other than that, the only large force, potentially within striking distance, would be the garrison by the forest where we are heading now. The garrison you led, to join with the legions, returned from Anglesey to defeat Boudicca.'

Regus relaxed as he was drawn in. He nodded, seeing the reasoning. They had read his strategy perfectly. Cut the rebellion off at the head had always been Roman tactics. He now realised how not varying a strategy played into your opponent's hands. It was a serious weakness, born out of the rigid Roman hierarchy and the harsh punishments for failure. He nodded and Bronwyn carried on.

'Boudicca had several weaknesses. She was not the true queen and did not have the support of the goddess. For that reason, she did not have the support of all the tribes, even those under Roman rule. We could call on all the tribes, even those in Alba and Cambrai. She also followed traditional British tactics of concentrating her forces and destroying the towns of her enemies. Once Camulodunum and Londinium were razed to the ground, she just left them and moved on. That meant the ports could be used again to reinforce Roman forces from Gaul. Finally, she overestimated her Berserkers. They are brilliant in a sudden shock attack or ambush but in a set battle or siege, where patient waiting is required, they are a liability. At the battle where she was defeated, the Roman commander simply waited until she could hold her Berserkers back no longer. And because she had concentrated her forces into a single army, one defeat was all it took.'

'I was there. Yes, I see your reasoning.'

Regus looked content for the first time in months. This was something within his grasp, that he could fathom, and it took his mind off the coming encounter.

'So, before proclaiming Salome queen, we set our plans. We made sure every Roman garrison was surrounded by hidden warriors. It meant that we couldn't take Camulodunum, Londinium or Verulamium but we didn't need to as we just needed to prevent you from getting reinforcements. After you were defeated, we could then pick them off at our leisure. You wouldn't get any reinforcements from Cambrai either because the tribes there would prevent it and it would take too long for you to assemble forces in Gaul and ship them over. Anyway, if you tried, you would have had a rebellion from Rivalin's cousin in Gaul to deal with.'

'What about the garrison by the forest?'

'Again, all we needed was to prevent it from being used for reinforcements, but we didn't bother with that. For a start, you had already moved most of the forces from there to Corinium. So, we just posted a few lookouts to monitor them. After all, the goddess would deal with them, if needed. You know her power now, so you know she could have.'

'But why did Miriam come to our camp then? There was no need.'

'Miriam would not cause harm to anyone if she could avoid it, whether that person was friend or foe. She went to your camp to avoid the necessity for war. A war in which some of her subjects would have been killed, true, but a war in which thousands of Romans would needlessly die. There would still be the necessity of coming to an agreement with Rome afterwards, whatever happened, and better a peaceful Rome, secure at being apparently in charge, than a belligerent Rome trying to regain its territory.'

Regus was silent, thinking. Bronwyn watched as he became first pensive, then he reddened, and then he cried. Something he hadn't done since he was a child.

'Will Miriam ever forgive me?'

'She forgave you long ago. She understood duty demanded you do what you did and accepted it for the sake of peace. The question is, will you ever forgive yourself?'

'I am not used to owing someone my life. I am not used to having a debt I can never fully repay. I am not used to someone sacrificing themself for me. I don't know whether I will ever be able to forgive myself.'

Regus sat in the boat and brooded. Towards the end of the day, he saw Miriam looking at him, with compassion in her eyes. He reddened, then burst into tears once more. Miriam was still there when his tears cleared, with concern on her face. Regus felt a change in himself, lifted his head and their eyes met. His heart was full of love for her. There was a queen he would willingly die for. He was hopelessly hers. Suddenly he understood Marcus Antonius.

Miriam came to him, kissed him lightly on the cheek, and whispered, 'It cannot be. I will always be Rivalin's even if I must share him with Coventina now.'

The tingle of that light kiss stayed on Regus's skin until he went to sleep that night. Strangely, he had sweet dreams for the first time since the dedication of the temple. The following day, he awoke without any fear. What did it matter what the goddess did to him now?

62

After the boat journey, they travelled along The Fossa for a time, with the women in a cart and Regus as a mounted escort. They then turned along a track for a few miles until they reached a large Roman fort on the edge of a forest. There the road ended. It had always puzzled Regus why the fort was there before he became its commander. There were no major settlements nearby. It wasn't even really on Roman territory. No roads crossed the woodland. All skirted it. It was central but, on The Fossa, a few miles to the southeast would have been more sensible. When he was commander, he thought it useless, only the Roman obsession with showing the superiority of their gods.

At the fort, he was told the now familiar reports of the appearance of the goddess, with one exception. No British warriors were seen, just enormous beasts emerging from the forest and roaming around the fort.

'It was bad enough seeing bears the size of a buffalo,' said the fort commander, 'but when we couldn't see them, only hear them, it was even worse.'

'Which way do we go to see the goddess?' asked Regus, hoping that the expected answer wouldn't come.

The fort commander looked at him in surprise and pointed to a gate opposite the one he had entered.

'That gate by the shrine. No Roman has ever gone that way and survived to tell the tale. We find their mauled bodies just outside the gate the following morning, but you know that. Even groups turn up dead, no matter how heavily armed. After the goddess appeared, three months ago, the only way I could keep the men here was to build that shrine to placate the goddess. Are you sure you want to go that way?'

'I know the reports from the commander before me. I am with the queens, the goddess's daughters. I am required to go. If I go to my death, then I go to my death, but go I must.'

'Leave your horse here, Regus. We walk from here. It is not far.'

Regus saw the fort commander pale, fall on his knees and shake with fear.

'The goddess,' he moaned.

Regus wasn't surprised when he turned to see Miriam.

'Alright, Your Majesty, let's get it over with.'

The camp troops had moved as far away from the road through the fort between the two gates as they could. Regus was forced to open the forest gate himself, pulling it behind him after Miriam, Bronwyn and Coventina had gone through. It was a pleasant walk by the stream which was a muddy red colour. Regus felt perfectly safe. Unusual for him. Woods were dangerous ground for Romans. You couldn't wield your shields well and every tree might hide an ambush. Roman battle formations didn't work well, as it was impossible to form a shield wall. Suddenly, he realised that he didn't have his sword, he had left it fixed to his horse's saddle. He felt naked without it.

'You don't need it here,' said a voice in his head. 'You are perfectly safe without it.'

Regus stopped and looked around to see who had spoken. He had a feeling it came from the small clear spring to one side but couldn't be sure. The women were almost out of sight, so Regus hastened through the dappled sunlight to catch up. The woodland suddenly grew dense, creating an impenetrable barrier to further progress. The women waded into the stream to get past. Regus followed them. Only a few feet further on, the river broadened into a large pool. To one side was a clearing with British huts. Steps allowed access from the pool to the village.

They were greeted courteously by the inhabitants, only three families, and shown to their quarters. Miriam, Bronwyn and Coventina to rooms behind the main meeting hall, Regus to a separate hut. There was no guard on his hut and Regus was free to roam around the village at will. There wasn't a great deal to see.

'Who are these people?' asked Regus, as they were served their evening meal.

'They are the goddess's attendants. Their sole duties are to look after people who come here seeking the goddess. At major festivals, they co-ordinate the events, with others doing the duties of cooking and feeding. This is as close as most people get to the goddess, but you will have the privilege of meeting her tomorrow.'

Regus slept uneasily that night and his soldier instinct was alert even whilst he slept. He heard nothing but the trickle of the stream, the beavers in the river and the breeze gently rustling leaves in the trees.

The following morning, he awoke late to find that Miriam, Bronwyn and Coventina had already breakfasted and that Coventina had left to see the goddess. Miriam joined him in drinking a strange, reviving hot brew. She told him it was made from acorns. Just then, Coventina returned and Bronwyn was taken to see the goddess.

'What happened?' asked Regus, like an eager schoolboy.

'Nothing really. She just reaffirmed what she had said at the temple but also reassured me that she would be there should I need her at any time.'

They were eating lunch when Bronwyn returned.

'There was not much to be said. I have my reward and honour,' she said, as she patted her stomach.

Then it was Miriam's turn. She returned just before dinner began. Regus reluctantly left his food behind.

'You look puzzled,' said Coventina.

'The goddess said that she had been allowed to bestow one extra gift on me. *The honour of Ruth* she called it. What could that mean?'

'Who is Ruth?' Bronwyn asked.

'Ruth was a woman from Hebrew history,' Coventina answered. 'She was not a Hebrew herself but married a Hebrew. When her father-in-law died, followed by her husband and brother-in-law, she returned to Judea with her mother-in-law to look after her, out of pity for her. There, she accepted marriage as a junior wife to a relative of her husband to secure her mother-in-law's future.'

'I see the parallel, but what is *the honour of Ruth*?' asked Miriam.

Regus did not return that night and he still hadn't returned when they started breakfast the following morning. They held lunch for him but gave up waiting. They had just finished, and Miriam was pouring a cup of acorn brew when she heard his familiar voice, 'Could I have a cup too?'

'There should be some food left over if you hurry. Before they feed it to the pigs.'

'The angel has kept me well-fed. I just need this brew and some sleep.'

Regus seemed more at ease than Miriam had ever seen him.

'Anything you would like to share?'

'It seems I am to get a soldier's reward. Another task, but one to my liking. I am going to be posted to Galilee. My job is to keep an eye on Tabitha and your daughter, plus a few other things.'

Try as she might, Miriam could get no more from him. It never occurred to either of them to question how the angel would arrange his reposting.

63

On return to Aquae Sulis, they were met by Quintus and, worryingly, by Eirwyn. Quintus was the first to give his news.

'Someone doesn't like you, Regus. Having given you the poison chalice here, they are now transferring you to Tiberius in Galilee.'

'That is fine, Quintus. I look forward to the challenge.'

Quintus's face dropped.

'That isn't a challenge, that is career suicide. The only worse posting is Judea.'

'It will be alright, Quintus, you'll see. And there are more important things than career advancement or are you regretting your marriage to Bronwyn?'

Bronwyn's face said he had better not be.

'Er, of course not.'

'Regus is playing with you, Quintus. The angel told him that he would be transferred to Galilee. He has been given a task, though he is being coy about what it is,' Miriam interjected.

'I told you, I am to keep an eye on Tabitha and your daughter Miriam, Miriam.'

Miriam frowned, 'Why do you keep doing that? You know it annoys me.'

'Not my fault that you Hebrews insist on calling your firstborn after their parents. If you must know, it involves getting married. Unfortunately, not to you, Miriam. Don't look at me like that, it is not my idea.'

'My daughter is still too young for you, Regus, if that is what is in your head.'

'It is not your daughter either. The angel says that Yahweh wants me to marry this person and who am I to disobey Him? This will be my last task. If I succeed, then I will go into peaceful retirement. If not, I will die a martyr.'

There was a stunned silence.

'That is enough of that. What are you doing here, Eirwyn?' asked Coventina.

Eirwyn presented her with a scroll. Coventina read it and her face went pale. Rivalin caught her to stop her from falling. He carried her to a couch. Coventina kept such a tight grip on the scroll that they couldn't prise it from her hand.

Rivalin looked at Eirwyn.

'Do you know what is contained in the scroll?'

'No, Your Majesty. The seal was unbroken. I just know that we were met in Carthage by Matthias, Salome's husband, who had bad news. They were tensely awaiting further news from Rome, for some reason. When the news came, Salome immediately wrote this message to Coventina and sent me here with it. Her hand was trembling as she wrote. I did see part of the message whilst she was writing but it was a script I didn't recognise, neither Greek nor Roman. I arrived, as you know, just after the queens left for the goddess's shrine. I do know that she sent a message to Sychar as well. Much briefer than this one.'

Coventina moaned, fainted, and dropped the scroll. Bronwyn knelt next to her and called Jenna and Rhian to help.

Rivalin picked up the scroll and looked at it. He passed it to Quintus, who passed it to Regus.

'I can't read it, but I recognise the script. It is Hebrew.'

Miriam held out her hand. Regus passed the scroll and Miriam read it.

'Poor Coventina, poor Rachel.'

She shook her head.

'What does it say?' demanded Rivalin.

'As you know, Coventina and Demetrius were betrothed. As the only way for us to achieve peace with Rome was for her to marry you, she had to give up her betrothal. The news they had from Rome, awaiting them when they arrived, was that Nero was persecuting Christians there and had ordered the garrison at Ravenna, under Demetrius, to go to Rome and help root out the Christians there.'

'Demetrius of Sychar?' exclaimed Regus.

'Yes, why?'

'He saved my life in the final battle against Boudicca. In fact, he won the battle for us. He told us about the Berserkers being on a drugged high so all we had to do was wait. When the Berserkers were released, we were hard-pressed to hold them until the drug wore off. Demetrius led a charge to relieve our position, just before we were about to be overwhelmed.'

'Demetrius refused because he is, or rather was, a Christian himself. They took Demetrius to Rome in chains and tried to make him renounce his faith. To try and force him, they had Photina, his mother, her two sisters and Alexander, Demetrius's brother, arrested in Carthage and taken to Rome as well. They lodged Photina with the emperor's daughter. She was so impressed by Photina that the emperor changed his focus onto her and had her thrown down a well. When that did not make her recant her faith, he had Demetrius and Alexander beheaded in front of her, then her sisters torn apart by wild horses. Finally, Photina was thrown back down the well and left until she died.'

Again, the phrase came into Regus's head, and this time he said it out loud, 'Roman honour comes cheaply. I wish I could have been there to save Demetrius as I owed him my life.'

Miriam put her hand to her breast.

'Not just Demetrius. His brother, Alexander of Sychar, was the third merchant, along with my first husband and Jairus, who saved your life in Judea. Rachel, his widow, has another third of your pendant. Now, all you men, out. Leave Coventina to us.'

Rivalin and Quintus knew to get going but Regus lingered.

'Is there nothing I can do?'

Miriam was just about to shout at him when she remembered that Regus had only known life in the legions and had never married.

'You need to prepare to go to Tiberius, Regus. You can do nothing for Coventina. Bronwyn and I will look after her with the help of our maids.'

Regus had never had much in the way of personal belongings. What fortune he had, rested with his father and he had always sent any share of bounty back there for safekeeping, living off his pay. He lived frugally, except for his occasional indulgence in Syrah wine. He only had a few bottles left of that, which he gave to Miriam.

'Parthia is close to Galilee, I will easily be able to get some more,' he said when Miriam objected.

On the morning he left, Miriam gave him a letter of introduction to Jairus in Capernaum and Rachel in Sychar. She also gave him her third of the pendant to prove that the letters were bona fide.

He then sailed with Eirwyn to Carthage.

64

Coventina didn't come out of her malaise until after her child was born, a son. Being Queen, she could have named him whatever she wished but asked Rivalin if she could call him Deedee, from the Hebrew. Rivalin agreed.

Once she slept again, with the baby in Miriam's arms, Rivalin asked why Coventina had chosen that name.

'It is what she called Demetrius when she was a child.'

Rivalin looked at Coventina with compassion.

'It is appropriate. In our language, it means *a beloved being*. Do you think she will ever be whole again?'

'Not entirely, but she will pour all the love she had for Demetrius into Deedee and that will help. I think she had some vague idea or remote hope that the child would be a girl and would be the new true queen, allowing her to leave her in our care, with us as regents. That, in her mind, meant she could go and live with Demetrius as his wife, in all but name. It would never have worked, of course. The Romans would not have allowed it, nor would our people. Demetrius's death seems the end of the world to her now, but she will be better in the long run without that hope.'

Rivalin was as disappointed as Coventina that the child was a boy. They needed a new true queen to prove to the people that they had the goddess's blessing. He was relieved as well though, as the child had brought Coventina out of her malaise.

Now, with Coventina and Bronwyn both nursing and settled, and their children six months old, he felt he could go back to Miriam's bed.

Miriam was relieved that Rivalin had come back, but apprehensive. She adored having him there, but she didn't want another child. When they celebrated Deedee's first birthday, Miriam had a problem. They needed a true queen, and it was coming up to the time when Rivalin should go back to Coventina's bed, but how could she tell Rivalin without seeming to reject him? In the end, Coventina solved her problem. They were sitting in the garden sewing whilst Rivalin played with the children.

'You really are a very good father, Rivalin, but we don't have a true queen yet.'

'Isn't it a bit early for that?' said Rivalin, hopefully.

'No.'

Rivalin tried to find an excuse not to, but couldn't.

'I will come back on the next full moon. That would be an auspicious occasion to do so.'

In his mind, Rivalin was thinking, 'We have only just passed the full moon. That gives me the best part of a month still with Miriam.'

Rivalin made love to Miriam every night for that period. She was surprised at his eagerness but pleased by his passion. He evidently didn't want to leave her for Coventina.

On their last night, Rivalin whispered to Miriam, 'I will be back just as soon as I can, but it will be a minimum of two months. I will miss every hour apart.'

Miriam smiled, 'So will I.'

Coventina was soon caught and it was under three months when they knew she was with child. Rivalin was delighted. He was a man who concentrated on one thing at a time so was disappointed to discover that Miriam was also pregnant.

'I am almost four months gone,' said Miriam. 'Must have been your eagerness pre-Coventina.'

She was then, promptly, sick.

'I don't understand this. I have never had morning sickness before.'

Rivalin worried for the next five months. He had never seen Miriam so pale. She was really having a hard time of it. Coventina and Bronwyn were worried too. Bronwyn was still nursing Sextus, Quintus's son. Although she could have another child, she wanted to nurse him until he was two. That was safer for the child and there wasn't any necessity for her to hurry, like Coventina.

To everyone's relief, Miriam was delivered safely. Another girl, Tara. Strangely, from the moment the child was born, Miriam seemed to regain her health. Coventina was delivered just over a month later. Also a girl, Nevanthi, who they hoped would be the new true queen. They would have to wait until her eyes changed from their baby blue to find out.

All attention was on Nevanthi for the next six months, but her eyes never changed. They stayed blue. Then one morning, they heard Miriam cry out. Worried because of her difficult pregnancy, the whole palace came running. By the time Rivalin got there, he found Miriam's room crowded with women. Bronwyn, Rhian, Coventina, Jenna, Miriam and Ffion were all cooing over Tara.

'Is there a problem with Miriam?' Rivalin shouted over the noise before noticing that everyone's attention was on Tara.

'No, not Tara!' he said, as he saw tears in Miriam's eyes.

Coventina lifted the child so he could see, 'Look!'

Rivalin was looking for a sign of injury or distress so earnestly that, at first, he didn't notice. Then he realised. Tara's eyes had turned a beautiful leaf-green. A new true queen had been born. Rivalin sank to his knees before his wives and daughter. The maids copied his action. Tara, the angel Coventina's new daughter.

Later, Rivalin, still marvelling, was talking to Miriam, Bronwyn, Coventina and Quintus in the garden whilst the maids looked after the children.

'Who would have thought it?' said Quintus.

'Actually, the angel told us, but we didn't realise what she was saying,' said Coventina.

'Yes. It is obvious looking back,' said Miriam

All eyes turned to her.

'Coventina was told that her children would wander free. Something she had longed to do. They wouldn't be able to do that as Queen. I was told that I would have *the honour of Ruth*. I thought that she was telling me that I had my reward. That I was, like Ruth, to be the foreigner who became the beloved junior wife. I was content. I forgot the real legacy of Ruth, that her descendants became the kings of Israel, starting with David. I was just thinking, in the usual way of things, that Coventina would be the mother of the next queen.'

'We all were. It has happened a couple of times before, but only when the true queen has died childless,' said Rivalin.

'How does this work out power-structure-wise?' asked Quintus, always the diplomat, always the political thinker.

'It doesn't change anything whilst Salome is still alive. The three of us are ruling equally as her regents. When Salome dies, Coventina becomes queen, but Miriam has equal status as the mother of the next queen. Actually, she has equal status now.'

There was a twinkle in Bronwyn's eye, as she said, 'You now have two senior wives to boss you around, Rivalin, and no junior wife that you can command.'

'What about Bronwyn?' asked Quintus, concerned for the status and feelings of his wife.

Rivalin smiled, 'Don't worry, Quintus. Bronwyn has got everything she ever wanted and more. A loving husband and a family. She will go down in the history of our people as a great queen, one of the three queens, Daughters of the Goddess, who sacrificed everything for their people.'

'Besides,' said Miriam, 'even when Salome dies, we will still need Bronwyn's wisdom and knowledge of British customs. Even if we didn't, she will always be a great queen in the hearts of her people.'

'Talking of customs, we have a problem,' said Bronwyn. 'Well, two problems really, but with a single solution.'

Everyone raised their eyebrows.

'Miriam is now the mother of a future true queen, but she is Queen of the Dobunni. She can't be both. In fact, by custom, she shouldn't be Queen now as she is not Dobunni, and not from a royal line. It has been tolerated because of her sacrifices for our people, and to keep the Romans happy that Rivalin is still King of the Dobunni.'

'And the other problem?' asked Rivalin, with trepidation.

'The next in line for the Dobunni throne is Jenna, as I can't be Queen, but she is not from our clan originally and her husband has died. If she marries outside the clan then Rivalin will no longer be King of the Dobunni.'

'I am not sure what we can do about that,' said Rivalin. 'It is her birth clan's right to decide which clan she marries into, as she doesn't have children.'

'I was just thinking,' said Bronwyn. 'We need to keep Rivalin occupied for the next two years, and we need him as King, to keep the Romans happy. There is no way, with the new queen having been born, that Miriam or Coventina are going to let him anywhere near their beds.'

'In my case, I am not letting him anywhere near my bed ever again. Period. Even if he is a great lover,' interjected Coventina.

Bronwyn suspected that Coventina might, eventually, soften on that but said nothing.

'So, I was thinking, we could use Rivalin in the role he plays best. Rescuing a maiden in distress. You know how Jenna dotes on him.'

Rivalin opened his mouth to protest but, before he could, Coventina put in, 'I suppose I could order the marriage. That would overrule Jenna's clan.'

Rivalin was speechless. He and Quintus were both shocked. Then they both burst out laughing, a slightly nervous titter at first, then a raucous laugh at the absurdity of the idea. When the women didn't join in, their laughter died.

Rivalin looked at the three women, 'You are kidding … aren't you?'

Part 3

Salome

65

When Salome arrived in Carthage, she was met by the Roman governor. He was all apologies and full of offers of help, *probably insincere*, but he had been instructed to make sure that Salome did not leave Carthage, by force if necessary. As a recompense for her enforced stay he would provide, at his own expense, a lady's maid.

So, we will also have a spy in the camp. Pity I can't travel. I so wanted to see more of the world, and another visit to the library in Alexandria would have been nice.

Salome went to the house they had rented in Carthage and found it empty. She was surprised but knew that Photina would have left some sort of message for her. In the end, the news came from a surprising source.

A week into their enforced stay, Salome's new maid, Nerilla, asked a strange question, 'Do you know Jacob, the Jew, from Rome?'

'Jacob is a common Jewish name. I know of a Jacob from Rome.'

'This one would now be in Carthage.'

'Then I don't know him. The one I knew is now living in Jerusalem if he is still alive. I haven't had any contact with him for over twenty years.'

Nerilla smiled, 'The one that sold you into slavery, you mean?'

That stopped Salome in her tracks.

'How do you know about that?'

'Photina told me. She is in Rome. Demetrius, her son, was ordered to Rome by the emperor.'

'What did Nero want of Demetrius?'

'There has been a great fire in Rome. He ordered Demetrius to Rome to round up Christians who were blamed for causing the fire. When Demetrius refused, he had him arrested and taken there. He had the whole family here arrested as well and taken to Rome. Photina is under house arrest, staying with the emperor's daughter.'

'Oh.'

Nerilla then drew a fish shape on the dust of the floor with her foot before quickly erasing it.

'How long are you to stay here, Nerilla?'

'I am permanent.'

'And you are to report back to the governor?'

'Only if I hear any news of you planning to leave Carthage. He is a lazy man and will do the minimum to comply with his orders.'

'You must be costing him.'

'Not at all. I was given to him as a slave when I was in my sixth year. I am surplus to requirements, so it is either here or he sells me. My father was a Christian martyr. They thought that they had caught me early enough to extinguish my faith. They felt it a better example to other Christians that the fate of their children was to be pagan rather than simply killing them. Hardly ever works but they still try. After all, who would convert to the faith of those who killed their parents?'

Salome then checked their warehouse. She discovered that everything was ready to be shipped out. Photina had left a list of the merchants that she had been dealing with, and when ships were expected to dock. The inventory of everything in the warehouse was detailed and accurate.

Oh well, I might as well take over. Nothing else for me to do, nowhere else for me to go.

'Nerilla?'

'Yes, Mistress.'

'Can you read?'

'No.'

'If I read out a list of names, would you know where I could find them?'

'Maybe.'

Salome started to read out the names of the merchants. Not only did Nerilla know every single one of them and where to find them, she knew all about their trading practices.

'That one is honest as the day is long. He shows you one thing and then tries to give you something else. This one has crooked measures. They are the best for Carthaginian metalwork and tools.'

When Nerilla had finished, Salome looked at Eirwyn, 'Did you get all that?'

'Most of it. I'll check with Nerilla before going to places. Perhaps I could take her with me.'

'Would be nice, but I think Nerilla had better stay with me.'

Eirwyn raised an eyebrow.

'The governor will feel less anxious if I am under Nerilla's watchful eye.'

Eirwyn chuckled, 'He has no idea of the deviousness of the people he is dealing with. We could have you halfway to Rome before he knew you had left Carthage, even with that goon who keeps following you.'

'I understand that one of your duties with Miriam was to distract the opposition during negotiations.'

'Only at first, until she developed her double act with Rivalin.'

'Oh, Miriam's double acts! She and Jesus could get their way any time anywhere with that double act. Is that how she got such a good deal on the spa in Aquae Sulis?'

'Yes. I am told that the governor's scribe was laughing for a week afterwards. Would have loved to have been there to witness it.'

'Well, you can take over those distraction duties again, in addition to being my bodyguard, but for now, you can do the dealing yourself.'

'What about you?'

'I am going to be occupied doing what I do best. I am going to educate Nerilla.'

Nerilla's jaw dropped, 'But I am only a slave, and I am not even your slave. Why would you do that?'

'It is not totally out of the goodness of my heart. You are going to be with me a long time and I don't need a maid. I have never had one before. So, this way, I get some work out of you whilst you are here.'

'So, what are you going to teach me?'

'We'll start with teaching you proper skills for a lady's maid and how to read and write. Your Latin is good, but you could do with learning Greek as well. That way, you can earn money outside of the house and perhaps, one day, buy your freedom.'

'How can I ever repay you?'

'Oh, well you could teach me Carthaginian Aramaic. It differs from the dialect spoken in Canaan.'

Eirwyn smiled. Salome had gotten Nerilla's devotion just as quickly as Miriam had gotten his. Within a month, Salome could take an unauthorised trip to Britannia and back, and the governor would be none the wiser, even if she took Nerilla with her.

A few days later, Matthias arrived from Galilee, exactly the day Photina had predicted. He was somewhat confused to find Salome there on her own.

'But where are Photina and her sisters and Alexander? And where is Tira?'

'Photina and party are in Rome. Coventina is in Britannia. I think you had better sit down whilst I tell you what has happened. By the way, meet Eirwyn, my bodyguard.'

When Salome had finished, Matthias looked non-plussed.

'Let me see if I have this straight. Demetrius, Alexander, Photina and her sisters are under house arrest in Rome for being Christians. You say Photina is staying with the emperor's daughter?'

'Yes.'

'Eirwyn here is from Britannia and is your royal bodyguard. You are Queen of Albion, but that is just the Greek name for Britannia. The Romans have exiled you here because they are worried about having another British queen to deal with, after Boudicca. As part of the same deal, Tira has married the king of the Dobunni, whoever they are, so that the Romans have her under their control. In addition to that, Miriam has come back from the dead and turned up as this same king's first wife. If I didn't know that you wouldn't, I would think that you were kidding me.'

'Well at least you don't have to worry about Coventina marrying Demetrius,' Salome laughed.

'What is this about Tina?' a familiar voice chipped in.

Salome looked around at the person who had just entered the warehouse.

'Pygmalion, how lovely to see you.'

'You had better tell him, Salome. I haven't got it straight yet.'

'Before that, would Your Majesty tell me why you are here? I was expecting you to stay in Britannia permanently.'

Matthias groaned, 'Does everyone know but me?'

'Change of plan, Pygmalion. Before I go through that again, I had better answer Matthias's other question. Britannia is made up of three areas. Cambrai, Alba and an unnamed area, referred to loosely as Britannia but which the Britons don't have a name for as each part is just named after the local tribe. You know, like Judea is named after the tribe of Judah. Since this is confusing for everyone, the unnamed area is usually referred to as Albion.'

Salome then went through her story again for Pygmalion's benefit. After she had finished, Matthias said, 'I still don't quite get it, but it will come to me in the end, I suppose. I need some sleep. I never sleep well on ships, as you know.'

He turned to go.

'Oh, just a minute, I thought you might like these.'

He handed Salome two large scrolls that he had been holding since he entered the room. Salome opened each scroll in turn, just a little.

'Plato and Aesop. How lovely,' said Salome.

66

Two months after her arrival in Carthage news arrived from Rome. Photina and all the family had been killed by Nero.

'Are you sure, Nerilla?' Salome asked.

'The news comes directly from Junia. She would not send it out unless she was sure. It says that she has sent word to Rachel in Sychar as well.'

'I will send news to Aquae Sulis with Eirwyn. I don't really need a bodyguard with the governor having armed men shadow us all day every day.'

Eirwyn arrived back a month later unexpectedly with Regus in tow. Regus called on Salome before going anywhere else. He seemed a little shy but asked if he could discuss something with her.

'Whatever is it, Regus?'

'Well, I have been posted to Tiberius in Galilee.'

'You need passage?'

'No, well yes, but that is not what I have come about.'

'I have been sent by the goddess er… angel to keep the peace in Galilee. Apparently, Judea is about to explode. I have a second task to protect Tabitha and her granddaughter Miriam.'

'So, you need, what?'

'I have a letter of introduction from Miriam in Aquae Sulis to Jairus and another to Rachel in Sychar, but I may need some independent advice when I am there,' said Regus.

'And you think that Miriam is too far away in Britannia.'

'No, not that. The angel specifically told me I was not to maintain contact with Miriam.'

'Ah, so you want advice from me. Well, my first bit of advice is that you take advice from Jairus and Rachel first. Only consult me if it is something that you can't discuss with them. Your first problem, though, is that you will still be viewed with suspicion even with Miriam's letter. Miriam is so strongly believed to be dead you might even be suspected of killing her. If I send Matthias with you, he can vouch for you on my behalf. Besides, we trade with Galilee a lot and Matthias travelling there will cause no comment. You taking passage on a merchantman to get to your new posting will also seem natural.'

'There is one thing I would like to ask now though.'

'Yes?'

'The goddess has told me that I must draw the sign of the fish in the dirt when I meet Jairus and Rachel,' Regus hesitated.

'Well after that I am to say, 'The bridegroom comes.' They will respond, 'His bride awaits."

'And?'

'Well, how will they react to the bridegroom being a Roman garrison commander? And I am not sure how I feel about marriage either.'

'If it is God's will, then it is God's will. Why are you worried about marriage? Are you married already?'

'No. I wanted to marry a Scythian woman, but she was a king's daughter, and we were not allowed. Then there is…' Regus stopped and his face coloured.

'You are in love with Miriam?'

Regus nodded.

'That, you must know, is an equally hopeless case.'

Regus nodded again.

'My advice is to just find out what is actually on offer, if anything, and then decide what to do.'

'Just remembered,' said Regus, 'Miriam gave me this letter for you. I am staying at the governor's house.'

Regus turned to leave.

'Hold on, Regus. Just let me read Miriam's letter before you go.'

A smile came on Salome's face.

'It looks like Miriam anticipated you,' said Salome, 'She has suggested that you keep in contact with me when you are in Galilee. I will pass any relevant news on to her. She will send news from Britannia. Anything relevant I will pass on to you. One thing she has asked me to emphasize to you is that neither Tabitha nor her daughter are to know that she is still alive and living in Britannia.'

So, I will not be on the periphery after all, but in the centre of things.

Matthias and Regus set sail with Pygmalion for Caesarea two weeks later.

67

When Salome received Regus's first letter from Tiberius, to her surprise, it was in Hebrew. There was a short introductory message in Latin in his hand. In the introduction, Regus said that Jairus had suggested that they communicate in Hebrew, as that was likely to be more secure. As such, all the messages would be written by his wife, Joanna.

When Salome read the main letter, she almost fell off her chair laughing. In it, Regus detailed his meeting with Jairus and Rachel. Apparently, the business about the bridegroom was a passphrase. However, as Regus needed a foot in both the Greek and Hebrew camps, they suggested that he marry Joanna. She was the daughter of a Greek, who had married Petronilla, Apostle Peter's daughter. Regus had bought her, Roman fashion, as his wife. In return, he had promised to release her after the crisis was over, with a dowry so she could re-marry.

The problem was that Regus didn't want to presume on Joanna and people were beginning to wonder whether the marriage was a sham. What should he do?

Salome's reply was characteristically terse.

What on earth made you get Joanna to write this letter when the obvious person to ask is Joanna herself? She is half-Hebrew and half-Greek. Though both Hebrew and Greek women know what is expected of a wife, the Greeks have no choice, and the Hebrews know their duty. In short, sleep with her, you idiot.

Salome then added underneath, in Latin: *Sleep with her, you idiot.*

About a year after that, news came to Salome of the Judean revolt. Apparently, Regus, through Joanna and Jairus, had managed to stop the rebellion from spreading to Galilee. There was then no significant news from Galilee if you discounted Joanna's second pregnancy. Obviously, Regus had taken her advice.

About three years after the rebellion, Salome started to think that perhaps what the angel, Coventina, had intended had already been achieved. She received a letter from Galilee, which she almost put aside to read later but stopped when she saw that it was not Regus's seal. Her curiosity was piqued, and she opened the letter immediately.

Regus knows nothing of this letter. He is caught in limbo by conflicting duties. We have learnt that Titus, the son of the new emperor, Vespasian, intends to carry out his father's plan to convert the temple in Jerusalem into a temple to Zeus. Regus feels that he cannot betray Rome by thwarting this and cannot let it happen either. If Titus succeeds, it will cause a rising of Jews from all over the empire. This would be disastrous, both for Rome and the Jews, and we could not keep the peace in Galilee as the angel intended.

We believe that Titus will prevail. He is a competent general and, now that the empire is in the hands of a competent emperor, Rome's internal strife will end. Add to that, the Zealots' insistence on not keeping a standing army and Roman victory seems inevitable. That leaves the problem of what to do to prevent a catastrophe. There is only one solution. We must make sure that the temple does not survive the Roman capture of Jerusalem.

We cannot use anyone from Galilee to destroy the temple, Greek, Roman or Hebrew, as that would shatter the delicate balance of peace we have, so I am asking if you could provide any assistance. We would need about a dozen men who would fit in without too much comment. Seasoned warriors who speak fluent Latin and Greek. The mission will be dangerous, perhaps suicidal, so I would understand if you feel that you cannot help.

Salome thought about it for some time. It wasn't Albion's fight but, if the worst happened and Titus succeeded, it would affect the whole empire, Britannia included. A weakened Rome would be seized upon by hotheads in Britannia to rebel. Her own sacrifice and that of Miriam, Coventina and Bronwyn would be in vain. Salome made a decision and called Eirwyn. She read out Joanna's letter to him, simultaneously translating it into Latin for his benefit. She heard Nerilla gasp in the background. Salome was so used to her always being there that she had forgotten about her presence. She turned and looked at her.

'I will say nothing,' Nerilla said. 'The stupid governor here would pass the information on, just to get kudos and promotion, without realising the wider implications, even though Joanna has been explicit as to what they are.'

She went to leave.

'Stay, Nerilla,' said Salome. 'You are Roman. Although brought up in Rome, I am not. You can give a much better Roman perspective on this than I can. For a start, what would be the main Roman view of this situation.'

'They will look on the conversion of the temple to the worship of Zeus as proving that the Roman gods are more powerful than Yahweh. It will be a necessity to do it, should they take the temple. If Titus didn't do it then the populace would call him a traitor, even though most don't believe in the gods anyway. They are arrogant enough to believe that they can easily contain any resulting rebellion.'

'Thank you, Nerilla, that is what I thought. It is my view, Eirwyn, that if the Jews all over the empire rebel, then others will follow. I think it likely that Gaul will follow very quickly and then it will be impossible to contain rebellion in Albion.'

'I agree.'

'I also believe that we cannot include anyone in Britannia in the plot, so as not to implicate Coventina, Bronwyn, Rivalin or Miriam.'

'Agreed. What you are really asking is whether I would undertake this mission, but you don't want to command me because of the dangers involved. You are my queen, Salome, whether you sit on the throne or not, and any request from you is as a command to me. Besides, with the recent news from Albion, I have no hopes left for a fulfilled life. I know of enough other Britons who look sufficiently middle-eastern to make up the numbers. They will all be single, like me. I would not willingly make anyone a widow for this.'

'Remember to mention to Joanna the recent news from Miriam. On second thoughts, I will put it in my reply to her.'

Eirwyn left.

Nerilla looked at Salome.

'What did Eirwyn mean by having no hope left?'

'He is in love with Miriam, just like Regus. In her last letter, Miriam said that her latest daughter has leaf-green eyes, like mine. That is the sign of the true queen of Albion. That means that her daughter will succeed Coventina on the throne of Albion. As the mother of a true queen, Miriam cannot marry anyone who is not of royal descent. To avoid dissent, she would not remarry at all should Rivalin die.'

'Oh, I see.'

68

Salome was worried. The news was that Titus had invaded Judea with the usual Roman brutality. Jerusalem was now besieged. It was four months since Eirwyn had left for Galilee. Salome's worry had started when Matthias had been late returning from his last trading trip. He told her that he had met Eirwyn in Alexandria. Eirwyn had left his ship there in the hands of a local merchant they knew hoping that, if he escaped Jerusalem, he could make his way to Alexandria. The Romans were allowing refugees out of Judea but had declared that, if Jerusalem resisted, everyone inside would be rounded up and sold as slaves. Eirwyn would either die or become a slave and be sent to the arena.

Matthias had continued his trading and was due back from his current trip. With local crops in Judea destroyed, the price of wheat had risen by sixty per cent. Miriam and Coventina had insisted that British wheat be used to stabilise the market in Galilee and Judea, otherwise, it would have doubled. Salome heard a familiar voice behind her.

'I have brought you my usual offering of scrolls from Alexandria; plus, another gift.'

Salome turned.

'Thank you, Matthias …'

She stopped as she saw a pregnant woman standing next to Matthias.

'This is Abigail. I will let her tell you her story.'

Salome was too surprised to speak for a moment then said, 'Well, Abigail?'

'My husband and I went to Jerusalem for Passover. I was pregnant so I was smuggled out. I was told by my husband that I should make my way to Alexandria and find Cornelius, a friend of our leader. He arranged for Matthias to bring me here.'

'Matthias, what is she on about? Whilst I am perfectly happy to help any Judean refugees, why bring her here?'

'I think you had better start again, Abigail. Salome knows what your husband is in Jerusalem for. So does Nerilla.'

'Oh. I had been told not to tell anyone, that is all. Rachel in Sychar made the arrangements. Twelve men were coming from Galilee. They didn't originate from there but needed to get into Jerusalem, without seeming out of place. It is usual for men married at this time of year to go to Jerusalem at Passover as a thanksgiving for their new wives. I, along with eleven other women from near Shiloh, was selected to marry them and go with them. Of course, we had to follow all the usual customs so as not to arouse suspicion.'

'Hence how you came to be pregnant,' said Salome.

'Yes. The men, and other women, have stayed in Jerusalem to carry out the mission at the appropriate time. The leader of the men, who is going by the name of Jonah, but whose real name is Eirwyn, said that he had been ordered to make sure that the temple didn't fall into the hands of the Romans.'

Salome nodded.

'Did you know what the mission was before you married?'

'Yes, and we were told that, as a last resort, they would burn the temple down rather than let the Romans have it.'

Not quite true. Their whole purpose is to burn down the temple. Probably better that Joanna was economical with the truth there though.

Their fathers would go along with the arrangement if they thought they were trying to save the temple, but not if the aim was to destroy it.

'Nerilla, your primary duty now is to look after Abigail. Before you go, though, how did you get out of Jerusalem?'

'There is a secret passage out from the temple precincts for the use of the Pharisees. Starts underwater at the Pool of the Angel, and then follows the watercourse from the pool as it leaves Jerusalem underground. Apparently, Paul told Peter about it. How that knowledge was kept, when most of the Pharisees were killed by the Romans at the time of the revolt and the rest killed by the Zealots after the revolt as Roman collaborators, I don't know.'

So, they don't know that Joanna is Peter's granddaughter.

'Are any other of the women likely to get pregnant?'

'None are showing any signs and we agreed that, after the wedding night, we would not lie together again.'

'Thank you, Abigail.'

69

Salome listened to the news coming out of Judea with interest and trepidation. Jerusalem held out for six months before the Romans managed to breach the walls. After that, events were swift. To Salome's relief, the temple had been burnt down during the final battle to take the city. There was talk of very few, if any, survivors amongst those inside. Salome was heartbroken. It was bad enough that she had sent Eirwyn and the other men to their deaths, but eleven brave young women had died alongside them.

Salome was dreading telling Abigail the news but would not hear of Nerilla telling her instead.

'The Romans have taken Jerusalem. The temple has been burnt down.'

'Was that Eirwyn?' asked Abigail.

'We don't know, as we have not heard anything, but the reports are that almost everyone in Jerusalem died in the last battle when the Romans tried to take the temple area.'

Abigail burst out crying and the baby in her arms cried in response. Nerilla moved to comfort her.

'My older sister, Seraphina, went too. She was married to Eirwyn as my father, Jeremiah, is the headman in our village. He has no other children.'

'I am so sorry. I am even sorrier that we cannot possibly hold a funeral for your sister. We cannot arouse suspicion.'

Abigail could not be comforted for the next week. Two months later, Matthias arrived from another trading trip.

'I have seen Eirwyn in Alexandria. He was fixing his ship after it was laid up for eight months. Said he will come back just as soon as he has found a cargo to bring with him.'

'How many have survived?'

'I don't know, I only saw Eirwyn briefly.'

'Typical of him to find a cargo before coming back. Ever the merchant.'

'He didn't seem too worried about profit, just about not looking conspicuous arriving in Carthage on a trading vessel without any goods.'

Salome was on tenterhooks, going down to the wharfs every day with Nerilla and Abigail, watching for Eirwyn's return. Finally, a fortnight later, Eirwyn's ship entered the harbour.

'Nerilla, your eyes are better than mine. How many are there on the ship?'

'I am counting now, Salome. Ten, eleven, twelve. Oh, I wish they would all stop moving.'

Suddenly Abigail let out a piercing scream, 'Seraphina, Seraphina is there.'

'Sera, Sera, Sera…,' she shouted at the top of her voice.

As the ship pulled alongside the quay, Eirwyn smiled.

'All present and correct, Salome, with just a few cuts, bruises and burns to show for it.'

Abigail couldn't be stopped. She handed the baby to Nerilla and jumped down onto the boat, into Seraphina's arms.

Both women were in tears.

Later, when the women had been settled in the British quarter of Carthage, Salome asked Eirwyn in private for his report.

'When we arrived in Tiberius, Matthias had forewarned Jairus, who told Joanna who I was. As I'd taken a letter from you, Regus was there. You should have seen his face when he saw me. It was a perfect picture of fear, but he was eager to know what you had written. Joanna only told him your news about Miriam's daughter. He was crestfallen and ...'

'Enough of that, Eirwyn. Back to the important stuff.'

'Anyway, Joanna sent us to Rachel in Sychar, who taught us some basic Hebrew culture and how we were to behave. She then took us to a village in northern Judea, close to Shiloh. The headman knew what our mission was, at least as far as us preventing the temple from falling into Roman hands. That was when we were told that they intended to marry us to the women, to get us into Jerusalem. I was to marry Seraphina, as she was going to be in charge of the women. I thought it unusual for an eighteen-year-old, but she has proved very capable. We supposed that it would be a sham marriage so were shocked when we found out it was for real. They said it was the only way to make sure 'that no one smelled a rat', whatever that means. Interestingly, they seemed more worried about the Zealots finding out than the Romans.'

Eirwyn paused and took a sip of water. Salome nodded and he carried on.

'We hadn't intended that any of the women got pregnant, but it was just as well that Abigail did. It enhanced our bona fides. It also enabled us to test out the escape route. Seraphina has been worried about her ever since. Strange that, as we were in greater danger. Anyway, we fell back, with everyone else, to the temple area when the Romans breached the walls. At the final Roman assault, we carried out Joanna's plan to burn down the temple.'

'How did you manage that with just twelve of you? It is a large building.'

Eirwyn chuckled for a moment.

'The plan was that we would dress as Romans and burn down the temple. We had set the various fires ready to light, but we thought it would be a miracle if we could manage it. Seraphina volunteered the women to help, but it was still going to be almost impossible.

Anyway, when the time came, we started lighting the fires. Then a band of real Romans arrived. Not knowing what to do, I shouted in Latin, 'Let us show these Jews whose gods are greater, burn down their temple.' To my surprise, they joined in. That is when I found out Seraphina speaks Latin. She shouted something in Hebrew. She later told me that it was, "The Romans are here, the Romans are here. Don't let them have the temple. It would be better that it burned." A large band of Zealots then appeared and, whilst some engaged the Romans, others started setting fires. More Romans arrived and then more Zealots, all setting fires as their countrymen were, without thinking about why the other side was doing it. At that point, we grabbed the women as if they were our prizes and dragged them away. As we left, Seraphina shouted something else in Hebrew. She told later me it was, "Leave us, we don't matter. Don't let the Romans have the temple. It is better it burns."

We got to the Pool of the Angel with no one stopping us, as we were then behind Roman lines. There we ditched our Roman armour and got out through the secret passage. We had wagons and other clothes waiting and joined refugees heading for Egypt.'

Salome smiled. She had heard enough.

'There is just one task left,' said Eirwyn.

'Oh, what is that?'

'We need to get the women back to their families.'

'I will have to think about that. I will need to talk to Seraphina first.'

70

Eirwyn brought Seraphina to see Salome the following day. She was surprised when Salome addressed her in Hebrew.

'Eirwyn has given me a good report of you, Seraphina. He also tells me that you are the leader of these women.'

'Thank you, Salome,' she answered in Hebrew and then turned to Eirwyn.

'Thank you for your good report, Eirwyn. It is appreciated,' she said in Latin.

'You have deserved it, Seraphina,' he replied.

'Eirwyn suggested yesterday that we need to get you and the other women home,' Salome continued in Hebrew. 'What do you think?'

Seraphina burst into tears and Salome was surprised when Eirwyn moved to her side and put a comforting arm around her. Seraphina responded by grabbing hold of his tunic like a frightened child holding her mother's dress. He whispered comforting words and Seraphina gradually conquered her distress. Salome waited patiently.

'I don't see how we can go back. We learnt in Egypt that there were very few survivors from the siege. That is partly because of the fires we helped to set. Those that did survive were sold into slavery by the Romans. If we go back, our miraculous escape will be the talk of Judea. That will raise suspicion. Also, the Romans started rounding up Zealots and their families in Judea to sell into slavery to compensate for the few prisoners they had from Jerusalem. It is known we were in Jerusalem. If we go back, not only will we be made slaves, but we will also put our families in danger.'

Seraphina burst into tears again and buried her head in Eirwyn's tunic. Again, Salome waited.

'That is what I thought. It will be dangerous if you are known as Hebrew here as well, but we could pass you off as any number of nationalities; Arab, Syrian or Phoenician. No, not Phoenician, you don't speak the language and Carthage is a Phoenician city. I thought of sending you all to Britannia, but your husbands are from seven different tribes. You would be split up, and it would be hard for you to adjust to the British culture. So, this is what I suggest, but the decision is yours. Yours and the other women. When you are ready.'

She waited until Seraphina nodded her assent and then she carried on.

'The best place for you to be is here, but you will need support. So, I suggest that you stay married to your husbands and we set up a community. I will put Eirwyn in charge of the men and you in charge of the women. We will have to make sure you can survive here so you will all have to learn Latin if you don't already speak it.'

'Only Abigail and I speak Latin, but we can teach the others.'

'You will also have to fit in with other communities here. The only way of doing that, without showing your ignorance of their culture and religion, is to become Christian.'

'Why Christian?'

'They are used to new Christians not knowing their religion and they come from many different cultures.'

Seraphina frowned, then shrugged.

'What do you think, Seraphina?'

'I will check with the other women, but we have no choice. It will be hard to adjust to men controlling everything, even our money, but they have all been considerate to us. When we escaped Jerusalem and could still hear the screams in the night before we started our journey the next morning, Eirwyn stayed up all night just holding me, giving me comfort. The other men did the same. How will the men react?'

'If they object, I will order them to.'

'Order them to?'

'Yes, I am their queen. And don't worry about the money. In British society, the wealth is controlled by the woman, not the man.'

Seraphina's jaw dropped.

She returned two days later, again with Eirwyn. Nerilla was with Salome and was signalled to stay. This time, Salome used Latin so that Eirwyn could understand.

'Have you decided?'

'Yes, we have all agreed to stay here. None of us is happy about becoming Christian but we see the sense of it. At least they worship Yahweh.'

Salome looked at Eirwyn.

'The agreement is that the women will stay in Carthage as your wives and integrate into society here.'

A broad grin came over Eirwyn's face.

'I was hoping Seraphina would stay but, under the circumstances, I didn't want to ask in case she felt pressurised.'

A matching grin came over Seraphina's face, as she threw her arms around his neck and hugged him.

'If you don't let go, Seraphina, you will strangle me and then you will be a widow.'

Seraphina laughed and stopped hugging him but caught his arm instead and held on tightly.

'What if the other men don't agree?' he asked Salome.

'It wasn't a request, Eirwyn.'

Again, he smiled.

'Anything else before we tell the men the dreadful news?' he asked.

'Just one thing. Do the women read and write, Seraphina?'

'Only Hebrew. We all speak Greek, of course. That was a condition of being chosen.'

'Looks like you have twelve new classmates, Nerilla. You can share some of the teaching duties too. Nothing like teaching others, to increase your understanding.'

Salome proceeded to give Eirwyn specific instructions on how she wanted things set up. When he and Seraphina had left, Nerilla carried on staring after them.

'Your thoughts, Nerilla.'

'I was just wondering how long it will be before Seraphina is pregnant.'

'An hour, two at the most, I would say.'

Nerilla sighed.

71

Salome wrote to Joanna to let her know of the safe arrival of Eirwyn and the women, as well as her decision to keep the women in Carthage, still married to their husbands. She expected to receive a reply from Matthias on his return, but he had just come back with his usual Greek and Latin scrolls from Alexandria. As part of the education of the women, Salome had them read out the scrolls and then copy them to practise their writing.

On his next trip, Matthias brought a message back from Joanna. In it, she said that she had contacted Rachel in Sychar, who had advised against letting the families know of the women's whereabouts. It would be too risky, as it might accidentally leak. She also said that Regus felt his task in Galilee was not yet done.

It was almost two years later when Salome next heard from Joanna.

After the Romans rounded up the remaining Zealots and their families in Judea, they were still not satisfied with the number of slaves they had taken, so ordered Regus to do the same in Galilee. The Galilean Zealots had anticipated that something like this might happen and only two had married. One of the two was David who, I am told, was Rachel's brother and married to Miriam, Queen Miriam's daughter.

Regus didn't officially know their hiding places and so kept his soldiers diligently looking in the wrong places for them. Unfortunately, one of the women was betrayed, so Regus had no choice but to take her and sell her into slavery. Jairus arranged for a Christian Roman merchant from Damascus to buy her. Luckily, she had no children.

Tabitha arrived back from Jerusalem, where she had been organising the reconstruction of the city and took control. She had Miriam and her young daughter bought by Alexander, Rachel's son, and taken to Sychar as his concubine. Alexander freed her on the way, and she is now safe in Sychar. Tabitha and David's father, Ezekiel, have both sold their businesses in Galilee to Jairus and are also living in Sychar, though both are currently working together on rebuilding work in Jerusalem.

Regus is very disappointed. He wanted to be the hero in Queen Miriam's eyes, by buying Miriam himself and sending her to safety in Britannia. He now thinks that his work in Galilee is done but is waiting for a sign of when to move on. Finally, he tells me that Queen Miriam knows why he was posted to Galilee and that it would be good for her to know that her daughter is safe.

Salome took the rest of the day to think about what to write to Miriam in Aquae Sulis. In the end, she decided on a short note with the briefest explanation of her daughter, Miriam, now being safe in Sychar.

She didn't hear from Joanna again. She only knew that Regus had moved on when the governor of Carthage paid her an unexpected visit two years later.

'I have come for Nerilla.'

'Oh, why?'

'I have been posted to Tiberius to take over from the governor there, Regus. His father has died, and he has decided to retire to an estate near Antioch. I don't need Nerilla to keep an eye on you anymore. You are not my problem.'

Nerilla looked at Salome, with fear in her eyes.

'Would you sell Nerilla to me?' asked Salome.

'It will cost you. She speaks Latin, Greek and Aramaic, and she reads and writes as well. A valuable slave.'

'Only because Salome taught me!' Nerilla blurted out before she could stop herself.

She expected him to hit her, but he just leered.

'It is tempting to keep you for other purposes, as well as your reading and writing abilities, but if Salome will meet my price …'

Nerilla cowered.

'How much do you want?' asked Salome.

The sum he asked was reasonable, below market rates for a slave with Nerilla's skills. Salome acted reluctant and asked if he would drop but agreed to his price in the end.

These Romans are out of touch with things because they leave too much to their stewards and underlings.

The governor left, with Salome promising to send the money to his steward by the end of the day.

His parting shot was, 'Pity in a way. She has grown into such a beautiful woman. I would have enjoyed having her as my latest toy. There again, I got her for a pittance in the first place and taking her would have ruined her sale value.'

Salome then summonsed Eirwyn. She sent him with the money to the governor's steward just in case the steward tried to increase the price and take a cut for himself. No one argued with Eirwyn. When he returned with the deed of sale, Salome asked him to accompany her and Nerilla to a local notary. She presented the deed of sale as proof of ownership and then had a deed drawn up, releasing Nerilla from her slavery.

'What do I do now?' asked Nerilla.

'You carry on as my maid, paid of course, until you find a suitable husband. That is what you want, isn't it?'

Nerilla nodded, with tears streaming down her face.

72

Suddenly Salome felt tired. It had been five years since the old governor had left. The new governor was a more amenable person. He took more interest in Carthage than the old governor had. He even instigated works to improve the harbour and had a library built. Having been told that Salome had the best collection of Greek and Roman scrolls, he immediately called on her.

'I need scrolls for the library. Would you be prepared to donate some?'

'Oh, I thought you had come about me being confined to living in Carthage.'

'No, I have seen the previous governor's arrangements for that. You could have given him the slip any time you wanted. The fact that you didn't, meant that you weren't going to. I understand that you have family both in Galilee and Britannia. Carthage is as good a place as any to live with those connections.'

'So, you conclude that I am staying put of my own free will. What if I wish to visit my daughter in Britannia or my son and grandchildren in Galilee?'

'I have discretion I can use, but I know that your son has already been here. He will soon be taking over from your husband, I hear. Now about those scrolls …'

'Oh yes, I have a better idea. I know of a dozen, or more, scribes who would welcome the employment of copying them for your library.'

'The Hebrew women, you mean?'

Salome was startled.

'I know all about what Regus did in Galilee or, should I say, Joanna? I was born in Carthage. My parents are Roman citizens, but we are descended from Phoenicians. I know what the Romans are like, and I know how Jews would have reacted to the desecration of the temple. You did what you had to do.'

'How did you find out?'

'My father, Pygmalion, told me.'

Salome laughed.

'If you ever need anything, let me know, and I mean that sincerely.'

Salome nodded her head.

'Your idea is a good one,' the governor continued. 'Would you organise it for me? The civic government will pay for it, of course.'

He stood up to go.

'You haven't asked me how much, Governor.'

'I don't need to. You will be honest with me.'

The previous five years had thus been taken up, with Salome, the Hebrew women, Nerilla and a few other scribes, copying scrolls for the library. Eirwyn had long since taken over running the business in Carthage. He and Seraphina had three children.

The youngest is only nine months. Seraphina will not try for another until he is weaned at two years old.

Her husband had died and her son, Matthias, had taken over the trade between Carthage and Galilee. Once a year, he would bring his wife and children with him, and they would stay with Salome until he came back on his next trip. She found she missed Matthias, her husband, but her son still brought scrolls from Alexandria, with each visit.

Salome was tired as she remembered all that had happened. She wished she could lie down and sleep, but there was the latest scroll to transcribe. Perhaps her tiredness was that she missed Matthias. Their marriage had never been close or passionate, but she had enjoyed his time at home when they could discuss business, or he could relate the latest news from Galilee. Much as she loved her son, it just wasn't the same. Perhaps that was why she felt so tired. Suddenly, she found Nerilla standing over her.

'Are you alright, Salome?'

'What happened?'

'I found you slumped over the scroll.'

'I am just tired. I must have been doing too much recently. I will go and have a lie-down.'

Nerilla took Salome to bed and then called Seraphina from the workroom. She was taking a break to feed the baby, anyway. She could still do that whilst keeping an eye on Salome.

Nerilla didn't bother finding a physician, since she knew what the problem was. She had been expecting it to happen at some time after she had noticed the lump on Salome's breast whilst dressing her. Just a bit sooner than she expected, that was all. It is why she had never married, despite numerous offers and having to pay the Roman unmarried woman's tax when she reached twenty-five.

When Salome next awoke, she found Nerilla sitting in her room, along with the governor.

'Sorry Governor, I will be with you as soon as I can. Nerilla, why didn't you wake me when the governor arrived?'

'Stay where you are, Salome,' said the governor. 'Nerilla, quite rightly, fetched me when you collapsed. She tells me that you want to die amongst your people in Britannia.'

'How…?'

Salome looked wide-eyed at Nerilla.

'I have known that you have been ill for years, so have been staying close-by overnight, to be there if you need me. There was a woman who had your condition when I was a child in Rome. I saw her die. For the last month, I have heard you talking in your sleep, repeating over and over, *I want to die in Albion.*'

'I will use that dispensation I am permitted. My father says he would like the honour of taking you home. It seems fitting to him that, as he took you the first time, he should take you again. Says it will be his last voyage. Nerilla will accompany you.'

73

They left for Aquae Sulis a week later, after Pygmalion had made his ship as comfortable as possible for Salome. He carried a cargo of Phoenician tools, more as ballast than as trade goods. He would bring British lead back for the same reason. Then he would give the ship to his second son.

It is about time he was his own master.

Salome looked on Aquae Sulis with wonder as they rowed upriver to the wharf. The place had totally changed. Before, there had been a few stone buildings surrounded by traditional wooden and thatched roundhouses. Now all the buildings were of stone. The spa-cum-temple dominated. The fort had changed as well. The wooden fort had been replaced by a stone one, though the unmanned wide-open gate showed that they feared no danger. Previously, the gate had always been shut with a sentry detail guarding it.

The reception party indicated that they were expected. Salome knew that Rivalin had set up a signalling system so that no one could pass the gorge by the estuary without him being notified. It was Pygmalion he addressed.

'Welcome Pygmalion, what brings you here? We haven't seen you for a long time.'

Pygmalion didn't answer but turned and looked in Salome's direction. Rivalin regarded Salome, perplexed for a few seconds before he saw her leaf-green eyes. He bowed.

'Your Majesty.'

'Just Salome please, Rivalin.'

Rivalin turned to the young man accompanying him.

'Brennon, go to the palace and let your mother know that Queen Salome has come from Carthage.'

The man stared at Salome for a moment. He had met her when he was a young child but barely remembered her. For most of his life, she had been a semi-mythical figure, always present in spirit but never there. He coloured and then bowed awkwardly, 'Your Majesty.'

He then left, running towards the palace.

'I am sorry for the inconvenience, but it would be best if Your Majesty stayed on board until we have informed the governor and he has given his permission for you to land.'

'Rivalin, please just use my name.'

'Yes, Your ... Salome.'

The wait was longer than anticipated. About an hour later, Miriam, Coventina and Jenna arrived, all dressed in their royal gowns, with their eight children accompanying them. Bronwyn and Quintus and their three children were five minutes behind. Pygmalion presented Salome's dispensation, which his son had given him, to Quintus. He read it and then smiled.

'Welcome home, Your Majesty. My apologies for delaying your disembarkation.'

'It is good to see you again, Quintus.'

Salome took Quintus's proffered hand and stepped onto the gangplank. As she did so, the weight she placed on him told Quintus that the queen was not well. Miriam also noticed. The maid behind rushed to steady Salome.

'Aoife, accompany the queen to the palace.'

A young grey-eyed woman behind Miriam, with dark brown hair and copper highlights, moved quickly to comply. Miriam signalled Pygmalion to follow.

Salome walked slowly to the palace, supported on her left by Nerilla, on her right by Aoife. The bustle of Aquae Sulis stopped as Salome approached, and people acknowledged the return of their monarch. She could hear it resume after she had passed. At the palace, they retired to a private room for a hastily prepared meal.

'I am sorry to spring this upon you suddenly,' said Salome, after they had eaten.

'We knew you were coming, Mother,' Coventina replied. 'The angel warned us. We just didn't know exactly when you would arrive.'

Bronwyn smiled.

'And just to make sure that we got the message, she told all four of us; Coventina, Miriam, Jenna and me.'

Over the following few days, whilst the arrangements were being made for Salome's onward journey, they had time to talk. Salome was delighted to meet her grandchildren finally, though they were initially confused as to who she was.

'I have been lucky,' Salome said, one morning. 'I have got to meet all my grandchildren, first those who live in Galilee, and now those here. I am also going to get to die in the place I wish, unlike Mary.'

They all knew about Mary. After Salome arrived in Britannia and was exiled to Carthage, Mary decided that she wanted to return to Galilee. She had travelled overland from northern Gaul, aiming to take a ship from Massilia, but had died on the way.

'Whilst Nerilla is not here, there is a problem that I would like to discuss,' Salome continued. 'She is unmarried and paying the tax. I do not need a maid any longer, being in

Albion. It is hard for Roman women to find employment and the tax will whittle away at her money until she is destitute.'

'That is easy enough to solve,' said Bronwyn. 'I know of just the right husband for her.'

Bronwyn looked at Rivalin. Coventina's eyes followed, as did Miriam's and Jenna's.

'No! Definitely no!' shouted Rivalin.

The four women laughed.

'I was thinking of Maximus, the garrison commander. He needs a wife of convenience so that he can evade the unmarried tax as well. It will be a good short-term solution for them both and then who knows …'

'That will require a dowry. You know that Maximus's family will never accept any other type of marriage for their son,' said Quintus.

'I will provide a dowry,' said Salome.

'In that case, if I stand in loco parentis, then I think it will work,' said Quintus. 'That way I can protect Nerilla as well, just in case.'

74

Salome and her daughter, Coventina, walked up the plank from the bank onto the waiting vessel. It was manned by sixteen men, with eight oars on either side. It was a barge with a shallow draught. The mast held a square sail, currently furled, as the wind was in the wrong direction.

The whole court, and most of the population of Aquae Sulis, were there to see them off. Miriam would have liked to have gone with them, but it was not a public occasion. It was a time for a mother and her daughter.

'I am still not sure why we aren't taking the road, Coventina. Why are we taking the river? It will take longer and cost more.'

'Yes, it does, but it is traditional to take the river. And the cost doesn't come into it when you are Queen. We will break with tradition when we get to the northernmost intersection of the road and the river and take the road from there.'

'Why will we do that if we are following tradition down here?'

'From there, the river quickly becomes unnavigable. We could go further by boat but then we would have to take a six-mile journey on a small dirt track to get back to the road anyway. This is easier and more comfortable. It is only a day's journey at the other end from where we alight, to our destination.'

'You haven't told me where our destination is yet, nor why we are going there.'

'I have told you as much as I am allowed, Mother. We are going to see an important person who is anxious to meet you at her home.'

'Couldn't she have come to us, after all, you are a queen, Coventina?'

Coventina smiled, 'She is very old and does not travel. Just think yourself lucky that we are not required to follow tradition entirely. That would require us to go all the way by the river, including wading the last section and pulling the boats along behind.'

Their luggage was brought up and unceremoniously dumped into the bottom of the boat. Salome was grateful that she had thought to pack her polished-copper mirror and not her glass one. She sat down in the back of the boat sullenly and Coventina gracefully seated herself next to her. At Coventina's signal, the oarsmen on the bank side of the boat pushed off and they set off down the river. They passed through the gorge at the river mouth and then turned upstream into a larger river.

Britannia, as Salome had already noted, was colder and wetter than Carthage, where she lived, or even Galilee where she was before that. Salome noticed that she had fallen into the trap again. Carthage was no longer her home. Aquae Sulis was her home now. The Romans had given her dispensation to join her daughter, now she was dying. Salome usually drove a wagon or rode a horse when she travelled so had the unusual luxury of being able to take note of the scenery.

The land was greener than she was used to. One advantage of more rain, she supposed. Unlike Carthage and Galilee, there were no stone houses. What houses she saw were round, with large posts in a circle and a central post. The walls were wickerwork, sealed with mud and moss. A group of these would be in a circular enclosure, surrounded by a low wooden palisade. Smoke rose from a few. Keeping out the autumn chill or cooking, Salome supposed.

All the buildings she saw were close to the river. After a narrow stretch of mixed-grazing land and crop fields, there was always woodland. Thin woodland at first, giving way to dark, impenetrable wood behind. Sheep grazed the pasture, and Salome thought she saw cattle amongst the trees. She looked avidly initially but soon lost interest.

'Is it like this, all the way?' she asked Coventina.

'Pretty much. We will come to the occasional Roman settlement, but this is it for the next eight days.'

Salome was soon bored and did what she always did when bored. She opened her pack, found a piece of fine linen and silks which she had brought with her and started to embroider. The last resort for Salome, who hated embroidering.

Coventina looked at her.

She never changes. Never idle for long. Just like when I was a child in Galilee. That is not one of her usual patterns, though.

'Why Naiads?' asked Coventina, 'I have never known you embroider them before.'

'I don't know,' replied Coventina, 'but they somehow seem appropriate.'

Perhaps Salome does know who we are going to see, subconsciously.

Coventina settled down to think of all that had happened since she had married Rivalin. Her surprise at her first summons. Her bigger surprise was when she found out that, though her husband nominally held the power, she was the one who was consulted and obeyed. The Romans didn't know that, of course, except Quintus. They were the only ones who thought that Rivalin was in control. His signature was on all the official documents, but the power lay with her. It was a marriage of state, for both of them, as their hearts were elsewhere since Salome, exiled by Roman edict, had gone back to Carthage.

Coventina had met her namesake on her first trip. They were going to see her now. Since then, Coventina had given birth to three children by Rivalin. They had grown to love each other, if only because they respected what each other had sacrificed for the sake of their people. The line of queens must go on. They had one son and one daughter. Both had blue eyes, like Rivalin. It had been unexpected when Miriam had given birth to the next queen. Coventina was content with that, though. It would give her offspring a freedom she had never enjoyed. Initially, Coventina swore that that would be it, but had been hit with melancholy after her father's death and had gone to Rivalin for comfort, leading to their third. She was now contemplating a fourth having decided that she liked being pregnant.

Coventina broke off her thoughts, 'Mother, why did you call me Coventina?'

'It was my grandmother's name. Like you and me, she had leaf-green eyes. Besides, it was the only British name I knew.'

'But do you know where it came from?'

'Of course. I didn't dare tell your father; he would never have allowed me to use it, had he known.'

It was eight days before they reached their landing place. There was a ford across the river where a track went from The Fossa to a small settlement. The ford was guarded by a small wooden fort. Bored Roman soldiers watched them get out of the boat. There was no honour guard for the queen, as none of them knew who she was. There would have been if Felix had been with them. His high official's uniform would have stood out and drawn their attention. Neither of the women was concerned by this. The wagon to carry them on to their destination awaited. Rivalin had wanted to send a chariot to honour their rank, but Coventina had vetoed that. She did not wish to attract Roman attention.

Salome wanted to get on, but Coventina assured her that it was a full day's journey. It was already late in the afternoon, so they decided to sleep on the boat and continue their journey in the morning.

The following day, they were up early. Salome wanted to be off as soon as they could. The sooner the tiresome journey was over, the better. Everything started as before on the journey. The trees cleared away from the sides of the long straight road. Scattered round homesteads. Nothing new. The road itself was well made, as all Roman roads were. Standard width-wheel gauge meant that the ruts steered the wagon without any real need for a driver. About fifteen miles north along the road, it all changed.

The driver turned off the road and onto a track. It was a well-maintained and well-used track, but it was not usual for a Roman trail. The trees came right up to the sides of their way, overhanging the wagon on occasions. Salome felt that they were being watched. The woodland itself seemed to have eyes. She looked at her daughter, anxiously.

'There is nothing to fear, Mother. This forest is protected. Even the Romans respect that. Where we are going, only one Roman has ever seen.'

'Rivalin?'

'No, Regus.'

'Why did Rivalin choose Felix as his Roman name? Britannicus is obvious.'

'Because he was in Gaul at the time of the Boudiccan revolt, so had not needed to choose sides. He felt lucky that he could come back and help restore Britannia, whoever won.'

At the end of the track, they came to a wooden Roman fort. It had obviously been larger once but was still a substantial size. The track took them into the fort. A guard of honour awaited them. It was a courtesy call only, Salome realised. They could have taken the track around the side of the fort if they had wanted to. The commander politely offered an escort, which was equally politely refused.

'I will be fine, Antonius, as I always am.'

'Your Majesty.'

Antonius bowed his head in acknowledgement.

They left, still in the wagon, through a side gate of the fort and turned left to the river. Salome noticed a shrine to an unknown goddess by the gate. A Naiad, maybe. She thought of her now-complete embroidery. A small clear stream went away at an angle to the northwest, a well-worn path at its side.

'What was that about, Coventina? It looked like a well-rehearsed play back there between you and the tribune. Some kind of game?'

'A game of sorts, yes. The Romans are not allowed out of the fort either in this direction or up the path by the stream without my permission. They have always kept to that treaty.'

'Not like the Romans. Aren't they curious?'

'Of course, they are curious. Hence the offer of an honour guard every time I come here. Equally, we don't want them here, so I give a polite refusal.'

'Still not like the Romans. They are usually more forceful in such offers. Particularly when dealing with a woman who has no escort. A treaty with you is not so precious to them, surely.'

'The treaty is not with me. It is with someone else. And of her, they are very afraid. They have tried to come up here. Absolutely. Every time there is a new garrison commander.

None have ever come back, alive. It is fear that holds the Romans to their word, not politeness or respect.'

They turned a corner of the track and arrived at what Salome assumed was their destination.

75

The village was a scattered group of roundhouses, arranged around a large central hall. Although the trees had been thinned out, they were still scattered throughout the village. Oak, elm, and ash dominated, but the edge of the village was marked by silver birch as if guarding it against the surrounding forest. On one side of the village, lay a pool with cool shady willows at its edge. In the pool swam many swans. Herons were in evidence on the farther shore, fishing, and a beaver lodge could be seen in the distance on the river, feeding the pool. Cows were grazing and pigs were rooting amongst the trees at the edge of the woodland.

All the villages Salome had seen on the way had been clear of trees and had a defensive ditch and picket and an animal enclosure. She supposed that with a fort containing a cohort of heavily-armed Romans blocking the way in, none was needed. There were enough dwellings here for thousands, but it was quiet, and Salome couldn't see how they could support so many.

She turned to Coventina.

'How do they protect their animals? There must be wolves and bears around.'

'The predators leave us alone. They have been commanded to stay away but have the leave to roam the rest of the forest.'

'Are there none around here then?'

'Some. They guard the village from the Romans.'

'So that's what keeps the Romans at bay?'

'That, their natural fear of forest and, of course, their fear of the wrath of the woman they have the treaty with.'

'That is the second time you have mentioned her. Who is she? Is Boudicca still alive?'

'It is not Boudicca, but someone far more powerful. You will meet her tomorrow.'

As they approached, men, women and children came out of one of the dwellings, about twenty in all. The two eldest, a man and a woman, stood in front. Behind, were four more couples, along with children in family groups. They waited until the wagon pulled up and Salome and Coventina had arrived. The foremost man came to Coventina, took her proffered right hand in his right hand, put his left hand onto his right forearm, did a semi-kneel with his right leg, bowed his head, and said something to her in a language Salome did not understand.

At Coventina's word, he stood up and they conversed. He looked towards Salome, who heard Coventina say something about Latin. He approached Salome. Coventina signalled her to put her hand out, as she had done. The man did, as he had done before, saying, 'Welcome Your Majesty', in Latin.

'Thank you,' replied Salome. 'May I ask, to whom I am speaking?'

He stood upright.

'I am Mael, the chief priest here. This is my family. My wife, Nevanthi, will look after your needs whilst you are here.'

With this, he indicated the woman at the front of the group.

'Thank you, that is kind of you.'

Mael gave a slight bow and moved away from her, to address the collected group in front of her. Then, one by one, they came and introduced themselves, the same way he had, first to Coventina and then Salome. First came Nevanthi, then the eldest son, Owen, and then Salome lost track. They all spoke in the strange language to Coventina and in perfect Latin to Salome, even the youngest.

After they had introduced themselves, Coventina took command and, to Salome's relief, spoke in Latin.

'Owen, Piran, Quade, Rivalin, unload the cart please.'

The four younger men immediately set to unloading. Then Coventina led the way to the great hall but, instead of entering the main hall, went into an annexe at the rear. Mael and Nevanthi followed them.

Nevanthi immediately set to, readying the place for their stay. Mael said something to Coventina in the strange language.

'Please use Latin when my mother is present, Mael.'

'Yes, Your Majesty. You are early this year, Your Majesty.'

'Yes, I was commanded to come early and bring my mother with me. We can drop the formality whilst alone, Mael.'

Mael glanced at Salome.

'My mother is to be treated with the same courtesy as I am, in public. In private, I think she will be happier with less formality.'

Salome nodded.

'We need you to guide us to the grove tomorrow, but I have been commanded that only Salome and I are to enter.'

Mael bowed.

By that time, the young men had started bringing the things in from the wagon, so Mael fell silent, except to request Quade to fetch an extra bed and mattress for the room, for Salome's use. When the preparation of the room was finished, they all left in a group, with Mael promising to return in the morning and Nevanthi that evening with a meal.

Once they had gone, Salome had a chance to look around the room. Apart from the two low wooden beds with straw mattresses covered in intricately woven blankets, there were two low divans next to a table, Roman-style and two stools. Nothing else. In the centre of the room, Nevanthi had set a fire in a small pit, the smoke from which curled up and out of a small hole in the thatched roof. Apart from the door by which they had entered on one short side of the room, there were two other doors. One was on the long side by the main hall and presumably connected to it. The other was on the other short side.

Seeing no privy, Salome asked what they were expected to do. Coventina indicated the door on the short side which Salome had previously seen. On entering, she followed a curving passage until she came to a pit. A wooden seat, with a hole in it, had been erected above the pit, with soft moss beside it.

After using the facilities, she noticed a bowl to one side, with a small wooden pipe above it, and a lever beside the pipe. On a stand, next to the bowl, sat soap and a length of linen. Salome guessed she had to pull the lever. She did so and water came gushing out, so fast that Salome had to jump back to avoid getting soaked. After washing and drying her hands, she looked around for a sluice in which to empty the bowl. Finding none, she emptied it into the pit.

On returning to the room, she found Coventina sitting on one of the beds, embroidering a fine linen cloth.

'Join me, Mother. I promise you that you will get so bored you will be tearing at the walls if you do nothing.'

'I could go out for a walk.'

'If you did that, everyone would feel obliged to stop work and attend to you. This is their busiest time of year. Interrupting their preparations for the autumn festival would not be kind.'

Salome sighed, got out her sewing and sat next to her daughter.

'When do we meet the rest of the village?'

'We have already met the whole village.'

'But there is enough space here for at least three thousand.'

'The village is empty, except for the autumn festival. People will start arriving soon. Firstly, people who live nearby with provisions for the feast and to ready the hall and all the huts. Then, those from further afield join in. Within a fortnight, when the festival starts, the place will be teeming.'

'Oh!'

They sat talking until Nevanthi arrived at dusk with the evening meal. It consisted of fruit and bread. She apologised for the simplicity. Coventina assured her that it was perfectly fine and that she knew how busy they were and that they seldom cooked this close to the festival. Nevanthi stayed until they had finished the meal, then cleared up the dishes and left. Since it was then after dark, and there was no light in the room except for the fire, they did their ablutions and then retired to bed.

76

The following morning, Salome was woken by the dawn. She saw that Coventina was already up. She had washed and was sitting on a stall, wearing a white gown with a white sash around the waist, decorated with gold edging. A second, identical gown, lay on the bed next to her.

'This is your dress for today,' said Coventina, indicating the gown next to her. 'Nevanthi will be here soon with breakfast and to prepare us for the day. If you go down towards the privy, you will see a door to your left. I have left it ajar slightly so you can find it more easily. Take the dress with you.'

Salome picked up the dress next to Coventina and took the wicker corridor towards the privy. She found the door that Coventina had indicated and left the new gown hung over it whilst she went to the privy. On her return, she picked up her dress and went through the door. She entered a strange room.

There was a wooden platform standing over a sluice. Two empty pegs were on the wall, on one side of the room. On the opposite wall, was a length of linen cloth and a stand with soap and a bottle of sweet-smelling oil. On the third wall, next to the platform, there was a lever.

Salome guessed that she needed to undress, stand on the platform, and pull the lever. She did so, putting her dress on the peg next to the white gown she had already hung up. When she pulled the lever, water came down on her from above, making her exclaim with surprise, let go of the lever and jump away. Thoroughly soaked, her eyesight blurred from water, she reached for the soap. After soaping her hair and whole body, she stepped back onto the platform, braced herself for the cold water and pulled the lever. It was not nearly as bad when she knew what to expect. She reached out to grab the linen cloth and almost, mistakenly, grabbed her fresh dress instead. Then she liberally used the oil, feeling like the queen she was for the first time in her life, and then she dressed.

On entering the Queen's Chamber, she found Nevanthi intricately braiding Coventina's hair.

'You might have warned me, Coventina.'

'More fun this way, Mother,' she replied, with a glint in her eye. 'I imagine the whole village heard your shriek.'

Coventina laughed.

'Come and sit next to me. Nevanthi will need to do your hair next.'

Then, when Salome was next to her, she gave her hand a slight squeeze.

'There is fruit and bread for breakfast and fresh milk from the goats. First, you might like some of that hot drink to warm you after your ordeal.'

Salome poured some of the liquid into a cup, and then smelt it suspiciously.

'What is it?'

'I don't know that it has a name. It is made from acorns. I find it pleasant at this time in the morning, especially when autumn sets in. It is a luxury though. Takes a lot of work to make.'

Salome took a sip. It had a slightly bitter, though pleasant, taste. She sat back to savour it.

'We have plenty of time, do tell. How is it made?'

'It is made from acorns, as I said. They collect the fallers, then wrap them in linen cloth and leave them in the river for three days. The acorns are then shelled, and the nuts roasted. They grind the roasted nuts between two stones like you would with wheat to make flour, and then they are roasted again until a dark brown colour. You mix the resulting powder with heated water to make the drink. Be careful not to empty your cup completely, as the powder accumulates at the bottom and doesn't taste nice.'

Salome looked at the cup thoughtfully. She could get used to life as a queen.

No, I won't. I don't have time. I am dying.

After finishing Coventina's hair, Nevanthi dressed Salome's in the same way. The same intricate pattern of braids. Salome looked quizzically at Coventina.

'It is tradition for a queen on formal occasions.'

'Thank goodness it isn't every day. It takes so long.'

After Nevanthi had left, Salome looked at herself in the mirror, very satisfied with what she saw. The interweaving of holly and mistletoe, with their red and white berries, gave her the look of wearing a coronet. Very regal, indeed.

A scratch at the outside door caught her attention. Coventina immediately responded, 'Come in, Mael.'

Mael came in and bowed, 'Your Majesties are ready?'

Coventina looked at Salome, who nodded.

'Lead on, Mael. You are to lead us to the grove but today it is a private audience so, once there, we are to be left alone.'

Mael simply bowed and led them out. They walked back down the path towards the Roman fort and then, just before they reached it, took a path following a tributary of clear water. At the edge of a clearing in the wood, Mael stood aside and let them proceed alone.

'This was easy enough to find. Why did we need Mael as a guide?' asked Salome.

'It is customary for the chief priest to guide the queen here. It is also customary for him to be present at all interviews. The fact that we have been asked to go alone will be a blow to his status. Using him as a guide, will keep that loss of status private.'

Salome's eyes took time to adjust from the dark woodland to the blaze of light of the glade. Once they did, she saw a woman at the opposite end of the clearing. The woman was completely naked, her milk-white skin appearing to glow in the morning sun. Though there was not a breath of wind, her jet-black hair waved behind her. The eyes held Salome's attention most, leaf-green like her own, but glowing in their intensity and kindly.

Well, Tirzah, Mother, she has leaf-green eyes like the queens. I guess this must be the goddess.

Salome gave a respectful bow.

As she came upright again, she saw her daughter smiling.

'Mother, meet my namesake, Goddess Coventina.'

The goddess spoke, though Salome could not discern any movement in her lips.

'Welcome, Salome. I have longed to meet you. Unfortunately, it has not been possible before, despite your long and loyal service.'

Salome was confused.

'I have done you no service that I am aware of, Your Majesty. Your Grace? Your Worship?'

She suddenly realised that she had no idea how to address a goddess. Coventina smiled.

'There is no need for honorifics here. Though you did not know it, you have served me well. You lifted yourself out of slavery; you faithfully taught Coventina, your daughter, and

Miriam the stories of our people; you became a merchant and brought your daughter to this land. Most of all, you were prepared to relinquish the throne in favour of Coventina for the sake of our people. That is your greatest service to me.'

Salome bowed slightly in acknowledgement.

The goddess continued, 'I cannot reward you for your service as it should be rewarded. Yahweh, as you know him, will not let me. I have been permitted this, though. You will preside at the marriage feast this week, as a joint queen with Coventina, then you will stay here for six months as a queen.'

Perplexed, Salome asked, 'Who is getting married?'

'Every year, at the feast, the queen is married to her people as a proxy for the goddess,' her daughter replied.

Salome was worried.

'Don't fret, Mother, it is purely symbolic. No marital duties are required.'

Salome let out her breath in a rush, unaware until that point that she had been holding it.

'In our faith, we believe that there is only one God, Yahweh. I always thought that you were just a fable, until now. Miriam always called you an angel.'

The goddess replied, 'It is true that there is only one God. I am an angel, as Miriam said. When people first came here, they had no concept of an angel, so I was portrayed to them as a goddess. I set a ruler over them they could understand and relate to; a queen, my daughter. They still call their rightful queen, Coventina's Daughter. Whilst they obeyed the queen, the land had peace and plenty, but when they went away from her, the whole land suffered. Your grandmother's brother usurped the throne. Boudicca's disastrous campaign and its aftermath was the culmination of that disobedience.'

Coventina let Salome digest that, then spoke once more, 'I need to converse with Coventina alone for a minute if you will wait with Mael at the edge of the grove.'

Once Salome had withdrawn, the goddess turned to Coventina.

'Thank you for your kindness to my mother,' the queen said, with a tear in her eye. 'She worked so hard and wanted to be Queen herself.'

'I would have done more if I could. This is not the end, though, not for Salome. She has not told you, but she is tired. She is dying and will never leave this place. I will give you sufficient warning for you to be present when she dies, but that will not be the end for Salome. Yahweh has granted that she will return and rule here once more, the last of Coventina's Daughters. She will be God's gift to this land one more time.'

The goddess's voice changed, almost wistful.

'As Christianity takes hold here, I will diminish. My job will be done. You and I will be forgotten, except by a few, but Salome's memory will live on. She will have her time of trial when she will need the strength of us both to help her through. Her legacy and her name, her new name, will live on. That will be God's gift.

Epilogue

The young woman stood beside a white horse, at the entrance to the courtyard of the manor house. A gentle breeze blew her brown hair across her face, the copper highlights catching the early morning sun. She moved her hand up to clear her face and tuck her long hair behind her shoulder. Her only garment was a colourless flaxen shift down to just below the knee. Then, taking the horse's halter, a simple length of rope, she took a deep breath and prepared to mount the horse's bare back.

The sound of footsteps behind stopped her. A young man with blond hair and blue eyes approached, wrapped in a fur-lined cloak, carrying a bag.

'Good morning, Husband. Have you come to satisfy yourself that I am fulfilling the terms of our wager?'

'You don't have to do this. I was drunk last night.'

'A bet is a bet. You agreed that if I rode through the streets of Coventry naked, you would reduce the city's taxes. As the lowest of the low, you said.'

'You could at least put a dress on, you only need to leave your finery off.'

'But that would not meet the requirements of our bargain. Your taxes are so high that many women walk around the city, day after day, in no more than I am wearing now.'

Leofric squirmed. He hadn't noticed anything when he rode around the city. Not, he realised, that there was anything for him to notice. His lords and retainers always cleared the streets before him, Earl of Mercia, a descendant of kings. He had lost touch with his people long ago. He had told himself for years that his building of monasteries and abbeys, in his territory, benefitted his people with new farming and animal husbandry skills. That he deserved a reward for his beneficence in the form of higher taxes. Until the night before, at the feast for his nobles, that is. His wife had confronted him, berating his lack of consideration for his people. In drunken jest, he offered her a wager. That if she demeaned herself to the lowest of the low, he would relieve the taxes. Her acceptance had instantly sobered him. He knew well enough that, once she agreed, she would fulfil her promise.

'You need a saddle on that horse.'

'Our people cannot afford saddles, so I will not use one.'

'If you ride bareback you will have to ride astride, and that shift will move up revealing your thighs. I will not have my wife going through the town with her clothing up to her thighs.'

Godiva's thoughts moved to her mythical ancestress, The goddess Coventina, who had been discovered in a grove a short distance away. There, where the River Sherbourne sprang up, the goddess had sat on a giant leaf, completely naked. Her leaf-green eyes danced with mirth, and she smiled at her husband.

'Would you prefer I took it off? It wouldn't be up to my thighs then,' she asked.

'No, definitely not,' he hastily replied.

'Why did you come, my lord?'

'I have prayed all night and made four decisions. I have sworn an oath to hold to these.'

Godiva cocked her head, questioningly.

'Firstly, I will relieve the taxes in all my territories as you asked, whether or not you perform the forfeit. Secondly, I will require my reeves to keep records of all taxes gathered in future so, if there is a dispute as to the amount owed, it can be remedied. Thirdly, since I cannot possibly return the money to those over-taxed because I cannot ascertain who they may be, I will pay for the restoration of the abbey at Leominster, established by Dewi Sant. I will also build a new church there. In addition, seeing you dressed as you are, I will add to that the purchase of a dress for any woman of Coventry who lacks one.'

'Restoring St David's Abbey will cost you far more than the amount overpaid.'

'I have finally remembered what my father taught me. To rule is a privilege that has its responsibilities. The chief of those responsibilities is to rule well and for the benefit of the people. I have been fooling myself for too long. You were well-named, Godiva, 'God's gift', for that is what you have been to me. The lesson has been learned. You have taught me humility and consideration for my people. Also, that a gift to God should be a devotion to Him and not for my financial gain.'

Godiva gave him a smile of love. *I wonder what he would say if I told him that I am so called because this second life was God's gift to me.*

'And your fourth decision?'

'That if I could not dissuade you from this enterprise, then I would join you in your humiliation.'

With that, Leofric opened his cloak to reveal a coarse tunic of sackcloth. A tear appeared in Godiva's eyes.

'Will you drop this project now?' he continued.

'I cannot, my love. We made the wager in front of all your nobles. If either of us breaks our word, we will lose their trust. You cannot ask them to do what you will not. Not only will you lose their respect but their support as well. It will become impossible for you to rule. From the lowest to the highest, they will say that a vow means nothing, a contract is a worthless scrap of parchment. They will say that as Leofric does not follow his own laws, why should they?'

Leofric did not reply. He took off his cloak, hung it on the hitching post by the horse, and opened the bag, revealing wood ash from the fire the night before. He emptied the bag over his head and then tossed it aside. Holding the rope halter with one hand, he held out the other to assist his wife onto the mounting block. Once on the block, Godiva lifted her right leg to mount her horse. As she mounted, a gust of wind caught the shift, lifting it. In catching the skirt, Godiva almost lost her balance. Once seated, she pulled the bottom hem down as far as she could.

'Ready?' asked Leofric.

'Ready,' she replied.

Leofric walked forward at a steady pace, leading the horse behind. As they passed through the courtyard gates, into the town, he noticed that the shutters were all closed on the wattle-and-daub-thatched houses lining the narrow streets. Unusual, even at that time of day. He breathed a sigh of relief. It might not be as bad as he had anticipated.

A sudden squall of rain came out of nowhere. Godiva was soaked in seconds, her shift clinging to her body. Water ran down Leofric's face making rivulets in the wood-ash. Leofric stopped, unable to see to go on. The squall passed as quickly as it had come. A last sharp gust of wind made Godiva shiver.

'Shall we turn back?' Leofric asked, hopefully.

'No, our people have to bear this weather, dressed as we are. We will too.'

Another squall hit, as sudden as the first. A final blow made Godiva shiver again. Leofric looked at her. She just nodded. Leofric led the horse on.

A warm, gentle breeze blew, drying Godiva's face and hair. In her clothes, however, sodden as they were, she felt like ice. The sun came out and warmed her exposed skin, she noticed, but only as part of her reverie. It seemed to her a tangible part of past fables. Of Coventina the water goddess, never cold even though never clothed. Of Coventina and Miriam, the reputed Roman queens of Albion, who put service to their people above everything. Their identities fused in her mind with her own and she became Salome once more.

Alright, Coventina, have it your way.

She lifted her covering up over her head and threw it away. Godiva rode proudly on, as the last of Coventina's Daughters, feeling that she was in the warm, safe embrace of her ancestors.

Author's Notes

Most of the characters in this book are fictitious. Some historical people are referenced, mainly for context. Where they are, I have tried to keep to known facts about them or researched tradition. In doing so I have used both Biblical and non-Biblical sources.

Actual dates are difficult to pinpoint in this period of history. The main events in the book are within a time period of about 30CE to 72CE. Taking the conventional dates:

Augustus becomes emperor 27BCE – Augustus made treaties with some British Tribes to support him in the event of an invasion which were then reneged on by the Britons.

> **Jesus's death** – between 30CE and 33CE (I have assumed 32CE)
> **Roman invasion of Britain** - 43CE
> **Boudiccan Rebellion** - 60CE
> **Judean Revolt** - 66CE
> **Roman sacking of Jerusalem** - 70CE

When I researched Celtic British society of 1st Century I came across a surprise. They were polyamorous, a group of men and women living together with there not being a one-to-one relationship between them. In some societies this is achieved by a woman and man pairing off for a year, but Roman sources indicate that this was not the case in Britain and that the men would be closely related to each other, and the women would come from other clans. This, combined with the fact that English, unlike other European languages, does not have the word for queen derived from the word for king, led me to believe that there was a more equal relationship between men and women and perhaps even a matriarchal society (status and wealth going through the female line). Roman sources indicated a patriarchal society, but the idea of pitting the very patriarchal Romans against powerful women was too good to pass over. Just before publication I was watching an archaeological programme. In this they highlighted a recent archaeological dig in southern England of a 1st Century, BCE, Celtic burial ground. All the high-status graves they found except one were of women, suggesting a matriarchal society.

There was common ownership of land by each tribe in Britannia. Also, there seems to have been no change of boundaries between tribes during the Roman era, each tribal district having their own administrative town with Colchester as the Provincial capital. Common land ownership continued with the Anglo-Saxons until the Norman Conquest in the 11th Century. This, along with a matriarchal society, raised questions about the Roman account of the Boudiccan Rebellion. Was Prasutagus king of the Iceni or was he Boudicca's consort? Did he make a will leaving everything jointly to his daughters and the emperor? If such a will were made, what would it have meant in a Celtic, matriarchal society? Certainly, it would not include Iceni land, and the seizure of land by the Governor of Camulodunum (Colchester) would be seen as an illegal land grab.

I have taken a liberty with the cistern at Ataroth (Madaba) as this was built later than the book's setting.

Short Glossary

Alba – Scotland, later called Caledonia.

Albion – Greek name for Britannia. Most of England was later called Britannia Primus.

Aquae Sulis – Bath, a spa settlement simply called Sulis existed prior to the Roman Conquest. Sulis was a water goddess. The Dobunni were the guardians of the sacred hot springs in Sulis.

Ardu – Arden in central England. There was a large Roman fort (the Lunt) here, at Baginton, near Coventry. They did send troops from this fort to join with Legions returning from Anglesey (Mona) to confront Boudicca in the final battle. I have used some licence here as they would probably have joined the returning Legions at High Cross (Venonae) where the Fosse Way and Watling Street meet. The fort stood at the confluence of the River Sowe and the River Sherbourne. The River Sowe flows into the River Avon, which flows into the River Severn and then into the Bristol Channel. The Severn Bore, in which large waves travel a long way up the river from the sea is a common natural phenomenon.

Ataroth - Madaba

Boudicca – Queen of the Iceni

Cambrai – Wales, later called Britannia Secundus

Camulodunum – Colchester, Roman capital of the province of Britannia.

Carthage – Now part of Tripoli in Libya. This was a Phoenician founded city and major trading port of the western part of the Roman empire.

Coventina – Romano-British/Celtic water goddess

Coventry/Coventina's Tree – The origins of the city are shrouded in mystery. There was a Romano-British/Celtic goddess of the name of Coventina; though whether the city derives its name from her, either directly or indirectly, is unknown. It is on the boundary between Dobunni and Corieltauvi territories. I have taken it to be in Dobunni territory, thus linking Ardu and Coventina's Tree with Sulis. Ratae (Leicester) was the capital of the Corieltauvi.

Corinium Dobunnorum - Cirencester, later the administrative centre for the Dobunni.

Dewi Sant/St David of Wales – 6th Century saint credited with founding many religious communities in Wales and western England including the original community at Leominster.

Fossa/Fosse Way – Originally a boundary ditch delineating the limit of Roman territory in Britannia it later became a major Roman road. It was built in 48CE or soon after.

Godiva – wife of Leofric, 11th Century Earl of Mercia. Name means God's Gift.

Hellenic Jew – A Jew who followed Greco-Roman customs. Often, but not always, a Roman Citizen.

Iceni – Celtic tribe living in modern day Norfolk, in the east of England. Their capital in the Roman era was Venta Icenoram, *Marketplace of the Iceni*, near modern day Norwich.

Joanna – Fictitious character but it is known that St Peter, her grandfather, was married. Peter was Bishop of Antioch for a time and there are still families in the region who claim descent from him.

Jubilee (Year of) – According to Hebrew tradition, every fifty years all land was left uncultivated for a year and given a rest. At the same time, all prisoners and slaves were released. The maximum period of slavery allowed in Hebrew tradition was seven years.

Junia – Female apostle mentioned in St Paul's letter to the Romans. She was a relative of Paul, but the precise relationship is unknown.

Leofric – 11th Century Earl of Mercia, husband to Godiva.

Londinium – London

Mary of Magdala/Mary Magdalene – Disciple of Jesus and known in the early church as *The Apostle to the Apostles*. I have mixed two traditions here. One that Mary fled with her daughter, Sarah, to Gaul (modern day France) and that Sarah married a local kinglet. A second tradition claims that she lived as a hermit in a cave north of Marseille and died and was buried there. There is a third tradition that Mary married St John.

Massilia – Marseille, originally settled by Phoenicians, but, by the 1st century, Greco-Roman

Mona – Anglesey, stronghold of the druids.

Naomi/Photina – Photina is the traditional name for the 'Samaritan Woman at the Well' at Sychar in Samaria. This account of her death follows Greek Orthodox tradition.

Petronilla – First century saint, believed to have been St Peter's daughter in some traditions.

Prasutagus – King of the Iceni, husband to Boudicca.

Ravenna – Port on the east coast of Italy.

Sherbourne – *means clear water.*

Verulamium – St Albans

Acknowledgements

I have gleaned information on first century saints primarily, but not solely, from Orthodox Church of America website. I am indebted to the use of All Nations Christian College library, Ware, for information on Hebrew customs in First Century Palestine (Levant).

Thankyou to the support of Micheal Heppel's Write That Book Masterclass members and particularly members of WTBBestsellers that has enabled me to bring this novel to fruition.

About the Author

Alan Rafferty was born in multi-cultural Coventry, UK. After a degree in Physics from University of York and a masters in Operational Research from University of Birmingham, he has worked in Medical Research where he has published papers on Diabetes; Operational Research and IT in UK and abroad.

His Christian faith was awakened at university after attending a lecture by Metropolitan Anthony. He has always had an interest in moral questions and questions of social justice.

After retirement he took up running to maintain his fitness and improve his social life. Two and a half years later he ran his first marathon. Still running, and living in Hertfordshire he enjoys, together with his wife, different cultures and travelling.

Buying Your Granddaughter

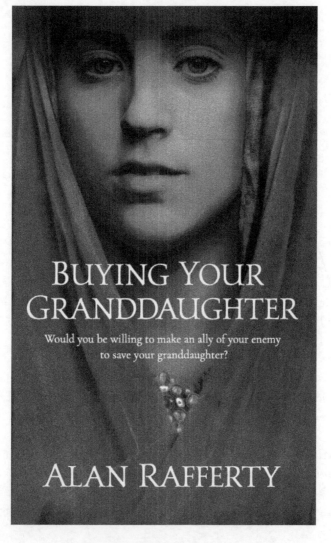

Alan Rafferty's debut novel

Now available from Amazon.